PRAISE FOR ADA

'A tense, original thriller that ⌐
suspense and shocks of *Silence of* ⌐

John Marrs, bestselling author of *When You Disappeared*

'A brilliantly original idea, with a terrifying villain at its heart.'
Claire McGowan, author of *What You Did* and
the Paula Maguire series

'*Trance* is a creepy, dark and highly original debut. I couldn't put
it down!'

Victoria Selman, author of *Blood for Blood*

'Fast, furious, and very scary, *Trance* is a hugely enjoyable and
original thriller. Adam's going to be one to watch.'

Simon Kernick, bestselling author of *The Bone Field*

MIRROR

ALSO BY ADAM SOUTHWARD

Trance

Pain

ADAM SOUTHWARD
MIRROR

THOMAS & MERCER

Text copyright © 2020 by Adam Southward
All rights reserved.

Published by Thomas & Mercer, Seattle

www.apub.com

Amazon, the Amazon logo, and Thomas & Mercer are trademarks of Amazon.com, Inc., or its affiliates.

ISBN-13: 9781542021036
ISBN-10: 1542021030

Cover design by Tom Sanderson

Printed in the United States of America

For Kerry, Isla and Daisy, who keep me sane and loved in these troubled times.

CHAPTER ONE

Eva stared through the grime. Droplets hit the windowsill outside, bouncing against the dirty glass and the metal bars, unable to wash away the filth. The garden drowned in the rain. She could make out the gravel path leading to the pond, and the red tulips planted alongside. The heads were closed against the weather, but they'd open again when the sun came out. Perhaps tomorrow. Eva loved the garden, although she was only allowed out once a week, if she'd been good. If she'd been bad, all she got to do was stare at it from the window.

Like today.

Eva hummed as she watched the water cascading down the window frame, a few droplets coming in under the sash, trickling on to the carpet by her feet. She hummed a lot. It was one of the few things that helped drown out the other sounds. Earplugs didn't work, neither did headphones, and nor did jamming her fingers into her ears until they bled. The voices always got through somehow, bypassing her ears and planting themselves in her head, constant and relentless.

She dipped her bare toe on to the sodden carpet. It was black and mouldy, like most of the rooms in her block. Her ward was the worst, she'd heard, although the person who told her was a patient, so unlikely to be reliable. All the women here were sectioned, which meant severe disorders, each and every one of them, Eva included. She knew that, but she didn't put much faith in the diagnosis.

Eva wasn't here because of the voices.

'Meds in ten minutes.' A real voice from a skinny man who stank of BO and called himself Nurse Stevie. He wasn't a real nurse, he was an orderly with three GCSEs. Nobody knew except Eva. Stevie poked his head into the 'quiet room' and smiled at its sole inhabitant. Eva faced him and smiled back.

'You're not supposed to talk in here,' she said.

Stevie thought she looked nice today. Eva could feel it, fragments drifting and forming. She hummed more loudly, conscious of her dress, which was too small and too tight. It was one of her favourites, though, one of her own, not some donated crap. The laundry had shrunk it, the fuckers.

Eva watched, listening as Stevie stared at her. He liked her legs. His vocabulary was limited, and his thoughts always the same. He stared and he thought about it, but he never tried it.

Stevie's thoughts were disgusting, but Stevie was harmless. Eva ignored him and gave the garden one more scan before heading to the communal lounge.

The queue to the pharmacy counter was long and slow. The girl in front of Eva had a severe dissociative identity disorder. Eva hadn't believed it until she saw and heard it for herself. Eva considered herself cursed, but at least she knew the voices weren't hers.

Tammy, the poor sod, didn't know who was inside her. Were both versions of her called Tammy? Did the other identity call itself by some other name? If Eva had bothered to talk to Tammy, maybe she'd know.

Or she could just sit and listen. Eva was good at listening.

The girl behind Eva in the queue, Andi, was mute and had been for years, but in her head she repeated a number sequence over and over. It changed every few days. Today it was easy to read and Eva did so, observing Andi's face – the arch of her eyebrows, the position of her jaw, the way her cheek muscles tensed as she mentally mouthed the words. Andi tilted her head and blood flowed to her lips, trembling under the thoughts.

Eva found herself humming along, turning away for several minutes while the queue shuffled forward. It became annoying. Noise in her head. Eva turned back to Andi.

Their eyes met and she saw it all in a heartbeat.

'Three, seven, nineteen, twenty-four,' whispered Eva.

Andi's eyes widened in shock and she began to shake all over. Her lips parted as she started to hyperventilate. Eva sighed and turned back around as the girl collapsed to the floor.

'Panic attack,' Eva said to Tammy. 'It happens to mental people all the time.'

Tammy snickered but didn't look round as a couple of the nurses rushed over to help. One of them caught Eva's eye. Her name was Susan. Her thoughts jumped out, wary and accusing. Suspicious as always, but unable to prove Eva had anything to do with it. Eva smiled. The nurse kept her mouth shut.

The queue sped up and Eva reached the front.

'Eva Jansen. Thorazine,' said the pharmacist at the counter. His eyes dropped to Eva's chest and back to her face. His thoughts didn't quite keep up, but Eva saw the familiar assessment. If Eva wasn't so dangerously mental, he'd definitely have a go. He thought the same thing every shift, and to be fair, he spread his perverted thoughts across all of the young women on the ward.

A go, thought Eva. *He'd have a go*. Wonderful. Would he think of his wife while he was 'having a go'? Doubtful. Frank the pharmacist only thought of his wife in vague and distant terms, like a permanent piece of him he couldn't shift. A wart perhaps, or a tumour.

Eva smiled and swallowed the two orange tablets, opening her mouth and waggling her tongue to prove they'd gone.

Yes, Frank, she almost said, watching his body shift subtly, his right hand going to his thigh, the left clenching on the desk, *my mouth is where you'd put it first. Of course you would, you bastard.*

Try it and see what happens.

Frank's thoughts shifted to his tedious routine, checking the person in front of him, checking their name on the list, checking the name of the medication. It was boring. Eva moved on.

She wasn't allowed to the bathroom after meds unless supervised. They didn't want her vomiting up the anti-psychotics – that would be naughty, and who knows what might happen?

Stevie and Frank had put her in a bad mood, and it wasn't even 10 a.m. Eva headed to the lounge, which today was supervised by female nurses. At least it gave her a break from the paedos. It wasn't that the women were any nicer, but at least they didn't want to screw every girl who walked into this place: St Anne's Mental Health Hospital, a refuge for the troubled. A secure unit for the violent. A place to hide people society didn't want around.

If only Eva belonged here.

Eva scanned the familiar faces seated at nests of tables, reminding her as always of some bizarre kind of primary school. A young woman, Maggie, sat on her own. Eva didn't know the diagnosis, but Maggie's mind was a swirling mess of paranoia. An event in her pre-teens had triggered it. Eva had seen it on their first introduction – a mass of painful memories that she couldn't be bothered to unpick. Eva wondered how long she'd been here, sat at her table, staring at a blank sheet of paper in front of her, never even picking up the pencil.

At the next table, Sarah and Nat chatted away like schoolgirls. They looked like schoolgirls, except they were both in their thirties and their juvenile features were a product of their incarceration. No sunlight, no make-up, no proper haircuts, daily sedatives and clothing that didn't fit.

Eva suspected that she herself looked younger than her own eighteen years, which was sometimes a blessing. On the odd occasion when an agency nurse did a shift, Eva was treated tenderly, like a child. It felt nice, comforting, but altogether alien, surfacing reactions she didn't understand. Anxiety, guilt, and the other thing. Eva couldn't help it, and she sure as hell couldn't control it.

Eva clenched her jaw and closed her eyes against her racing heartbeat. She waited until the thumping settled in her chest before opening her eyes and shifting her gaze to the window and an old woman called Bobby. Bobby claimed she was sane, but preferred to stay here with 'her girls'. Harmless towards the other patients, Bobby had a habit of lashing out whenever an assessment was due. Her last assessor had gone home with half a thumb. Bobby had insisted on swallowing the other half, and then smiled for the rest of the day, refusing dinner. The blood still stained the carpet in her room. No one had bothered to scrub it out.

Eva's eyes moved on, landing on a group of girls in the corner. Nasty, that lot; Eva quickly averted her gaze. She then wished she hadn't, because she now found herself looking directly at Dr Naylor, who was standing by the TV, arms folded. Her head was cocked to one side, her eyes narrowed, staring at Eva.

Dr Naylor was tall, thin with dark hair. Her white coat hid her body, but Eva imagined it made of wire, twisted and barbed, just like her mind. Dr Naylor's face was gaunt, with a mouth fixed in a permanent wry smile. Her eyes were huge and piercing. Eva hated her.

Dr Naylor continued to stare, but didn't beckon Eva over. Naylor was careful when it came to Eva, rarely coming close, and when they met for their weekly sessions she always insisted on an extra dose of Thorazine plus a shot of Promethazine, a strong tranquilliser. Forced to lie on her back, out of sight, the voices faded and Eva became almost normal.

Eva was used to knowing everybody around her, the superficial and the deep – from whatever was on the tips of their tongues to their gravest secrets, the things they would never utter. That was her thing; that was her secret.

But Eva had never managed to read Dr Naylor, and it worried her. The odd emotion showed itself, flutters of fear or suspicion, but Dr Naylor's desires were carefully hidden.

A silent mind was a threat, and Eva was scared.

CHAPTER TWO

'You beat your wife unconscious. You threatened to kill her.'

Alex Madison watched the face of the man in front of him. The cell was bright, the sun managing to find its way through the small window and bars, casting a glow over the prisoner.

'You need to answer,' said Alex, shifting his weight from right to left foot, wishing he'd taken the prison guard's suggestion of an interview room.

But this man couldn't help Alex. It was a dead end, and to make matters worse, Alex still had to complete the parole assessment.

'Why should I answer?' The prisoner, Jacob Cohen, seemed to sense Alex's discomfort, leaning back on his bunk, arms and legs splayed.

Alex sighed. 'The hearing won't proceed until I've completed my risk assessment. The parole board meets once a month. You'll miss it.'

'It's personal,' said Jacob, sniffing and turning away, looking at the window. He scratched at his crotch, pulling his trousers lower. Alex saw a huge scar across his lower abdomen, jagged and rough.

'My assessment is confidential,' said Alex. He leaned back against the wall, taking the weight off the balls of his feet, rocking back on to his heels, hearing the click of his leather soles on the concrete floor.

Jacob turned. His face dropped, his lips curling at the edges. 'Confidential? Bullshit. You put it in your report, every fucker reads it.'

'Just the board.' Alex rolled off his heels. Jacob's agitation was increasing. The original prosecutor had described the man as a pressure cooker: a faulty one that exploded every few days. He'd served two years for ABH. Not enough, in Alex's view, but Alex could tell the CPS had got lucky. Jacob was a violent serial offender. He just rarely got caught.

Alex could see the rage barely contained within the huge hulk of muscle sitting in front of him. What bred anger like that? Alex had many theories and finding the answer would take time – something that unfortunately was not available in this case – and wasn't his purpose here, officially or otherwise. His remit was a straightforward risk assessment for which he'd been allocated half a day. If released, did Jacob Cohen pose a threat to himself or the public? Simple. Alex suspected he would take the same path as most psychologists in his position: err on the side of safety.

This man was staying in prison. Luckily, Alex wouldn't be the one to tell him, but he still needed to write something in the box.

'Will you seek out your wife? Yes or no?' he said.

Jacob pulled a thin smile. His muscles clenched and he tilted his head over to the left until it cracked.

'Has your wife ever fucked anyone else, Doctor?' he said. The smile widened.

Alex swallowed, keeping his expression firm. *Not while she was my wife*, he thought. After he and Grace split up, however, Alex preferred not to think about it. 'I'm not married,' he said, 'and you just have to convince me you won't go after yours.'

Jacob's smile dropped. Another neck-crack. Alex resisted the urge to write anything on the form. He checked the door, which was unlocked but pulled to. The guards were at their station at the

8

end of the wing. He could call them, hammer the door, run. They'd be here in ten seconds, maybe fewer. Alex wondered how much damage this man could do in that time.

'I'm trying to help,' he offered, dropping the clipboard to one side. He tried to catch Jacob's eye but couldn't keep it. The man's pupils were dilated and darting to and fro. Alex watched as Jacob crunched his knuckles, first on one hand, then the other. An addict, but at the wrong end of the scale.

'Then let me the fuck out of here,' Jacob said. 'I've served what they said I'd serve. What's the problem?'

'That was based on good behaviour,' Alex said. 'No altercations. No violence. No drugs. Plus you have to answer my questions.'

Jacob twisted his lips into something approaching a smile before clearing his throat. 'Last time you asked me a lot of questions about my supplier,' he said, tilting his head. 'If I was the suspicious type, I'd say you were after your own fix, not to stop me getting mine.'

Alex swallowed, holding his expression neutral. 'Answer my question and I'll go,' he said.

Jacob held Alex's gaze for a few seconds before his smile widened. 'If I get out of here,' he said, leaning forward, resting his elbows on his knees, 'I won't go near her. Skank bitch filed for divorce anyway. She doesn't deserve me.'

Jacob's eyes burned but his expression remained grim. Truthful? Alex couldn't say. He had no experience of this man to read any subtleties of his body language. Alex could only read the obvious, namely that Jacob was simmering inside and, given half a chance, would go back and finish what he started, which was assault and battery of his wife in a drug-induced rage while his three-year-old daughter watched. A neighbour had called the police after hearing the screams. Two years later, and here they both were.

Alex wouldn't risk that happening again, and Jacob was of no other use to him. He'd read his file and done his own digging, as he did with every referral with links to drug trafficking, but it was another wasted effort. Jacob's narcotics suppliers were small-time, and they led nowhere.

'Well then, that concludes our session,' said Alex, making a brief illegible scribble on the form. 'Thank you for your time.'

Jacob kept eye contact as Alex backed towards the door. 'Let's hope they make the right decision, Dr Madison,' he said. 'Let's hope you do.'

Alex paused, but Jacob arched his back and lay on the bunk, staring at the ceiling. He scratched his crotch again and started humming. Alex tried to make out the tune, but the sound was quickly buried in the din from the other cells. Shouts and taunts were thrown at Alex as he headed out of the cell and towards the gate.

Alex sucked in the fresher air of the open space, trying to purge his lungs of the foul odour of Jacob's cell. His clothes would smell too; he'd taken to wearing cheaper suits for these visits, throwing them in the dry-cleaners the following day. What he couldn't remove was the unease certain patients left him with – patients like Jacob, where Alex's interventions made zero difference to their mental state, only to their physical situation. Even then, he wasn't convinced it made much difference. Jacob would be out in another year regardless, having served his maximum sentence, and Alex very much doubted he'd be a changed man by that time.

He'd file the paperwork for his assessment tomorrow. The parole board would receive it as part of their pack the following week. Jacob would get the news at the end of the month. Alex's work on this patient was done.

It was time he turned his attention to more pressing matters.

Later that afternoon, Alex locked the door to his study and checked it twice. It was unlikely anyone would come barging in; the receptionist would call him if anybody entered the foyer and the clientele at his private practice were of the naturally polite variety. Nevertheless, it had become a ritual, a habit, and not without good reason.

Locked inside his study in one of the most opulent parts of London, the feeling of safety eluded Alex. It barely registered when the packet of Xanax anti-anxiety medication slipped out of his pocket. He tapped a pill from the foil and stared at the small white dot, contrasting against the dark polished mahogany of his desk. It wasn't enough, and hadn't been for months, but it was all he had. A more fundamental solution was necessary, but he'd resisted this long, and today was not the right day. It never was.

Memories, distant voices from the past. The minimal information he possessed triggered little more than a gradual increase in his paranoia. But still, he investigated when he could, pushing a little harder each time, trying to scratch beneath the surface of his recent past.

Victor Lazar. A serial killer with a bizarre ability, who had disappeared two years ago without a trace.

Mia Anastos. A woman with a tragic past and a deadly affliction. The violent soul who tortured her victims, extracting every last twist of agony before turning inward, almost killing herself in a frenzy of pain.

But hers wasn't a standard case of psychopathy, just as Victor Lazar hadn't killed eleven people merely for the thrill of it. Some monsters are born, but others are created. Alex's last couple of cases had dealt firmly with the latter – two instances of people who

11

had been brutalised and experimented on before being unwittingly unleashed on the world.

What bound these cases together consumed Alex's thoughts. So far as Alex was concerned, he'd stopped them, but hadn't explained what lay behind their actions. Victor had disappeared. Mia was safe. The people behind their deeds had vanished into the ether, leaving nothing except for death and silence.

Until now.

Alex waited, tapping at the desk while his MacBook booted up, feeling the Xanax dissolve on his tongue. The search results, as expected, revealed nothing new. The vast reaches of the web had not yet caught what he was looking for. Six months of searching university archives, library records and company filing information had produced nothing useful. Nova Pharmaceuticals – the organisation that had created Mia, and the only lead open to Alex – had disappeared behind a wall of red tape and political threats.

But he'd clearly made someone nervous.

Alex pushed away from the desk and stood by the window, pulling the blinds open a fraction, scanning the street below. He squinted as the sun reflected off the rows of Audis and Mercs, black and silver, bumper to bumper. He knew what to look for. The oddities he'd become increasingly aware of over the last few weeks. Black SUVs with shadows inside, sitting and watching. Tinted windows, the same car driving first one way, then the other a few minutes later.

His house, his office, his movements.

The street remained quiet, the traffic light and flowing. The sun obscured the interior of the parked cars, the reflections hiding all manner of secrets. His gaze landed on a large BMW parked at an angle at the end of the street. A disturbance in the air suggested the car was hot, engine running.

Alex's mouth went dry. He pulled his shoulders back, feeling the tension pushing forward. He drew the blinds open further, staring at the car, daring it to move. The featureless glare of the windscreen stared back. He watched it for another moment before stepping back, releasing the breath he'd been holding. The blind closed with a snap and he watched it quiver, trembling in its frame until he released it from his grip.

CHAPTER THREE

'Did Katie tell you?' said Alex. He gripped the phone in one hand, the other resting on his mouse, scrolling through the week's appointments. A fresh week. A fresh chance.

'She did,' said Grace, huffing at the other end. 'A vacation sounds wonderful, but it's not that simple.'

'It can be.'

Alex could hear Grace breathing. Her silences were hard to read, and Alex found himself crossing his fingers.

'I don't think so, Alex.'

His fingers snapped apart. He laid his hand flat on the desk. He wanted to argue, but knew it wouldn't help. He'd spent this long trying to get close – he couldn't risk pushing her away. They'd been divorced for so long, it would be hard to rebuild. He mustn't rush things.

'I understand,' he said, wondering if Grace knew how hard it was for him to say. She probably did. She could read him even at the end of the phone.

'Thank you,' she said. 'You and I . . . we're complicated, Alex. You're always welcome here and Katie needs to see her dad. But she's going through a difficult time at the moment. A holiday together . . .'

'It's OK,' he insisted. 'It was a step too far. I'll drop it. You two should get away, though. Do you remember the villa in Pollenca?'

'I do, but . . .'

'Take her there,' said Alex. 'You pay for yourself and I'll pay for Katie.'

Another pause. 'Deal,' she said. 'As long as you promise to take a break too. You've been flat out for months. You're distant at the moment, always working.'

'Nothing exciting,' said Alex. 'Lots of CPS assessments. Tedious, mostly, but it's building my forensic experience back up.'

Alex neglected to mention the long evenings spent on his own research, his increasing desperation at the lack of progress, and the more worrying side effects of his stress – the recent onset of panic attacks and the failure of his medication to combat them. Grace couldn't know any of that and neither could Katie. As far as they were concerned, his anxiety was under control with regular therapy sessions. If they knew the truth it would push them away beyond reach.

He also failed to tell her about the other things – the recent shadows following his every move, the sense he was being watched, tested, *threatened*. But he had nothing substantial to offer, and the thought was never far from his mind – that he could be imagining it all.

'Speaking of work,' he said, feeling the phone vibrating, 'I have another call. Speak tomorrow?'

'More like Thursday,' Grace said. 'Are you taking Katie to see your mum at the weekend?'

'If she'll go,' said Alex, peering at the screen. His heart jumped at the caller's name. Not a routine call. Not from this man.

'Gotta go,' he said distractedly. 'Thursday, then.'

'Bye, Alex.'

Alex hung up.

He paused, taking a sip of water, watching the phone vibrate for a few seconds longer before answering the incoming call.

'Larry?'

Dr Larry Van Rooyen was one of Alex's oldest and most trusted colleagues. A good psychiatrist, authentic and caring. They'd been close friends in the past, until Alex had required more of him than was reasonable, coercing his involvement in something he should have dealt with on his own. Together they held a secret that could never be shared, the sort that could only grow with time. They hadn't spoken in months, and the last Alex had heard, Larry had moved out of London and was now heading up a department at Southampton University.

'Alex, hi. It's been a while.' Larry's voice was friendly but tired.

'It has,' said Alex. 'How's the family?'

Larry paused. 'Good, thank you. Healthy and happy – that's all we want, right? How about Katie? Grace?'

'They're both well.' He didn't mention Katie's spiral a few months ago into near-crisis, her latent trauma emerging in a flurry of anger, most often directed at Alex. He deserved it, every bit, but it didn't make it any easier. Larry didn't need to know about that. He hadn't called to ask about Alex's family. *Spit it out*, he thought.

Alex heard Larry take a deep breath. 'Look, I'm not sure if I should have called,' he said, 'but I spoke to someone yesterday. Something strange in one of our psych wards.'

Alex's heart fluttered. Larry knew Alex's special area of interest. He also knew not to call unless it was serious.

'I'm listening.'

Larry hesitated. Alex could hear footsteps and a door closing at the other end of the phone.

'An old colleague of mine,' said Larry. 'Susan Halsey. A psychiatric nurse at St Anne's Hospital in Sussex.'

'OK,' said Alex, casting about for his pen, 'is this regarding a referral?'

'Not exactly.'

Alex found the pen and pulled his notepad towards him. He wrote Susan's name at the top.

'What, then?' Alex wondered if any of his patients ended up in Sussex. Probably, given the lack of beds and money. Mental health patients in the UK were shipped all around the country at the tap of a calculator.

'She wanted my help.'

Alex frowned. 'A whistle-blower? Why did she call you? Why doesn't she take it up the usual routes?'

'It's not . . . it's not that straightforward.'

Alex cleared his throat. 'It's about a patient?'

'Yes.' Larry sounded stressed, his voice tired and concerned.

'What did she say?'

'Not much, but what she did say piqued my interest. I immediately thought of you. She talked about a patient. Name of Eva Jansen. Violent and disturbed, but with something much more unique about her. *Special, truly special*, were her exact words.'

Something in the way Larry said it caused the hairs on Alex's neck to stand on end. He shivered. *Truly special.*

'So what's special about her?'

Larry cleared his throat. 'The patient doesn't have the condition they think she does. The history is nonsense, the diagnosis is wrong. Her behaviour is bizarre and notably curious . . .' He tailed off. 'Alex, you know my feelings about these lines of inquiry. I agreed to pass her concerns on to you – I told her I had a colleague who specialised in this sort of thing. I think it's best if you call her direct.'

'Specialise in what sort of thing? You haven't told me anything.'

'Speak to her,' said Larry, 'that's all I'm suggesting. Ask her to tell you what she told me. Then, please, leave me out of it.'

Alex tried not to push him too hard. He understood Larry's reluctance to talk. His friend hated discussing things like this openly. Every time they spoke it was a risk.

'The numbers, Alex,' Larry said, 'that's what caught my attention, made me think of you. Of us.'

'Why?' said Alex. 'What can she do with numbers?'

Larry cleared his throat. 'Look, I've got to go. I have clinic starting in five minutes.'

Alex squeezed the phone in frustration. Larry had been determined enough to make the call, then sufficiently panicked to leave him hanging. He heard a knocking sound at Larry's end.

'Is it worth my time?'

Larry paused. 'I think so,' he said, 'but be careful, Alex. I know you're searching for answers, but some are best left hidden. Don't get in over your head. Don't let it happen again.'

Alex pinched the bridge of his nose. It might be nothing more than a jumpy nurse and a creepy patient, but this was exactly what he'd been searching for – the smallest hint of the inexplicable. Alex was careful with his inquiries, ruthless in his attention to detail. The tipping factor was simple – this had come from Larry, and that made all the difference.

Dr Larry Van Rooyen had helped Alex hide Mia Anastos. Larry knew precisely what Alex was searching for.

'Give me her number,' he said.

Larry reeled off the digits. Alex heard a door being opened, banging against a wall.

'Excuse me . . .' he heard Larry say. 'Who are—?'

Alex waited. He heard hushed voices. The phone crackled.

'I have a clinic now,' he heard Larry say. 'You'll have to come . . . Oh . . .' There was a pause. 'Well, in that case, I'll be two—' The line went dead. Larry had hung up.

Alex stared at the screen for a few moments. He redialled Larry, listened while it rang three times before going to voicemail.

Alex hung up. A ripple of unease spread across his chest. It was probably nothing – Alex had lost count of the number of times Larry had hung up on him in order to care for a patient.

He'd call him back later. In the meantime, Alex stared at Susan's number, his unease replaced by a tingle of excitement.

A lead. Finally the hunt was back on.

CHAPTER FOUR

The voices.

Always buzzing, surging and fading. Eva hardly ever slept, despite the drugs. Hours of staring at the ceiling, tracing the cracked plaster to the cobwebs in the corners, running her eyes down the walls, searching for an object of focus. On the rare occasion she did sleep, the dreams snapped her awake in cold sweats. By 4 a.m., sometimes earlier, Eva would wrench the thin sheets off her body, feeling the cold air on her drenched skin. The light would be on – always on – Eva insisted on it, but still claustrophobic and suffocating, she would lose the dream, giving her nothing to reflect on, nothing to blame.

'It's only me,' said a timid voice. Nurse Susan stepped over the threshold, hands on her hips.

Eva was immediately on guard. The lounge had been empty this early in the day, open to all – one of the few unrestricted rooms. The plastic chairs and tables scattered, the month-old magazines ripped and left on the floor, which was just as well, because they covered the worst of the stains. The mould wasn't as bad in here, probably because they cranked the heating right up, even in summer.

Eva had drifted, alone with her daydreams. She didn't particularly dislike Nurse Susan, in fact the poor woman tried to be friendly, but she was suspicious with it, too probing. That was partly Eva's fault, but the woman just wouldn't let things go, and it made Eva angry.

What the hell did the woman want from her?

'I want to talk about what you did the other day,' said Susan. Her voice wavered, but held. Eva shifted on the sofa, straightening up. She sniffed, watching the nurse, feeling the anxiety seeping out of her. Susan kept her face in the shadow of the door, tilting it downwards. Eva squinted, trying to make out the fine movements of her jaw, the muscle twitches, the static through the air and the vibrations through the floor. She sniffed again.

'I don't know what you mean,' said Eva. This was not confession time. Susan would just have to deal with it.

'You know what you did,' said Susan. 'When I was working in here last week, doing my paperwork, you said something to me. Something hurtful.'

Eva slipped off the sofa and stood. The floorboards creaked in protest. She looked over at the table she'd seen Susan at. The nurses often worked there, like they didn't have any other place to be. Didn't they have homes to go to or a study to work in?

This was not going away. Eva cursed herself for what she had done. So obvious, so risky. But the woman wouldn't shut up in her head.

'I'd like to go to sleep now,' said Eva, faking a yawn. 'Please get out of my way.'

She crossed halfway to the door. Susan shrank back a little but remained in the doorway, blocking her exit.

'I want to talk,' she said. 'I want to know how you knew such hateful things about me. Why you said them. Who told you?'

Eva laughed. Perhaps Nurse Susan wasn't so clever after all. Or perhaps this was a ruse. Either way, she'd get nothing out of Eva, other than more of the same. Eva stepped forward again.

'Hurtful or hateful? Make up your mind.'

Susan just stood there. She swallowed, her neck wobbling. Her right hand fidgeted.

'Go away,' said Eva, but as she did so, Susan's face came into the light. Eva saw a flash, an admission. It presented as guilt, but resolute, gaping and loud. She said it in her eyes, and her cheek bones, which wouldn't stop shaking. She said it in her lips, which quivered in pathetic synchrony.

Eva followed these almost imperceptible movements and found it, the thread of thought snaking its way out. She caught it, teasing the end, following its delicate path. Her mind fluttered in response. A name tumbled out.

'Who is Dr Van Rooyen?' said Eva.

In that moment Eva knew her mistake, but the anger returned with a vengeance. Susan's eyes widened, and Eva rushed forwards, lunging as Susan backed out of the door. They stumbled through into the corridor together. Susan hit the opposite wall, arms up in defence. Eva's temper was rising, out of control. She needed to get away before . . .

'Stop!' The boom of a voice behind her.

Eva felt the sharp scratch of a needle in her upper arm. She turned and saw Dr Naylor pulling the needle out. She held Eva by the scruff of her neck, pulling her away from Susan. Behind her stood Nurse Stevie, his eyes firmly on her chest, his impulses messy and wild.

Eva's vision at once began to swim, but she held Naylor's eyes, and in that moment saw a combination of curiosity and anger, a fragment of suspicion creeping out. Naylor glanced at Susan, her eyes saying it all. Nurse Stevie was a simpleton, but how long had Dr Naylor been standing there, and what had she heard?

The answers to both would have to wait, as Eva's legs gave way and her head clouded with fog, as she slipped into unconsciousness.

◆ ◆ ◆

Fuck!

Eva caught the thought before she said it. She stared at the ceiling. Back in her room, the familiar position meant she was in her bed, the rough leather straps holding her arms and legs. Her head throbbed and she felt woozy – that would be the promethazine.

'What did you tell her?'

Fuck! she thought again. Dr Naylor's voice was quickly followed by her face, leaning over the bed, but only for a second before she darted away. The doctor's arms were folded. Defence or contempt, Eva wasn't sure.

'Does she know?' Dr Naylor sniffed, her thin nose squeaking as the air rushed in.

Eva listened, but her eyes weren't working properly, as the drugs won their usual battle. She couldn't get a grasp on Naylor. Her facial expressions would have been readable, if only Eva could see her clearly without the room spinning. The woman's movements and smell were masked and she kept her eyes hidden, out of focus and carefully averted.

'We restrict your leisure time,' said Naylor, 'but you find trouble anyway.'

'She came to me.' Eva knew that getting defensive didn't work with Naylor, but she couldn't help herself. 'This is my room.'

Naylor sniffed. 'Wrong. This is *my* room. You're a guest. Or at least, you were.'

Eva paused. Moving on so soon? It usually took more than a few broken faces for them to shunt Eva to another home, another ward, another asylum.

But there was something odd about the doctor's behaviour.

It was for that reason that she kept quiet. Perhaps this came as a surprise to Naylor because the doctor paused and leaned in, and

23

in that second Eva read a snippet, a fragment of her intentions in among the haze.

A good price.

What the fuck did that mean?

Naylor stepped back. Eva waited, but Naylor shuffled out of sight, still sniffing through her beaky nose. Eva didn't strain her neck or try to move. She was confused.

'You forced my hand,' said Naylor. 'This is your fault.'

Why? Eva wanted to ask, but didn't. Naylor left the room before she had the chance to say another word, leaving her strapped to the bed, closing the door with a muted click.

CHAPTER FIVE

Dr Larry Van Rooyen led the elderly gentleman through to his office. The request was odd, but Larry had a forgiving nature, one that his wife had always said made him work too hard – at the expense of his own well-being. Well, what could he say to that? To be a doctor of the mind was never to push anyone away, to be forever inquisitive, to take every possible chance at improving a life, discovering a condition, making a mark on the world.

'Please,' he said, 'sit down.'

Larry walked around the other side of his desk and poured two glasses of water, before seating himself in his leather chair. It creaked under the strain, or was it his hips that creaked? He could never be sure.

He examined the man in front of him. Elderly, in his eighties perhaps, but physically sharp, his posture and movements unstrained, like those of a much younger man. He remained standing, reaching down to brush a fleck of dust from his tailored suit. Larry peered at the man's shoes: polished brogues, not even a scuff.

The man clasped his hands together and stared. He whispered something, perhaps to himself, his mouth trembling. Larry met his gaze, puzzled not just at the man's reluctance to sit, but at the sensation creeping up from his own stomach: one of unease, faint nausea, tinged with anxiety.

Low blood sugar, he thought. When had he last eaten? He'd be late for clinic if he stopped to eat now. He needed to find out what this man was after – something about another patient, confidential – *could they chat in his office?*

'I'll stand.' The man's face twisted into an unpleasant frown, his leathery skin stretching, deep lines etched into his forehead.

A complaint? Larry didn't get many complaints, and was unused to dealing with them. Should he get a colleague in to hear it? HR? He couldn't even remember the proper protocol in such cases.

The man murmured something else, not in English, but Larry couldn't make it out. He frowned and his throat tightened.

'I can only give you a few minutes, I'm afraid,' he said. 'I have a clinic. Perhaps if you go to the desk, make an appointment?'

The man stepped forward, leaned in, placed his hands on the edge of Larry's desk.

Larry felt a flutter in his chest. Pins and needles in his scalp, his forehead cold.

'Who did you tell?' said the man.

Larry shifted backwards in his seat. The intensity of the man's gaze was unnerving. Larry was used to dealing with damaged minds, troubled personalities. He'd faced all manner of violent and manic disorders over the course of his career. And yet this man had managed to trigger his basic defence mechanisms in a split second – Larry recognised the primitive parts of his brain kicking in, alarm bells sounding. What threat was his body so certain about?

'Who did I tell about what?' said Larry, trying to keep his voice calm. He didn't manage it. Why was his throat so dry? He swallowed, trying to conjure a drop of moisture.

The man leaned in further. A brief pain seared across Larry's chest, starting at his left shoulder, ending somewhere beneath his diaphragm. It caught him off guard and he drew a sharp breath.

'You know *what*,' said the man. He sniffed, pulling out a hand-kerchief, dabbing the end of his nose. 'The girl. Who else did you tell? What did you record?' He folded the handkerchief away neatly, tucking it into his top pocket.

Larry's throat constricted even further. The girl. This man had appeared while he'd been on the phone to Alex.

A thousand thoughts presented themselves, most of them useless, ones of regret. Larry quickly worked out why this man was here.

He should never have got involved. He should have told Susan to ignore it and move on. And now they'd come looking for him. These people that Alex sought, that he was certain were out there.

'Nobody,' he said, the first thing that came to mind. Denial. Stupid. This man wouldn't be here if he believed that.

'Nobody *else*?' The man emphasised the point. Larry's chest squeezed, the breath forced out. The pain in his shoulder returned, and fluttered violently. Larry's ears popped with pressure, increasing as each second passed.

Larry shook his head. It was the truth. Is that what they wanted? Larry had told Alex, nobody else. Who would he tell? The girl was interesting, weird, an anomaly, but Larry wanted to stay well out of it. His last foray into Alex Madison's world had ended with an illegal act he'd always be burdened with – he was not about to repeat it.

'Nobody,' he whispered. He shook his head again, slumping. His flesh began to crawl, the pins and needles spreading. His stomach flipped with a fresh rush of fear, a creeping sensation through his body.

The man leaned forward further still. His face dominated Larry's vision.

'Nobody,' the man repeated. His voice was also a whisper, seeping into Larry's head, bringing with it a wave of white noise and pain.

Larry put both hands on the desk, trying to keep himself upright. His chest tightened, unbearably so. His breathing laboured to the point where he doubled over, unable to draw another gasp. Pain shot through both shoulders, grasping his neck and jaw, which was now so tightly clenched he could feel his molars chipping under the pressure. The crushing pain enveloped his torso and a rush of heat flooded his face.

Vertigo took him as the realisation of what was happening brought on a surge of panic.

He tried to focus, could almost hear the slowing of his heart, the electrical impulses disrupted, the muscles unable to contract, the organ unable to function.

He counted the seconds, each thumping with a fresh surge of pain. As they passed, they took all hope with them, and he began to pray, soft murmuring against the background thumps in his head.

When his heart finally stopped, he had a last fleeting moment of consciousness, face down on the desk, during which he saw his wife's face and that of his son, etched on the brown, scratched surface. He whispered goodbye to them and watched them fade. Grey to black.

The white noise cut out in an instant, and so did the pain.

CHAPTER SIX

Natalia Volkova stood at the hotel desk while the clerk checked her details and assigned the room key. He handed her Russian passport back with a smile. Volkova wasn't Natalia's real name, but it was as good as any. She didn't have a last name – it, along with everything else, had been stripped away from her by the orphanage.

The '80s were a cruel period for abandoned children in Eastern Europe, and all the more so if, like Natalia, they happened to find their way to the Comănești orphanage in Romania, one of the many facilities run by her current organisation.

Natalia's memories of the orphanage were never far away – no mind can bury that much – but today, standing in the hotel reception, she experienced a fresh rush, fragments and flashes of a darker time. Even darker than now.

The orphanage was where it all began for her, but her organisation originated from long before that.

She knew precisely why these memories were resurfacing. With each new assignment came a corresponding wave of conflicting thoughts and arguments, her purpose questioned and her loyalties tested to the limit. Natalia knew very well the requirements of her role, but as the years rolled by her conviction had wavered and her motivation had wandered. Maybe this assignment would break the spell at last.

'Your key, madam.' The man finally broke into Natalia's musings. She turned and smiled, plucking the key card from his outstretched hand.

'Thank you,' she said. 'The elevator?'

'Over there, to the right. First floor.'

Another smile, and Natalia grabbed her suitcase and walked off. She didn't trust the concierge with her bag, and she was in good enough shape to carry ten suitcases if she had to.

As Natalia waited for the lift, she gazed through a picture window out on to the restaurant terrace and pool. She hadn't been to Spain for years, maybe a decade or more. The air was dry and warm, such a contrast from the northern latitudes of Russia, where the cold and damp pervaded everything and everyone. Even her bones felt damp at times and her persistent cough was relentless – did her lungs ever feel clear these days? This morning, however, she already felt warm and relaxed, the Madrid climate casting its arms around her in a delightful embrace.

She savoured these moments, for they were rare in her job. The lift pinged and the doors opened. She left the view behind.

Four stars, not five, but the room was luxurious nevertheless. Things had improved over the last couple of years. Early assignments had seen Natalia dropped off in foreign countries with no more than a fake passport and a hundred dollars – told to figure it out or not to come back. Living in stolen cars and hostels, she'd suspected she wouldn't live beyond the next job.

But she'd proven herself, and with that came elevated status and perks. She was respected and feared, and found worthy of a hotel with a spa and a view.

The first phone call came in before she'd even had the chance to unpack. Three matching bikinis lay on the huge bed, still with tags on. The rolling designer suitcase held the rest of her holiday clothing, expensive and chic. She pulled out a pair of Louis Vuitton flip-flops with interest, turning them over in her hands. Her personal shopper had gone to town, and Natalia wondered if she'd get a chance to wear any of it.

'Yes?' she answered.

'The details have been sent through.'

'She was one of ours?'

'We believe so, yes.'

Natalia's chest tightened. Involuntary, and unfortunate. It meant the assignment was confirmed. She was committed.

'Origin?'

'Like I said, read the details.'

'So why this charade?' Natalia opened another section of the suitcase, revealing a selection of designer dresses. She plucked out a sheer black number, holding it against her body, wondering how anyone could even think of wearing something so small and transparent. Did they think she was some kind of hooker? She crumpled the dress and threw it in the wastebasket beneath the dresser. The cleaner could have it.

'Well?'

'Read the notes, OK?'

Natalia huffed. 'How long have we got?' she asked.

'Twenty-four, forty-eight hours. Maybe longer. What do you care? You get to sit in the sun. I get to sit in mud and Siberian shit. Be grateful.'

'Sit in the sun?' Her tone was suddenly icy, and her handler was lucky he was three thousand miles away. They might own her, but she had enough power to demand respect from him. He caught her tone and appeared to realise his mistake.

'I'm sorry,' he said. She heard him swallow. 'I meant no immediate action is required. You can—'

'Act professional, like I always do. We don't get to *sit in the sun*.'

The man cleared his throat. 'I'll call again when we're ready,' he said.

'Goodbye,' said Natalia, hanging up. She sniffed, regaining her composure, then looked back at the bikinis on the bed. After a few moments she decided on the red one. Slipping it on, she admired herself in the mirror for several minutes, wondering what the other guests would make of the deep bruises on her legs and arms, a souvenir of her last training session. The needle marks scattered across her back told of earlier battles, and the sight of them brought back memories from even further back.

She tore off the bikini and threw that in the wastebasket on top of the dress. *Sit in the sun*, she thought, a faint smile on her lips, grabbing a bathrobe from the rail and wrapping it around her naked body. She sat on the bed and opened her laptop. It was time to read up on her real reason for being here.

It was time to read about the girl.

CHAPTER SEVEN

Alex kept to the speed limit as he headed south. His fondness for fast driving had been tamed by Katie's relentless campaigning – YouTube videos of car crashes, pitiful stories about the victims, accounts of distinguished professionals locked away for reckless endangerment. Katie asked if he'd prefer to die speeding or, instead, kill somebody else while speeding and then die in prison? She assured her dad she loved him and his stupid car, but he really should know better.

Alex didn't point out that he'd always known better. He knew better about many aspects of his life, but still managed to screw up much of it. On this topic, however, he listened. He kept to the speed limit and his thoughts turned inward, back to the photo of a patient – Mia Anastos – sent to him via a secure online lockbox from the secretive private clinic where she was being treated. A high-resolution photo of her strapped to a wooden bed, along with this month's invoice. Mia's condition was stable, but otherwise, nothing new to report. Progress in her cognitive and medical therapy was slow, and she was still unable to receive visitors or be discharged. Too high a risk – they'd barely begun to reverse the damage. Alex was paying for a patient he might never see again, for a purpose he might never get to exploit. But she was safe, and he knew it was worth the money for that alone. The clinic urged him not to share the photo with anyone else. If only he could.

Mia's presence there was a secret that could never be revealed. Alex knew well enough what the inside of a prison was like without wanting to live in one. Mia was still wanted by the UK police for seven murders, and officially Alex had no idea where she was. Officially, his confidant, Larry, didn't either. The lies persisted but never got easier. The secrets he held weighed him down.

Alex took a breath, watching the countryside give way to the city, keeping the pressure in his chest at bay.

He had called Susan and agreed to meet at a pub not far from St Anne's Hospital in Sussex. She couldn't get to him in London, and although he barely had enough information to justify a day out of the office, she intrigued him. He couldn't ignore it.

The satnav announced his arrival and he parked, double-checking the address before heading inside. It was almost empty at this time in the morning, with only a few yummy mummies chattering over their lattes alongside baby buggies and the odd toddler, and a solitary man at the bar sipping a glass of pale beer.

'Dr Madison?'

Alex turned. A woman waved at him tentatively from one of the booths on the left wall. She was short and stocky with shiny black hair, her face creased with worry. Alex walked over, noticing the whites of her knuckles as she clasped her hands tightly together.

'Susan?' said Alex. He placed his jacket on the chair and slid his bag in before sitting. A waitress appeared and took his order. He glanced at Susan's half glass of water and ordered a Diet Coke.

'Thank you so much for coming,' Susan said. She paused, her eyes darting between Alex and her hands.

'It's my pleasure,' said Alex, sensing her anxiety. 'Larry's an old friend. If he referred you to me, I'm listening.'

Susan nodded. 'What is it you do, Dr Madison? I mean, your specialty.'

Alex paused. He used to think it the most banal of questions – one people always asked when he mentioned he was a psychologist – but here with Susan, he realised it was of the utmost importance. What was his speciality exactly? The obscure, the macabre? The cases that slipped through the net – those patients who defied any standard diagnosis and demanded something more? Or was it his relentless pursuit of the other thing? Not the patients themselves, but the cause of their afflictions. The endless evenings hunched over his laptop in his darkened study, searching for answers. Was that his purpose now?

'I deal with forensics,' he said, clearing his throat, 'and I've practised as a clinical psychologist' – the correct answer, although perhaps not the fullest – 'for almost fifteen years.'

Susan nodded again, her shoulders relaxing. Her mouth twisted into a timid smile. 'I wasn't sure if I should bother Larry, but I know what I saw.'

'OK if I take notes?' said Alex, pulling out a pad.

Susan nodded. 'Of course. Will you keep my name out of it, please?'

Alex met her eyes and recognised genuine fear. He'd seen this numerous times before in patients, but rarely in a clinician.

'It depends what you tell me,' he said. 'I'm sorry, but that's the way it is. If this is a case of abuse, it has to get formal. I would give your name to the police, but they'd keep it confidential. Whoever your complaint concerns would never know.'

Susan put her hands together, taking a breath. She shook her head. 'I work on bank hours. You know what that means?'

'Zero-hours contract, yes.'

'I can't afford for my hours to be cut, Dr Madison. I'm a single mum and I find it hard enough to pay the bills working sixty hours a week. If she finds out I told anyone, my career is finished.'

'She?'

'Dr Naylor,' said Susan, spelling it for Alex. 'She runs the department.'

'And where is she now?'

'Away. At one of her many conferences, supposedly. Madrid, I think. She won't be back for a week.'

Alex scribbled it down.

'And the patient?'

'Eva. Eva Jansen.'

Alex nodded. 'How old is she?'

'Eighteen, according to her record, but I'm not sure. She looks very young.'

Alex frowned. 'The record is wrong?'

Susan shrugged. 'So much is wrong about her, Dr Madison—'

'Alex, please.'

'OK then, Alex. Eva's medical record – what the nurses were allowed to see – was unremarkable, but I'm not sure it was accurate.'

'What do you mean?'

Susan took a sip of her water. Alex watched her eyes nervously jump from the table to his face.

'Tell me what prompted you to call Dr Van Rooyen,' said Alex.

Susan struggled to get started, swallowing hard. After a few deep breaths she seemed calmer, more thoughtful.

'I called because I don't trust the hospital . . . our department . . . to do its best for her, but it won't make sense unless you know why.'

Alex nodded. 'OK.'

'All of the patients I care for are troubled,' said Susan. 'That's why they're locked up. Sure, not all are violent, but many are. It's often triggered by the most unlikely of events – at least . . .'

'I've worked on psychiatric wards for thirty-odd years. Patients come and go. Some are interesting, some are sad. Most just need a plan. But every now and then I get a patient who doesn't belong. Either the diagnosis is suspect or something else doesn't feel right. Eva Jansen is one of those. She doesn't belong in our ward. I'm not sure where she belongs, but we're doing nothing for her. Her behaviour . . .'

'What's her diagnosis?' asked Alex, picking the first salient point.

Susan shook her head. 'A severe form of IED – intermittent explosive disorder,' she said.

Alex frowned. IED was a well-understood condition, but seldom resulted in someone being sectioned long-term. Medication and psychotherapy were the usual treatments, although they tended to have mixed results.

'Did this diagnosis come with her to St Anne's?'

Again Susan shrugged. 'I'm not sure.'

'But you don't agree with it?'

'Eva is violent, yes,' said Susan, 'sometimes incredibly physical – very tough. She learned how to fight at a young age.'

Alex nodded. There was no shortage of young female patients with a history of violence, normally inflicted on them by somebody older, somebody they trusted. Some learned to fight back; most didn't.

'But it's different with Eva,' said Susan. 'IED patients are impulsive, grossly over-reactive, but it doesn't last, and they are full of regret afterwards. Eva . . . She's driven by something else entirely. Her rages are meticulous, but with an inner fury she struggles to keep under control. There's more to it, I think . . . There were rumours she'd done more than just hurt people at a previous facility. Two patients ended up in a coma, I'm pretty sure. She doesn't have IED.'

Alex nodded, swallowing. 'OK,' he said, tapping his pen, digesting the violence, comparing it with his previous patients. It didn't change anything, but it was useful to know. 'So, you disagree with the primary diagnosis. But what's the big deal? The diagnosis isn't your main concern, is it?'

Susan shook her head. Her eyes glanced rapidly around the pub. She stared past Alex's shoulder towards the door for a few seconds before refocusing on Alex.

'Eva pays a lot of attention to other people. She studies them, staring, listening . . . I don't know . . . Some of the patients don't care, but many do, and I can see why.'

Alex raised his eyebrows.

'She *studies* them, Dr Madison.' Susan paused. 'She studies us too – all of the nursing staff, the pharmacist, the porters. The kitchen staff shun her. I think they're scared. Eva's been with us for less than a year, but she's already one to watch.'

Alex took a sip of his Coke, feeling the bubbles on his tongue, hoping the caffeine would stop the headache that was threatening to develop. He could feel it creeping out from the back of his eyes. Too little sleep and too much time in front of the laptop the night before.

'Scared of what?' he said. When clinicians are scared of a patient it typically signifies something odd, something inexplicable.

'That she'll find out too much about them. Their personal lives. Their innermost secrets.' Susan chose her words with care, clamping her lips together and nodding, as if it all made perfect sense.

Alex stopped tapping his pen. 'What do you mean?'

'They're scared she'll blurt something out,' said Susan. 'And they're right to, as I found out myself.'

Alex shook his head, confused. 'Sorry, I'm missing something. Back up. This patient—'

'Eva Jansen.'

'Right. Eva. People are scared of Eva because she asks them lots of questions about themselves?'

38

'No,' said Susan. 'She never asks questions. She barely talks at all, only when she gets angry, and then it's mostly shouting.'

'So how does she learn people's secrets?' asked Alex.

Susan met his gaze, holding it for a few seconds before shifting away. 'I don't know,' she said. She chewed the inside of her cheek, clasped the sides of her water glass, her face strained.

Alex leaned back in his chair. He needed Susan to relax, or this would be a wasted trip. All he'd learned so far was that Eva unnerved both the other patients and the staff. Hardly a revelation when it came to a violent mental health patient.

'There's another girl on the same ward with severe dissociative disorder. She's obsessed with number sequences, writing them down or circling them in magazines. Very withdrawn, she rarely speaks to the clinicians, and never to the other girls in the ward.'

Alex leaned in. Larry had mentioned the numbers in the telephone call. What was it that Eva could do? Alex had a reasonable idea, and, apart from one rather awkward detail, had a sinking feeling this might be a wasted trip.

'Eva knows the numbers,' he said, making a brief note on his pad.

Susan looked up, surprised, and stared Alex in the eye. 'Not just that, but . . . You don't think it's strange?'

Alex finished his scribble. 'It's odd, but not unheard of. We're all capable of reading one another in various ways, with a huge tool-kit of mechanisms evolved over hundreds of thousands of years—'

'Do me a favour,' Susan said, her eyes flashing with frustration, 'and don't patronise me. I understand perfectly well how to read people. It's psychology one-oh-one and even us lowly shift nurses learn it. Body language, posture, eye movement, lip-biting, emotional presence, energy – everything a patient says and everything a patient does. I know how to get information out of people who don't trust themselves, never mind me. I also did my own research on cold reading and all the tricks that performers use. Nothing comes close to what Eva can do.' Susan paused for breath and folded her arms around her body.

'Eva has an . . . ability. It's bizarre and it's unique. I've never seen anything like it in my thirty years of psychiatric nursing. She can read . . . more than emotions and stress. More than the odd word you were already mouthing. More than some song you were humming under your breath.' Susan frowned, clearly irritated at his lack of insight.

Alex put his palms up in apology, acknowledging that he was talking to a psychiatric nurse with more years' experience on the wards than himself. But still . . .

'People in our profession and with our experience understand the methods,' he said, building a bit of flattery and common ground into his apology, 'but we can still be surprised when we see things in practice.'

Susan nodded, narrowing her eyes. 'Then I'm not explaining myself very well. Eva doesn't *cold read* people. She doesn't empathise with their *feelings* – in fact she displays an alarming lack of empathy. But she can *read* them. Like an open book. She thought she was doing it in secret, that no one was paying attention. The staff are all too busy and the rest of the girls too disturbed to analyse anybody other than themselves. But Eva picks on each person she meets in turn and finds out secrets that simply could not be revealed through some trick or misdirection. It scares people – it scares me.'

Alex watched the sincerity in Susan's eyes. She was telling the truth as she saw it. No exaggeration either. If anything, Alex could tell she was holding back.

'How do you know this?' Alex asked. Susan's account was interesting, sure; creepy, yes. But how serious was it? Was this something Alex should be pursuing?

'Because she did it to me,' said Susan gruffly. Alex watched as her eyes welled up, but she quickly brushed the tears away and sniffed. 'She could see things I've never told a soul.'

Alex wrestled with his initial reaction versus the obvious honesty and conviction displayed in front of him. Plus, he shouldn't forget who had referred her to him in the first place. Susan must have told Larry all of this, and Larry had thought it worth Alex taking a look. Alex's judgement had maybe been a little hasty. He tried to put his scepticism to one side and just listen.

'I'm sorry,' he said. 'Please, tell me what happened.'

Susan paused for a second. 'My secret is that my husband was unfaithful to me,' she said. 'Last year: a work trip. I found out all the gory details. Long story short – it was a very difficult period for us. Ian left in the end and I . . .'

Susan swallowed hard, more tears forming. Alex passed her a napkin. She took the thin tissue and dabbed her eyes.

'I've never told a soul and neither has he, both of us out of shame. Nobody at work knows. They think I'm still married.'

Alex took a long breath. He wanted to say that cold readers are adept at preying on people in emotional turmoil. That although she might not have told anyone, Susan's emotions would show through. It was probably a lucky guess – Eva had run through a number of possible reasons as to why somebody of Susan's age would be so devastated, and picked one.

Alex said none of these things. He waited for Susan to continue.

'I was writing up some notes in the lounge one afternoon,' said Susan. 'It's nicer than the office, warmer, and the girls leave us alone when we're working.

'My thoughts drifted to Ian, as they often do when I'm tied down with mindless paperwork. I was thinking about the night he betrayed me – he met the woman in London and they stayed at the London Bridge Hotel. Fancy, I've heard. He never took me there. Anyway, I have this recurring vision of them both kissing, not at the hotel but on London Bridge itself. I put myself there, watching from a distance. The ultimate betrayal played out in full view of the city.'

Alex nodded. These things had a terrible way of finding their way into your thoughts when you least needed it. He offered Susan his most sympathetic smile.

'But something caught my eye, in my peripheral vision. I looked up and saw Eva, standing six feet away in the common room, staring at me. She started singing – do you know what it was?'

Alex shook his head, puzzled.

'*London Bridge is falling down, falling down, falling down.* She kept at it, over and over, staring at me, no expression on her face. She repeated the same lines for a minute or more. My insides were in turmoil and my head was spinning with what I was hearing. Why would she sing that? How could she possibly know? It wasn't a coincidence. I'd never told anybody. But she was singing *at* me.

'I lost my temper and shouted at her to be quiet, screaming over the sound of her voice. Eva stopped singing alright, mid-sentence, but I could see my rebuke had triggered her anger. She stepped over to the table and hissed at me, *I bet Lydia doesn't scream like that. Except perhaps when Ian's on top of her.*

'The words caught me like a blow to the face. I was speechless. Lydia was the name of the woman Ian had slept with. But nobody knew that here. My mouth hung open and I saw in Eva's eyes she knew she'd gone too far. She was angry, but she checked it. Her expression changed, the smirk disappeared and there was conflict in its place. I could see her fury bubbling to the surface – something she was scared of, something she couldn't control. She swallowed and muttered something, backing away, her fists clenched. She ran out of the common room, muttering to herself.'

Susan paused. Alex realised he was on the edge of his seat, leaning halfway across the table. He let out the breath he'd been holding, his heart thumping, the significance of those few short moments taking hold.

'So what did you do?'

'I left. I jumped from the table, ran out of the ward, the hospital, and sat in my car for over an hour, trying to stop the tears. When I returned, Eva was in her room and under sedation. She'd turned violent and hit one of the porters.'

Alex watched Susan for several seconds. His mind was whirring, churning through what she'd said, looking for holes, looking for an easy explanation. None arrived, and the hairs on the back of his neck began to stand. *Don't get excited*, he said to himself. *This may be nothing.*

He took a sip of his drink, his mind sifting through the last few years. Victor Lazar with his incredible hypnotic ability. Mia Anastos with her deadly empathetic sense of pain. Bizarre and macabre, but rooted in medicine. Two patients who had been pushed to the limits of human psychology and physiology, damaged and left out in the cold.

There were more such patients out there, Alex was convinced of it.

But was Eva one of them?

Alex ran over the details again, and then a third time to be sure. He'd been seated for less than thirty minutes, but Susan was already checking her watch and finishing her drink.

He paused to massage his wrist, which ached from the frantic note-taking. He had a hundred questions for Susan, but the most pressing was also the most straightforward.

'What do you expect from me. From Larry?' Alex examined his notes, carefully assessing his duty of care and the risks he was willing to take in order to investigate Eva. The girl was a target, certainly, but Alex must calculate his next move with the greatest of caution.

Susan nodded and hunched down, her eyes flicking back to the door.

'Larry was the only person I thought I could trust who wouldn't immediately kick off an internal investigation and land me in trouble,' she said. 'Call me selfish, but I need to keep my job, Dr Madison, and Dr Naylor scares me. A nurse at my level in the pecking order is easily dismissed, and along with that go any chances of more work.'

'She scares you how exactly?'

Susan clasped her hands together tight, shaking her head. 'Something's not right. Eva's drug regime is all over the place. Her curfew is erratic. Her record is restricted.'

'Restricted?' Alex knew it wasn't unheard of to restrict access to medical records from all but a few clinicians, but it was certainly irregular. 'Why?'

Susan checked her watch again. 'I don't know. I just know what I saw and what I heard – with Eva's strange . . . ability, whatever it is, and then what she did. Like I said, I called the only person I trust. Larry has influence, he can make things happen – maybe Eva can be transferred, treated in another hospital. She can't stay where she is.'

Alex stopped writing and sat back, digesting everything he'd heard over the last half hour. Yes, Larry could make things happen, but he'd chosen to pass it to Alex, suspecting the worst – or the best, depending on which way you looked at it.

If Eva was indeed capable of what Susan claimed, the girl was right up there with Alex's previous cases. A damaged enigma, and almost out of reach. Alex hadn't even begun to figure out what her condition might be, but the behaviour, if Susan was accurate, was extraordinary and demanded his attention.

But she was young, so young. Somebody's child. Somebody's daughter. Katie's face popped into his head. He shivered. It wasn't the same, and yet it provoked a similar reaction in him. Who would protect these damaged souls if people like Alex did nothing?

'You'll do something, won't you?' said Susan, grabbing her handbag. Alex saw the guilt in her eyes. Reporting it up the chain within the hospital was protocol – it's what Susan should have done, although Alex was glad she hadn't. Coming through Larry gave Alex a head start.

'Of course,' said Alex. 'Let me make some calls. I—'

'Then I'll go,' said Susan, rising to her feet and picking her coat up from the chair. 'I'm due to collect my son.' She paused. 'Alex, I really appreciate you coming here, I do. It may be nothing, but I want Eva to be safe . . . Just leave me out of it if you can.'

Alex nodded. 'I'll do my best.'

He watched Susan exit the pub, the door swinging closed behind her. Alex needed time to process everything she'd said. It could all just be some innocent misunderstanding, or something altogether more sinister, but it was a simple question to ask.

What or who was Eva Jansen?

Alex finished his drink, scanning his notes before gathering them up and slipping them into his bag. He opened the maps app on his phone, checking the traffic. It was all clear as long as he left now. Time to go.

He was just pulling on his coat when he heard a screech outside the pub and a dull thump, followed by the breaking of glass. The other patrons fell into silence. Alex stared at the waitress, who stood frozen near the bar, a tray of empty glasses in her hand; they shared a puzzled look.

Alex ran to the door, increasing his pace when he heard the shouts outside.

It took only a second to process the scene – two men standing over the body of a woman in the centre of the road. One was on the phone, the other crouched down, checking for a pulse. Alex ran out to them.

'Susan!' he shouted.

'It just swerved out from the kerb,' said the man. 'A big SUV. It clipped that parked car in the process, then straight across on to the wrong side of the road. It hit this poor lady full on.'

Alex crouched next to Susan. She was lying on her side, still alive, although her breathing was laboured. Her left arm was bent at an awkward angle. She tried to push herself up with her right hand, her legs shifting as she did so.

'What colour?' said Alex. 'What colour was the SUV?'

The man shrugged. 'Dark – black, I think. It turned in off the main road. It's long gone.'

Alex's heart skipped a beat. 'Stay there,' he said to Susan. 'Please! Don't move.' He heard the man on the phone, talking to the ambulance dispatch.

'You'll be OK,' he said, casting his eyes over her body. No blood, no open wounds, and she was conscious, but he had no idea what internal injuries might have been caused. A car that size could have inflicted all sorts of internal trauma. He checked her pulse, which was slow, then sat and held her hand as the sirens wailed in the distance.

'Did you see them?' he asked. 'The people in the car.'

Susan shook her head weakly.

'Have you seen them before? Dark SUVs? Any similar types of car?' Susan didn't respond, and Alex was aware of a puzzled glance from the man on the phone.

He sat back on his heels, still holding her hand, head spinning.

The ambulance arrived and the paramedics took over. They quickly assessed Susan and announced she was stable enough to be moved.

'I'm a friend,' he told one of them. 'We'd just had a drink.' He waved weakly at the pub behind him.

The paramedic nodded, distracted. He spoke to his colleague, reeling off a list of concerns. His partner was on the radio, presumably to the emergency department. A haemorrhage was evident in her lower abdomen and she was now floating in and out of consciousness.

Alex bent over the stretcher as they lifted her into the ambulance. She opened her eyes and gazed at him.

'I'll come with you,' he said, not knowing what else to do, an irrational guilt over what had happened, not wanting to leave her on her own.

She shook her head again, insisting he leave her. The paramedic assured Alex they had her emergency contacts from her purse. They'd call her son's school along with her sister. Alex wasn't family – there really was no need for him to attend the hospital. If he wanted, he could follow them to Brighton General.

Susan shook her head. *No.*

Alex backed away. The crowd began to disperse as the first police officers on the scene took statements from the two men who'd found her and from anyone else who claimed to have seen the car speeding off. Alex gave his name. Because he hadn't seen anything useful, he was told they'd be in touch if they needed anything further.

'Thank you, Doctor,' said the police officer. 'Bloody four-by-fours,' he added. 'They race through here. Chances are, the driver didn't even see her.'

Alex shook his head. They'd seen her alright. He was convinced of it.

He opened his mouth, but the words escaped him. What could he say? What could he possibly tell them without offering up a much longer story? One that started with his legitimate role work-ing for the Met police, but finished with him hiding a wanted murderer, complicit with the doctor who'd given him Susan's name, bolstered only by his own drug-fuelled fear? That was not a story he was willing to tell some traffic cop in the street, no matter how serious the situation. Not today.

Alex closed his mouth and edged away. The officer shrugged and moved on to the next person, one of the barmaids from the pub. Alex heard her start a dramatic recounting of the screech of the car as it sped off. Her voice was interrupted by that of an older woman who'd apparently seen it all from the Co-op store across the street.

All eyes were focused on the road, the police and the depart-ing ambulance. Everyone present at the scene of the accident wore expressions of sympathy and shock.

All except one man.

Alex spied him at the back of the crowd, standing no more than twenty yards away, at the corner of the road. Elderly, but standing tall, and dressed in an immaculate suit, the man surveyed the scene with a scowl, arms crossed. He watched the police officers for a few moments before his eyes settled on Alex.

Alex found the man's stare piercing, unnerving, but held his gaze. The noise of the street faded as Alex's focus intensified. He felt a throbbing behind his eyes, pressure in his temples.

The man tilted his head to one side, then straightened it. He unfolded his arms and gave a small shake of his head, before turn-ing and walking around the corner, out of sight.

Alex blinked several times before moving. He jumped for-wards, colliding with the group in front of him. He apologised, barging his way through, heading after the stranger. As he rounded the corner he stopped. The road stretched on into the distance, but the pavements were empty in either direction.

The lone watcher, whoever he was, had disappeared.

CHAPTER EIGHT

Alex tried dialling again. For the third time he got Larry's voicemail. He hung up, scrolling through for the number of the psychology department at Southampton. Even the main hospital switchboard would be worth a try.

He'd got very little from the emergency department where Susan was being treated in Brighton. He couldn't claim any special relationship with her – all he could tease out of the nurse was what he already knew, that Susan had suffered internal bleeding at the scene of the accident and remained in a critical condition.

He found the number, pausing, a sudden tremor taking his hand. Good old-fashioned shock, except it was worse than that. Alex just couldn't shake the sight of Susan lying on the ground. The shadows he ran from – the ones he knew were watching him. He tapped the edge of his phone, trying to squeeze out the thoughts that screamed at him.

His first firm link to his research in over a year. An accident, or mown down in the street after revealing what she knew? If the latter, it confirmed what he already knew: a sickening display of power, a cowardly act. Should he see it as a threat? Would speaking to Larry again place him in similar danger? Was Alex prepared to risk that?

He should go to the police, to DCI Hartley, tell her what he suspected and what he'd seen.

A detective chief inspector, Hartley had worked with Alex on the cases of Victor Lazar and Mia Anastos. Her acceptance of their bizarre nature was tacit – never openly discussed, not even when it was just the two of them. Hartley trusted Alex's assessments of the inexplicable and the macabre and she used him where she could. She was honest and hardworking – something Alex had to respect – and they had a solid working relationship, although Alex knew her side of it was edged with a suspicion of his own motives and actions. She openly considered his empathy for the perpetrators as misplaced, his interest in their origins useful only if it meant catching them more quickly.

But the consequences . . . How could he tell Hartley anything without revealing the whole of what he knew? If this was indeed Nova's doing, did they know what he sought? Did they know about Mia? Did they know what he'd *done*?

Alex moved his thumb away from the screen. He'd brought this on himself. Hiding Mia had been a one-way ticket. He could never again be one hundred per cent honest with the police, and had known that when he whisked her away into a new life on foreign shores. When he embarked on this dark pursuit of Nova, he had given up their full support, able now to call on them only when he had something tangible, something obviously criminal, and most importantly, something that could not be linked to his private affairs.

He needed to tread with the utmost care, and that meant delving deeper. Once he had more information, he'd have more insight. He'd go to Hartley when he was ready, and not a moment before.

Alex placed his phone on the desk, stared at his blank monitor for a few minutes, keeping his breathing in check, calming himself. He reached into his pocket and took a single Xanax, crunching it between his front teeth, feeling better as the anticipation of relief turned into the real thing.

Calm took him and he was finally able to focus. The vision of Susan lying in the road refused to leave him, but he had no intention of stopping his inquiries into Eva. Susan had said all she wanted to, and given him a plea, a challenge, one that he felt bound to follow up. He hoped to God that Susan would pull through, and when she did, he wanted to be able to assure her he'd done all he could for her patient. If she didn't, well, it didn't bear thinking about.

◆ ◆ ◆

By the time Alex pulled up at his house in Ealing the anxiety had subsided and a distant, hovering worry had taken its place. Staring at his home, he wondered if he'd ever one day come home to find someone waiting for him – a loving partner who opened the door and welcomed him in. Alex remained single, living alone and trying to prove to Grace and Katie that he was serious about rebuilding the family he'd single-handedly demolished in the preceding years. Family came first, work second and his own need for female companionship a distant third. He wondered how healthy or realistic that statement was. His period of reckless short-term girlfriends had ended, but Grace was still encouraging him to go out and meet people. Did she know how much it hurt when she said such a thing? He supposed that had always been the problem – that he still loved her more than she loved him. Or perhaps she was simply a realist, and he was a dreamer, stuck in the past.

They'd been divorced for five years now. Grace had insisted on moving on. Alex couldn't.

He slammed the car door and rummaged for his house keys. Alex punched in his PIN at the alarm panel and waited for the green light, then used his phone to check the cameras. He had cameras to the front and rear of the house triggered by motion sensors, with one inside covering the open-plan kitchen–diner. He tended to leave the alerts switched off and settled for checking the feeds once a day when he got home.

A quick flick through today's footage revealed nothing out of the ordinary. No visitors, no suspicious-looking cars stopping outside. Nothing.

His mind was full and pulsating with nervous energy. He needed to find some calm, let the Xanax take its effect and chill out for a while before starting work. He could go for a run, but the earlier panic had sapped his energy. Not a great excuse, but a reasonable one. Instead, he grabbed his phone and stretched out full length on the sofa. There was one voice that never failed to bring him back from the brink.

'Dad.' Alex heard various muffled words at the other end. 'Are you calling about Gran? I said I'd go and see her. Just not this week. Or next. Maybe . . . the week after.'

Alex read her tone – impatient, borderline hostile. Not just teenage hormones.

'I wasn't calling about that,' said Alex, the sound of his daughter's voice penetrating deeper than any drug or alcohol seemed to, reminding him of his purpose, and of the debt he owed. He stretched his legs over the end of the sofa, feeling the tension ease in his calves. 'I just wanted to catch up. See how you are. See if you need anything.'

The reality was that he worried more than he let on. Katie's therapy had started after the case of Victor Lazar, who had kidnapped Katie and held her at knifepoint. She'd escaped any physical hurt, but the trauma was real and the damage needed addressing. That had been a couple of years ago, and, initially at least, she had made good progress, failing to exhibit any persistent symptoms. Alex had dared to think she'd come through unscathed.

This year was different, however. Katie had begun to spiral, her therapy sessions unearthing all manner of issues which had started to manifest in new behaviours, both at school and at home. Neither Grace nor Katie blamed Alex. Not openly. Not officially.

He thought he heard her snort, before taking a deep breath.

'You're checking up on me, Dad,' she said. 'Stop it. I'm *working it through*, as Dr Amir keeps telling me.'

'She's a wise doctor.'

Alex had kept Katie's therapy separate from his own practice and never pried. Dr Amir was a former colleague, experienced in child trauma and with a track record of good results. Alex paid for all the treatment – one small way in which he could try to make amends – and promised always to be there if Katie wanted to talk. Sometimes she did, sometimes she didn't.

'I guess. So I'm OK. What's yours like?' asked Katie.

'Mine?'

'Your therapist. Mum said you were seeing her this morning.'

The panic surged in his chest again. His muscles tensed. Ah yes, therapy. The fake therapist he'd told Grace about and the imaginary therapy sessions he was attending in an effort to tackle his lifelong generalised anxiety disorder and benzo habit, the latter of which was satisfied via illegal prescriptions.

That therapy.

'Umm,' he said. 'OK. She's OK.'

The guilt slapped him and his cheeks burned. He expected honesty from Katie, yet he lied straight back. He hated it, but the alternative was being honest with Grace. He'd promised to get help, and there were only so many reminders he could take from Grace before he'd finally agreed to see someone. He'd phoned a clinic, in front of Grace, and made an appointment. That was six months ago, and every week Grace asked him how it was going. Each time he assured her that while progress would be slow, he was on the right road. He would talk about it when he was ready.

He'd cancelled the appointment the same day, in the car on the way home, figuring he'd rebook it when he was in a better frame of mind. He wanted help, he needed it, and he fully intended to get it. But not now. Not while he had so much on. The thought of opening the lid on his own mind at the moment didn't bear thinking about. The lie had persisted and grown. And now it was too late to come clean without the risk of pushing Grace and Katie further away.

'Fine,' said Katie, sensing he wasn't going to elaborate. Another sigh. 'Mum's out, if you wanted to talk to her. She told me about the holiday.'

'You deserve one,' said Alex, eyes clamped shut, his face flushed.

'Yeah, maybe. She said maybe one year you might come with us.'

Alex's eyes popped open. 'She did?'

'That's what she said.'

'Well, that's . . .'

'After you've had a chance to work through your issues,' said Katie. 'Once you're in a better place emotionally.'

Alex took a deep breath. Why was he doing this? The most precious thing in the world to him. Lying to her, after everything she'd been through, because of him, felt like the ultimate betrayal. Grace too. She'd understand if he came clean. They both would.

'Katie,' he whispered. 'Look, I—'

'Hang on a sec,' said Katie. Alex heard a shuffling at the other end and the line went blank. He'd been put on hold. He let out a breath, thinking about the words he'd use: how to tell her.

'Dad, gotta go. Bonnie's on the line – I need to organise next week.'

'Oh,' said Alex. 'OK. I just want to—'

'I know, Dad,' said Katie. She was frustrated, hormonal, angry, but still his little girl. 'Speak soon, OK?' She hung up.

Alex dropped the phone on to his chest and closed his eyes. The moment was gone. With Katie's voice still in his ears, the panic came on again, rising from his stomach, forcing his breathing into shallow gasps. He wrestled with it, begging it not to overwhelm him.

He rolled on to his side, pulling a pillow under his head as the room spun. He lost focus on everything, his mind a swirling mess. Lying to Katie, lying to Grace. Lying to the police about what he truly pursued and why. How many lies can a person stack, one on top of the other, before they tumble?

Not just panic – something else.

A memory. A flashback of the abandoned orphanage in London where Victor Lazar had made his last stand. Then darkness. Pitch black. Katie was safe, but something lurked behind, a whisper bringing a thud of confusion to the fore.

The memory switched. Alex's hands were now covered in blood – the blood of Mia Anastos, the girl Alex had carried to safety against all odds and against the law. He had saved her life but could never admit it. The whisper again, a voice in the darkness, teasing him.

A female face appeared next. Featureless and hollow, it grew in shape and presence until Alex could feel it in the room.

Beauty and danger. The Russian woman with the beautiful eyes who'd pointed a gun at his head but let him escape.

She was looking at him, probing his soul. Alex opened his eyes, blinking furiously, but her face remained burned into his vision. How many times had he seen her like this? Too many to count. Why was she here again, flooding his mind with such dread? She raised her hands up. They too were drenched in blood, palms dripping. She tilted her head and parted her lips, whispering. Alex heard nothing.

He rolled on to his back, not sure whether his eyes were open or closed. Stars danced at the periphery of his vision. A drop in blood pressure, he thought. No, something else. He focused inwards. Alex could hear the whispers; they crowded his mind as he tumbled. He blinked and her face reappeared with each flash. Her lips still moving, her eyes silent dark holes that stared through him, back to the distant past.

Alex floated and he breathed. Four in, four out.

The daydream ended as quickly as it had begun. Alex's phone rang, the piercing notes jolting him out of his trance. The face disappeared in a flash and the whispers faded. His ears popped and reality appeared, the washed-out colours of the living room growing more vibrant as the fog cleared.

Alex sat up straight on the sofa, realising he was holding his phone. It vibrated in his hand, rang three more times and then stopped. Releasing his fist, he watched the sweat evaporate from the screen. He forced his breathing under control, closing his eyes as the last of the vertigo settled. His galloping heart slowed to a dull thudding in his ears, replacing the whispers.

She was gone.

CHAPTER NINE

The girl looked so young in the photograph, so pretty and pure, yet her blue eyes betrayed her. Natalia recognised the pain – it was the same pain she saw every day in her own reflection. This girl had suffered in a similar way. And this girl, like Natalia, would never forget.

The dossier was disappointingly light. One recent photograph, taken by the hospital on admission. Over the years, Natalia had met many despicable people. A woman who sold young girls for profit wasn't the worst by a long way.

Natalia put the phone back to her ear. She lay back on the sunlounger, in the shade, hidden on her own private balcony, where she'd spent most of the last two days simmering in boredom and room service. The bikinis remained in her suitcase, unused.

'How the hell did they end up with her?' she had asked. Her questions had been relentless and she was growing frustrated at the vagueness of the answers. Her handler, Tomas, did his best, but only told her what he thought she needed to know.

'They didn't realise,' he said. 'The girl was lost to us, like so many of the others.'

'How long did they have her?'

Tomas cleared his throat. 'There were far worse places than Comăneşti, Natalia.'

The words triggered hurtful flashes of Romania and the cold dormitories of the orphanage. Natalia could hear the screams from behind the metal doors, the begging and the cries. She struggled to imagine a worse place, but nonetheless could believe they existed.

'Most of those places were abandoned, forgotten,' continued Tomas, 'although some were still running until very recently. The products were scattered. She has been found and we're bringing her in.'

Natalia remembered her own homecoming, long after the Romanian orphanage had been razed to the ground, when she'd been plucked from the streets and offered the life she had now. There had been no choice in the offer back then; there wasn't now. What were they bringing this poor girl home to?

'How do they know what they've got?'

'I don't think they did, not for years. The seller stumbled on her and knows she's got something special.'

'Special?' Natalia snorted.

'By their standards, of course. By ours – well, we'll see.' Tomas cleared his throat.

Natalia paused. There was a lot that could go wrong with their current plan.

'There's no other way?'

'The organisers already have her. They are not a fight we want to pick right now.'

'Right.' Natalia had already reviewed the background information. A Spanish trafficking ring was organising the sale. They were big, established across the mainland with links to both Russian and Italian mafia, and down into Libya. Her organisation was not against making enemies, but it chose them strategically. Picking fights with trafficking thugs was too noisy and too risky. Openly challenging the police, or killing them needlessly, was always avoided. Operating in the shadows was the preferred option.

'We've narrowed the field,' said Tomas. 'We ran regular interference. Most bidders have pulled out already. There are a few we can't affect. Those are the variables.'

Natalia nodded to herself. Being the only bidder would have been perfect, but they wouldn't have got that lucky.

'So the seller, this *doctor*' – she spat out the word – 'is a regular?'

'Apparently so. Her products are damaged girls. Teenagers, children. Sold for sex. Sold for anything. We looked into her. She's provided two others this year through the same ring.'

Natalia nodded. She was long desensitised to hearing such things, as was Tomas. The act of selling a child for sex was one of many grotesque realities of the underworld in which she operated. Given permission, she would kill the people who committed such crimes in a heartbeat. But she must wait for permission.

'But this time, the doctor was marketing something different,' she said.

'That's what we picked up on the chatter. A peculiar talent. You know the rest.'

'The other bidders?'

'Nothing yet. You'll know as soon as I do.'

Natalia sighed. She closed her eyes, feeling the warm breeze on her bare skin. Perhaps she'd try and stay on for a few days when this was all over. They wouldn't let her, of course, but she could still ask. One day they might say yes.

'Once this is dealt with,' she said, 'what happens to the doctor?'

Tomas cleared his throat again 'Don't agitate the sale,' he said. 'She's a loose end.'

'Please stick to your instructions,' said Tomas. He paused, then in a softer tone, added, 'Afterwards . . . I'll ask.'

Natalia nodded to herself. She couldn't think of anything else, so hung up, dropping her mobile on to the towel.

◆ ◆ ◆

The day reached its hottest point and Natalia daydreamed, listening to the bustling streets below and the cry of the birds fighting over the rooftops. The relentless blue sky was mesmerising; she was used to impenetrable grey and white.

Sleep was harder to come by, and not because of the noise. Something in Tomas's tone bothered her. Natalia had a great deal of autonomy – she was one of the original *păpușars*, a puppet master. Her ability was not in question and she was deployed on the most difficult and sensitive of assignments, yet she sensed things were changing. Her organisation was shifting, exposing itself more readily, becoming more ruthless in its objectives.

Natalia knew she had a black mark against her for the disappearance of a young woman the previous year. Mia had disappeared into thin air, according to Natalia's report. A valuable asset, damaged, but not beyond repair. They'd wanted Mia terminated at first, but had then decided to bring her in. Natalia had made a different choice, one that played easy on her conscience but hard on her professional reputation. As far as her organisation was concerned, Natalia had screwed up. Only Natalia and one other individual knew the truth.

The thought of this individual stirred something else in Natalia, an excitement and a fear. A man she'd deceived, befriended and taken as a lover; a man who didn't know her identity or whether she even really existed.

She'd kept her eye on Alex Madison, off the books, a small operation, competent but restricted, and they reported only to her. It was for her own safety, and, if she was honest, for her own curiosity. Such a normal individual, by Natalia's standards, yet he was a man who had managed to distract her from one of her most difficult tasks, his moral compass and his anxious idiosyncrasies attracting Natalia in a way few others could.

But not in *that* way. Their moment of passion had been a mistake, long forgotten, and he never even knew it had happened, Natalia had made sure of that. Her own feelings were confused and amplified by the nature of her existence and the life she lived – Natalia had no friends, no regular lovers, certainly no love. She existed in a covert world of suspicion and fear, where she gave and took in equal measure. Alex was interesting to Natalia in regard to what he stood for, particularly given his father Rupert's role in her organisation – this apple had evidently fallen far from the tree. She felt an affinity with him and his actions.

An affinity that could get her in a world of trouble if anybody found out.

She sat up and reached for her laptop. It lay under the table, out of the sun. A tickle caught her throat and she coughed, feeling the familiar pain as her lungs erupted into a fit. It had been getting worse over the years, but so far she'd resisted medical treatment back home. A visit to the authorised medical centre would throw up red flags and curtail her activities. A visit to an unauthorised doctor would result in immediate retirement – the products of her organisation must not be examined by the medical establishment in any country, that much was obvious.

She assumed it was simply the result of the damp Russian air. Perhaps this country would clear it up. Maybe she'd leave healthier than she'd arrived. Most of the people she'd meet over the next couple of weeks would not be able to say the same.

The coughing subsided and she opened up her laptop, browsing through her emails. She sat up, alert. One of them was red, urgent. A warning.

It was from her man in London. She scanned the usual activity and paused. Natalia knew what Alex was looking for, and wasn't surprised at what she read. The good doctor had been travelling south, to a psychiatric hospital in the UK. He was hunting the same thing she was. He was on the same trail.

But it was the last few lines that left her cold. Her lips parted as the air escaped, her skin prickled despite the scorching heat.

They're watching him. Pavel has taken it as a personal assignment. He's cleaning up.

A shadow from her past, Natalia was never quite sure whether Pavel had come from Comănești, or some other hell on earth. His age suggested something older, something closer to home. The Soviets had been the prime mover in their shared history, and Natalia wondered what had created him, this man who was feared across the organisation as dangerously unpredictable and unflinchingly powerful. Many had gone up against Pavel and lost, their tattered minds and bodies strung up as examples of rank disobedience. His position in the hierarchy was higher than Natalia was ever likely to reach, and he restricted himself to matters of state and global interest. He also ran *that* place as his own institution in the East – that particular hell on earth that not even Natalia could bring herself to think about.

Pavel used Natalia and her comrades as trained dogs to conduct the lower-level work – to clean up the messier aspects of their operations and keep the cogs turning.

For Pavel to emerge from Russia meant he was taking a special interest.

Cleaning up. Natalia scanned the brief bulleted observations. The people who'd been targeted so far.

These were overt warnings, meant to strike fear.

But why Alex Madison? Why now?

Awaiting instruction.

Natalia thought quickly, but there was nothing she could do. She typed out the briefest of replies: *Stand by*, before closing the lid.

Alex, she thought. *Shit. Once was lucky, second was charming, but three times will be your downfall. I can only protect you so much, and if Pavel is after you, then God help us all.*

CHAPTER TEN

Nurse Susan's first sensation was noise, an intermittent hissing, interspersed with the beeping of a monitor. She recognised these sounds intimately. A respirator, an ECG machine. The smell came next, the distinct hospital blend of bodies and chemicals, each one trying to cancel out the other. The metallic tinge of blood flooded her nostrils as she drew a long slow breath. Swollen nasal cavities, a thick, dry mouth. A tube pressing down on her tongue.

She tried to move, to shift up on the bed, but her body failed her. No strength to speak of, not yet. How long had she been out? Where was Noah, her son? Which hospital was this?

The memory appeared, unchallenged, flooding back. The call she'd made, the visit by Dr Madison. She'd left the pub, deciding she'd said too much, regretting her involvement. She wanted the young girl to be safe, that's all.

She'd hurried out into the street, hadn't looked properly, focused on the screen of her phone. The impact had knocked the wind out of her. At first, that's all it was, then the pain grew inside, and with it, the sense of more severe injury. Faces looking down at her, then nothing.

Tears formed. It wasn't the pain but rather the emotion, the realisation of what had happened to her. So close. So stupid. Her son could have ended up alone, her life snuffed out in one careless lapse of concentration.

She drifted for a few moments, trying to collect her thoughts. She glanced to the bedside table, looking for her phone, for the call button.

The door to her room clicked open. She tilted her head to the side for a better view. A dark-suited man stepped in. She didn't recognise him. By his age, she guessed the consultant, or surgeon perhaps, on his rounds. What news did he have for her? Could she leave? Would her path to recovery be swift? Or was there some more catastrophic message to be delivered? Her heart started to thump with anticipation. What if she was left permanently injured? She wiggled her toes, felt the sheets shift across her bare legs as she moved them.

The man moved closer, his smart shoes clicking on the hard floor. He didn't look at the screen of the ECG or check the chart at the end of her bed. He reached out, placing his hands on the edge of the mattress, leaning towards her face.

His lips moved, just a fraction, a whisper of sound escaping.

Susan's thumping heart began to strain. *Just nerves*, she thought, but couldn't read his expression. It was wooden, with a slight frown. Was this the face he used to deliver bad news?

'Doctor,' she said.

The man smiled, but shook his head. The smile was strained, disingenuous. Susan felt a shiver, felt herself grasping the bedsheet, drawing it closer.

The whispering stopped.

'Who else have you spoken to?' the man asked. His voice was low, with a strong accent. Not surprising – the NHS was staffed by all nationalities – it was what made it a world leader in so many disciplines. Yet this doctor somehow didn't fit the profile.

'I've only just woken,' said Susan. 'You're the first person I've spoken to.' Her throat stung, too dry.

The man nodded. 'Before. Who *else?*'

Susan shrank back as he leaned in, his face unprofessionally close. This was not an examination.

'I don't know what you mean.' Susan's voice quivered. Her heart continued to race, accompanied by a tightening of her chest. 'I haven't spoken to anyone.'

The man closed his eyes, his grip on the bed tightening. Susan saw his knuckles turn white with effort, his wrinkled and hairless skin revealing thick blue veins. She saw them pulsate as he shifted his weight.

The ECG alarm went off as Susan tensed, her legs twitching, involuntary and uncontrollable. The twitching moved upwards, her stomach muscles clenching. Pins and needles took her hands, creeping up her arms like a thousand small spiders, reaching her neck, covering her face. She shivered from top to toe, her face growing cold, detached.

The man opened his eyes, reached over and tore the ECG pads from her body, flicking the device off. The alarm fell silent.

She winced, her eyes begging, but the man just stared, the wooden expression returned, his eyes glazed. He whispered a few more incoherent utterances. He wasn't here to help her. Quite the opposite.

The nurse in her screamed. These symptoms, so rapid, so specific. Not a result of her injury.

'Please,' she said, reaching out, trying to move, but her arms remained weak and limp, her hands wracked with spasms, the pain in her chest growing, tight, central. Her basic training flooded back to her. All the signs she knew to look for.

Her heart was failing. She was going into cardiac arrest.

The man nodded, the movement sinister in its banality, his expression unchanged as he watched her body writhe in pain. 'I believe you,' he said.

The tension spread to her neck, her jaw clenched and her back ached. Not just tightness, not mild discomfort, but twisting, acute pain. The nausea and vertigo hit at the same time, sweat beading all over her skin, the final reactions of a dying body as it struggled to deal with intense trauma.

The man stepped back, releasing his grip, watching her intently. Susan's vision was fading now, the man's body waning to a silhouette, a shadow of death, come to take her.

Some people imagine they'll have time to reflect on their lives during their final moments, their loved ones, their successes and regrets. It rarely happens that way in practice, particularly during acute trauma, and Susan was no exception. In her final moments, her only thought was one of understanding, the confusion suddenly clearing – of why this man was here. Susan had been right about Eva, the girl under her care with the bizarre ability. Eva's uncanny grasp of people's inner dialogue – their thoughts and emotions – were not in Susan's imagination, they were real, and this man was proof. He could do the same, and worse, and his actions were no more than that – the demonstration of a phenomenon beyond Susan's comprehension or control. She had no option but to succumb.

As if in understanding, the man raised one eyebrow at Susan as her heart thumped to a halt. He nodded one last time, then disappeared into the darkness.

CHAPTER ELEVEN

The entrance to St Anne's Hospital in Sussex opened into a small lobby. All the wards were restricted and the corridors were security card access only, so Alex was forced to queue at the main reception desk. It was staffed by a thickset woman protected behind a grubby glass barrier.

'Dr Alex Madison,' he said. 'I have an appointment with Dr Naylor.'

The woman smiled and turned to her keyboard. Her face showed the expected confusion as she searched for his appointment.

'I'm sorry,' she said, 'they haven't put you in the system. Let me call her PA.'

Alex nodded and smiled, as if this happened all the time. 'It was last minute,' he added. 'My fault.'

The receptionist spoke on the phone for a few moments. She was obviously being told the same story – Alex didn't have an appointment. The woman glanced at Alex a few times before putting the phone down.

'Kathy will be right with you,' she said. 'She doesn't have it in her diary either. Take a seat and we'll sort this out.'

Alex thanked her for her time and walked over to the visitor waiting area: a steel bench bolted to the floor with plastic seats on top. He placed his bag on one and sat on another, stretching his legs out, feeling his lower back crack in protest.

The drive from London had been quick. Alex had taken the back roads, avoiding the motorways, watching the morning sun as it cut through the mist on the South Downs National Park. Once or twice in south London he thought he saw somebody following him. It was probably nothing, but he took a fast exit off the M25 and pulled over into a layby to make sure. Nothing passed him. Nothing stopped.

He thought of Susan in her hospital bed and felt his heart skip a beat.

Choices. He couldn't see any alternative. Susan had given him a thread – he must pull it until it broke, or until he unravelled something bigger. Eva Jansen was too intriguing to let go.

'Dr Madison?' A young woman leaned through a set of double doors.

Alex stood and picked up his bag. He showed Naylor's PA his card and followed her through the doors and into a long corridor. It was cold and dreary, the walls painted a dark grey, pocked and marked with age.

'I don't know why she didn't tell me of your visit,' Kathy said. 'Have you spoken to her recently?'

'A few weeks ago,' said Alex. 'Dr Naylor and I met at an NHS workshop a few years ago – we share a lot of common research subjects. She invited me down today to talk about one of her current patients. She was after some advice on treatment plans.'

The lies came easily, and Alex followed them with his practised smile.

Kathy sighed. 'I do my best to keep her diary in order,' she said. 'I can't help it if Dr Naylor doesn't tell me these things.'

'Of course not,' said Alex. 'Hopefully she'll see me anyway.'

'Well, that's the thing,' said Kathy, swiping through another set of doors and turning right. 'She's not here – she's in Europe at a conference. She's not due back until Friday.'

'Oh.' Alex looked as disappointed as he could. 'Oh,' he repeated, 'that's a blow. I've driven all the way from west London this morning. You're sure?'

'As sure as I can be,' said Kathy. 'Her clinic is clear all week. She's moved everything. I booked her plane tickets. She left at the weekend.'

'Anywhere nice?'

'Madrid,' said Kathy. 'You doctors do like to pick the best destinations.' She sighed again, but this time with a smile. 'This is us,' she said, walking past a reception area towards a cluster of offices.

Alex nodded. Just as Susan had said. Madrid didn't feature prominently on the medical conference circuit, but he'd look it up.

'Give me a sec.' Kathy approached her desk and keyed in the password on her computer, scanning through what looked like the staff roster.

'OK,' she said, 'it looks like Dr Morgan's covering clinic today. She's free for a few minutes if you wanted to talk?'

Alex appeared to consider it. 'OK, that would be good,' he said. 'I don't know how this mix-up happened, but if I can help with the patient while I'm here, it won't have been a wasted trip.'

'Take a seat in Dr Naylor's office,' said Kathy, indicating the door behind him. 'I'll call Dr Morgan and tell her you're waiting.'

Dr Naylor had a large office overlooking a courtyard at the centre of the hospital. The room was spotless and ordered. Her desk sat in front of the window facing three chairs and a couch. Along the back wall stood rows of filing cabinets, and the opposite wall was empty except for a selection of certificates hung at varying heights, all bearing Dr Naylor's name. To the right of Naylor's desk was a wastebasket and a large shredder. There was no clutter in sight, no files or notebooks.

Alex closed the door and sauntered over to the filing cabinets. As expected, all were locked. The desktop PC on the desk was switched off and would require credentials to log in. The three drawers under the desk were also locked.

He glanced at the door before searching the wastebasket. It was less than half full, containing a few items of junk mail. He crouched to look at the shredder. The window on the side indicated it was empty, but to make sure, Alex lifted the top off. Paper dust wafted up, but other than a few scraps, it was clean.

He placed the lid back on and stepped away. He hadn't expected to find anything, but you never knew. He couldn't glean anything so far. Naylor might be a naturally tidy person, or she might have something to hide.

Alex sat and waited for Dr Morgan. He took his pulse, trying to avoid the spiral of self-examination – the curse of every anxious person. His pulse was high, but reasonable considering he'd entered the hospital on false pretences. His anxiety was bubbling but kept at bay by his morning dose of Xanax. He felt an irrational desire for coffee but decided to wait. His stomach rumbled and with it came the faint hint of nausea – he should have eaten a proper breakfast.

Alex paused, taking a deep breath. This could be nothing. Susan could have it all wrong. But what if?

The door swung open, startling him. The woman stuck her arm out.

'Holly Morgan,' she said, with a wary smile. 'Kathy told me why you're here.'

'I'm Alex.' He shook the doctor's hand. She was middle-aged, with laughter lines on her face and short black hair. She moved with the speed of someone always running from one place to the next, careful never to get comfortable. She sat, her small frame perched on the edge of one of the chairs, facing Alex.

'Thank you for seeing me,' said Alex, settling back into his seat. 'Dr Naylor invited me here to discuss a patient.'

Alex noticed a slight twitch in Holly's eyes at the mention of Dr Naylor. He paused. 'You work with Dr Naylor?' he said.

Dr Morgan shook her head. 'Barely. I've only been here six months. I've started to cover her clinic when she's away.'

Alex noticed an air of disapproval in her tone. 'She goes away a lot?'

Dr Morgan shrugged. 'Privilege of her position, I guess. There's always a conference somewhere.'

Alex smiled. 'I guess there is,' he said.

'And you?' said Dr Morgan. 'You're . . . close colleagues?'

'No, no,' said Alex, sensing she wasn't Dr Naylor's biggest fan. 'We've only met once, corresponded a couple of times. It was the patient that brought me here.'

Dr Morgan frowned. 'Which one?'

'Eva Jansen,' said Alex. He saw the reaction in her eyes.

'Oh,' she said. 'Oh dear. Well, this really is a wasted trip. Didn't Dr Naylor tell you? I suppose she didn't.'

'Tell me what?'

'Eva Jansen passed away.'

Alex froze in his seat. 'Sorry,' he said. 'Eva *Jansen*. She's a young woman – eighteen, I think. She's in the secure ward here.'

Dr Morgan frowned. 'Yes, I know the name, but I'm sorry.' She stood and walked over to Naylor's PC, tapping in her credentials. She stared at the screen for a few moments. 'Yes, the night before last – sudden cardiac death caused by . . .' She clicked the mouse a few times. 'They think an underlying inherited disorder.'

Alex was dumbfounded. He struggled to piece it together. 'Dead?'

Dr Morgan looked at him, then frowned again. 'I'm sorry, Dr Madison. It was unexpected. Did you know Eva well?'

Alex shook his head. 'No. No . . . I.' The room seemed to shrink and the air grew thin. His flesh begin to crawl with the exact same unease as when Susan had been carted into the ambulance. Her nurse in critical care, and now Eva dead.

'Has it been filed?' he said.

Dr Morgan frown deepened, but she glanced back to the screen.

'The medical certificate was filed by Dr Naylor on the same night. She pronounced it and dealt with it all on her own. She circulated the news – we normally get a memo. Eva had attacked a member of staff, been forcibly restrained, but . . .'

'What?'

'Nothing,' she said, scrolling through something on the screen. 'It's nothing. It's just . . . something wrong with the system.'

'What?'

She shrugged. 'Her main medical record is missing. It happens sometimes. IT issues.' She logged out and sat back down. 'My sympathies,' she said, 'but—'

'Were you working at the time?' said Alex.

Dr Morgan's puzzled expression remained. 'No,' she said. 'I was on another ward. I got the memo from Dr Naylor – everyone connected to her clinic did.'

'Did you treat Eva?'

'No,' said Dr Morgan. 'I'm afraid I had no involvement with Eva's treatment or assessment.'

'So you didn't see Eva on the day she died?'

She sat back, clasping her hands together. A step too far? Alex hastily backed up, trying to control his sudden panic.

'Sorry,' he said, 'I'm studying her condition – IED – and any link to underlying physiology would be very valuable for my research. Anybody who saw or treated her on the day of her death might be able to offer some insight.'

Dr Morgan nodded and the frown disappeared. 'Dr Naylor was running the ward that day. You could ask the nursing staff but . . . nothing was recorded.'

It seemed a strange thing to say. 'How do you know nothing was recorded?' said Alex.

She looked uncomfortable. 'I . . . It's nothing.' Her eyes darted again to the PC and she bit her lower lip.

'Please,' said Alex, watching her. 'Anything you know might help.'

Dr Morgan stared at him for several moments. Alex waited, holding her gaze. He saw she wasn't entirely comfortable with their discussion, and wanted to know why.

'Our discharge rate is higher than average,' said Dr Morgan. As soon as she'd said it, she shook her head and made to get up from the chair. 'I really need to get going—'

'Please,' said Alex, extending his hand, indicating for her to sit back down. 'I'd like to know what happened to the patient. To Eva. Here are my credentials.' He rummaged in his jacket pocket and produced his ID badge. 'I'm on your side.' He let those words hang. The doctor was clearly uncomfortable about something, but like Susan, she was reluctant to get involved.

Dr Morgan slowly sat.

'It's probably nothing,' she said, 'but our discharge of young female patients is faster than the average.'

Alex frowned. 'What do you mean?'

'I mean some of the female patients we have on this wing are transferred out more quickly than I'd expect. I was interested to know why they're being discharged so early back into the community. It suggests extremely successful treatment . . . much better than average outcomes.'

Alex sucked in a breath. Why would Naylor have a higher than average discharge rate?

'I don't understand.'

'Neither do I,' said Dr Morgan. 'And I'm not claiming anything, but I'd taken to reading all of the discharge reports in Dr Naylor's ward over the last few months. That's how I know what gets recorded.'

'But Eva won't have had one.'

Dr Morgan paused. 'She had a preliminary one but it was withdrawn.'

'By whom?'

'I don't know.'

'Why would it be withdrawn?'

Dr Morgan shrugged. 'Many patients can't function beyond the walls of this place. It's not uncommon. You'd never offer the prospect unless you thought the patient was ready. Perhaps Eva was reassessed as unsuitable.'

'Was she? Suitable?'

Dr Morgan puffed her cheeks and blew out. 'Not by a long way, from what I'd read.'

Alex tried to organise his thoughts. They still didn't make sense. And now she was dead.

'What about the other discharges? What was strange about them?'

Dr Morgan shook her head. She looked troubled, as if she'd revealed too much. 'I can't discuss the other patients with you.'

'But—'

Dr Morgan's pager bleeped on her belt. She checked the screen. 'I've got to go,' she said. 'I've told you all I can. I'm sorry this was a wasted trip. I'm so sorry about Eva, whatever your connection to her.'

She stood and smoothed her jacket, then nodded, as much to herself as anything. She extended her hand. 'It was nice meeting you.'

'Are you sure you can't tell me anything else about the clinic,' Alex asked. 'About Dr Naylor?'

Dr Morgan once again met his eyes. Alex saw the uncertainty, but sensed she had said all she was willing to divulge.

'I'm sorry,' she said. 'There's nothing else concrete to tell you.' She emphasised the word *concrete*, with an apologetic shrug.

'Can you do me one last thing?' he said. 'Send me Eva's medical record when the IT issues are sorted? I have permission from Dr Naylor. Now that Eva's deceased, there are no remaining issues regarding data protection.'

Dr Morgan considered it for a second. 'OK. When I've finished clinic, I'll dig out what we have and email it to you.'

Alex thanked Dr Morgan and followed her out of Naylor's office. To linger would have looked strange, and although his visit would no doubt raise awkward questions at a later date, he didn't want to be escorted off the premises by security.

CHAPTER TWELVE

Alex exited the building and slumped into his car, still not believing what he'd heard. Eva could simply have been a troubled young woman with an unfortunate and fatal physical condition. But something didn't feel right about her death. The timing – what with Larry's call and Susan's whistle-blowing – was too much of a coincidence. He couldn't even call Susan to get her input, and Larry was bound to stay out of it, particularly if the patient was now deceased. He certainly wasn't returning any of Alex's calls. *Move on*, he'd say. *Let it go, Alex.*

What had Dr Morgan been holding out on? He'd taken away a couple of crucial points. First, she was suspicious of Dr Naylor, or at least saw behaviour that concerned her, which bolstered the fact of Susan herself having suspicions. Second, there was this odd situation of the rapid discharging of female patients. Why would Dr Naylor seek to get patients out of hospital and out of the system?

Alex pulled on to the main road as his phone rang. He read the display and took the call.

'Grace,' he said.

'Hey, Alex.' Grace's voice cut through his train of thought. He slowed down a little.

'Listen . . . can you talk?'

'Sure,' said Alex, puzzled at her tone and wondering what was up.

'Well, I had a strange call from a home security company today – ADT? They said they were booking in a time to fit the alarm and cameras?'

Grace left it hanging. She sounded more than a little peeved, and perhaps rightly so. Alex hadn't expected them to contact her so quickly, and had planned on raising it at the weekend when he picked up Katie.

He'd rehearsed his rationale, ready to speak to Grace, although put on the spot, it failed to form coherently in his head. His explanation was that his job carried a low-level risk – the criminals he was exposed to were in and out of prison, and he just wanted to make sure his family was safe.

What he wasn't going to tell them was the other side – that somebody was watching him. They'd ask who, and he couldn't give them a clear answer without revealing far more than he should. Grace and Katie didn't know about Mia; they didn't know about the Russian. They didn't know of his research and his certainty that he'd only scratched the surface of something far deeper-reaching. They'd insist he went to the police, but the police would ask the same questions, explore the same avenues. Alex would be exposed, and he couldn't afford to be. Not now. Not yet.

'I . . .' Alex's thoughts spiralled and he wasn't quick enough for Grace.

'What's happened?' she said. 'Why do we need security?'

'Nothing,' he said, trying to sound as confident as he could. 'Nothing's happened, and you probably don't need it. I'm being extra-cautious. Loads of people have it these days—'

'None of my friends do.'

'But they don't live on their own,' said Alex, wincing as he said it. Grace and Katie's situation was his fault, and Grace's new partner, John, seemed to be off and on. Grace didn't like talking about it, but Katie gave him the low-down. John remained living the other side of town and Alex was always delighted to hear it. The only downside was that it left Grace and Katie in a big house all alone.

'And they don't have a family member who works for the police on violent crimes,' he said.

Grace paused.

'It's precautionary,' said Alex, hoping to God it was true, no longer sure if that was the case, 'and when I booked it, they said it would be a few weeks before they'd get to you. I was going to mention it this weekend.'

Grace sighed. Alex pulled off a slip road on to the motorway.

'I can't help thinking . . .' Grace paused. 'You're being very . . . cautious at the moment, Alex.'

'Cautious?' He knew what she meant, but he'd tried not to make it so obvious.

'If there's nothing for us to worry about, then this is more about you than any outside threat.'

The words hit Alex with their insight. Grace knew him so well, but even so, she was starting to put together a pretty damning analysis of his current mindset.

'I'm not paranoid, if that's what you're thinking, Grace,' he said, trying to dismiss it. 'Please just trust me on this one. I'm paying for it all.'

'I didn't say you were paranoid,' said Grace. He heard her take a breath, as if to continue. She cleared her throat. 'Have you spoken to your therapist about it?'

It was Alex's turn to pause. Grace had reached a very quick and very reasonable conclusion. She was wrong, but Alex couldn't tell her without revealing everything.

'No,' he said, which was true, notwithstanding the bigger lie of there being no therapist to tell.

'Maybe you should? Ask what they think about it?'

Alex indicated to overtake a lorry, accelerating well past the speed limit before forcing himself to slow down.

'If I tell my therapist, will you have the equipment fitted?'

'Deal,' said Grace. She paused. 'I'm proud of you, Alex.'

'OK,' said Alex, feeling the habitual lump in his throat, touching the brakes as the traffic thickened up ahead.

'You're still coming around on Saturday?' said Grace. 'Katie said 3 p.m., which sounds a bit early for pizza, but what do I know?'

'I'll be there,' said Alex, thanking Grace in his head for ending the call on a pleasant note. She always knew what he needed to hear.

He pulled up in a traffic jam. He inched along the motorway as the guilt crept through his mind. It was constant these days, nagging and tiring, but a necessary consequence of what he was doing – or at least he convinced himself that was the case. He had to, or everything would fall apart, and he'd be lost.

The traffic began to thin a little, the outer lane moving at last. Alex indicated and pulled out, accelerating, checking his rear-view mirror.

That's when he saw it. Three cars back. A black BMW also changing lanes, weaving across, getting closer.

Distracted by his phone call, he hadn't been paying attention. Had they followed him to St Anne's? Had they been there the whole time?

Alex gripped the wheel, his fingers on the paddle shift, his foot resting lightly on the accelerator. The traffic was speeding up, but still three lanes across. He was in the fastest, going just 50 mph. He tried to peer ahead, while at the same time glancing in the mirror.

How many people in the car? He could make out one shadow, but it was hard to tell from this distance.

A flash of memory. Susan on the road, then carted into the ambulance. Was that what awaited him?

His hands trembled on the wheel. Fight or flight. Should he just pull over and get out? Surely nothing would happen – could happen – in front of all these witnesses?

Except that if this was Nova, he could be handing himself to them on a plate. Their surveillance might have been building up to this moment. Maybe it really was his turn now. He'd witnessed their agents in action, knew what they were capable of. His mouth went dry. The BMW shot across lanes again, making up the distance. One car away.

It was now or never.

Alex tapped the left paddle twice, sending the gears down into third, and at the same time stamped on the accelerator. The car leapt forwards, rear tyres struggling to maintain contact. Yanking the wheel to the left, he darted across a gap in all three lanes on to the hard shoulder – the lane reserved for emergency services.

The Mercedes accelerated rapidly, its V8 engine growling as the gears automatically shifted upwards. Seventy, ninety. Cars honked their horns as he shot past them. He relaxed his foot a fraction, slowing before he hit 100 mph.

He checked his mirror and took in the scene behind him. The BMW was half a mile behind, hurtling along the same lane, accelerating, closing the distance. They weren't just watching him, they were chasing him in broad daylight.

Alex planted his foot once again and his car sprang forwards, and as the speedo approached 120 mph, he knew he still had plenty in reserve. The upper limit was 155 mph, but he'd never reach that, not along a crowded motorway.

The futility of his actions hit him as the gridlocked cars flashed by on one side, the crash barrier on the other. To simply outrun them might be possible, but they knew where he lived, where he worked. Escaping them now would mean nothing. And yet his foot remained planted on the accelerator. He couldn't help it – the need to escape was deeper than his rational brain telling him to stop.

A bridge appeared in the distance, a slip road off the motorway. He had no option but to follow it, but was forced to slow, weaving in and out of two cars and a truck; all three blew their horns as he narrowly missed clipping one of them. Checking the mirror, the BMW was much closer now, taking advantage of the slower speed.

Down to 60 mph. The slip road terminated in a roundabout. It raced up to meet him and he made a quick choice, hard left, tapping the brake momentarily to give him a chance. The Merc's tyres screeched, the traction control alarm screamed, taking over, reducing the throttle to stop the car losing grip. Alex swore, but the car gave control back to him a second later, and he floored it, picking up speed.

The BMW was right behind him now, matching his pace. The road was clear ahead, but winding, cutting through the country-side, leaving the busy motorway behind, deep into the forests of the South Downs. Alex struggled to get much above 80 mph in the straights, before slowing for a series of tight corners.

Again the traction control took over. Alex stared at the central console for a moment or two, taking his eyes off the road. Where was it? He jabbed at a series of buttons near the top, one of which would turn off the traction control. A light came on the dash to confirm.

He accelerated hard through the next corner, feeling the tyres bite. A quick check confirmed the BMW was even closer, the driver more skilful than Alex, the car equally powerful.

Alex's heart thumped, speeding up with each turn. This was a mistake. He owned fast cars but didn't know how to drive fast. The motorway had been full, busy, full of witnesses. This country road was deserted – just the two of them hurtling along, with no one else to witness how it ended. What madness was this?

His car thundered. A signpost flashed by. Ten miles to the next village. Would he make it that far? And then what?

The next corner they took together, as if connected. Alex felt the back end of the car shift on the road, and instinctively took his foot off the pedal. The car slowed, just a fraction, and the black SUV filled his rear-view mirror, right on his tail.

In a panic, Alex stamped on the pedal again, pulling away, giving it everything the Merc could deliver. The stretch of road was straight but rough, the bumps making the car skittish and light. Alex edged into the middle of the road to give himself more room, trying to ignore the trees blurring to his left, trying to ignore the fact that coming off the road here would be fatal. No hard shoulder, no room for error. Just tarmac and the solid, immovable bulk of the forest.

But still he accelerated. He was pulling ahead, the BMW struggling to keep up. He kept his eyes on the mirror. If he could do this on each clear stretch of road, he might yet stand a chance.

The road climbed more steeply, disappearing over the top of the hill, the trees thick and dark. But as the car hit the incline, the sun shone directly into Alex's eyes, dazzling him for a second before he tugged the visor down. He blinked, missing the first sign indicating a sharp right turn, spotting the second, but a fraction too late.

The car reached the limit of its grip as he hit the brakes, and without automatic control to maximise traction went into a skid. The car shuddered, the tyres skipping over the bumps in the road surface as Alex yanked the wheel over to the right. The bend tightened further still, and worse, dipped over the top of the hill, causing the inertia of the heavy Mercedes to lift the car off the road.

The road slid away from him in slow-motion, as did the gravel speed trap positioned to catch cars that had taken the corner too fast. Beyond the gravel was a steel crash barrier, intended to prevent cars from plummeting over the edge of the rocky outcrop and into the valley below.

Alex hit the barrier side-on, the inside of the car exploding in a series of deafening bangs as the multiple airbags deployed. The crash barrier held, but shifted, the car screeching to a stop in a cloud of dust and debris.

Alex shook his head, taking a few breaths to clear the dizziness, shocked by the airbags more than the impact itself. His right shoulder screamed in pain, the seat belt digging through his jacket. He looked to his left, saw how close he'd been to the edge of the small precipice.

His hands were still clutching the wheel, but both were shaking, the adrenaline flooding his body, the reality of the crash taking hold, and the near-miss of the cliff edge a few feet away.

The engine of the Mercedes had stalled in the crash, but now he heard another, the deep bass of a powerful engine, winding down the revs. He looked to his right at the road, and the sight of the BMW appearing at the top of the hill. It stopped. Its engine revved. Alex could see nothing more than the reflection of the sun on the windscreen.

Another growl from the engine and the car suddenly shot towards him. Alex realised too late what that meant. On the edge of the precipice, with the barrier damaged from one impact, it wouldn't take much to send him over.

There was no time. Alex braced himself, holding the door with one hand, the wheel with the other, as the huge car bore down on him. With only ten yards between them, he closed his eyes.

A shower of gravel hit the side of his car in a series of cracks and bangs. Alex peered round in surprise. The BMW had stopped, inches from the driver's door, the bonnet of the SUV reaching the top of his low-slung car. Alex could see nothing except the radiator grille, the air shimmering from the heat of the engine.

The BMW revved one last time before reversing, inching backwards until it was in the centre of the road. It turned, stopped, its tinted windows still hiding the driver.

Alex swallowed, unable to move or speak, his heart thumping its way out of his chest.

Several moments passed before the BMW shifted into gear. It moved off slowly, making a U-turn in the road, heading back the way they'd come.

Alex waited another few moments until he felt calm enough to open the door. He stood back, watching the road, half expecting the BMW to reappear, to finish what it started. But the only vehicles to appear came from the other direction, two in quick succession. They both slowed to see what had happened, the second one pulling over.

'You OK, mate?' the driver shouted, looking with concern at the smoking wreck of the Mercedes.

Alex nodded, unsure, but certain he didn't have any major injuries. The car had shed energy rapidly as it slid sideways, the gravel trap doing its job. The airbags and crumple zones had done the rest. The car might be totalled, but on this occasion Alex would walk away.

'I've called a tow truck,' he replied. 'Took the corner a little fast. Thanks, anyway.'

The driver nodded and pulled away, slowly gaining speed as he passed over the crest of the hill, disappearing into the distance.

CHAPTER THIRTEEN

Alex cleared his morning appointments, spending the first hour of his working day on the phone, paying the tow-truck company, sourcing a temporary car while his was assessed and repaired, filing an accident report with the Sussex police.

But that's all he said it was. An accident.

Shocked, yes. Scared. But also angry. He had been watched, chased and trapped. Trapped, but then spared, left alive. Not even a scratch. He'd been given a very clear message – as if Susan's hit-and-run wasn't enough. It didn't take a genius to figure it out.

You're getting too close, Alex. Which meant Eva Jansen was exactly what he was looking for.

This was not a time to lose his nerve, and given everything he'd been through in pursuit of Nova over the last couple of years, they were grossly mistaken if they thought he'd heed the warning. He couldn't disregard Susan's cry for help. He owed it to her as much as to himself to find out everything he could about Eva.

Alex could withstand threats. It was failure he couldn't deal with.

He tapped his packet of anti-anxiety meds, and then smiled, despite everything. Bravado was so much easier after two of his small white pills. Maybe he'd feel differently if he ever allowed himself to see things in the cold light of day, to acknowledge the risks with a clear head. To stop and think about what was important, what spiralling pain awaited him.

But not today. He wasn't ready to face reality yet.

He focused on the anger, the frustration, tried to blank out the moments of terror he'd experienced in the car. It would serve no purpose.

He stared at his monitor, refreshed his email. The new notification pinged. He sat up, feeling the tension pulling across his shoulders, then held the stretch, tilting his head to each side. The effect of stress on the body was something he preached to his patients on a daily basis, and he was speaking from painful experience. The muscles in his back howled in protest from the impact the day before, not helped by the nagging worry that had kept them tensed all night.

He lifted his lukewarm coffee to his lips and took a long sip, followed by a deep breath to clear his head.

The email was from Dr Holly Morgan, with a single document attached. The message itself was brief – apologies, but she'd searched the records at St Anne's and, other than the death certificate, Eva's entire record still appeared to be missing. All she could find was the referral sheet from a previous facility. She could find no evidence of any recent hospital care plan for Eva.

No offer of anything else. No suggestion he might talk to Dr Naylor. Alex thought she was making her position clear – she would rather stay out of it. He didn't blame her.

He frowned. Eva's medical record from the hospital had disappeared at the time of her death. He opened the document and pulled his chair in.

The document was two pages long with an appendix, handwritten – a scanned paper form. There wasn't much, but Alex read between the lines – it was signed by a Dr Kaleb at the Canterbury Mental Health Hospital and was dated six years ago.

A tentative diagnosis of PTSD was written with a question mark next to it, below which was a bulleted history. Alex frowned as he scanned the page – there was little of substance and the text was scattered with question marks.

Eva had turned up in the UK health system at age nine. No history before that age, no details of any parents or carers, only that she had been in 'instable' foster care placement, and before that, plucked from the streets. She spoke fragments of English, Dutch and German. She had been committed to long-term psychiatric care in a children's facility following a violent incident at a state school – details overleaf – and bizarre behaviour indicative of several other conditions. She'd been moved regularly – more than twenty institutions listed, and counting. Dr Kaleb had scrawled a note to follow up on this. His notes indicated he was just as frustrated at the lack of a coherent history.

Alex scrolled straight to the appendix. It was a copy of a police report from Hackney, east London – a transcript of the interview with Eva's class teacher, Mr Shawson. Eva had attended Hackney Community Secondary School for three weeks, after which she'd been permanently excluded and handed over to the medical establishment.

Alex read only the first few paragraphs at first. The temperature in his office seemed to drop; he shivered and the hairs on his neck prickled. It was the familiarity that struck him cold – the nature of the attack, the behaviour of the subject. This was extreme violence, but not caused by any normal condition.

It wasn't what she had done, but why.

Alex hunched over the desk, scanning the transcript between the police officer and the teacher.

Officer Wilks: So Eva attacked first?

Mr Shawson: Well, yes and no. She accused the girls of something. She yelled at them.

Officer Wilks: Yelled what?

Mr Shawson: To shut up, I think. Yes, she definitely said to shut up. To all of them, but to Juliet in particular.

Alex scanned further down. The teacher had witnessed the beginning of the altercation, but hadn't expected it to escalate so quickly.

Officer Wilks: So Eva struck first?

Mr Shawson: The other girls crowded around Eva. Juliet was the ringleader – always was . . . is, I mean. Will she be OK?

He noted the description of Juliet's injuries below. She'd been admitted with an array of head wounds – a skull fracture, a fractured jaw, fractured cheekbone, and four teeth missing. Extensive bruising to her eyes and lips. The rest of her body was unharmed.

Mr Shawson: I saw Juliet stagger away and fall. The circle of girls widened out, suddenly wary, with Eva at the centre. She was holding her own head, shaking it violently – I mean, really violently – pulling it left and right, grabbing her own hair in her fists.

Officer Wilks: So Juliet didn't strike Eva?

Mr Shawson: I think if Eva had any injuries, they were self-inflicted.

Officer Wilks: What happened next?

Mr Shawson: Eva went wild. Feral, would be the best description I could think of. I've never seen anything like it – bear in mind, these girls are only eleven years old. She leapt on Juliet, wrapping her arms and legs around her. Punching, biting . . . She was going for Juliet's head, always the head. Screaming while she was doing it – 'Shut up, shut up, shut up.' She kept thumping Juliet in the head until . . . I got there as fast as I could. You understand? I had difficulty pulling Eva off. Juliet's friends all scattered – I was on my own.

Officer Wilkes: But you got Eva off, and then what happened?

Mr Shawson: I tried to calm her. She was holding her own head. She looked at me and . . . I knew immediately that Eva had some deep disturbance inside – she was damaged, deeply traumatised. I was completely out of my depth and so was the school.

Officer Wilkes: Did she say anything to you?

Mr Shawson: She just kept repeating the same thing. 'I can't stop them.' And she said something else – before she clammed up and went silent for the next few hours. 'Please help me,' she said. 'Please make them stop.'

Alex read the sentence again. *Please help me. Please make them stop.* Eva, an eleven-year-old girl, was possessed by something she couldn't control: an urge. *I can't stop them.*

What couldn't she stop?

Alex felt his hand flutter, tremble. At the same time Katie's voice sounded in his head. Her frequent pleas for him to change, to emerge from this, not to go deeper. But what choice did he have? Eva had needed saving, even back then. She'd been left at the mercy of the care system. Until now.

The pieces slotted together. Eva could read people, hear them. But the violence . . . Alex was interested in the violence – who wouldn't be? And the next section sent a fresh shiver down his spine.

The other schoolgirl, Juliet, had suffered not just physically, but had never recovered. She'd been found unmoving on the playground. When the paramedics arrived, they reported her eyes as dilated and fixed. She had appeared able to hear them but was otherwise unresponsive. Six days later Juliet had been admitted to the child psychiatric ward at Great Ormond Street Hospital in London. Persistent psychosis was the tentative diagnosis. A brief note was attached, with observations from the consultant psychiatrist, as requested by the police for the report and subsequent medical record.

> *Eleven-year-old girl presents without previous psychiatric or medical history. The patient is conscious but cannot engage in meaningful communication. Appears to be experiencing auditory hallucinations and displaying disorganised speech and behaviour. Complains of pain in right temple but can't accurately describe it. Toxic screening shows no alcohol or illicit drugs present. Physical examination findings are unremarkable and mild trauma to the head is inconsistent with presenting symptoms. Recommend admission for full evaluation.*

No other information was recorded, but Alex stared at the paragraph, pondering the possible causes.

Flashes of Victor appeared. What could he do to people's minds? Compel and coerce. Could he also destroy? Mia Anastos had only her own mind to worry about – the girl who'd stabbed herself almost to death out of her craving for pain. Alex had seen her eyes and watched her frenzied body. Mia had no control over her urges.

What had Eva done to Juliet?

The transcript finished. Alex scrolled back up to the summary.

Following that day, Eva had been taken out of foster care and placed in a juvenile facility where attempts at sedation had worked – anti-psychotics and a combination of other tranquillisers, but a longer-term plan had yet to be developed. She had jumped from home to home – Dr Kaleb's was just one of them. The final bullet point on the sheet was the only useful addition, and Alex read it with interest, reaching for his notepad.

Dr Kaleb had observed Eva's alienation of her fellow patients and the nursing staff, with numerous deliberate attempts by nurses to change shifts to avoid caring for her. Even one of the psychologists had applied to change ward in an attempt to keep away from her. Alex jotted down another note – this certainly corroborated Susan's concerns, without offering any further detail. Dr Kaleb had found this puzzling and commented that he also intended to follow up on this. Eva was held in a secure room until a review could be arranged. Then came nothing further.

Alex sighed, tapping his pen on his notepad, concluding he wasn't going to find what he needed in the official medical records. He filed the document away on his computer and tapped out a brief acknowledgement and thanks to Dr Morgan. He leaned back in his chair again, feeling the adrenaline bite.

The most disturbing patient since Mia. Exactly what he was in search of and yet she'd slipped away already. He had a couple more lines of inquiry he wanted to pursue, but his next step needed thinking through. He checked the time. He'd make the call tomorrow. In the meantime, he had another place he needed to be.

CHAPTER FOURTEEN

Alex slipped his hire car in behind a small hatchback, a little down the road from Grace's house. He switched off the engine and slouched back in his seat, staring towards the building he used to call home. Before he ruined it all.

It had started as the odd visit. Rarely at first, and then with increasing frequency. Grace would be mad if she ever found out. He knew what it looked like, parked up in his ex-wife's street, staring at his old life, but his behaviour was nothing to do with jealousy or possessiveness. He'd always found the activity somewhat cathartic, relaxing against the soft leather, letting his mind drift while he imagined a possible future. Hope, that's all it was. A daydream. A strange counter to his increasing levels of anxiety. Not as good as Xanax, although it did offer some minor respite.

He could just knock on the door – Grace would invite him in, she always did. He could pretend he was passing this part of town, and make small talk.

And not say the things he really wanted to say.

It wasn't as if he didn't see them. Grace, every week at a minimum, and Katie whenever she liked, which admittedly was less and less these days – she was a busy teenager, and her troubled dad no longer her number-one friend.

But it wasn't enough. It would never be enough. Not until he'd repaired the damage. It was just so hard to do that from a distance.

His thoughts wandered and he almost missed it. A dark SUV, creeping along the road, slowing further as it passed Alex, pulling in against the kerb a couple of houses down from Grace. The windows of the SUV were blacked out and Alex couldn't see the driver. The brake lights flashed and it came to a halt.

Alex held his breath. He put his right hand on the car door, tensing his legs against the seat. It was a BMW X5, new model. His heart leapt into his throat.

The same car? They were here. So not just him, but his family too.

What threat could he hope to offer against a determined assailant? His chest began to tighten, the anxiety causing a flutter in his throat. Flight wasn't an option, not with Grace and Katie at risk. Do something! He grabbed his phone, placed his thumb over the emergency call button.

The door of the SUV opened and a man stepped out – tall with light-coloured hair, dressed in a pale blazer and trousers. Was it the same man from the scene of Susan's accident? It could be. Same height and build. Hard to tell from this angle. The man paused, as if testing the air, before leaning inside the car to retrieve a briefcase.

It would all be over before the police arrived. Alex threw open his door and jumped out on to the pavement. He ran the short distance to the BMW, reaching it as the tall man turned towards him.

'Who are you?' Alex blurted out. He stepped back, catching his breath, assuming what he hoped was a safe but intimidating stance, with absolutely no idea of what he'd do if the man turned violent. 'Leave them alone!'

The man's face clouded. He glanced towards his car and back to Alex. He squared up, holding his briefcase in front of him, across his legs.

'I beg your pardon? Who are you?' The man's voice was puzzled, irritated. Alex tried to read his eyes.

'I asked you first,' said Alex, 'and I've already called the police. They'll be here in two minutes.' He hadn't dialled, and had left his phone on the seat when he leapt out. He knew his face would betray the lie, but his chest was bursting, the adrenaline rushing through his body.

The man's face twisted. Confused, not scared. He glanced around, turning towards the row of houses and across the road. He dropped his briefcase on the pavement.

'What the hell are you talking about?' he said, putting his arm out to swing shut the door of his car. As it closed, Alex spotted Katie. She was walking out of her driveway, approaching them both. The man stood between them. Alex was about to shout when she called out.

'Hi, Mr Wareford,' she said. 'I see you've met my dad.'

The man glanced over his shoulder at Katie. 'Oh – hi, Katie,' he said. He turned back to Alex. 'Dad?'

Alex let out the breath he'd been holding and held his shoulders high for a second longer before they sagged. His face flushed with embarrassment, but the relief was overwhelming. He swallowed a few times, clearing his throat in the process, and his ears popped with the pressure.

Shit.

'Yes,' said Alex, feeling his heart thump, this time with humiliation. 'You must be—'

'The new neighbour,' said the man. 'Tony Wareford. Just moved in. Sorry, what's this about the police? What on earth's happened? Are you OK?'

'The police?' said Katie, nipping past Tony and giving Alex a hug. 'What's happened, Dad?'

Alex closed his eyes. A rewind button would be so perfect right now. A few seconds, that's all he needed. If only. He took a deep breath.

'Nothing's happened,' he said, turning to Katie. Her lips smiled but her eyes pierced into his, searching for the truth. 'Mistaken identity.'

He extended his hand to Tony. 'I'm Alex, by the way.'

Tony examined his hand for a second before shaking it. He looked Alex up and down. His face relaxed a fraction. 'So, the police . . . ?' he said again.

'Aren't coming,' said Alex, pulling his best fake smile. 'I . . . was—'

Tony's eyes narrowed before widening with recognition. He nodded, offering a genuine smile now, as if it had all suddenly clicked into place. 'Don't sweat it. I've met Grace – lovely woman. Her and my wife, Beth, hit it off immediately. They've been chatting quite a bit. Don't worry, I've been through it with my ex. I understand.'

Alex cocked his head. Just quite what Tony thought he understood was intriguing. Had Grace been filling Beth in on their affairs? Telling Beth about her mad ex? That wasn't like Grace, but then who could blame her? Alex certainly didn't get to dictate such things these days.

'Good,' was all Alex could offer. He tried in vain to return the smile, but settled for a weak grin.

Tony nodded again and retrieved his briefcase from the ground. 'Well, it was nice to meet you, Alex. Next time, let's leave the police out of it, OK?' His broad grin was honest, and although Alex wanted to punch his face, he was lucky Tony was being quite so relaxed. Being accosted by a stranger outside your own home was enough reason for Tony to make a far bigger deal of it if he wanted to.

'No police,' said Alex. 'I promise.'

Tony strolled off up his driveway. Alex watched his front door close behind him, before he grabbed Katie and pulled her into a giant bear hug.

'What are you doing out here?' he said, feeling her small body wriggling against his chest.

Katie struggled, pushing him gently away. 'What's wrong, Dad?' she said, her voice releasing a wave of guilt and sadness in Alex.

He released his hug, holding her by the shoulders. He wasn't sure how to start.

'I saw you out here acting weird,' she said. 'Where's your car? Why are you parked down the road? Why not in our driveway?'

Alex shook his head. He couldn't tell her why.

'Something's wrong, isn't it?' She cocked her head. 'Is therapy not going well? It gets worse before it gets better, you know. Isn't that what you tell your patients? Isn't that what you tell me?'

Katie's maturity only served to deepen his guilt. Alex sagged some more. Lies and more lies. But not to her. He couldn't lie to her. He knew what that felt like – his own father had lied his entire lifetime, right up until his death. It had never helped Alex.

He walked over to the low wall of the neighbour's house and leaned against it. Katie followed. She stared at him with curiosity and suspicion.

'Therapy,' he said, watching her eyes. 'I don't . . . That is, I haven't . . . been going.'

There, he'd come out and said it, the confession tumbling out, watching its effect, judging the hurt he was causing.

Katie's eyes narrowed. She frowned. 'For how long?'

Alex closed his eyes for a second. 'For ever,' he said. 'I never started it. I planned to, of course, but I never managed to make the appointment. I will, of course I will. It just isn't the right time.'

Katie's face dropped. She looked away from Alex, staring at the pavement. 'You lied,' she said in a small voice.

'I know. But Katie, listen, I—'

'I don't understand. We talked about your sessions. What you said to the therapist and how it was helping. Did you . . . did you make it all up?'

Alex struggled to respond, his body failing him as he watched his daughter's hurt, her mind frantically replaying all of the conversations they'd had, where she'd shared her experiences of therapy and he'd shared his. He swallowed. His eyes met hers, but hers were already filled with tears.

'How could you?' she said, backing away from the wall and Alex. 'You lied to me. To Mum.' She waved her hands, pointing along the road. Her face twisted with more confusion. 'And this. You come here, *spying* on us? Picking a fight with Tony. What the hell are you doing, Dad?'

Alex shook his head, glancing at his hire car. 'This . . . No, it's not what you think. I was just passing. I . . .'

Katie raised her eyebrows. Alex could see she was still processing his lies, her jaw clenched in anger and disappointment.

'You lied about the therapy, and now you're spying on me and Mum?'

Alex had no words. He kept shaking his head, but felt a fresh desperation, one he'd never felt before, the most important relationship of his life falling apart. He'd fractured it, driving a wedge in where there never needed to be one at all. He could have been honest and she'd have understood. There was nothing they couldn't have tackled together.

But he'd chosen to lie, and he must deal with the fallout.

'I'm sorry,' he said, his eyes welling up at the sight of his daughter betrayed. 'Really. Please, Katie.'

But Katie was backing away, her face streaming with tears. 'Don't,' she said. 'Your words mean nothing to me now.'

She gave him once last glance, and Alex saw a whole new world of damage he'd created. Katie disappeared into the driveway. He heard the door slam a few seconds later. Alex remained on Tony's wall, clenching his fists together, feeling the beginnings of a panic attack coming on.

He made it back to the car before it arrived, waves of panic mixed with grief and fury at himself. He swallowed a Xanax and rested his head on the steering wheel, fighting to control his breathing, gasping in air as he trembled.

The panic attack lasted five minutes before releasing him from its cruel grip. He waited another five before starting the engine, then drove off without looking back.

CHAPTER FIFTEEN

Holly Morgan turned off the tap and tested the water. She wondered whether to light a candle, but decided the bath oils were enough, the rather pungent fragrance already filling the air and steaming up the windows. Besides, lighting a candle for herself alone seemed rather sad. Clive wouldn't come knocking tonight. He had a double shift and would sleep at the hospital. They wouldn't see each other for four more nights, their shifts overlapping. Such was the life of a medic.

She slipped off her robe and dipped a toe in the bath. Hot enough to boil her alive almost, but she pushed through the shock, dipping in at an awkward crouch, letting her skin adjust to the searing heat.

Lying back, the rush of relief was intense, the hot water flushing out all the stress. This day, this week, had been more difficult than most, the lack of senior staff and the influx of patients pushing them to breaking point, turning away desperate people, sending them to far-flung corners of the country in search of a free bed. Worse, some patients were left in prison cells until a bed could be found locally. Not the best start to their mental health treatment, but with increasing frequency an unavoidable one.

But a hot bath made it all better, didn't it? It tempered the uneasy feeling Holly had at work these days, in her ward under the management of the evasive Dr Naylor. The suspicion that something wasn't right, that the assessments were rushed, incomplete, missing, the drug recording inconsistent. It was odd and played on her mind, especially since the doctor from London had visited and asked about a specific patient whose record had revealed all the same inconsistencies.

She'd managed to keep most of her thoughts to herself. Malpractice was not a word anyone liked to utter in an over-stretched hospital where the vast majority of clinicians were doing their best, but the whiff of it was also something no one could ignore.

She'd told Clive all about it. He was junior to her in the pecking order, but his dad was on the board. Maybe a quiet chat might reveal something and a discreet investigation be possible without her being directly involved.

Or perhaps she should simply move on, apply for a rotation at a different hospital, except that then she'd see even less of Clive. Her hopes for something more serious between them would be ruined.

She drew a deep breath, the steam tickling the back of her throat, and stretched. Her right foot touched the tap and made a squeaking noise. She ran her toe down the cold metal, enjoying the contrast of temperature. A huge, cold drip ran down her foot, causing her to shiver. At the same time she heard the creak of floorboards, on the staircase and then along the landing outside the bathroom.

Holly pulled her knees together, shuffling upright.

'Clive?' she called. He had a door key, one of their more recent agreements. She still didn't have one for his apartment, but he'd promised to get her one cut on his first day off. 'Is that you?'

She looked over to her towel, hanging on the rail, beyond reach. But why cover up? These moments should be grabbed whenever possible. She was already naked, relaxed. That saved them several minutes at least, didn't it?

She stretched her legs back out, tilting her hips sideways, arching her back, exposing her chest above the waterline. She felt mildly ridiculous, but it was fun all the same. She closed her eyes as the door creaked open, wondering what he'd do first.

She managed to keep her eyes closed as the footsteps approached the bath. Hard soles, whereas Clive would normally be wearing soft surgical shoes. They stopped.

She waited. Felt a strange tingling in her legs. Anticipation? No, more uncomfortable, like cramp. The longer she waited, the more unpleasant it became. Her hip started to grind into the bottom of the bath as her right leg twitched.

She gave up and opened her eyes.

'OK, I—'

The scream didn't get past her throat. She tried, and her lungs were full of breath, but her jaw clenched and her vocal cords spasmed into silence.

Her body tensed, her muscles contracting in symphony, her back arching further still, painfully extended. The back of her head slammed against the rim of the bath as she convulsed.

The man standing over her had his hands spread wide, palms down. He was whispering something, inaudible, his wrinkled lips moving in minute twitches. His eyes moved all over Holly's body, starting at her legs, moving up to her stomach, her breasts, her face. He peered into her eyes, his expression impossible to read.

Holly's body gave another convulsion. She let out a groan, a whimper, the terror catching hold, her brain struggling to process the possible outcomes. A strange man in her house. She was naked, on her back, and as much as her mind screamed at her, she couldn't move.

'Please,' she said, through gritted teeth. She'd heard stories of home invasions, the rape of single women. She'd treated patients who'd been through it, their stories as devastating as they were mundane. In the kitchen, cooking dinner. In the bedroom, sleeping. In the bathroom, cleaning. The victims often struggled to forgive themselves for letting it happen. *Letting it happen.* They left the door unlocked, they left the lights off, they should have fitted an alarm.

The absurdity of the guilt often played on her mind, and yet right now she wondered what she'd done to deserve this – *deserve this* – as though anyone ever did. She was careful with her private life, careful around her patients, even her colleagues. Even Clive.

So who would want to do this? Who had decided Holly was their target for this evening? What gave them the right, the power, to terrify her like this?

'You told him,' said the man. Even in the small bathroom, his voice sounded distant, echoing against the hard floor, the porcelain fixtures. He cocked his head, as if listening to her reply.

'You have a loose tongue,' he said, nodding, as if it made perfect sense.

Holly shook her head, but the movements were small, her neck muscles rigid, unyielding.

'I . . .' she started. Did he expect her to reply? To beg? Should she just let him do it? Get it over with? Perhaps if she didn't fight, he wouldn't hurt her. He'd just do what he wanted and then leave.

Frozen with terror. It was supposed to be a figure of speech, not a reality. Why couldn't she *move*?

The man sniffed. He reached up, taking a handkerchief from his breast pocket. He dabbed at his lips, then his nose, then his forehead. The movements seemed so sinister in the circumstances, so banal. Holly whimpered again. *Just get it over with.* Another internal scream, but her lips trembled in silence as he tucked the cloth back into his suit pocket.

The man took a step back. He opened his mouth, cracking his jaw, before returning his gaze to Holly's face.

This time the convulsions were immediate and severe. Her feet stamped at the far end of the bath, kicking the tap until she felt the crunch of broken bone, her big toe snapping out of place against the metal spout. Her cry was smothered by the cramps in her chest, a squeezing of her lungs, a shooting pain from her collarbone through her body to her lower back, repeating, waves of pain intensifying, burning, forcing the air from her lungs and the bile from her stomach, burning her throat as it spewed from her mouth.

Her head slumped forward, chin against her chest as she slid down the slope of the bathtub. The fragrant water crept up to her neck, then her chin, and over her lips. It bubbled around her nostrils as she breathed. Her chest drew in the liquid and then protested in a fresh spasm of coughs as it flooded her lungs.

Holly had no coherent last thoughts. No memories. No flashes of light or moments of euphoria. Her last moments were a primitive battle of pain and panic as her heart stopped and her lungs filled with fluid, her body unable to combat either.

By the time the darkness descended, her eyes were already closed.

She didn't see the man frown. She didn't see him curse to himself as he walked away.

CHAPTER SIXTEEN

Alex's calls and texts went unanswered until the following day. Grace sent him a brief message at lunch, expressing her disappointment. She didn't offer advice or rant about his lies – he was suffering enough, and she knew it.

Katie finally texted him a few hours later. Her message was longer and Alex almost cried again on reading it. She said she understood why he'd lied, but that it upset her. She asked him to promise never to lie again, and then they could talk.

Alex was forced to pause before replying. When a parent lies to their child it's generally out of necessity – protection from the things they shouldn't need to worry about – but he had crossed the line. Lying about therapy was due to his own demons: his fear of what it would reveal and how long his journey would be. He could never tell Katie how terrified he was of confronting the long decades of pent-up anger and confusion waiting within . . . Or was that another lie? Katie was growing up fast, maturing in ways he hadn't anticipated. But she was damaged too, and he carried the burden of blame.

But parents were supposed to be rocks, weren't they? Whatever suffering you yourself endure, you protect your children from the worst of it. Distract, misdirect and lie if you have to – because if they don't think you can cope, how on earth can they?

Alex knew the truth and yet still he couldn't do it. The position in which he now found himself – or had placed himself – was not a world he could expose to Katie or Grace. Not yet. There was so much he didn't know. Too much. The sinister machinations of his father and the group he had worked for towered above all else. Alex was utterly trapped by his mission to find out what and who they were. In the meantime, his precious family must be distanced, protected and in every way kept blind to what he was doing. It was the safe option. The only option.

I promise, he texted back, loathing himself a little, but convincing himself it was for her protection. If she ended up hating him but safe, that was preferable to putting her in danger, however much it might hurt them both.

Alex prepared fresh coffee and settled himself at his desk, preparing for his next move. The first call would be quick. He'd searched online and found nothing about a psychiatric medical conference in Madrid. That didn't rule it out – some of these events were closed, sponsored by pharmaceuticals or private medical facilities, but Alex wanted to be sure. Something was bugging him about Naylor's departure so hot on the heels of Eva's death. He'd be reluctant to talk, but there was someone who might be able to help him.

He got Larry's voicemail, again. This time he didn't give up. The hospital switchboard led him through a series of redirects, until he finally heard a human voice.

'Good morning. Psychological medicine.'

'Ah, good morning,' said Alex. 'I'm trying to get through to a colleague. Dr Van Rooyen. He's not picking up.'

There was a pause. 'Dr Van Rooyen?'

'That's right.'

He heard the tapping of a keyboard. 'Can I take your name, please?'

'Dr Alex Madison.'

The line was placed on hold and Alex waited a few moments in silence before it clicked back into life.

'Dr Madison? This is, uh, Dr Pohl.' The doctor's voice was hesitant, wary.

'Morning. I'm trying to get hold of Larry. I can't seem to get him on his mobile.'

Dr Pohl cleared his throat. Alex could hear him shuffling some papers. 'Ah, there you are,' he said. 'You're on the list. Let me check you off.'

'List? What list?'

'We've compiled a list of everyone we need to notify. You obviously haven't heard.' Dr Pohl cleared his throat again. 'I'm terribly sorry to tell you, but Larry passed away the night before last. Heart attack. Out of the blue. He was found in his study, still at his desk.'

Alex felt a shiver. A lump forming in his throat. A sudden tremor took his hand. He transferred the phone to the other one, watching his fingers.

'Heart attack?' he asked. Larry was fit, healthy, body like an ox, mind sharp as a scalpel.

'It was a shock to all of us, Dr Madison. He was an excellent physician, a good friend . . .' Dr Pohl's voice began to crack. 'He'll be missed, terribly. We haven't got around to informing everyone in his professional circle yet – it was big. He had a lot of friends, a lot of contacts. If you wouldn't mind telling people, it would be appreciated.'

Alex murmured his reply, his thoughts spinning, his first conclusion unbearable: a heart attack was hard to fake, but not impossible. Tracing Eva to Susan to Larry to Alex. But they'd let Alex walk away.

'He was found at his desk?'

The question caught Dr Pohl off guard. 'What? Er, yes.'

'Will there be an autopsy?'

A pause. 'Why would there be an autopsy?'

Alex had to bite down, clench his jaw to avoid the flood of his thoughts from tumbling out.

'You're right, there wouldn't be,' said Alex. 'Sorry, it's just he was so healthy . . .'

Don't say it, Alex, he thought. Don't drop any more breadcrumbs. Don't expose yourself any more than you need to.

'I'm . . .' He couldn't offer anything else.

'Were you close?' said Dr Pohl.

'Close?' said Alex, thinking back, flashes of Larry's face as a younger man, a teacher, a mentor. A confidant. 'Yes. Yes, we used to be very close. I trusted his judgement. I'll . . .' Alex found his own voice cracking. This was different to Susan. More personal, more damaging. And yet, it could still be a coincidence. A heart attack was not a hit-and-run. This might have just been Larry's time to go.

So why then did Alex's flesh crawl in disagreement?

'Thank you for telling me,' said Alex. 'Please inform me of the funeral arrangements.'

'That's for the family to sort out,' said Dr Pohl, 'but they have the list of his colleagues. It won't be for a few weeks, I don't think.'

'Thank you.'

Alex hung up. He dropped the phone to his desk, nausea biting at his throat. He struggled to draw a full breath, his chest tight.

He thought about their last exchange. A briefer conversation than Alex would have liked, but the emphasis in Larry's last words still resonated. Larry had cautioned him – he feared what would happen if they scratched beneath the surface. He'd been wiser than Alex. Wise enough to let sleeping devils lie.

Except that Alex had woken them.

He dialled Brighton General emergency department in a dream-like state. He asked after the victim of the hit-and-run, not fully listening as the nurse put him on hold. He tapped his fingers on the desk, swallowing, feeling the lethargy of the stress taking hold.

It took an age, but when the nurse came back on the line, he closed his eyes as she told him the news. Susan Halsey was dead. Cardiac arrest. The nurse was very sorry. There was nothing they could have done.

Alex's next call would be the one to set things in motion – the formalities would begin and there would be no going back. But he'd hit the tipping point. He'd spent the last twenty minutes wrestling with his decision, making notes – a timeline. It was the right thing to do. Eva deserved it, and if Susan's and Larry's deaths were indeed related, he must throw everything he could at it.

Maintaining separation between a police investigation and his own was paramount, but he'd managed it before. He could do it again.

Alex found the number and dialled.

'Alex,' came the reply, 'to what do I owe this dubious pleasure?' DCI Hartley's tone was the same as ever – professional but with the dark humour that develops over years of working on murder cases and dealing with the monsters other people pretend don't exist.

They had a good relationship and she valued his contributions. She reluctantly brought in outsiders, and Alex was a regular. He had worked on several cases for her over the last couple of years, mostly profiling and minor assessments for the CPS. She trusted him more than most, something he was banking on.

'I have something for you,' said Alex. 'Can we talk?'

Hartley sniffed. 'That's not normally how this works, Alex. I'm supposed to call you. I'm sure most people give you that message.'

Humour from Hartley meant she was in a good mood. Very rare. He should take advantage.

'Do you have five minutes then?'

Another sniff. 'For you, Dr Madison, I have ten. But try and get it done in five if you can.'

Alex checked his notes on the desk. It was important what he told Hartley, the order of events and the details.

It was also important what he left out.

Alex started at the beginning. Almost. He proceeded to outline the nurse's account of a troubled young girl and the suspicious actions she'd witnessed at the hospital. He mentioned the hit-and-run, then described his visit to St Anne's, the death of Eva Jansen and his own reservations about Dr Naylor. He mentioned that he'd been tailed leaving the hospital, leaving out the extent of his own race through the countryside – circling his notes with a big question mark. He could reveal that later, depending on what route Hartley took. His carefully ordered narrative leading to his suspicions about the Madrid conference took a little under five minutes.

At the end he paused. He could hear the sound of Hartley breathing in the background and thought he could also make out the scratch of a pen on paper, mingled with the odd tap on a keyboard.

'You haven't tried contacting Dr Naylor again?' she said finally.

'No,' said Alex. 'I thought it was best to speak to you.'

'OK,' said Hartley, digesting his story. 'OK.'

Alex paused.

'Did you ever meet my colleague, Larry Van Rooyen?'

Hartley clicked her tongue. 'I don't think so. We have records of your associates, contacts, etcetera. Standard stuff. We never met.'

'He died a few days ago. I'd like you to request an autopsy.'

Hartley paused. 'Even assuming I could, which I can't, why would I want to do that?'

Alex struggled. His relationship with Larry had ended with their illegal actions in hiding Mia. He had to give Hartley the bare minimum. 'He knows about this case. Eva Jansen. The timing was odd.'

Hartley sniffed. Waited. 'That's not enough, Alex. Not enough for me to open a file on him.'

Her tone suggested she knew there was more. But that was all Alex could offer. He didn't bother asking about Susan.

'You'll investigate Eva?' he said.

'I didn't say that. You describe her as *special*. Do you have any other interest in her?'

'Such as?' Alex hoped she wouldn't force the issue.

'Did the nurse, Susan, call you only because she'd seen your name online, or was there another reason?'

'That's what she said. No other reason. However, I'd like to understand the patient's condition a little better.'

'Why?'

'Professional curiosity,' said Alex, trying to get himself on an even keel, trying to present his case professionally. Trying to keep the emotion out of it. 'We've seen enough strange cases together to have a certain inquisitive streak, haven't we? First and foremost, I think the two deaths are suspicious. I'll butt out if I must, but thought you might keep me in on this one. Understanding Eva's condition might help us clarify the circumstances surrounding her death and even exonerate Dr Naylor. This is my world – doctors and the institutions they manage is my bread and butter.'

He tried not to overdo it. The last line was a bit of a cliché, but he hoped it would do the trick. He forced himself into silence and waited for Hartley to bite.

She took her time.

'Give me a few hours,' she said. '*Don't* pursue any of this on your own, and if anyone contacts you about it, refer them straight to me. Got it?'

This was a good outcome. Not only would Hartley mobilise her significant team and influence, but she'd do it without Alex needing to reveal any of the rather more fantastical details about the girl.

'Thank you, Hartley,' he said. 'I've got it.'

It was less than two hours before Hartley called him back. Alex had remained in his study, figuring he'd put his precious time to good use. Thoughts of Katie and Grace dominated, or rather, surges of regret. He could have handled the situation more smoothly, but as a result was faced with a long journey trying to win back their trust while at the same time maintaining his hidden agenda. He must continue on both fronts, and hope for a breakthrough in either.

'To what do I owe this dubious pleasure?' he said, leaning back in his chair. Hartley couldn't have found anything much this fast, but Alex was pleased – she'd got straight on the case.

'I'm sorry, Alex. You're not going to like this.'

Alex shifted back in his chair. 'What?'

'I checked the files on Dr Naylor and Eva Jansen. I added all the information you gave me and ran a few checks of my own.'

'And?'

'Dr Naylor was flagged already. The National Crime Agency are investigating her. I got a call within the hour telling me to back off. They appreciate the heads-up on Eva Jansen, but they'll take it from here.'

Alex frowned. The NCA was the UK's main national law enforcement agency, much like the FBI in the US. Organised crime; human, weapon and drug trafficking; cybercrime – all the big stuff. They handled all the most serious regional, national and international investigations. If Dr Naylor was on their radar, she was up to something major. The hairs prickled on Alex's neck.

'I need to be involved,' he said. 'They can run it, fine, but they need me.'

'They don't, so they say,' said Hartley. 'They have their own team, their own investigation. They were very clear.'

'And you're happy with that?' Alex's grip was slipping away. Unless this case was assigned to Hartley, it left Alex out in the cold.

She sighed. 'Happy? I'm rarely happy, Alex. But listen, if the NCA are running this they have more resources than I do. If the doctor acted improperly, they'll prove it. That's what you want, isn't it?'

Alex paused. 'Yes, of course, but—'

'No buts, Alex. Their instructions were very clear and I have no grounds to challenge them. Listen, I've got to go. We can chat later in the week, but as it stands, we're out. That means you, Alex. Understand?'

Alex cleared his throat. He glanced at his notes on the table, the article on his screen and the locked filing cabinets along the wall of his study. He clenched the phone, his frustration building.

'Tell me you understand, Alex. Thank you for the tip-off, but stay away from this. Don't risk it. Don't risk your career.'

Alex's stomach sank, anxiety and desperation creeping in at the edges. He'd been cut out of the investigation before it had even begun. This was not part of the plan. In calling Hartley he'd pushed his chances at discovering Eva's background and any possible links to Nova even further away than before.

He paused a moment, collecting his thoughts.

'I understand,' he said, ending the call.

CHAPTER SEVENTEEN

The movie was playing in the background, with Grace and Katie on one sofa, Alex on the other. He watched their faces more than the movie, observing the small glances, the hurt and closed expressions from Katie.

The Saturday-afternoon film had become a regular event, and Grace hadn't cancelled on him – he had to give her that. She'd said what she needed to, and left it to Alex to repair the damage. So far, he hadn't made much impact, turning up with a bottle of red and a promise to order whatever pizza Katie fancied. The food had arrived, the film had started, and conversation had ceased.

Alex sipped his wine, watching how Grace held her glass, spinning it by the stem. It was still full – she had only accepted it to keep him company.

'Enjoying the film?' he asked, forgetting what it was called – some unremarkable comedy about a modern, dysfunctional family. Very apt, he'd thought. Katie shrugged. Grace gave him a thin, sympathetic smile. She raised her eyebrows and turned back to the TV.

Alex watched her for a few seconds, sensing the familiar tug at his heart, just a little, enough to remind him of what he'd lost. He shifted his gaze back to Katie. Her young face was tense, the hurt still very much evident. She watched the film without enthusiasm, one hand on her phone, checking it every few minutes, responding to messages from her friends.

The conversation with Hartley played on his mind. He'd been told to stay away. Hartley was clear on that and so were the people she reported to. But they didn't know what he knew. They weren't interested in the same way he was.

He tried to keep his mind on the present. 'Maybe next week we could watch some sci-fi,' he said. Katie loved science-fiction as much as he did. Grace pulled a face and put her glass on the coffee table.

'You can count me out, then,' she said, smiling at Katie.

Katie shrugged. 'I'm not feeling too well,' she said. 'I might go and lie down.'

Alex glanced at Grace, then turned to Katie.

'Are you OK? Headache? Stomach? Are you hot?' He stopped as he realised. Katie didn't look ill at all. She looked like a teenager who didn't want to be sitting in the lounge with her parents, one of whom she was still mad at.

'Ah, OK, sweetie,' he said. 'This film is making me feel fairly nauseous too.'

Katie couldn't stop a small smile escaping before quickly suppressing it. She slid off the sofa and faked a yawn.

'Bye, Dad,' she said, leaving the room.

'I love you!' Alex shouted after her. The only response he received was the faint stomp of footsteps and the slamming of a bedroom door.

Alex turned back to the TV and slumped in his seat. He took a large gulp of his wine, feeling the heat in his chest and a sharp bite in his throat. The pizza sat uneasily in his stomach.

'Time, Alex,' said Grace. 'It'll take time, plus . . .' Her eyes said it all.

'I know,' he said. 'And I'm sorry for lying to you both, I truly am. I just . . . I'm finding it difficult to focus at the moment.'

Grace shrugged. 'I'm not going to fight to convince you, Alex. You're the psychologist. Look in the mirror and figure it out. Katie will always love you, but she's at a complicated stage in her life. Her therapy is unravelling things she needs to process. Watching you self-destruct isn't helping. It isn't helping either of us.'

Alex frowned. He'd been called self-destructive before – at the time of their marriage breakdown. Had he not changed since in Grace's eyes?

'Your behaviour is all we have to go on,' said Grace, as if reading his mind. 'Change that and the rest will follow. Katie will want a normal relationship with you when she's had time to deal with her past, the damage. But you . . . you seem more distracted than ever. If you won't let us in, we can't help.'

Alex nodded, struggling to keep his pride in check. To be a respected psychologist and yet fail at the most basic of tasks – so open and easy to analyse.

'I should go,' he said, heaving himself off the sofa.

'You don't have to,' said Grace. Her expression was sincere, but all Alex could see was sympathy. He wanted to see more in her eyes. He wanted to see the same regret he felt. He wanted to see love. He wanted all the things he wished still existed between them – a happy marriage and family.

But with each visit those things became more distant, and he was making it so. The thought that he and Grace would get back together was something he kept a lid on – forced to the back of his mind as a detached but certain event in his future. He always assumed it would happen.

But time marched on. Grace was in a steady relationship with John, and despite Alex's determined attempts to hate the man, he had to admit he wasn't so bad. John provided stability for Grace, space when they needed it, and most annoying of all, John encouraged Katie to spend time with Alex. He even made himself scarce when Alex visited.

John was altogether a wonderfully modern man. Alex wished he could hate him. He also wished he was more like him.

Grace watched Alex for a few moments as he paused at the doorway. 'I'll get the home security,' she said. 'If you want us to, we'll get it.'

Alex nodded his thanks. He'd feared she'd say no, not knowing the risk. What that risk might entail, Alex still didn't know, but he couldn't hide his relief.

'I'm sure you won't need it,' he said. 'It's only precautionary. Everyone has security these days.'

Grace raised her eyebrows but said nothing. She picked up her glass, took a small sip and let out a long breath. 'I'll trust you, Alex,' she said. 'I don't know what's going on. I won't beg you to tell me, but . . .' She spun the glass between her fingers again, examining its dark contents for a moment. 'Just be careful. Make sure it's worth it. Make sure you can find your way back again.'

Alex lowered his gaze, not daring to meet her eyes. He nodded one final time and then backed away, letting himself out of the front door.

Grace's insights had always been spot on, her understanding of Alex better than his own. She was wiser than he, yet he knew he wouldn't listen. Like the addict he was, Alex was hooked. His distraction, as she put it, was all-consuming, and they both knew it.

Alex paused at the garden gate, rummaging for his car keys, hoping he wouldn't bump into the neighbour. He'd only drunk half a glass in the end, so decided to go for a drive. Solitude was rarely helpful, but it wasn't like he had a raging social life to attend to.

He made it as far as the end of the road before his phone rang. He checked the display and hit the answer button on the steering wheel.

'If you're calling to warn me off again, there's no need,' he said. 'I'm going home to wallow in self-pity.'

'Quite the opposite,' said Hartley, her voice filling the car. 'I've just had a call from the NCA. Somebody wants to see you.'

CHAPTER EIGHTEEN

Sunday morning. This particular building in Vauxhall was busier than most in the vicinity, the buzz of activity infectious and urgent.

Detective Laurie spun around on her chair and stared at Alex, examining him from head to toe with a critical look. Alex shut the door to her office and stood rooted to the spot, staring back.

'F-F-S,' she said.

'What's that?'

'It means *for fuck's sake*, Alex, keep up. I meant it as a joke.' Laurie stood, putting her hands on her hips. 'You're not the joke, exactly,' she said, 'though I'm sure you can be funny when you try. That suit's a good start.'

Alex smiled, dropping his bag on one side. Laurie hadn't changed a bit. She was still the same bundle of sarcasm and wit he'd grown to love during the Mia case, just over a year ago. Alex had often struggled to work out if she was insulting him or not, but soon realised he didn't mind either way. Laurie's style was cutting and derisive, but she was sharper than any detective he'd ever met. Her powers of deduction put her several steps ahead of Alex in most conversations, and she often had to wait for him to catch up, making a point of doing so in the most impolite and obvious way possible. Seeing her gave him a much-needed boost.

He opened his arms to her.

She pulled a face and frowned, before her mouth broke into a huge grin. She stepped forward and they embraced. She relaxed in his arms and both lingered for a fraction longer than strictly necessary. She was first to pull away and leaned back against the desk, smoothing her jacket, taking a moment before looking him in the eye.

'It's good to see you, Alex,' she said, without a hint of sarcasm on this occasion.

'You too, Laurie,' he said. 'And it's good to have you on this case – if that's what this is.'

Laurie frowned. 'We'll see,' she said. 'Oh, and it's my case you're on, not the other way around.'

Alex sighed. 'And I like this suit,' he said, making a mental note never to wear it again.

She nodded at him. 'Of course you do. But chinos will be fine. They suit men of your age.'

Getting so personal so soon. Laurie was a few years younger than Alex and looked younger still. Her blonde hair was tied back in a ponytail, with a few wisps escaping around her face. She wore corporate-looking grey trousers with a simple black top, her trademark brogues standing out in rebellion. More formal than before, thought Alex, but he tried to avoid staring, knowing it would only invite a fresh attack.

'So,' he said, casting his eyes around the small office, trying in vain to find any personal items that might give some insight into her current personal life – a photo, a boyfriend . . . anything. 'The NCA, huh?'

'Huh, indeed,' she said. 'They had to fill a quota or something.'

Alex raised his eyebrows. Hartley's call had been curious. That the NCA wanted to speak to Alex after warning him off had raised all sorts of alarm bells, until Hartley mentioned who had requested it. Alex hadn't known she'd transferred, but Detective

Laurie's promotion to the National Crime Agency was not a surprise. Modesty was one of Laurie's more obviously likeable traits, and her promotion here was entirely down to her own skill and professionalism, nobody else's.

Alex hoped to turn the surprise into a situation that could work in his favour.

'Quota. That's what they told me,' he said.

She punched him on the arm and sat back on her chair, indicating he take the other.

'You work alone?' asked Alex, shuffling on the hard plastic seat. He grabbed his bag from the floor and pulled out his notes.

'No, with a partner,' she said, 'but they're based out of Manchester.'

'What's his name?'

'Hannah.'

'Oh,' said Alex, realising his mistake a fraction too late.

'Wow,' said Laurie, opening her mouth in shock. 'Shit! Yes, I see what you mean – two female officers operating without a man in sight. How the hell do we even function? I hope nobody higher up has realised.' She glanced around the room. 'Tell you what, let's keep it a secret between us, and when we get stuck, we can ask you for help. You're a man, aren't you?'

Alex couldn't stop another laugh from escaping. He'd have to do better than that around Laurie. 'Good idea,' he said. 'I'm always available. Ask me anything.'

'Good to know,' said Laurie, trying but failing to suppress her own grin. 'But you're not available, from what I've heard.'

'Heard?'

Laurie blushed. Only just, but Alex caught it.

'Oh, do shut up,' she said, turning back to her laptop.

Alex kept his eyes on her for a few moments. He couldn't help it.

'Stare at something else while your brain catches up, Alex.'

He shifted his gaze, closed his eyes and took a few breaths. Laurie was several leagues above him and had already given him the opportunity to be closer than colleagues. He'd failed to take it, of course, caught up in his attempts to win Grace back, but that had been over a year ago. It was a blip, a non-event. They both should have moved on.

'So you warn me off, then invite me in for this lovely chat,' he said.

'I didn't warn you off,' said Laurie. 'Nobody did. We simply declined the Met's offer of assistance. That was until the email was passed my way and I saw the mention of your big ugly name.'

Alex tilted his head and smiled. 'You're welcome.'

Laurie returned a thin smile. She shook her head. 'Tell me what you know, Alex. No secrets. Then perhaps you can be useful.'

Alex paused. Laurie's eyes were piercing, full of curiosity and suspicion.

'I don't have much,' he said, 'but of course I'll share my thoughts. Seeing as you asked so nicely.'

On the drive in, Alex had already decided to give Laurie more information than he had given Hartley. If Eva's death was suspect, then finding out the truth was the priority, but close on its heels was *what* she was – an innocent troubled teenager or a product of something much bigger? Was Nova the shadow lurking behind her? The shadow following him?

Alex was wary of giving everything away too soon. If he told them the full extent of his suspicions, they might thank him for his time and wave him goodbye. Alternatively, if curious, which Laurie was, they might also inquire as to his determined interests in such things and why he hadn't phoned it in the minute he'd spoken to Susan, or even to Larry. They might decide to dig a little deeper into Alex's own work and financial activities, which wouldn't stand up to full-blown scrutiny, particularly from the NCA.

Alex was treading on thin ice. He wouldn't survive a focused examination. Sooner or later they'd stumble across Mia, and that would be it. Game over.

'This is everything I have,' he said, spreading out the papers he'd prepared on the desk. 'Where do you want to start?'

Laurie lined up her laptop, pausing for a few seconds while she flicked through a document. She ignored Alex's papers.

'So what did Hartley tell you about Dr Naylor?' she said.

'Nothing,' said Alex truthfully. 'Only that you're watching her. You'd be taking it from here, were her precise words.'

Laurie nodded. 'The name flagged up against our alert system. Dr Naylor has been under investigation for six months, but so far we've failed to obtain any concrete information.'

'Regarding?' said Alex.

Laurie paused. 'She's connected to a Spanish trafficking network. Interpol caught a financial transaction linked to Dr Naylor through an offshore investment fund and notified us several months ago. We traced the money but then hit a dead end. It's nigh on impossible to track this sort of thing, and the money disappeared into a network of private banks, who are being unhelpful, to say the least.'

Alex took a moment to consider the significance of such a find. A psychiatrist with links to trafficking. Young vulnerable women under her care. Complete power over their activities, drug regime, treatment . . .

'Shit,' he said. 'But . . . assuming we're talking about girls under her care . . . that should be easier to trace? People can't just disappear from the system. This is the National Health Service we're talking about.'

'Tell me about it,' said Laurie, rolling her eyes. 'But you're wrong. People can disappear, and psychiatric patients can disappear very easily. They often have nobody on the outside keeping tabs. They can disappear in the system, or once they've been discharged into community care. In the latter, they're as free as you or me, and can vanish just as easily.'

Alex nodded. It hit him plain as day. He understood perfectly. The most vulnerable people in society were at the mercy of a few people with power over them, who were often accountable only to themselves. Dead or discharged . . . they were just gone.

Like Eva Jansen, with no medical record, just a brief twisted history and a death certificate.

'You'll check for a body?' he said.

'We will,' said Laurie, 'but I don't think we'll find one. Cremation records can be forged just as easily as death certificates.'

Alex closed his eyes. He had to force his thoughts in order. Gradually, they clicked into place.

'I spoke to a Dr Holly Morgan at St Anne's,' he said. 'She said Dr Naylor's discharge rate out of hospital was higher than average.'

Laurie raised her eyebrows. She tapped away on her laptop. 'Dr Holly Morgan?'

'Yes.'

'OK,' said Laurie, nodding. 'We haven't spoken to her yet. There are a lot of people we haven't yet spoken to, in fact. I've just emailed one of our team – asked them to make contact, see what she says. We didn't want to spook Naylor until we had something. Arresting her would disturb everyone else in the chain and the anti-trafficking operation would collapse. Six months sounds like a long time but we've barely scratched the surface.'

Laurie paused. She appeared to be considering things. 'OK, before I continue . . . Your turn, Alex. How did you come to know the delightful Dr Naylor? I know this won't be boring. It's why I insisted on speaking to you.'

Alex gave a brief account of his involvement and thoughts surrounding Susan and her concerns over her patient Eva Jansen, in much the same way as he'd described it to Hartley. He relayed his rehearsed story but this time left out Larry. That could wait.

Laurie remained silent, making notes, checking her laptop and shooting him the occasional look of puzzlement. 'And you're thinking what I'm thinking?'

Alex's mind churned with the consequences. 'I am now,' he said.

'So?'

'So . . .' Alex struggled to spin this around. Susan's concern about Eva might have been justified, but for altogether different reasons, at least initially.

'You think this is straightforward sex trafficking?' he said. In which case, where did Nova fit in? They weren't traffickers. Working with them, or against them?

Laurie looked at him with contempt. 'Nothing about trafficking humans is straightforward, Alex.'

'Not what I meant,' he said. 'I mean, Eva . . . if she isn't dead, she's being sold for sex?'

Laurie frowned. 'Unless she has some other major talent, it's sex. That's what these people do. Sex sells, or hadn't you heard?'

Alex cleared his throat. Just the right amount of information. Just enough to keep him involved. 'Remember Mia Anastos?'

Laurie did well to hide her reaction. She folded her arms, leaning back in the chair, her eyes narrowed.

'Of course I do,' she said. 'How could I forget our winning teamwork? Oh, hang on. She escaped, didn't she? Disappeared into thin air.'

Alex's heart thumped through his chest. He kept his expression neutral. 'But what we discovered about her. You remember? The medical experiments. The result?'

'Of course.' Laurie's arms remained crossed over her chest, but her face twisted with curiosity.

'I think Eva may have suffered something similar,' he said.

'The same condition?' Laurie sat up a little straighter. The murderous rampage undertaken by Mia Anastos was not an easy thing to forget.

'Not the same, no, but perhaps linked. And I'm not altogether sure she's harmless.'

'Experimented on by Dr Naylor, you think?'

Alex shook his head. 'No. Before. But I think Dr Naylor might know. That would explain her behaviour. It might explain all of this.'

'Linked how?' Laurie now unfolded her arms and leaned forward on the desk. She flicked her laptop back into life. 'To Nova? They disappeared into the wind. We never made any progress there and any assets they held just disappeared. Exactly like Mia.'

Laurie's eyes were still piercing. Alex's face flushed as she stared. She didn't know. She couldn't. Whatever suspicions she might have were no more than that. There was no proof.

'I don't know,' he said. 'But the nurse, Susan Halsey . . . her account suggested Eva was suffering from the result of something unnatural in origin. Her condition was . . . undiagnosed.'

Laurie pulled a face. 'What the hell does that mean? You're not going alien on me are you, Alex?'

'Not yet. I mean drugs. Conditioning. Psychological or physiological manipulation. It's a leap, but I wonder if she was maybe subjected to it in a similar way to Mia. Given what you've said about Naylor's activity, that might be why she's being sold.'

Laurie continued to stare. She tapped her fingers on the desk. Alex didn't doubt that her intellect was whirring away.

'Are you going to tell me what it is, or do I need to guess? I hate guessing games, Alex. I get grumpy, and when I get grumpy, I can be horrible to be around. Trust me. What do you mean *not altogether harmless?*'

Alex described Eva's condition in broad strokes, keeping it high level and plausible to someone as sceptical as Laurie. He emphasised the documented violent outbreaks, and the fear shown by all those treating her.

Laurie's face twisted dramatically into several different expressions. She ended with her hands on her cheeks, framing a puzzled appearance. 'She's an empath?'

'No. Or at least . . . what do you mean by an empath?'

'I don't know,' said Laurie, shrugging. 'It's what Mia had, wasn't it? A distorted perception of empathy. A heightened sense of it? That's what drove her to hurt people.'

Alex paused. Laurie was accurate about Mia, but that's not what Eva displayed, or at least not from his minimal information. 'I don't think so,' he said. 'She can read people, but it's not empathetic. It might be nothing more than showmanship and misdirection, but I think that's what her talent is – not sex. If she's not dead, and she's being trafficked, it's on the basis she can do something else.'

Laurie appeared to consider this, her eyes remaining on Alex. 'And the violence?'

'That's more troubling. I simply don't know. The information is in the notes I brought with me.' He indicated the papers on the desk. 'I need more time. Ideally, I'd meet her and find out.'

He said it without thinking. Laurie picked up on it immediately.

'Yes,' she said, tapping the notes with her hand. Another of her expert silences followed. Alex thought she could probably hear his heartbeat.

'I appreciate you're not a cop, Alex,' she said. 'Your heart's in the right place, though, and so is your professional compass.' She paused, her palm still resting on the desk, gazing at his face as if in search of the answer.

'Here at the NCA we pursue criminals,' she said, smiling. 'If your psychological assessment and insights can help us catch them, you're with me. But if your interests lie too far the other way, to the detriment of the case, we'll need to part company sooner rather than later.'

Their eyes met and he saw how her suspicions ran far deeper than mild doubt. Laurie knew Mia hadn't disappeared, but for whatever reason she'd decided not to pursue it with him. She'd let a year pass and done nothing. This, however, was as strong a hint as he was likely to get.

'Mia got away,' he said, maintaining eye contact. 'Eva doesn't have to, and neither does Dr Naylor.'

Laurie's lips twisted into a crooked smile as her eyes continued to search his face.

'Very well,' she said, leaning back. She closed her eyes as if suddenly tired, stretching her arms behind her head. 'Time for coffee. Let's take a break.'

CHAPTER NINETEEN

Laurie hurried off to make a private call, insisting Alex stick around – they weren't finished. Alex strolled back to Laurie's office from the vending machine, blowing into the small plastic cup, uneasy, his mind whirring with what had transpired. If Eva wasn't dead, then this became a completely different game. His dealings with Laurie must ensure he didn't get thrown off the case before it even started, and in the process also reveal the extent of his own criminal actions. Quite a challenge for a Sunday morning.

The only positive to the whole thing was how much he was enjoying seeing Laurie again. Her direct and ruthless approach had a surprisingly calming effect on him. She was good for his mental state. He hoped he wouldn't let her down.

'The wheels are in motion,' said Laurie, sweeping into the office before he'd had a chance to sit.

Alex waited for her to continue, rather than be ridiculed for asking a stupid question. He sipped his coffee, wincing at the bitter plastic taste.

Laurie sat checking her laptop screen, her mobile beside her on the table. Satisfied at what she saw, she crossed her legs and spun towards Alex. 'Dr Naylor is headed for Madrid. And yes, I know you know this.'

Alex opened his mouth and shut it again. He'd already told Laurie his suspicion about the psych conference. Best not to interrupt.

'Contacts on the ground say it's a handover and a new auction,' she said. 'We're familiar with the location and we have access to the auction.'

Alex's mouth stayed open this time. A new auction? Eva? 'What do you mean?'

Laurie sniffed, shuffling in her seat. 'I'll tell you only what you need to know, Alex,' she said. 'We need to tread carefully. The official channels through the Spanish police are time-consuming and . . . let's just say, not altogether reliable.'

Alex got the gist. 'Bribery?'

'We don't hold any evidence. Without that we have no actual jurisdiction on the Spanish mainland, although we may take action regardless. It's been authorised. The traffickers have been operating on UK soil so it's in our interests to pursue them.'

Alex's heart rate increased. He sat a little straighter, mirroring Laurie's posture. Her face remained calm, but she radiated a seriousness he hadn't seen in her before, in stark contrast to her chirpy welcome only an hour before.

'You know how they move these girls?' he said.

Laurie nodded. 'We will do. We have officers on the ground – the trafficking group was compromised a few months ago. We don't have anyone on the inside, but we do have access to the sales.'

Alex realised what this meant. He raised his eyebrows and Laurie nodded.

'You want to buy Eva back?'

Laurie chewed her bottom lip. '*If* she's alive, there will be limited opportunities to find her and Naylor. Many girls disappear before we can even mobilise. Storming in is out of the question.

Tipping off the Spanish police, in our experience, would mean both Eva and Dr Naylor disappear for ever.'

Alex's hands shook. This was the opportunity he needed.

'There is, of course, the question of exposure,' Laurie continued. 'In other words, we don't want any. What we do want is to save this girl, if she can be saved, and to discreetly retrieve Dr Naylor, bringing both of them back to the UK. If we achieve that, we can work outwards again, using Interpol to bring the network down. This is a small off-book operation. Do you understand?'

Alex nodded. He couldn't have asked for more. 'I need to go with you,' he said.

Laurie examined him for several seconds, until finally she smiled. It was small and tired, but honest.

'I'd already decided that was the case,' she said. 'Given the nature of the crime and the people involved, we've been advised to have a psych consult with us at all times. You're it, Alex.'

Alex returned the smile. 'Thank you,' he said.

'We leave for Spain on Monday,' said Laurie. She replaced her smile with a frown. 'Don't let me down. And pack some chinos.'

Alex excused himself, leaving the room under the ever-suspicious eye of Laurie, heading home to grab a weekend bag.

'You still need to tell me what's in that head of yours,' called Laurie, as he slipped down the corridor.

Perhaps he did, but he needed to get his narrative straight first. How much to explain? How much to hide? His story was a mess, with threads hanging, spoilers looming.

He'd get it together by the time he got on the plane with Laurie. He must.

The corridor ended at the lifts. Alex stepped in, watching the doors close. At the last minute a hand appeared, forcing the doors open.

An elderly man stepped in and stood next to Alex, facing forward. Alex glanced sideways – an immaculately tailored suit with polished black brogues. A senior officer, perhaps? Civil Service? His grey hair was thin, but neatly combed. Alex felt something. A stir.

Recognition?

The lift moved downwards.

Alex felt a flutter in his chest, heat radiating outwards. His shirt felt tight, his chest pushing outwards. The lift shook. Where had he seen this man before?

The man stood straight. Alex kept his gaze on him, watching the side of his face, the wrinkled skin, pale and withered, yet he held himself in a rigid posture. The man started to whisper, soft murmurings to himself. Alex couldn't hear the words, found himself leaning in to listen, the whirr of the lift fading into silence, white noise taking its place.

The lift pinged. Stopped. The doors opened to an empty corridor. The white noise faded and Alex's ears popped. The doors closed and his flesh crawled, the unease palpable, an intense rush of fear, of hopelessness, creeping up his body.

Alex put his hand out against the wall of the lift. His chest tightened and his breathing grew laboured. A pain shot across his shoulders, grasping his neck and jaw. A crushing pain enveloped his chest and the heat disappeared to be replaced with cold. Sweat beaded on his forehead and he felt a sudden vertigo.

Something screamed at the back of his mind. *Symptoms of cardiac arrest.*

The lift stopped again. Pinged. The doors opened.

Alex gasped, staggering backwards into the corner, leaning against the wall, propping himself up. 'Please,' he said. 'Please help me.'

His vision swam as the man turned to him. He tilted his head to one side, examining Alex, before moving closer. He reached out, putting a hand towards Alex's chest. His palm rested lightly on his shirt, and he leaned in, until their faces were mere inches apart.

'We know what you've done, Alex,' the man said, his voice low, barely a whisper. Alex couldn't place the accent, the pain in his chest almost unbearable, his head spinning, his breath coming in short gasps.

'We only give you so many chances,' said the man. 'Take one. It will be better for you, and the ones you love.'

The man whipped his hand away and stepped back. He sneered, contempt and anger in his eyes. Alex saw the man's jaw moving, clenching, releasing, some inner dialogue playing out. Alex couldn't move, his weakened body frozen, still pinned against the cold metal of the lift.

The lift pinged again, the doors opened and the man stepped out.

Once the man was out of sight, Alex's symptoms immediately evaporated. His heart thundered in his chest, but the tightness began to release and the pain subsided. He gulped in huge breaths of air as the lift descended.

He stepped out on to the ground floor. It was busy, with officers milling around, a queue of visitors waiting at reception, behind the access gates or shuffling through the metal detectors.

Alex staggered over to a row of visitors' chairs and collapsed on to one. He took several minutes to compose himself, avoiding the odd stare, taking deep, slow breaths in and out, surreptitiously swallowing a Xanax, closing his eyes while his body adjusted after the shock.

He managed to pull out his mobile phone, which slipped out of his pocket and into his trembling hand. He stared at it for a moment. The urge to call Laurie and have the building locked down was tempered only by the voice of the man replaying in his ear. *We know what you've done, Alex.*

Mia. He was talking about Mia. Alex had hidden a murderer, and they knew about it.

Nova knew about it. Of that, Alex had no doubt.

So what did that leave him with? A confession? He'd be arrested immediately and his pursuit would be over. His relationship with the police would be over. His life would be over. No truth, no justice, no recompense for all those people who'd suffered at the hands of his father or for those he worked for. Nova would once again be free.

The alternative, then. Twice now they could have killed him and twice they had let him go with a warning. There was no rhyme or reason, but he was being allowed to live.

The people who threatened him were capable of so much more. The threads he pulled were tangled, and yet they were allowing him to follow through.

They were complicit in his search, but he didn't know why.

His phone buzzed. Incoming call. Alex focused on the screen. It was Grace. He answered it in a daze. Her voice snapped him out of it, shrill and impatient, and edged with fear.

It was Katie, she said. Katie had been approached in the street. Approached by a man in a black SUV.

CHAPTER TWENTY

No, Katie wasn't hurt. No, she wouldn't explain on the phone, but he had better get his arse around there pronto.

Speeding through London was impossible at this time of day, but he gunned the hire car down the side streets, trying to burn away the myriad of pressures building in his head.

How could he have been so blind? Was he blind? Or just selfish? What did he expect would happen, poking the hornets' nest? The last time he got Grace and Katie involved in his work, it had ended in disaster – his mistake, because he hadn't figured things out fast enough.

He had promised it would never be repeated.

He'd broken that promise already.

Alex pulled up outside Grace's house, noting the neighbour's car, ensuring that he parked well away from it. As he approached the front door, he heard raised voices and leaned in, trying to catch the gist, but as he did so the door flew open.

'Come in,' said Grace, leaving the door swinging as she walked back through the hallway and into the kitchen. Alex followed her and found Katie perched at the breakfast bar. She'd been crying, her eyes puffy, her face red.

Alex paused, assessing the situation, suddenly in the moment. Grace looked angry. Katie looked upset. It wasn't what he'd expected.

'Looks like I missed something,' he said. Katie's failure to return his smile suggested he'd read it wrong.

'Don't you always?' said Grace. Her tone was fierce. He wiped the smile from his face.

'Will you tell him?' Grace glanced at Katie, hands on hips, although her anger seemed to be projected towards Alex, not Katie.

Katie shrugged. 'It's not a big deal. I *told* you.'

'It is a big deal!' shouted Grace. She turned to Alex, pointing at Katie. 'Your daughter was out late last night, way past her curfew.'

'Mum—'

'Which wouldn't be a big deal, except that someone tried to pick her up.'

Alex frowned. 'Someone?' He turned to Katie. 'Somebody hit on you?'

'Not hit on me, Dad.'

'In a car,' said Grace. 'An old man. He tried to get her in his car. On the high street.'

'He wasn't hitting on me. He didn't try to get me into the car!'

The temperature dropped. Prickles on his neck.

'What did he say? What did he look like?' His voice was loud, too demanding.

Katie looked pleadingly at him. 'It's not my fault!'

'If you'd come home on time, he wouldn't have been there.' Grace was pacing now, shaking her head.

'How do you know?' Katie screamed back at her. Alex saw the tears welling up again. He clamped down on his own panic. It was his fault, but he didn't want to scare Katie by saying it in front of her.

'Did you call the police?' asked Alex.

Katie and Grace glanced at each other.

'I called you,' said Grace.

'Why not the police?'

Grace huffed.

'Because he said he knew you,' said Katie. 'That's what we've been arguing about.'

Alex let out a long breath. 'Knew me how?'

'I dunno. He said he worked with you. He said to say hello. He said he'll always be around, keeping an eye out for us.'

He. Nova. The man in the lift. A direct threat to Katie. Open and arrogant.

'I said thank you, but no,' said Katie, 'then I walked off. I got to the corner of our road and ran home.'

'I've been so stupid,' Alex whispered under his breath.

'What?'

'Good,' said Alex. 'Good girl. You did the right thing.'

Grace looked incensed. '*Good girl?* Is that all you have to say?'

Alex could see her biting down on her frustration.

'Do you know this person or not?' she said.

Alex shook his head. 'I . . .' His mind whirred. How many warnings would he get? Had they been watching Grace and Katie all this time? Surely, they'd know the police would be called. Alex paused for thought. Except the police hadn't been called. So did they bank on Alex hiding it?

We know what you did, Alex.

But if he'd wanted to hurt Katie, he'd have done so. A polite *thank you, no* would hardly have dissuaded him.

'Christ, Alex,' said Grace. 'Katie – go to your room for a bit. I need to talk to your dad.'

Katie slipped off the stool. Alex tried to give her a hug as she passed but she shrugged him off.

'Leave me alone, Dad,' she said, slamming the door behind her.

Grace stopped pacing, stood hands on hips again. 'So?'

Alex leaned on the worktop. He had to tell Laurie. The question was how much to tell.

'I'll speak to the police.'

'That's it?'

'Did you get the cameras fitted? The alarm?'

'You're scaring me, Alex.'

Alex took a deep breath. His heart was jumping, his throat swelling. Could he take the chance?

No. Not with Katie and Grace. Never with them.

'Is Kerry still local?' He thought of Grace's best friend from university. Katie got on well with her daughter, Josie.

'She's in Harrow, yes.'

'Could you and Katie stay with her for a few days?'

Grace's face fell. She closed her eyes. 'Who are they, Alex?'

Alex shook his head. He was beginning to feel dizzy, nauseous.

'It's a big case, organised crime,' he said, taking a glass from the shelf. He ran the tap until it was cold, then filled the glass. 'It's possible they know where I live. Where you live.'

'How?' Grace looked scared, but furious with it. 'How the hell does that happen?'

Alex shook his head. 'It happens. Look, if they'd wanted to harm Katie, they would have done. I—'

'That doesn't make me feel any better!'

'But it's true. This was a warning – a stupid, scary warning, but that's all. It's for me, not for you. I think you're both safe, but to be sure, go and stay with Kerry. I'll have the police on it first thing. It'll never happen again.'

He regretted the words as they tumbled out of his mouth. It had happened before. Victor Lazar had taken Katie, and Alex had sworn then that such a thing would never be repeated. His work and his family would never clash again.

And yet here they were.

'Is it worth it?' said Grace. She perched on a stool, shoulders slumped, hands fidgeting. 'Is it serious?'

Alex sidled over, standing in front of her. He clasped her shoulders.

'I won't let anything happen to Katie, OK? This was a mistake. My mistake, but no harm was done.'

The doubt was clear in Grace's eyes.

'Don't patronise me,' she said. 'Not ever.' She shrugged off his hands. 'We'll go and stay with Kerry. I want to know it's safe here before we come back. I want a proper guarantee from the police. OK?'

Alex nodded. 'I'll wait while you pack your stuff,' he said. 'I'll follow you to Kerry's.'

Two hours later, Alex sat in his car outside Kerry's house and dialled Laurie's number.

'Laurie.'

'Alex. You OK? You sound out of breath.'

Alex swallowed, his careful thoughts suddenly muddled.

'I need a protection unit for Grace and Katie,' he said, 'but I can't tell you why, not yet. It's related to this case, but I just need you to trust me. Will you do that for me? Before we leave? I can't go to Madrid without it.'

He heard Laurie take a deep breath, her mind no doubt whirring through the possible scenarios. Several moments passed, while Alex tapped impatiently on the steering wheel.

'Related?' she said.

'Please?' he said.

'I—'

'Please,' he repeated. 'Don't make me beg. Just do this for me. I'll explain when I next see you.'

Laurie paused. The line hissed. The noise of the passing traffic crowded his head.

'You still there?' he said. He was pushing their professional relationship to the limit, their friendship too.

'OK,' she said finally, her voice cautious. 'Calm down, Alex. I have no interest in hearing you beg. Whatever's just happened in that head of yours needs describing, but for now, I'll do as you ask. I'll put a watch on them. I'll do it now.'

'Thank you,' said Alex. 'Thank you, Laurie.'

'But you'll need to explain properly, Alex. Protection costs money. I'm not saying I don't trust you, but this isn't the way it works. We need some honesty between us. Don't screw me around, OK?'

Alex forced a few slow breaths. He was teetering on the edge, but he'd come back from it. Everything so far – his history, his research, the threats to himself and his family, the attacks on Susan and Larry – it all pointed in one direction. Nova was cleaning up, removing traces, removing *people*. They'd done it before, and if Alex wasn't careful, they'd do it again, disappearing beyond his reach, beyond the law, fading into the ether.

This is what they did. This is what he couldn't let happen again.

The only thread he had was Eva. He was sure of it.

This was his only chance of pursuing them beyond the shadows. If the NCA could bring her home, he might lure Nova out again, to give him another chance, another shot. And this time, somehow, he'd be prepared.

This was all about Eva now. His focus was resolute.

'I understand,' he said.

CHAPTER TWENTY-ONE

The temperature dropped a few degrees as the evening drew in. Natalia paced her room, paced the balcony, her own unease forcing her into a cycle of nervous research and wild conclusions.

Her man in London had reported in. Pavel was departing the UK. Whether it had anything to do with the twenty-four-hour police protection suddenly appearing around Alex Madison's family, her contact couldn't be sure, but it made sense. Pavel might not wish to expose himself any more than he already had. With his final bargaining chips now out of reach, he might have decided to cut his losses. Whatever the reason, he was heading back east. Where and what for, Natalia was left guessing.

She slumped on one of the balcony chairs, clearing her throat, her lungs still protesting, slowly clearing themselves in the warm and humid air. She sipped at a cold glass of lemonade, casting her eyes down to the restless streets as the city came to life with shouts from a group of excitable teenagers, cries from a baby, and strains of music from nearby restaurants, opening up for the night's business.

Waiting.

Natalia sighed. She closed her eyes. Complications flooded her otherwise straightforward mission. Or rather, one particular complication by the name of Alex Madison.

Pavel had lashed out ruthlessly, clearing Eva's history quite unnecessarily. These people had not been a threat to Nova, implying that their deaths represented a warning from Pavel himself.

And yet . . . Alex Madison had not been frightened off. So far, Natalia had kept her knowledge to herself, not even telling her handler. Alex's motives were misguided but his goals were noble – in comparison with those of Nova, at any rate. His tenacity was infectious, and Natalia found herself wanting to follow his next move.

Pavel had underestimated his determination, his resolve to track them down. A scare like that would work on most normal people – in Natalia's experience, most men and women were weak and self-centred. Faced with real danger, they'd scamper away to hide, not daring to incur the wrath of the monsters that chased them. But not Alex. It didn't work. And now, with his family under armed protection, he would be steadfast in his pursuit.

Alex was following the girl, his only concrete lead. Arrogance should be the natural response – Natalia's organisation was well prepared and a small British police unit was not going to get in the way. But Alex wasn't done yet. His encounters with Natalia's world had nurtured an obsession to uncover more. She had often wondered at what point her masters would call time – concluding his curiosity had run its course.

But Pavel had ventured to the West and revealed himself, and Alex's time had not been curtailed. So far.

She slammed the glass of lemonade down on the table. It cracked, with a hairline snaking from the base up to the lip. Fragile, ready to shatter at any moment, yet still holding. She watched it for a second, the bubbles surging to the surface, away from the damage.

Natalia's frustration grew because she had no answers. Once again, the unpredictable nature of Alex's involvement threatened to ignite the chaos that was never far away from her world. Pavel could have killed Alex in an instant – in his sleep, at his office, in his car. The fact that he hadn't bothered Natalia almost as greatly because she couldn't fathom why.

She focused on her rising anger, pinpointing its root cause: a combination of fear and helplessness. Natalia was used to fighting worthy adversaries – it was her job, and she was good at it. But Pavel was in a different league entirely.

If she ever came up against Pavel, she'd lose. She knew that for a fact.

It wasn't his overt ability that worried her – his talents that extended far beyond hers, inflicting all manner of psychological and physiological damage on his subjects. Natalia could counter and block, maybe even run and hide.

But she couldn't hurt him. Pavel was one of Nova's directors, the elite, the voice of power. He, like all those at his level, were immune to the lesser abilities Natalia possessed. They were the origins, the patient zeros, and they had nothing to fear from within. Still human, flesh and blood, but protected from their wards by decades of training and conditioning.

Pavel was a monster. Worse than that, his personal motivations were unclear.

Another deep breath. A song drifted towards her on the warm air, the thumps of the drum breaking her stupor, the delicate Spanish words lifting her spirits, if only for a few seconds. But long enough.

She'd figure it out. That was her job, figuring out the darker problems, ensuring the future of her group and the masters who played their games. Even Pavel. She was in control at the moment, and Alex's fate would remain connected to hers.

To protect Alex would be her job. Powerless to do anything more than watch him, the best path she could take would be to complete her mission. Success, with any luck, would mean Alex's trail would go cold. He'd be out of the picture, left to his dark studies and his hopeless searching.

CHAPTER TWENTY-TWO

Eva focused inwards. The pitch black gave her nothing to see in the real world, her senses dulled. The chafing of the rope on her wrists sent the occasional stab of pain up her forearms, but she could ignore that. Eva was used to filtering out discomfort. The darkness sent her heart racing, but at least it was quiet.

The horrible realisation thudded into her mind, along with deep regret – she had been careless. More than that, arrogant. She'd been safe for so long.

What had been the final straw? The friendly nurse with the philandering husband? She'd told somebody. No, the nurse was too kind and would never run to that witch, Naylor. Was it Andi? Or one of the other girls? Had they been telling tales on her? Eva thought back over the last few weeks and realised she'd been studying them all and then been loose with her tongue. She could blame boredom, perhaps, or frustration. Eva knew her temper was uncontrollable once it started, but she'd been in fewer fights lately. Why?

Dr Naylor, that's why. The bitch was always there, always intervening. Eva swore under her breath. She had thought she was studying them. She'd been so stupid not to figure out that Naylor was studying her.

The promethazine – Naylor always gave her a shot *to calm your anger, dear*. But it also rendered Eva unable to read the doctor. That had been no accident. Plus, she always made Eva face the other way. Out of sight, out of mind.

'Stupid, stupid,' whispered Eva.

Eva strained at her wrists, but they held fast. Her anger would do her no good here, and she was aware it wasn't just anger now. Fear was creeping in around the edges.

Dr Naylor was the first person in a long time to unnerve Eva, and Eva hadn't paid attention. The fear and fury swapped and circled each other like enemies, jostling for position. The voices were silent. Her dreams were absent. Her blindfold hurt, tied so tight it caused flashes in her eyes when she moved. It caught the top of her right ear, squeezing the flesh against her skull – a sharp pain that had numbed in the hours since she'd been beaten to the floor of her bedroom and sedated.

She sensed a gentle swaying, unmistakable. As a child she'd travelled this way, tucked into a container in the bowels of a ship, stuffy and humid, until the journey was over. The sickness she'd felt back then threatened to return as more than a memory – and she swallowed down the faint taste of bile at the back of her throat. Her hands were tied behind her, but she managed to shuffle herself into a seated position, leaning her head against the cold wall, turning so that her head rolled rather than pitched with the motion.

But not since childhood had she been off the mainland. They didn't tend to offer foreign holidays as part of the psychiatric package in most of her institutions. The fear welled back up – fear of the unknown.

The blindfold was telling, her early suspicions reinforced. Naylor knew what she could do, and was taking all the necessary steps to weaken her. Eva needed sight more than anything. The smells, movements and impulses she sensed were nothing without her eyes to put the puzzle together. Eva watched the words assemble before they appeared in her ears.

But here she sat, shackled in darkness. Where were they taking her?

From the south of England – she could assume that's where they had departed from – they must be heading for France or Spain. Possibly Belgium or the Netherlands. Or north towards Norway? Unless this was just the start of a journey to somewhere altogether further – a new continent. Asia? The Americas?

Eva shook her head. Speculation wouldn't help, and only increased her unease. Instead she sat, feeling the motion, trying to settle her thoughts. Unfortunately, now that she was upright, the need to urinate came on with a sudden urgency. She crossed her legs and tensed her muscles, but she wouldn't last long. *Pissing myself in a dark room on a ferry*, she thought. Fucking wonderful.

'Hey!' she shouted, the sound echoing in the room. Her ears picked up the reflections. It was a small space, metal walls, low ceiling. A cabin, perhaps, or a cupboard. 'Hello?'

Nothing except the dull vibrations spoke back. Eva shuffled on her bottom, trying to move around in the confined space. She managed a few inches before her legs tugged in refusal. Straightening them one at a time she realised they were also tied, fixed to something in the room.

Eva kicked out a few times, jerking her body against the restraints, then stopped suddenly. A scraping sound, a door opening. Eva went limp.

'You're awake.' A female voice, croaky, old, English. Not Naylor. 'Are you hungry?'

Eva relaxed a fraction. Her mind raced. You didn't feed people you were going to kill. She nodded. A few moments later the blindfold tugged against her skin as it was dragged up on to her forehead. She blinked a few times. The light was dim but it still flooded her eyes. A woman was staring at her with curiosity. She was dressed in loose trousers and a thick jumper, her dark hair tied back, speckled with grey. Her face was weathered, making it hard to judge her age, but Eva saw that whatever life she'd lived, it had been hard so far.

Eva took a breath. She read sadness coming from this woman. Regret, but also resignation.

Pretty, thought the woman. *She'll sell quickly.*

'Who will buy me?' said Eva, without thinking.

The woman looked startled. Her face screwed up in confusion, but relaxed a second later.

'You already know,' she said. 'Ah well, probably for the best.'

Eva bit her tongue. Naylor had thought she'd get a good price. Eva had struggled with what she'd meant by that.

The woman's thoughts clouded as she laid out a tray of food and a bottle of water on the floor. A bucket had been placed to one side. She appeared to study Eva for a few moments.

'If I take off your restraints, will you behave? There's nowhere to run to. Not here. Unless you're a very strong swimmer.'

Eva paused, nodding her agreement. She couldn't swim and knew the woman was joking, the comment coming within a whirl of mixed emotions, words jumping out but then burying themselves away. The threads were frayed and Eva struggled to hold on to them, to grasp her intentions.

The woman reached over, loosening the ropes on Eva's wrists before stepping back. Eva rubbed some life back into her aching flesh.

'Promise you'll sit there if I release your legs? I'm not the only person looking after you, but I'm certainly the kindest.'

Again, Eva nodded. Once untied, she sat cross-legged, tucking her dress between her legs, realising how hungry she was. The tray contained a lump of dark bread and some fruit, a chocolate bar and some biscuits. Eva picked up a banana and devoured it, pausing to drink half the water.

'Make sure you take your tablets,' said the woman.

Eva glanced at the two orange pills on the tray and shrugged. 'I need the toilet,' she said, feeling the cold water in her stomach and her bladder swelling in protest.

'I'll leave the bucket,' said the woman. She shrugged. 'Sorry, but you don't leave the room.'

It wasn't the first time Eva had been locked in solitary, but usually the facilities flushed. Her childhood and teens had been full of spells locked in on her own. Her earliest years remained a blur, but Eva wondered if captivity was written in her stars.

She glanced at the woman. Her emotions were getting clearer to read, the voices more persistent. Eva reacted. She tensed her legs. It wouldn't take much.

Hopefully, they won't spoil her too much first.

The thought took Eva off guard. The woman's eyes were on Eva's legs, exposed thighs. Spoil her? It took Eva a second to realise what the woman meant. Their eyes met. Eva saw the woman's turmoil, her thoughts tumbling. Was she an ally? No. The woman owed a debt that would never be repaid. She couldn't leave and she knew it. They'd kill her.

Who were they?

Eva was about to speak when the door creaked open again. A man stood in the doorway, huge, bearded, and dressed in what looked like fishing gear – a thick woollen jumper and waterproof trousers.

He paused, glancing at the woman, who shrunk in his presence, before casting his eyes over Eva. Eva shuffled, trying in vain to pull the dress further down.

'She's supposed to be blindfolded,' said the man. His accent was English too. Eva's eyes darted between him and the woman. The man's thoughts jumped out, vile and aggressive, hitting Eva with force. Both the woman and the man together created a cacophony in Eva's head and she fought to suppress it.

'And we're not supposed to talk to her.'

The woman stepped forward. 'I was just trying to—'

The man cut her off with a backhanded slap to her head. The woman staggered and hit the wall, barely managing to keep on her feet.

Eva's natural reflex was to lurch backwards. Unrestrained, she scrambled away from the man but hit the corner of the room, still in a crouch.

'Don't touch me,' she said, her breaths growing more shallow as the adrenaline pumped.

But the man made no advance towards Eva. His eyes were narrow, darting. Fear seeped out of him. He'd been warned, threatened with dire consequences. He pulled away, grabbing the woman and throwing her out the door.

'Blindfold,' he said to Eva. 'Put your fucking blindfold on.' He backed out himself then, slamming the door shut behind him, his eyes on Eva until it closed.

Eva heard bolts being shot into place, then a cry, muffled by the thick metal.

Her confidence wavered and she shivered, folding her arms around her thin body as protection. This wasn't like playing games with the patients or nurses. For the first time in her life, Eva felt utterly powerless.

The voices were gone and so was her anger. The adrenaline pumped and Eva started to shake.

CHAPTER TWENTY-THREE

Alex stared through the small window at the sprawl of Adolfo Suárez Madrid-Barajas Airport. The air was hazy and hot, shimmering off the taxiways. The noon sun scorched down, baking the expanses of metal tubes bearing thousands of people off on their adventures, commutes and lazy holidays.

'It looks warm,' he said, waiting for the sarcasm in return. It never came. He turned to see Laurie already out of her seat and struggling with the overhead storage locker. She yanked her bag so hard it shot out, hitting the seat in front on the way to the floor. A few people glanced her way and she stared back, her winning smile convincing the other passengers to mind their own business.

'That's why we brought you along, Alex,' she said. 'Nothing gets past you.' She lifted her bag on to the seat. 'I'm going to keep you with me at all times.'

Alex packed away his own possessions – a paperback and a set of noise-cancelling headphones. He tucked them into his bag, checking his medication pouch for the fifth time. He'd brought enough benzos to keep an elephant sedated for the week, but even the thought of being without his precious pills caused his throat to swell with panic.

He brushed the thought aside as he rose to standing, perching in the awkward stance necessary in economy seating when the person in the aisle seat won't move. Laurie appeared quite happy with this and stayed right where she was.

Alex cast his eyes around the other passengers but couldn't see any sign of her colleagues. She hadn't introduced him to anyone at Stansted Airport, maintaining her usual 'need-to-know' approach. Alex really couldn't spot anyone who looked the remotest bit like a British police officer, but he supposed that was the point. NCA officers operating undercover would be quite good at it.

The doors opened and the plane emptied. The airport – one of the largest in Europe – was heaving, and Laurie and Alex queued through Customs, both travelling as tourists. Alex felt a rush of adrenaline as his passport was checked and they were waved through. Laurie's face remained perfectly calm. She gave Alex several sideways glances as they retrieved their luggage and headed for the exit.

'Stop smiling,' she said. 'It's disconcerting. You do know why we're here, right?'

Alex adopted a more sombre expression as they queued for a taxi. He had no doubt the next few days were going to get serious fast, but being asked to accompany the NCA was a huge vote of confidence. It took him off the sidelines and into the action – and was a step closer to Eva.

Laurie's relentless questioning on the plane had been partly satisfied by Alex's carefully crafted answers. An initial probe into Larry's death, suggested by Alex, had indicated something amiss – a strange security breach, an odd CCTV recording in Larry's department in the hours before his death. Combined with the inability of the Sussex police to track down Susan's hit-and-run driver, Alex had managed to raise the possibility that whoever had taken Eva was not averse to cleaning up witnesses in the UK. Alex insisted that he didn't fear for himself, but that his wife and daughter were easy targets if the shadowy kidnappers should learn of Alex's involvement.

Laurie had relented. The watch on his family would be maintained. They'd be protected. And that gave Alex the confidence he needed.

He had a chance now to make a breakthrough, one way or the other. This time it would happen on his terms. This time his family were safe from the outset.

Alex felt the same rush he always got at the turning point in a case – sensing progress along with professional pride. He couldn't help the way it made him feel, although his ever-present anxiety tugged deep down despite the elation. He'd need to keep it in check around Laurie and her team. No panic attacks. Not for the next few days.

The drive into the city took thirty minutes and they restricted their conversation to the sights and sounds of Madrid – not daring to talk openly with the taxi driver listening in. Alex wondered why they couldn't take an official car, or hire their own, but reminded himself that the fewer traces they left, the better. Laurie had explained that public transport was full of cameras, which ruled out the metro and the bus. Alex didn't get a straight answer as to who she thought might be watching them, but was assured that paying for a taxi in cash was the best compromise.

'Are your friends joining us later?' he asked, wishing the driver would turn the air con up a touch. He was beginning to sweat. Laurie seemed unbothered by the heat, still dressed in dark trousers and blouse, cool as a local. She gave him an amused glance as he shifted around on the seat.

'My friends will be there already,' she said. 'They came in on an earlier flight.'

Alex nodded, staring through the windows. The barren industrial zones to the east were giving way to brightly coloured buildings as they entered the city centre. Madrid was beautiful and he regretted his first visit under such circumstances. Another time, perhaps, he might enjoy the sights without the pit of his stomach churning at what lay ahead.

'And where is "there", exactly?' he said.

Laurie gave a warning glance, her eyes darting to the back of the driver's head.

'The villa?' she said. 'I thought I told you. The same rental as last year. It's very central – great for exploring.'

Alex nodded, embarrassed. For the rest of the short drive he kept his attention focused on the urban scenery, holding his rising sense of unease in check, while Laurie kept checking her phone, tapping out frequent messages with increasing urgency.

CHAPTER TWENTY-FOUR

Eva didn't remember sleeping, but woke to the stench of diesel fumes, stifling heat and the drone of an engine. The swaying had stopped. Bound again and blindfolded, she struggled to make sense of her surroundings. She shuffled to left and right, stretching her limbs, concluding she was cramped into a container with the dimensions of an upended coffin. Trying to rise on to her haunches confirmed this as her head struck a hard surface above.

She sank to the floor, the terror biting. Eva had suffered from claustrophobia for as long as she could remember. Her panic rose with every breath. She forced it down, trying to breathe through the foul-smelling rag across her face. The movement increased, acceleration, harsh bumps. A van or truck, possibly the trunk of a car.

She screamed, but the sound was muffled by the rag and drowned out by the noise of the engine. She screamed again, kicking out with both her legs against the wall of the container. All she got back was the steady drone and the vibrations through her body.

Forcing her breathing into a slow, controlled rhythm, Eva tried to calm herself, but she wasn't stupid. A lifetime of incarceration might have shielded her from many things, but she wasn't entirely ignorant of the world. She knew slavery was alive and well – she just hadn't expected to be sold by her own physician.

The motion of the truck was nauseating. Eva closed her eyes and memories of other doctors found their way into her consciousness. Not Naylor. This was before. From a long time ago. Fragments and snippets – Eva must have been a small child. But some of them were vivid. And painful.

You're not listening, Eva.

The familiar rebuke. They shouted it at her on a daily basis.

The doctor wore a white coat with a badge; Eva couldn't remember what it said. His tie was yellow and his face was mean. He tried not to shout at Eva, but Eva knew he was mad with her. She could tell by the way he smiled. Eva held her toy rabbit, Josie, close to her chest, squeezing the matted fur.

'*Listen* to him, Eva,' said the doctor.

Eva glanced at the window to her left, smudged with handprints, showing a separate but identical room. A different man sat on a chair. He had no white coat, just grey trousers and a tatty blue jumper with holes in the sleeves. His hair was messy and his eyes were red. He looked scared. He *was* scared. Eva could feel it.

'Where's my mum?' Eva couldn't even picture her mum's face, but had a vague longing for the comfort of soft skin and hair that smelled of lemons. Eva hadn't seen her for ages.

The other doctor, the blonde one with huge glasses and the mole on her chin, stood by the wall, writing something on her clipboard. Her whites were grubby, showing dark stains around the collar and cuffs. She was one of the worst – her thoughts so simple in their savagery. She cared for nothing but the programme and would only tolerate Eva's disobedience for so long. Then she'd send Eva away for punishment.

You're not a child, you're a monster. And you'll be treated like one.

Eva didn't know what the punishment was expected to achieve, but she remembered the sensations.

A flash of pain, lasting and profound. Eva's heart raced, and the smell of diesel and the drone of the engine jolted her out of the dream. An unpleasant sense of loss settled on her. The memory was new and disturbing. Not the usual repeating dreams of anger and torment. She closed her eyes, trying to focus. The room with the doctor. What did he say?

She drifted.

'*Watch* him, Eva.' The doctor's voice was stern and impatient. He pointed at the man through the window. 'Tell me the numbers. Do as you're told.'

Eva stared at him first, feeling the fear in her own small body. She looked at her dress, which was dirty, and at her bare feet. She was cold.

'Tell me. What do you *see*, Eva? What do you *hear*?'

The doctor was scared too, his voice pitching and wavering. Eva felt the tiny impulses twist out, thin and long, like strands of cotton spooling across the air towards her. The doctor wanted this to be over. He was thinking of his own daughter, Phoebe, and every time he thought her name the fear increased. Eva kept the daughter's name to herself. She searched, but the doctor didn't know where her mum was.

The blue-jumper man's eyes darted around and found hers. He didn't look at her like most people looked at a little girl. He looked at her like she was an animal. A tiger, perhaps, or a wolf. Why did he think she'd hurt him? Was he afraid the same thing would happen to him as the others?

He had strands of cotton too, tangled around him, crackling with nervous energy. The information was snarled and knotted – a puzzle, but not a problem. She reached for the outermost threads, and when they touched her, she saw three numbers. The information was reflected in the curve of his mouth, the tension in his cheeks, the way he blinked. So clear.

Eva turned to the doctor. She paused, watching his eyes, listening.

'I don't know,' she said.

At the back of the room, the blonde doctor sighed, and Eva read her intentions as clearly as if she'd shouted. *Punishment.*

The orderlies picked her up and dumped her in a wheelchair, the arm straps hanging as threats. She turned and watched their faces, their mouths trembling, jaws grinding with stress. She could hear them thinking as they pushed her, desperate, guilty, full of hatred at what they were doing. But they shared her fear. They had no choice.

The tank dominated the room, a huge grey cylinder, its door already open, ready to devour her. The air was hot and sticky and she could smell the salty water. It was part of her conditioning. Sensory deprivation, whatever that meant – part of her treatment. They all knew she screamed until her breath failed her. It didn't faze them.

Sometimes she passed out in terror, other times she'd curl up and pray. Either way, they'd leave her, returning much later, when her world had caved in and all she could hear was the screaming white noise from her own head. Her body floated and her visions dominated, dancing in front of her eyes, whether they were open or closed.

She remembered the sound of the door, waking her from the darkness. A scrape and a bang, metal straining against metal.

Back to reality.

CHAPTER TWENTY-FIVE

'This is nice,' said Alex, staring at the grand villa in front of him. It had a high-gated front garden filled with lush shrubbery obscuring the street-level windows. He waited for Laurie, feeling the heat from the pavement radiating upwards, drifting in the slight breeze – although not enough to cool the sweat beading all over his body.

'I'm sure it is,' said Laurie, as she watched the taxi disappear into traffic around the nearest corner, 'but it's not ours. It's a few minutes' walk from here.'

Alex sighed. He should have guessed. Laurie grabbed the handle on her small case and dragged it behind her. Alex followed, puffing with exertion. The few minutes turned out to be twenty, enough time for them to have left the neighbourhood of spotless pavements and grand villas and to head further south, into the working-class neighbourhood of Vallecas, and into a maze of side streets filled with apartment buildings.

Laurie stopped at a rather drab example, checking the building number and the apartment list. She pressed the intercom for number forty-three.

'*Qué?*' A quick reply.

'It's me,' said Laurie. She glanced at Alex. 'And the doc.'

The outer door buzzed and clicked open. Alex wasn't surprised to find the inside even hotter than outdoors, and he headed to the lifts, thinking that four floors of stairs in this heat might just about finish him off.

'The Foreign Office rents an apartment here on a permanent basis,' Laurie explained, as the lift hummed upwards. She didn't explain further, still distracted by her phone, which buzzed incessantly.

The apartment itself was spacious, the cool terracotta tiles of the hallway opening into a large room with comfortable seating at one end and a dining area at the other, with a kitchen and several bedrooms leading off a further corridor. Large ceiling fans did their best to circulate the heat. The sliding door on to the balcony from the seating area stood wide open, a net curtain wafting in the breeze.

Alex dropped his case and bag to one side as the three other occupants of the apartment stared at him from the dining table. Each had a laptop in front of them and was surrounded by swathes of paperwork.

'Alex, meet the team,' said Laurie. 'Josh on the end in the awful T-shirt, Terry with the awful hairstyle, and Hannah, perfect in every way and the only competent one of the three.' She directed a thumb behind her at Alex. 'And this is Dr Alex Madison, our revered psychologist.'

The three smiled at Alex, raising their hands, clearly used to Laurie's complimentary introductions. Josh looked the oldest, with thin grey hair, wire-framed glasses and a bright Hawaiian T-shirt. Terry looked no older than Alex but sported a long ponytail, no doubt a lasting mistake in Laurie's company, and too late for him to fix. Hannah's smile lasted longer than those of the others. She had close-cropped dark hair and was busy tapping away at her laptop. She paused to give Alex a thumbs-up, before returning to her work.

'Bedrooms are through there,' said Laurie. 'I'm bunking up with Hannah, and Josh and Terry are in together. You get a bedroom of your own.'

'Thanks,' said Alex. 'I can bunk down wherever,' trying to think of the last time he might have used the term 'bunk down'. Probably not since private school. Probably not ever.

Laurie gave him a sardonic wink. 'Of course you can, dear.'

They took a few minutes to unpack their luggage before Laurie gathered them at the dining table. Josh poured fresh coffee, which Alex welcomed, scooping in several sugars and lots of milk.

As he raised the mug to his lips, his hand quivered, enough to make him pause. He lowered the cup and watched his forearm twitch, ever so slightly. Tiredness, he thought, simple fatigue. He'd taken his normal dose of Xanax that day, no more, no less. It could be the heat, or the act of dragging his suitcase through the cobbled streets for so long.

Or it could be his body following his mind.

Quivering and fracturing, day by day.

'OK?' Laurie's face was curious.

Alex swapped hands and took a gulp. He gave a reassuring smile. 'Fine,' he said. 'Tired and hot, but fine.'

Laurie held her gaze on him a moment longer before turning to her colleagues. She glanced around at the scattered papers, including a large map of Madrid in the middle of the table, mounted on a wooden board. There were several coloured pins stuck into the map.

'I've told the team why you're here, Alex. I don't have time to give you the full background on our operation, but I'll give you the basics. Try to keep up. What do you know about prostitution?'

'I—'

'Don't answer that. The sex trade, let alone the trafficking elements, is massive business here. Prostitution is legal – decriminalised in 1995, and worth in the region of twenty-five billion dollars a year. There are roughly three hundred thousand women affected by it.'

She let it hang for a second. Alex was forced to admit he had had no idea of the scale of the activity. He thought about Eva, one solitary girl among that huge number, but unique in her particular reason for being there.

'So it's big business,' she continued. 'The players are serious and they have more resources than we do. It's also a fast business – faster than most of the consumer goods businesses you're used to back home. Women are sold and moved across borders within hours and days. They're hard to track and even when they can be will often choose to remain in their new life out of fear. They're controlled and exploited through debt, violence or psychological manipulation. Families are threatened and the threats are often carried out.'

Laurie paused. Alex could see the passion and anger in her face as she described the abhorrent situation. He understood why she was here, why they all were, but at the same time worried they were after different things.

'The group we're observing – their name translates as "The Black Vipers" – is part of a cartel focusing on the international trafficking of women into Spain. This lot set up transport and auction.' Laurie tapped her fingers on the table, her eyes glued to the map.

'And they have Eva?' asked Alex. 'How did Dr Naylor come in contact with such people?'

Laurie glanced up. The concentration in her eyes wavered and she shrugged. 'We don't know how exactly, but she did, and we think more than one girl has come via her through the Vipers. What we've lacked until now is enough proof for a convincing arrest.'

Alex nodded. He gazed at the other three around the table, all with their eyes lowered. They'd heard all this before. Hannah tapped distractedly at her keyboard.

'So what happens next?' he asked.

Laurie sighed. She nudged Josh. 'Wanna show Alex what happens next?'

Josh looked reluctant, but spun his laptop round so Alex could see the screen.

'Most girls go straight to the streets, to legal brothels, clubs, etcetera, but . . .' he said, tapping at his keyboard to open a folder on the desktop, 'some girls are sold to order: individual sales based on a buyer's preference, or a special asset they figure they can run an auction on.'

Alex gulped. He hated the use of the word 'asset' to describe a human being. He guessed it helped these guys to keep an emotional distance. 'What marks a person out as special?'

Josh raised his eyebrows. 'Several things. Children are kidnapped to order, as are girls with particular features, abilities, disabilities . . .' Frowning, he looked over at Laurie, then back at Alex. 'I thought you knew all of this?'

'I do,' said Alex. 'I did, but . . . it's one thing to read about it, another to be part of an operation. I'm sorry.'

Josh's face softened. 'Don't worry,' he said. 'We're all a little snarky at the moment.'

Alex nodded. He sipped at his coffee, composing himself.

'We never know where the girls are being held,' continued Josh. 'They're moved around constantly and the auctions are online – profiles with photo and video. See here.'

Josh opened a document and tilted the screen up.

Alex leaned in. It took him a few minutes to register what he was looking at. His mouth went dry, the anger and horror rising with each moment he stared.

This wasn't concerning a child, but horrific nonetheless. It could have been a dating profile – an introduction followed by measurements and vitals. A playful statement on what the young woman supposedly liked doing, and a collection of photos. The face was clear – heavily made-up, hair styled immaculately – but her naked body had been blurred and greyed out.

'We redact the pictures after they've been filed,' said Josh, scrolling to the end of the document. At the bottom was an obscure Internet address.

'Dark Web?' said Alex.

'Good,' said Josh. 'So you do know something.' He winked. Alex tried to smile, but couldn't, the bile burning the back of his throat. He had a sudden new respect for Laurie and this team of officers, exposed to this repugnant practice every day. Alex had seen his fair share of horrors, but the business of trafficking made his flesh crawl. He wasn't sure he could do this day in, day out. Had he made a mistake in coming here? Was his race to find Eva hopelessly naïve?

'The Dark Web portal is for bids and queries,' said Terry, tugging at his ponytail with one hand, examining his fingernails on the other. 'Impossible to trace – UK and US cyber teams have tried for years, but it changes with each auction.'

Alex continued to sip from his mug, trying to wash down the rising nausea. He had to ask the obvious question.

'And you have one of those' – he indicated the document – 'for Eva Jansen?'

Josh closed the profile and searched for another document. 'No,' he said. 'From what the boss told us, we think she's one of the more obscure orders.'

Alex looked up.

'I'm the boss,' said Laurie, nodding. 'In case you didn't know.'

'Obscure?' asked Alex.

Josh flung around a few more files on his desktop. 'The trafficking groups focus on demand for the sex industry, but on occasion they'll take other orders. They have all the infrastructure and the contacts, so it's easy for them to move anything. Or anyone.'

Alex frowned. 'Like what?'

Josh looked at Laurie before continuing. Laurie nodded again, going back to staring at the map. Alex had never seen her so serious – her usual quick-fire sarcasm subdued.

'Commercial kidnapping,' said Josh, 'for ransom or auction. North Korea has been known to buy talent – scientists, academics, those sorts of people.'

'Russia used to do it,' said Terry. 'Not so much these days.'

'Right,' continued Josh, 'but the most dangerous type of auction is military or intelligence assets.'

'People or weapons?' asked Alex.

'Both, but I'm talking about people. Clandestine operatives who've been caught operating on foreign soil. These agents can be sold . . . it's very rare. Most often they're kept and used to secure the release of other agents. There are regular horse-trading arrangements between most governments for that sort of thing. Intermediaries are only used when things go pear-shaped and the asset can fetch more on the open market.'

Alex swallowed, considering the implications. He caught Laurie's eye. She already knew.

'Eva is being sold as a—' said Alex.

'This need-to-know thing works both ways,' said Laurie. 'The team here are not briefed on Eva's full background, other than that she's a British citizen. That's enough. Josh, continue.'

With barely a pause, Josh resumed his summary.

'The NCA got wind of a new auction,' he said. 'No photo and no name, but yes, the asset is being sold as high value, British.' He paused. 'You think it's this Eva Jansen of yours?'

Alex opened his mouth to speak, unsure of what to confirm or deny. Laurie cut him off before he had a chance to do either.

'Tell us about Naylor,' she said.

Josh shrugged. 'Naylor, as far as we know, always accompanies her assets to the sale. We assume she wants to secure her cut in person.'

'What, and they let her?' said Alex. 'I mean, see them? Talk to them? I assumed they'd be rather more discreet about that kind of thing.'

'Why?' said Josh. 'She can't hurt them, and they don't want to hurt her – she's a source of young assets, often with no family or friends to come looking. Unless she screws up, there's no reason not to deal face to face with her. It's just business to them.'

Alex took a breath. Just business. Except Eva wasn't a normal asset, and even the team didn't know it.

'So . . .' He took another sip of coffee, which was now luke-warm. The panic rose in waves and circled, knowing what was at stake. 'So what's the plan?' he said. 'How do we get Eva back?'

The team looked at Hannah, who finished whatever she was typing before leaning back in her chair. She rolled her head from side to side, before extending her arms out for a final stretch.

'We register our interest, or rather, we already have. We've done it under the guise of a South African commercial military com-pany. It exists – it's a British shell company. Our bid is as a broker reselling military assets to the highest bidder. We check out – our colleagues in SA detected a background trace on our fake business activities. We believe our cover is intact.' She chewed her lower lip.

'And?'

'And . . . we've been invited to a viewing of the asset,' she said, not looking so happy about it. 'Location to follow.'

Terry and Josh both screwed their faces up. 'A viewing?' said Terry. 'That's irregular.'

Alex glanced at Laurie. He knew why. How better to sell Eva than to demonstrate what she could do? Nobody would believe it otherwise. The traffickers had obviously confirmed it or they wouldn't be arranging the meeting. That meant it was real. Eva was real, and alive.

'Let me go,' he blurted out. Laurie shook her head.

'Alex—'

'No, listen. I'm the only person who understands her condition.'

It was a stretch, given how little he knew about Eva, all of it second-hand, but it was still the truth. 'I can test Eva, if that's what this viewing is about, and verify not just who she is but precisely what she's capable of.'

'Alex,' repeated Laurie, 'no way. You're not trained for undercover police work. You're not trained for police work, full stop. The plan will be to secure Eva and catch Naylor at the handover – that's all the hard evidence we need. I'll value your contributions once we have Eva in safekeeping, but until then you stay in the apartment.'

'You don't understand,' said Alex, aware that his voice had grown louder, the urgency seeping through. 'This girl is damaged. She's had a lifetime of institutions and mental anguish. If she can do what I think she can . . .' Alex glanced at the others seated around the table, and seeing the warning in Laurie's eyes, chose his next words carefully. 'Then she'll know you're police officers as soon as you meet her. She won't speak to you and won't comply. She may even blow your cover.'

Josh and Terry shuffled on their seats. Alex suspected that a police officer caught by the traffickers would not have a pleasant time of it, and with no official British support, the outcome could be catastrophic.

'Trust me. Inmates of secure mental health facilities distrust authority figures, and the police are about as bad as it gets – it's institutionalised fear. You don't want to put a police officer in front of Eva if you want to get her back. Nor if you want to get Naylor.'

Laurie looked unconvinced. 'But psychologists are trusted friends?'

'Sometimes. We're often the only friend these people have. We talk, we listen, we try to establish trust.'

Laurie stared through him. She was clearly thinking hard, no doubt weighing up all the risks, even if she agreed in principle.

'If she trusts me,' said Alex, 'I can try to swing it our way and you can be ready to pounce on Naylor. I presume we have funds?'

Terry cleared his throat. 'Kind of. Yes. They'll never receive it, but we play a good hand.'

'Then let me go. Let me build the initial relationship. If she trusts me, not only will it help get her back, but I can smooth the way to finding out more about the traffickers from her. That's what we all want, isn't it?'

Again, Laurie's eyes narrowed. She knew Alex's motivations ran further than capturing Dr Naylor and the trafficking ring. Alex was in it for Eva and whoever had created her. Laurie knew he didn't care about much else in this case.

She pushed herself away from the table and walked over to the window. Alex watched her go, feeling the tension, waiting for the decision that would fundamentally alter the course of the next few days. He was *this* close to Eva.

'Hannah,' Laurie said over her shoulder, 'do we have passports for all of us?'

Hannah replied without looking up, 'We're all South African. Even the doc.'

Laurie continued to face the other way, staring out at the streets and the surrounding blocks of apartments that obscured the view of the city.

'Let's break for twenty,' she said. 'I'll think about it.'

CHAPTER TWENTY-SIX

The blindfold stayed on. Eva had heard little and felt nothing, her captors practised and ruthless. If only she could look at them, *feel* them. The thousand clues people never realised advertised their emotions, their intent, and their pointless, selfish thoughts about their own irrelevant existence. Without her sight, she was vulnerable.

Pushed into a chair, her hands were fastened behind her back. A door slammed, close enough to make her jump.

Silence. The passing of time slowed. Occasional fragments of speech seeped into the room, but meant nothing. Emily hovered in conscious oblivion, feeling the tendrils of anger and panic tangle.

She sensed the door open before she heard it: a change in pressure and temperature.

An intake of breath, whistling, constricting through a beaked nose.

Naylor.

'How are you feeling, Eva?'

Naylor's voice was firm, but she kept her distance across the room. Eva turned her head to make out the direction. Naylor remained by the door.

Eva chose not to answer. What could she say? She knew why she was here and what might happen. Naylor didn't care how she was.

'I apologise for the rough journey,' said Naylor. Her voice didn't sound apologetic. 'But here we are, and you're going to do as you're told.'

'Fuck you,' said Eva. A dozen further expletives readied themselves, but she bit them off. Her breathing grew shallow. She could feel her heart thudding in anger.

'You have two options, Eva,' said Naylor, 'and you won't like either, but at least one gives you a chance to do something you're good at. You know I've been watching you since you arrived under my care. All of our sessions together, all of your fights with the other girls, your conversations with the nurses. I've watched everything, Eva, and I know.'

Eva clenched her jaw tighter. Hearing it from Naylor's mouth was a punch in the gut. *Stupid*, Eva. *Stupid*.

'Once upon a time I might have kept you for myself, but this was the better option. For you. For both of us.'

Eva heard Naylor move. The doctor walked, creeping to the left, maintaining her distance, pacing the room. Eva moved her head as far as she could until Naylor was behind her.

'You've shown *me* what you can do.' Naylor's voice hissed over her shoulders. 'Now it's time to perform. Your talent is valuable, Eva, and if you play your cards right over the next couple of days, you might just have a good life. Better than most of the useless girls who come my way. Those girls are beyond help, Eva, suitable for one thing only. But not you – you're special.'

The words grated in Eva's ears. The honesty with which Naylor described her deeds was sickening, although it came as no surprise. Eva had met enough psychopaths in her life in institutions to know the signs.

'People want to use your talent, Eva. People with money. People with influence. And . . . I think you should do what they ask.'

'Fuck you.' It was all Eva could do not to scream. 'Fuck you, fuck you, fuck you.'

Naylor let out a short laugh, a snort. It snapped off quickly. Eva felt breath on her left ear.

'I know how you hate the blindfold, Eva,' Naylor whispered. 'I know how you hate to be deprived of your sight, of sounds, of *proximity* to others. I know why this is, probably better than you do. You need it and you crave it, no matter how unbearable the voices become.'

Eva tensed. Her secrets. Her dreams. *Her confinement.*

'You need your senses, Eva,' Naylor continued. 'Your talent relies on them entirely, and so does your fragile sanity, what's left of it. Shutting your senses off would be a cruel way to lose your mind, now wouldn't it?'

Naylor paused, her nose squeaking with each breath. 'Which brings me to your other option. What did you think of the box you were brought here in? Did you like it?'

The very mention of it made Eva's throat close up, the claustrophobia clamping her chest in panic.

'I can keep you in a box indefinitely, Eva. Every day and every night, locked up in a small, dark box. No room to even turn around. I think battery chickens are kept in similar conditions, but at least they can see each other. We'll feed you and keep you alive, if your heart can take it, but you'll never see anything, ever again. That's an option for you.'

Eva's breathing shortened into shallow gasps. She forced her diaphragm down, drawing in air, her chest screaming in protest. Her concentration wavered, visions of her past lurching to the fore.

Cutting off her senses, isolating her in the darkness.

The memories returned.

Get in the tank, Eva.

Eva clutched her arms against her small chest. The voice came over the speakers. The orderlies waited by the door. She was older now by a whole year. She was supposed to do as she was told – supposed to know the routine. They shouldn't have to keep forcing her into the tank – restraining and holding her while she screamed and begged.

But for Eva, the treatment hadn't become easier with practice – quite the opposite. It angered the doctors. They argued about the length of time she was kept in isolation; some wanted longer. *Distillation*, they called it, refining the pathways – cleaning out the noise.

Distillation.

Darkness.

All alone with nothing except her thoughts.

And her screams.

Naylor's voice snapped Eva out of her dream.

'Although, I guess there is a third option,' she said, another snort coming from her nose. 'One word to the people outside this room and I can have your eyes taken out. It would make for a different type of sale, a more traditional one, if a little niche. Someone will buy a pretty young girl like you with no eyes. You wouldn't believe the sort of requests they get here. It wouldn't even be the strangest.'

Eva's head spun. Nausea joined the panic as the threats took hold. She'd rather die. Anyone would rather die, wouldn't they? But Naylor wouldn't do it. Couldn't.

'So . . .' Naylor paced around to the front. 'Which is it to be, Eva? Option one, two, or three?'

Eva thought she was going to vomit. The bile rose into her throat, burning at the back of her mouth. Time. She needed time.

She thought back to the man on the boat. These people were serious. Naylor's threats weren't empty.

Eva didn't need to read her to know this, and her possible fate if she made a mistake.

'One,' she whispered, trying hard to swallow.

There was a pause. A sniff, the nostrils squeaking in victory.

'Good choice,' said Naylor, her voice suddenly soft and warm. 'Good choice, Eva.'

CHAPTER TWENTY-SEVEN

Natalia opened the photo on her phone. It had been taken from a distance, across the road from the terminal at Madrid-Barajas airport. Alex Madison looked just the same, although the stress lines and his tiredness were clear. *That's what you get for delving into my world*, she thought. The years would not be kind, if you got to survive them.

She examined the woman he was travelling with. Without question a police officer – she carried herself too formally, was too rigid in her body language.

Natalia frowned. The doubt lingered and Alex's photo brought it back with a vengeance.

She needed focus. She opened her laptop to review the latest information, received that morning. Background on the girl's condition, which should have been available earlier. Kept from her until necessary, she suspected, its contents reviewed and assessed for risk. But Natalia was trusted. She could handle the truth.

There were far worse places than Comăneşti.

Her handler's comment, hiding so much in so few words. Of the multitude of operations over the decades, some had failed before they produced anything, some had been caught by the law. Some continued to this day.

Natalia scrolled through the document, looking for warnings, looking for handling advice. Eva Jansen was not the first of her type, but she was rare – a child of a faction based in the Netherlands. The group had closed suddenly, some twelve years ago, scattering its products into the wind, desperate to avoid detection. Most of the products had been terminated, but some had found their way to the authorities and then been lost.

Until now.

Natalia totted up the years. Eva would be seventeen or eighteen years old. The age was significant in most cultures, often signifying the end of innocence, the beginning of life's struggles. Natalia knew Eva would have lost her innocence many years beforehand – if she had ever had it. If Eva's journey had been anything like Natalia's own, innocence was something to be exploited. It was a weakness, quickly crushed out of you.

Natalia's hell had been Comănești in Romania. Eva's was Westpoort in the Netherlands, where her captors had made what were described as *significant breakthrough contributions* before being disbanded.

'Breakthrough' was apt, she thought. How many children had been broken in the process? How many mind and bodies devastated in pursuit of that elusive talent? Those overarching objectives, known only to the people who commissioned such things. The sponsors, distant and elusive. God-like in their ambition. Devastating in their execution.

Natalia took a breath, closing her eyes, trying not to see the visions floating into her consciousness – the dark corridors of the orphanage and her days at Comănești. She remembered the treatment rooms, dark and foul-smelling with the single chair in the middle, her reclining in it, eyes staring at the ceiling. Two white-coated doctors standing over her, stabbing her arm with a blunt needle – the burn of the fluid entering her bloodstream and the chaotic thoughts that followed soon after.

She opened her eyes and controlled her thudding heart, drawing deep breaths, forcing the thoughts back into the box in the dustiest corner of her mind. Never forgotten, but somehow contained.

The primary drug for the Westpoort children had been a super-concentrated version of MDMA, which ramped up production of serotonin, dopamine and noradrenaline. Natalia was intimately familiar with these neurotransmitters and their effect. The children would be stimulated to the point of hallucination, with increased levels of energy, empathy and pleasure. Toxic reactions were noted at twenty per cent due to the dose and frequency. These reactions had a hundred per cent fatality rate. Those children who tolerated the inordinately high dose of MDMA were given a shot of a second compound drug, a blend of psychoactive substances and opiates. The compound was tagged with a sequence of numbers and letters.

Was it the same or different to what Natalia had been filled with? She had never been told the exact details of her own experimentation. It was not considered appropriate or beneficial to her reintegration with Nova.

Details of the Westpoort conditioning therapy followed in the report. Subjects were placed in water-filled isolation tanks for hours, sometimes days, at a time. The purpose was to stimulate hyper-awareness, with all senses removed. Brain activity was monitored, scanning for new neuron pathways activated in the brain's amygdala. Subjects displaying positive results were subsequently honed using more traditional training methods.

This had continued for months. Many subjects had died. Some had survived.

And thus the product was created.

So what was Eva? Natalia shivered at the possible capabilities of such an experiment. Eva had received much of the same training as Natalia, but the drugs were more advanced, the isolation treatment more refined.

She scrolled on, but there was little more in the file. Just one warning note, tucked away in the observations – a side effect witnessed in ninety per cent of the children: *Extreme and explosive violence disorder presenting intermittently. Immediate sedation with promethazine hydrochloride is authorised. Staff are to take adequate precautions – possible permanent damage (frontal lobe function) to those in the immediate vicinity. Further research pending.*

Natalia frowned, scrolling back to the top. She considered the girl in the photo, cast out before her teens, probably with no idea of the extent of her abilities. Her treatment had been cut short and she had bounced around the UK's mental health institutions until falling under the care of one particularly corrupt psychiatrist. They had Dr Naylor to thank for finding Eva.

Natalia very much wanted to thank her in person. Perhaps with a bullet to the head.

Perhaps with something worse.

A knock at the door broke into her thoughts. She frowned. She hadn't given explicit instructions not to be bothered, but had assumed the hotel staff would leave her alone. She approached cautiously, checking the peephole. A man stood outside, dressed in the hotel uniform. Natalia recognised the man from reception.

She pulled her robe together and fastened it at the waist before opening the door.

'*Holà*,' she said, presenting her warmest smile. She checked his name badge. '*Eduardo.*'

'*Holà*,' said the man. 'I'm sorry, madam, for the intrusion.' He looked past Natalia into the room, and then back to her. Natalia raised her eyebrows.

'We were concerned. Nobody has seen you since you checked in, only your room service trays left outside. We were worried you had been taken ill. The manager asked me to check you are OK.'

Natalia sighed. So annoyingly attentive. In her country you could die in a cheap hotel and be eaten by rats before anybody thought to check – as long as you'd paid in advance.

Spain was different. They were used to tourists and treated them like actual human beings. How annoying. Raising suspicion of any kind was careless. She was better than this. She should have made at least one daily appearance downstairs, in the restaurant or out in the lobby with the concierge.

'Easily fixed,' she said.

'Pardon, madam?'

'Look at me, Eduardo.' Natalia met the man's gaze. She muttered a few words, whispering across the threshold. She touched his arm, caressing it as she spoke.

His face relaxed at her touch, his pupils dilating. He leaned in a fraction, his lips parting, his breath panting. His mind was open, inquisitive, and Natalia took swift control. He went under with barely a blink.

Natalia took a moment. If she so wished, she could send this man flying off the edge of her balcony, or running through the streets naked. She could send him into a trance so deep he would never awake, warping his mind until it fractured into a million memories, never to be stitched together again. She could leave him in a walking coma for the rest of his days, such was the power she wielded – the ability she had honed since those days at Comăneşti. They had given her this power, but it was her own gift to use it.

She teased and flexed her thoughts. None of that would be necessary. A harmless soul, just in need of a little direction. A correcting of facts, as it were.

'I have been out of my room,' she said, gazing deep into his eyes. 'Every day, in fact, strolling around the city, seeing the sights. I asked you for directions to the Prado yesterday. You remember. You gave me directions and wished me a wonderful day. Your eyes lingered a little too long on my *culo* as I walked away, but we'll put that down to the heat.'

She gave him another gentle nudge, just enough to help him along. She watched his mind accept the instructions, the thoughts slotting into place, the logic flowing and the emotion following.

She waited. It only took a few moments.

His face broke into a frown. Confusion. He stepped back, embarrassed, his cheeks flushing.

'F-Forgive me,' he said, his eyes darting left and right. 'Of course, I remember. I've seen you every day walking through the lobby. I wasn't staring at your . . . I, um.'

'Forget it,' said Natalia, with a playful laugh, her hand still resting on his forearm. 'Fetch me a Mojito and a lunch menu, and we'll forget you rudely interrupted me when I was trying to rest.'

She gave him one last squeeze, whispering a final goodbye, before relinquishing control. She spun on the balls of her feet and turned back into her room.

'Right away, madam,' she heard Eduardo utter as he closed the door.

Natalia paused at the balcony. She drew a deep breath, pulling more of the warm air into her body. Did she feel healthier here, or was it just her imagination? Her cough persisted, but it was less severe, barely waking her in the night, only troubling her in the morning now, as her lungs cleared themselves from slumber.

Closing her eyes, she dared to dream of what it must be like to walk the streets of a city like Madrid, free from her burden. Free from her history. She allowed herself these fantasies once in a while, when the tension was rising and the stress began to bite.

She would wear a long summer dress and flat sandals. Not because it was part of a persona or somebody had told her to, but because she wanted it. She'd feel the soft fabric against her skin and enjoy the bursts of sunshine as she weaved in and out of the side streets, seeking out nothing but the pleasure of an unexplored city – the art and the architecture, the shops and the culture. She'd sit and watch the people – innocent men, women and children as they lived their carefree existence, dancing through their lives, never knowing what lurked in the shadows. Never having to.

She breathed several times, the picture perfect in her mind.

The fantasy was cut short as Natalia's pocket vibrated. She pulled out her phone. A message. One word: *Tomorrow*.

She turned her back on the sunlight and her visions of the city. It would keep until next time.

Less than twenty-four hours. At least the waiting was over.

Another knock at the door delivered her drink and today's lunch menu from a very apologetic Eduardo. She thanked him without a smile this time. Her mind was elsewhere and his had been tampered with enough.

She closed the door and stared at her suitcase, picking out her outfit and approach. There was no foolproof plan. She had virtually unlimited funds at her disposal, but there was no guarantee of success. With this type of auction, there were too many variables to predict how it would fall.

She considered forcing it. Natalia could use her own talent to get Eva out without bloodshed, but the repercussions were considered too high. They could be exposed and it would close the door on future business with this particular trafficking group. She'd been advised by her handler, Tomas, to pursue the old-fashioned route.

Money would be the start – she'd get her instructions tomorrow, meet the asset and place her bid – but Natalia wouldn't rely just on that. She had another persuasive element up her sleeve, one which only she could offer. It relied on Eva being who they claimed she was, with the ability to match. It relied on Natalia opening her mind just enough to give Eva something she would want. Something to tip the scales in her favour without arousing suspicion.

Eva's history. Her story of origin.

Natalia was offering more than money, although the auctioneers wouldn't know this.

She was offering answers.

CHAPTER TWENTY-EIGHT

Eva had her sight back, not that there was much to see. The room was windowless, illuminated by a single dazzling bulb. The walls were painted pale blue. Two chairs faced a leather sofa.

She took a seat on the edge of the sofa, hearing it creak under her weight, wondering how many girls had sat on it, draped themselves across it, curled up and wept on it.

Eva waited. Then she waited some more. Another hour or so passed before the door opened, and it began.

A first man appeared in dark glasses, thin and impeccably dressed. A dark grey suit, tie and gold tiepin. His black hair was slicked back and his face covered with a thick beard.

A second man stepped in after him. Large-framed, also wearing dark glasses and a suit, this one's gaze flicking around the room, sizing it up, judging it. The first man glanced back and the second man nodded his approval. They took the seats facing Eva.

A flood of thoughts hit Eva from both, but mainly the first, smaller man. He was fascinated by Eva, excited. He cast his eyes over her face and body, looking for damage, for appearance, simple curiosity. He took off his glasses, focused on her face, and his deep brown eyes gave away the rest.

He wondered if she could do it, his head full of curiosity. *Can you?* The threads of thought were easy to grasp; words formed and faded in his head.

The man rubbed his beard, pulling the hair. He stared deep into her eyes. Eva flinched at first, but met his stare, sucking in a sharp breath. She saw exactly what he wanted her to.

She pulled at the threads, gently at first. She saw corridors and metal doors, bars on the windows, blood on the floor. Underground, in near-darkness, she heard screams, the pleas of men and woman, begging for their lives. A room, not unlike this one: a naked man strung up by his hands, a chain hanging from the ceiling. Blood poured from the man's face, his breath hissing weakly. Another man stood over him with a thick baton, shouting in a language Eva didn't understand. He rained blows down on the hanging figure, shouting the same thing over and over. It was a question – he was demanding an answer.

The thoughts changed; the vision flickered. The same room – a car battery on a table, thick wires attached, crocodile clips at the end. The clips were attached to the hanging man's body – one to his groin, one to his right ear.

The sounds intensified. Shouting and pleading, the screams emanated from this man's mind and echoed through hers.

Eva couldn't hold his gaze any longer. She turned away, releasing the threads, blinking at the gruesome thoughts until they faded. Drawing several deep breaths, she turned back, saw the corners of the man's mouth turn into a smile.

Is it true?

'Did you see it?' he whispered.

Eva clamped her lips together. She tried to control her shaking hands.

'Tell me what you saw,' he said. 'Tell me.'

Eva tried not to move, but found herself shaking her head. The torture of a man. The person in front of her seeing it, knowing it. This man was a criminal, a beast. He tortured these people. Better or worse than Naylor and the people who had brought her here? Eva didn't know, but the calm opening of his thoughts – his intentions – was sickening. What did he want with Eva?

She could guess. She could see. With Eva they wouldn't need to use such force.

With Eva the questions would get answered.

A human lie detector.

She shook her head.

'I didn't see anything.' Her defiance sounded weak. She was lying and the man's widening smile indicated that he suspected it. More thoughts of excitement tumbled out, but this time they were greedy, sinister and manipulative. He was thinking of how to secure her, to take her with him. What would it take? What price for this mind?

He paused, continuing to stare. A crack. He wasn't yet convinced.

Throw him off, Eva. It won't take much.

'I saw a beach,' said Eva, finding her voice, trying to stabilise it. 'You were on a beach, with your family. Playing in the sand.'

The man's smile wavered, his eyes narrowed.

'I saw an office,' she continued. 'Corridors, desks and chairs. Sunlight through the windows. People arguing and laughing. Computers and numbers.'

Eva swallowed, getting a grip, seeing the doubt forming in front of her.

'You sit in a leather chair, running a business from your office. You're wealthy, but struggling. You wish you were still on the beach.'

183

She had him, but barely. Her terror scarcely contained, Eva watched his initial excitement fade, to be replaced with confusion and irritation. Conned. Duped.

What is this?

Give up, she wanted to say.

'You're thinking of the beach,' said Eva, grasping the leather of the sofa, her hands clenching into fists, desperate to convince him. She stared him in the eyes, watching the strands of his thoughts twist in confusion. She was too fatigued to pull any harder and her anger had been subdued by fear, but she was convincing him nonetheless.

'You're thinking about me,' she said, forcing a smile. 'About getting me home. Taking me to bed. What you'll do to—'

'Stop!' the man shouted. His face transformed; anger poured from it. He stood and the second man stood with him, turning to hammer at the door.

Eva heard the initial shouts as the door opened, but they were muffled as the thick door then closed and was locked.

She watched the door for several seconds before unclenching her fists, letting out a shaking breath, sinking into the sofa. The shock took her in waves. So far out of her comfort zone, Eva wrestled with what she'd done. Shouldn't she have told him the truth? Gone with him? Avoided the box Naylor had promised her?

But she saw his mind, and her likely future. The reality would be even worse. She still had time, didn't she? Time to figure it out. Time to manipulate and escape.

The creak of the door made her jump. Naylor entered, holding the door wide enough for two others, rough-looking men in combat trousers and tight black T-shirts.

Stupid little bitch. Naylor was furious, edged with panic. Eva saw the uncertainty flood from the doctor. She was losing control.

One of the men approached. He had a black hood in his hand. The other stood to one side, ready. No place to run. No time to read anything except the force with which they'd take her, and the punishment that was due.

'I warned you,' said Naylor, as the hood was forced over her head, tied roughly around her neck. Her legs were pinned and tied, arms behind her back. She didn't even have the energy to kick out.

'I warned you, Eva.'

CHAPTER
TWENTY-NINE

Alex paced the small living area, his concentration shot from all the nerves, trying not to drink too much of the insanely strong coffee Josh kept brewing. His panic symptoms thus far had been suppressed by distraction more than anything else, the Xanax holding a background level of calm. It wasn't enough. He'd seen it in his patients enough times – simmering, ready to blow.

A *breakthrough* was what some therapists called it, rather than a breakdown. Alex wasn't prepared to allow either. He needed to keep his shit together long enough to finish this. He held his left wrist with his right hand, shielding the trembling from view.

'I'm already regretting this,' said Laurie, eyeing him from the kitchen. She'd changed into something more fitting for a summer break in Madrid, her dark clothes ditched in favour of a white linen suit. Her relentless sarcasm was still welcome, but her constant examination of Alex only served to increase his worry.

'I'll be fine,' he said, rehearsing his story in his head. 'We're based out of Johannesburg, right? Not Cape Town?'

'It doesn't matter,' said Laurie, huffing for the umpteenth time at him. 'You won't be asked unless you act or do something stupid, and then it'll all be over. They've already vetted us and they'll expect a professional business transaction. You turn up, identify yourself, check the asset and you leave. We'll place the bid online.'

'Check the asset?'

'Check the asset, Alex.' Laurie glared at him. The others were still hunched around the dining table and Laurie hadn't yet shared any of the more unique details about Eva. 'I'm sure you'll think of a way.'

'If we're bidding online, why do we even need to attend the auction? Can't we just outbid everyone else?' Despite his insistence on being the one to meet Eva, and Laurie agreeing to it, he could suddenly see all sorts of holes in his brave plan. Like being captured and killed, for instance. Traffickers were not his usual fare.

'That's not how these specialist transactions work.' Josh piped up from the table. 'Straightforward girls can be online only, but this is the commercial military business. It's old-fashioned at heart. People do business with people. They'll want to see the whites of your eyes – put a face to a name. If we don't present ourselves to view the asset, we'll be an instant red flag. We'll be removed from the auction and it'll disappear. We'll lose the asset and the traffickers until they resurface.'

Alex nodded his understanding. So this was it. He'd got what he wanted, and he must deal with it, despite his throat wanting to leap out of his mouth in protest.

'Noon?' he said to Laurie.

'Noon,' she confirmed. 'You'll make your own way, as we discussed. No wire, no surveillance. You'll take this burner phone' – she pointed at an iPhone on the kitchen worktop – 'which has my number and an array of random others. Call me when you're done. We'll be close by.'

Laurie picked up the iPhone and spun it around in her hands. 'Alex, if my superiors—'

'I know,' he said. 'They'd insist you go. But I meant what I said – I'm the best chance of getting Eva on side. You know it, or you wouldn't even consider letting me do this.'

Laurie huffed. She threw him the phone and he caught it awkwardly in his left hand.

'You've got find-my-phone switched on?' he joked.

Laurie looked as if she was in pain. 'Alex, dear, if they decide to move you somewhere against your will, your phone will be the first thing that gets killed.'

Alex wished he hadn't said anything. Apart from a brief snort from Josh, a sombre silence now descended on the group.

Two hours until the operation turned hot.

CHAPTER THIRTY

Eva woke lying on her back, unable to twist around. The panic surged as she wrenched her arms, trying to free them. The rope held fast and a crushing weight descended on her. Her legs were free and she kicked out, finding the limits of whatever container they'd forced her into. Smaller than she'd thought – she couldn't even bend her legs at right angles, her knees hitting the top of whatever coffin they'd placed her in this time, even when she twisted at the hips.

Nausea flooded her body, her face flushing.

'Shit, shit, shit,' she moaned, raising her head until her forehead touched a hard, rough surface.

'Please,' she said. 'Please!'

She screamed, writhing as the panic attack took hold. The container grew smaller, her body thumped against the walls, the air turning thick and useless.

Naylor had carried out her threat. Eva could see nothing, hear nothing.

Punishment.

Her head spun. Vomit surged into her throat before seeping back down, burning on its way. She swallowed and dragged another breath into her lungs.

Her mind floated and her body detached. Time became meaningless, reality and memory overlapping, competing for conscious thought. She saw flashes in front of her eyes, bright blues and greens. She blinked rapidly, but it made no difference. Her eyes couldn't detect anything real. Her ears registered only the thuds of her body against the walls and her laboured breathing.

Suffocating. Hyperventilating. Her lungs sucked at nothing and she moaned as her body shook in spasm.

Is this the end? a small voice cried above the white noise in her head. Would they keep her like this, in this? How long until she went insane? An hour? A day?

Would going with that man have been so bad? Whatever he wanted, whatever he was going to use her for, would be better than this. Any existence would be better than this.

She kicked, thumping the soles of her feet into the solid wall until she was exhausted. She paused. A loud bang answered her, resonating through the floor and into her bones.

A creaking sound and a blinding light.

The lid was lifted off.

Eva gulped, sucking in the rush of fresher air. She saw roof rafters and corrugated iron, with a skylight, the sun shining. A figure silhouetted against the light. Eva squinted as Naylor's face came into focus. It leered down at her.

'Enough?' said Naylor.

Eva tried and failed to get a grasp on the doctor. Her eyes watered and her body shook. She averted her eyes, lifting her head to examine the wooden coffin she was lying in.

'Another hour?' said Naylor. She nodded across to somebody out of sight. The lid came back into view, sliding over, already cutting off the light.

'No!' screamed Eva. She stared at Naylor, pleading. 'No. Please.'

Naylor raised her hand. The lid stopped.

'I'll do it,' said Eva. 'I'll do it.'

CHAPTER THIRTY-ONE

The same room. A different day. Eva assumed she'd been sedated overnight, allowing her to wake in her coffin. Worse than any nightmare. A waking terror. Naylor knew it wouldn't take long. The bitch knew it. And Eva could do nothing but beg.

The door creaked open.

Eva sat, as before, on the edge of the sofa. Her clothes had been replaced with more of the same. Her hair had been brushed. She looked presentable for the next bidder. She tried to keep her expression neutral as her heart rate spiked.

The woman who entered was a stark contrast to the men who'd come before. Tall and dark, with stunning features, she paused inside the room. Dressed in a black trouser suit, the woman cast her eyes around for a few moments before settling on Eva.

Their eyes met, and Eva felt a strange sensation – a shiver, followed by a tingling down her spine. Odd, yet not unpleasant, Eva felt warmth – *comfort* almost. She relaxed, her fists unclenched, her thighs sank into the soft sofa as she leaned back. She let out a long breath. Her fear seemed to evaporate with it.

'You must be Eva,' said the woman, tilting her head, keeping her lips parted. She wore a dark pink lipstick. It glistened in the light.

Eva was tongue-tied. She nodded, aware that the sensation was growing. Her whole body felt numb, but pleasantly so.

'I'm not going to threaten you,' said the woman. She paused, concentrating. 'But I need to confirm you are what we think you are.'

Eva found her voice, but kept her lips sealed while she probed for a way in. The woman was relaxed, her face calm and her body open. She took a seat, crossing her legs.

Eva searched. She watched the woman's chest rise and fall, and her hands fidget on her lap. She watched the muscles in her jaw and her neck move this way and that, clenching and relaxing. She stared into the woman's wide eyes, waiting for the inevitable flood of inner dialogue, of raw emotion and intent.

She waited for the threads to emerge.

The realisation took several moments to hit Eva. It rose up like an ocean swell, sweeping away the feeling of comfort and leaving a shiver of fear in its wake.

Eva waited, and nothing arrived.

No thoughts, no emotions. No fragments of intent, and no whispers of memory. Nothing.

The woman's mind was blank. Wholly. Completely.

Eva could see nothing, read nothing. The woman's mind wasn't empty, but it was hidden, closed. The very fibres of her mind were wound tight and forbidden.

And she knew it.

The woman's lips curled into a smile. Her eyes shone more brightly, dancing in front of Eva, teasing her. She leaned in, towards Eva.

My name is Natalia.

The woman offered this one solitary thought, then she closed her mind. Nothing to grasp, nothing to follow. Silence in its wake. The woman's smile didn't waver, but nor was it real. Eva had seen enough fake smiles in her life to know the difference.

Eva shuffled against the back of the sofa, unease creeping over her body like a swarm of ants. The shivers increased. Who was this woman? What did it mean? Had they drugged Eva? Stifled her ability? Disabled her? No, that's not what this was. This woman was in control, and Eva was being played with.

'What's my name?' asked the woman.

To answer would be to play the game. To refuse would be to invoke Naylor's wrath. Another night in the coffin. Another hour. Another minute. None would be bearable. Eva knew she had no choice.

Whatever smiling monster this woman was, she had to be better than the alternative.

'Natalia,' whispered Eva.

The woman's expression softened. She leaned back again in her chair, letting out a long sigh. She clasped her hands together, entwining her fingers, bit her lower lip. Again, the gesture was false, meant to indicate nervousness, meant to endear her to Eva. And yet, Eva sensed this woman was not altogether sinister. An array of strange signals emanated from her body, but without access to her mind, Eva could make no sense of them. *This is what normal people have to deal with*, Eva thought. It fucking sucked.

'Good,' said Natalia. 'Thank you, Eva.'

Don't thank me, Eva thought. *You're buying a young girl at auction, so you're still mostly a bitch. A bitch with talent, though.* This woman could hide her thoughts from Eva – the first person ever to do so, the shock of which was sinking in.

'What do you want?' said Eva. If this was the extent of her trial, then so be it. But this was a sale, wasn't it? She was supposed to fetch a good price, and that meant competition.

Natalia's face dropped, almost imperceptibly, but Eva caught it. The smile was pinned even more firmly.

'I want you,' said Natalia.

'The last person in here wanted me to help him torture people,' said Eva. 'At least, that's what I think he wanted. He was sickening, violent, open.'

Eva noticed Natalia's face waver again. She wasn't perhaps as good at this as she thought she was.

'And I am closed,' Natalia responded. The smile dropped away. 'As I'm sure you've noticed.'

Eva nodded, then shook her head. 'How? I—'

Natalia put a finger to her lips.

Not for now. Time is precious, and I want to secure this – Natalia looked around the room, pulling a face of disgust – *whatever this is. I want you, Eva, and I want you to come with me, and nobody else. You must refuse to perform for the other bidders.*

Eva shrunk under Natalia's gaze, which had lost any sense of friendliness, false or otherwise. Her thoughts were so clear, voiced in perfect harmony. Eva had never read anyone in this way before. It was as if Natalia was projecting directly into Eva. There was barely any movement from Natalia, and yet the clarity was exquisite.

'But I—'

And I will give you something in return.

Eva bit back her shock and initial reaction. This is what it came down to. What could this woman offer her except further incarceration? She wasn't going to buy Eva and then set her free, was she? Eva was a slave, being purchased for a reason. The woman was certainly intriguing, but Eva wasn't picking a new best friend. Why should she help her?

In answer, Natalia leaned in again. Eva wanted to resist, but became lost in the woman's eyes. The warmth flowed over her once again, her skin tingling in response.

Finally, Natalia's thoughts came tumbling out.

And Eva gasped as she read them.

CHAPTER THIRTY-TWO

Natalia had given the men a slight nudge on the way out, nothing that would be remembered as anything out of the ordinary, but enough to keep her in their minds. Careful not to force the auction, but a small jolt in the right direction. She was confident Eva would do the rest.

She needed the walk back to the hotel, so shunned the offer of a driver and strode through the seedy district into the city centre with a mind full of conflict and a face full of angst.

The lies came so easily to Natalia. So many years of practice, weaving fiction with reality until it was impossible to unpick. It wasn't all false, but the picture she'd painted for Eva was far from the truth. She'd thought about the experiments in Westpoort and the treatment of the young assets. She'd thought about the toddlers torn from their parents.

She'd let the information flow, careful and controlled, watching the reaction from the young girl as she absorbed the shocking, brutal truth about her own history.

Natalia had left, promising a different future for Eva if she cooperated. A life of answers and freedom, of sun and choice. A life where she would be nurtured and developed.

Natalia had promised Eva everything she'd been assured of herself when she'd been brought in from the cold all those years ago. They'd promised her a different life from her current one – one of homelessness and starvation, the life of a fugitive. They'd offered hope and comradeship.

At the time she'd been wandering the frozen landscapes with her only friend in the world, a boy called Freak who was true to his name. They had lived in hiding, always hunted, always on the run from Comăneşti: the place, the name and the legacy. As teenagers, she and Freak had struggled through the winters, practising their skills and most often failing. She remembered watching the snow fall, looking enviously at the warm lights of the houses in the towns and cities, dreaming of being the other side of the windows, looking out.

But her skills had been incomplete and fragile back then, much as Eva's were now. She'd been receptive to the men when they came to her. They'd understood what she was suffering in a way nobody else could. They showed her the other side. They said her dreams didn't need to remain dreams any more. She could have a different existence.

A different life.

Different was no lie. But the reality for assets like Eva was ambiguous. Things might get worse before they got better if Natalia's own experience was anything to go by. Life in a facility on the freezing slopes of a Siberian mountain was *different*, but not exactly desirable for a teenage girl with a deadly psychological condition and a head full of questions.

The doubt lingered.

As the hotel came into view, Natalia pulled out her phone and texted a short message. It was done. The asset had been confirmed as viable, and the bid had been placed.

Now, they waited.

CHAPTER THIRTY-THREE

The journey across the south of the city was short and quick. Deep in the Carabanchel district, the taxi weaved through the narrow streets. As instructed, Alex ditched the taxi several blocks from his destination and walked the rest of the way. The sweat beaded on his forehead and soaked his collar. His left hand was still trembling. He paused, sheltering in a doorway, getting some brief respite from the midday sun, and extracted one anti-anxiety pill from his jacket pocket. He swallowed it dry, wishing he'd brought a bottle of water with him.

He watched several old cars drift by. None of them slowed. None was interested in Alex.

Another couple of blocks and Alex found himself in a maze of almost identical apartment buildings. He kept his eyes on the road signs, checking against the maps on his phone. The destination was up ahead.

A ground-level entrance, deep in shade. Subtly different from the rest. Alex counted the windows, each with bars on the inside, visible through the hazy glass. Ten on the ground floor. Did this entrance serve the whole building? In which case, this wasn't an apartment block, it was a single huge residence. Housing what?

He didn't get a chance to knock. The door opened within seconds of his arrival. Two men crowded the entrance. The larger guy asked Alex for his ID in curt broken English. Alex produced the South African passport naming him as Ethan Pretorius.

He tried to stop his hands shaking as he handed it over. The man stared at the passport photo and at Alex, repeating the act several times, much as a customs officer would do at passport control. He took a fine-nibbed pen from one pocket and tested it on several pages.

Satisfied at last, he nodded, handing the passport back, before beckoning Alex to follow him inside. He indicated for Alex to stretch his arms up and gave him a rough pat-down, shoving his hands into Alex's armpits and groin. Laurie had been correct. The man didn't ask him a damn thing.

The smaller man remained behind on the inside of the door, perching on a stool. He unfolded a newspaper and started to read, producing a cigarette and a lighter from his back pocket.

The larger man headed along the corridor, beckoning Alex to follow.

The air was a few degrees cooler than outside, but not enough to reduce Alex's profuse sweating. Was it only from the heat? Alex wasn't sure. He began to feel light-headed.

After twenty feet or so the corridor opened into a wider space with several chairs, a coffee table and a water cooler.

'Wait here, please,' said the man, indicating the row of chairs. He disappeared through a door at the end. Alex could hear hushed voices behind it, but his Spanish wasn't good enough to catch what was being said.

Alex poured himself a cup of water, followed by a second. The icy water soothed his throat, sloshing down into his stomach. His chest tightened and his throat fluttered. He breathed through it all – four in, four out – managing his body's reaction to the increasing anxiety.

The door swung open and the large man appeared again. Alex took the opportunity to examine him in the light. He was dark-skinned – Spanish, he assumed. Muscular but dressed in tailored trousers and a fine cotton shirt. His face was stubbled but groomed. Neat. This was no thug, or at the very least he was a thug with standards and a decent income. Big business, Alex reminded himself. And he was about to get embroiled in it.

'Apologies for the . . . the lack of facilities,' said the man, stuttering over his English. 'Our usual residence is unavailable. We'll keep this quick and to the point, yes?'

Alex was surprised. He'd been expecting . . . Well, what had he been expecting? Violence, threatening behaviour, intimidation? He reminded himself these were salespeople, albeit the lowest of the low. He was a customer. It wasn't pleasant, but Alex didn't feel in danger. Not yet. He cleared his throat.

'I'm ready when you are,' he said.

The man nodded. 'Very well. Please – your phone.' The man held out a plain manila envelope, open at the top. 'It will not be touched until you leave,' he said.

Alex had been told to expect this, but nevertheless experienced a fresh bolt of anxiety as he handed it over. No way in which to call for help. No way to track him if they destroyed it.

'This way,' said the man, turning to the door.

Alex was taken through to a separate waiting room. Marginally less shabby than where he had previously waited, this room had a line of hard plastic chairs along two of the walls and a fire extinguisher in one corner. The floor here was tiled, the grouting clean and fresh. Another door stood at the far end.

His anxiety notched up a fraction more. Was that the purpose of these rooms and spaces? Alex had a faint recollection of a psych experiment involving this type of arrangement – the subject's unease would increase with each waiting point. What was the purpose here? To test the resolve of the buyer?

'Two minutes,' said the man, disappearing again, back through the door via which they'd entered.

Alex didn't take a seat, but instead focused on his breathing and crossed his arms to keep them from shaking. His focus was Eva, not the traffickers. Laurie would deal with them later. All he had to do was confirm that Eva was capable of what they suspected, and then try to convince her to trust him.

He had a brief panic. Trust. The sort of thing his daughter should have in him. Something she should have absolutely no doubt about. If he couldn't even get that right, how on earth did he expect a complex girl with psychological trauma to trust him?

The door opened again.

The man smiled.

'Through the other door,' he said. 'No cameras, no listening devices. You have ten minutes.'

He nodded and exited the room. Alex turned, staring at the far door.

Ten minutes to get this girl to trust him.

The first thing Alex noticed on entering the room was the faint smell of perfume. It seemed to ooze from the walls, rather than from the petite young girl sitting in front of him. He took a deep breath, pausing to compose himself.

The girl squirmed on the dark sofa, watching his every move. She looked fearful, angry, but also defiant. An image of Katie flashed into his mind. Strong, independent. This girl was the same, except this girl had been abused, kidnapped and put up for sale. Katie had Grace and Alex. This girl had nobody.

'Eva,' he said, closing the door, seating himself on one of the chairs. He'd considered how to prepare for this moment, but there was no precedent, no case study he could use. Extraordinary patients required an open mind, and although his many years of psychological training and practice would be invaluable, he had no strategy to open with Eva except the very simple.

To open his mind.

If she could do what Susan claimed, she'd know his purpose for being there and his intentions. The risk was that she'd expose him to the traffickers. It was a reasonable risk, but Alex considered it low. Alex gambled on Eva hating the people who held her. Stockholm syndrome would not have set in yet, so she'd be hostile, scared and open to rescue. She'd be looking for anything better than the situation she was in. Alex could honestly offer that. There was no dishonesty on his part towards Eva, only towards the people who held her. If she could see that, then maybe his job was done.

That relied on her ability, of course. If she lacked it, Alex's strategy was sunk. It seemed likely that their interaction in this room was being observed. He couldn't tell Eva what he was doing there. He could only think it.

He paused, realising his mind was racing, realising Eva's face was twitching, turning. Her eyes were narrowed, she was concentrating. He paused.

'How old is Katie?' said Eva.

It caught Alex off guard. Shit. He didn't mind Eva knowing about Katie, but not the people watching or listening. How stupidly naïve of him.

'I'd rather not talk about her,' he said quickly.

Eva's eyes widened. Her face dropped. She understood. He saw her bite her lower lip, as if punishing herself.

'She's just your secretary,' Eva said, raising her head. 'So you screwed her. So what?'

Alex stiffened but admired her quick thinking. To say such a thing exposed so much about her already. She too suspected they were being watched and saw Alex as an ally. She had realised her mistake and moved quickly to protect him.

Eva nodded. She sighed, seemed distracted.

Alex's spine tingled.

Can you read me as easily as that? He spoke the dialogue in his head, but kept it there.

She stared at his lips. Micromovements? Alex knew they existed, but to read them was impossible at this speed. It would take a lifetime to learn such a skill.

'Not as easily as you think,' she said, 'but you aren't even trying to hide it.' Her voice was quiet yet firm. Alex recognised the voice of someone who'd spent a lot of time controlling their outbursts, training themselves to speak softly. A lifetime of institutions and medics telling her to stop shouting.

Her eyes narrowed.

'You're wrong,' she said, but Alex could see the resentment. How did she sense that? He hadn't even spoken in his head, not consciously, but he would have given other clues – his lips, cheeks, the dilation of his eyes. Subtle changes in his posture, his breathing – even his heart rate. Could she really see all of that?

She huffed. Turning away.

Alex paused, unsure of what to do. He realised he was in shock. Eva had demonstrated the depth of her ability within the first few seconds of him being there. A psychological ability never legitimately witnessed before in the history of his profession. Never observed, never documented. His mind churned at the possible causes – heightened empathy, elevated oxytocin, perhaps – as with Mia. But he couldn't even begin to understand the mechanisms.

This would take time. Months. Years. He'd need to study Eva, explore her physiology, take her under into deep-trance hypnosis, delve into her past.

'You want to lock me up and study me?' she said.

Alex shook his head, trying to clear it.

'Yes. No. That's not what I meant. My thoughts are . . .'

'Jumbled,' she said. 'Messy.'

Alex stuttered. 'I-I . . .' *I'm with the UK police. We've come to take you home.* Was that clear enough?

She narrowed her eyes. 'I thought so.'

And to lock up Dr Naylor. She'll pay for what she's done.

Eva's face twisted again, not unpleasantly. She looked like she was trying to smile.

Alex desperately tried to organise his thoughts, his history and his experience so far. He couldn't help visions of Victor and Mia springing to the fore, their abilities and their deeds. Flashes of the havoc they had wreaked, and the chase by the police. He watched Eva's smile disappear, to be replaced with confusion. The fear was back.

'No,' he said, trying to keep his voice in his head. 'I helped her. I saved her.'

Eva put up her hand, silencing him. She waited. He saw the picture in his mind of Mia in her bed at the facility. Safe, recuperating, under treatment. He thought of the monthly fee and the drain on his savings. He thought of the lies he told and the secrets he kept from the police and his family.

He thought of everything and nothing, his consciousness like a sprinkler, casting its wares far and wide.

He realised with increasing hopelessness that Eva might see all of this, all of his failings and his inadequacies. She'd know he wanted to save her, but also that he wanted to pursue the people who had made her like this. His motives were not entirely selfless, although he wished her no harm.

Katie stole his mind again, her face and her innocence. If he could save another girl, would it make up for the damage he had caused to his own flesh and blood?

The door thumped. Three knocks.

'Two minutes!' came the muffled shout.

Two minutes. Alex's mind focused. There was a twinge in his temples and a headache simmering in the background. *Validate and trust.* The first step was complete, but Eva showed no sign of trusting him.

Time was running out and he was failing fast.

CHAPTER
THIRTY-FOUR

Eva watched Alex's eyes. He had nice eyes, and a reassuring expression on his face, all things considered. Eva struggled at first to understand his presence here, until she read his intentions and his role with the police. He seemed woefully underprepared, but his intentions were decent.

His mind and body together were like an open book, and she devoured every last word.

It was refreshing, she thought, to meet a man who didn't instantly examine her body and think about screwing her. Alex looked at her and thought of his own daughter. He had a need to save his daughter and Eva. Both of them in trouble. No. His daughter was safe, but distant. His feelings for his family were complicated, messy, but a sense of debt pervaded. He owed his daughter, and this was his way of repaying it. He wanted to prove something, prove his worth, prove that what he'd done wasn't for nothing, that the damage he'd caused wasn't selfish. His presence here was his punishment, his pursuit of the truth a personal journey of pain. He worried it would never be enough. He worried if he lost this, he'd lose his family too.

She looked deeper and saw that he also carried a darkness about him, self-inflicted, a suffering she couldn't identify. He was driven by anguish, not just mental, but physical too. An addiction. Eva had seen it in enough girls. Perhaps that was it.

Alex had arrived as her hero, her rescuer, her saviour, although in his own mind it was more desperate than that. He didn't see himself as a hero, simply as the only person who could help her. He trusted the police, but only to an extent. The police were pursuing her captors, the Vipers – his face contorted as he mentally formed the word – while he was interested in her specifically.

His offer was clear. She could be purchased by the UK police, of all people, and delivered back to England. Safe and sound. Back in her room.

Back in her cell.

Back on the drugs.

And she would have welcomed all of that, her nightmare over, had it not been for Natalia. The Russian woman's mind, in contrast, had been closed and controlled. Eva had no idea how she'd done it, but the woman had offered a very different future for Eva.

What Alex sought, Natalia already knew.

Their two worlds separated by Eva. Did they know how close they were to one another? Did Natalia know about this polite and harmless man, intent on pursuing her and her people?

But Eva's thoughts darkened. Along with Natalia's offer had come information about her own childhood – not laid bare, not all of it, but a carefully released stream of information, shared for one purpose only.

And it had worked.

Eva was hooked, and there was only one possible path for her now. Alex Madison had come too late, his offer too little – mere safety and a return to the status quo.

But Eva wasn't interested in safety. The simmering noise in her head couldn't be quenched in some NHS hospital with a nice doctor asking her questions. She needed a vent. Answers. Natalia had offered her the beginnings of her story, and Eva wanted the rest.

This man, Alex, was a person she might trust, given time. He was damaged, but he knew it and made no excuses for it. A kindred spirit, perhaps. She watched his eyes. They were so intense she felt the heat from his body and the sparks in his mind, flashing with furious activity, mirrored in hers. She saw a thread, an intriguing one, so far untouched. Something in the darkness, some trauma, a distant noise he didn't even know was there. The more she probed, the more it became real. A primal caution stirred within her and the back of her neck prickled.

The door thumped. He blinked. His mind changed. The darkness crowded his thoughts from view. His face creased with worry.

Eva wasn't sure what she'd found in Alex, but his time was up and now she'd never know. His pain must continue; his quest was not the same as hers.

'You don't need to save me, like you did her,' she said, needing to offer him something. A brief gesture of understanding.

Alex frowned, a second of confusion before it cleared. *Mia*, he thought. *She means Mia.* He kept rubbing his temples – a headache. One of the signs. She needed to let him go.

'Thank you anyway,' said Eva. 'You did the right thing, but I won't be coming with you. You must let me go.'

CHAPTER
THIRTY-FIVE

Natalia ventured from the hotel later that day. A request from a friend. A surprise, but not altogether unwelcome. She dressed in one of the more discreet designer summer dresses from her suitcase and took a taxi to a small café in the central district – the crowds providing the cover and protection needed for her next conversation.

She arrived first, ordering a double espresso and a small glass of water. She took a seat in a corner booth with a view of the entrance, bar and rear exit, keeping an eye on the crowds flowing in and out, along with her thoughts.

Until this point she had performed exactly as asked, with years of perfecting her own warped talent and years of doing her masters' bidding. There had been no choice and so she had never looked for an alternative. The people she was asked to find – the scattered damned, as she thought of them – were mostly monsters. Natalia could handle the process because these people were never meant to be out in the world. They couldn't survive and all they caused was chaos – violent chaos. On balance, removing them from the wild was a public service, even if that public never knew they were being saved.

But what was it she had seen in Eva? What had been different with her? Those eyes, some innocence still remaining. An awakening, triggered by the sight of the vulnerable girl wrapped in a black hoodie, defiant and angry, fearful yet hopeful. Natalia had seen what she'd always dreaded finding – a younger version of herself, ready to be caught and brought in from the cold.

Promised a different life.

That was it, but not all of it.

Natalia's foundations were starting to shake, and she worried for her future. She also wondered who might possibly be able to help her.

The strong coffee slipped down her throat. Proper coffee, not the shit they produced back home. She'd miss this when she left. Another day or a week, then back to the mould and the damp and the forever winters. Maybe she could smuggle some back. Brew coffee and dream of this other world.

The door jingled and a large man with a thick beard and unsuitable clothing entered the café, standing a head taller than most of the other customers. He saw Natalia and paused, staring through her for a few moments before his face broke into a smile – a vivid Russian smile with no room for insincerity. He strode over.

'You're looking well,' he said, trying to keep his naturally booming voice from deafening the other patrons. He cast his eyes up and down her. 'Perhaps too well. Do you ever eat? You need some flesh on those bones of yours or you'll never survive the winter.'

Natalia waited for Tomas to sit. He waved the waiter over and ordered a double espresso.

'There's a place not far from here,' he continued. 'The best Iberian *jamón* in Madrid. Melts in your mouth. Eat some of that and store it up. Your hips can take it.'

The waiter served his drink at the table. A group of women took the booth next to them, engrossed in conversation, their eyes and words turned towards the windows.

'Your hips seem to have been lost long ago,' Natalia said. 'Perhaps *ensalada* for you? Then *you* might survive a few more winters.'

Tomas chuckled. Natalia watched him. He was a subordinate, technically. A handler – a glorified PA, responsible for passing messages and ensuring that assets such as Natalia could go about their business with minimal disruption. However, the handlers had power granted from above. One word from him that Natalia was stepping out of line and his orders might change. He stood no chance against her one to one, but he could make things very difficult for her until they had time to despatch somebody else. Someone who did stand a chance. Thoughts of Pavel caused her to shudder.

So far, Tomas had been genuinely friendly. He understood his role, just as Natalia understood hers. His own life was only as precious as their masters decided at any one time. That, they shared.

She wanted to treat him as an ally but, unfortunately, she couldn't share her thoughts. Her current crisis of faith must remain internal. Her next steps must be by the book, and ruthlessly efficient, as was expected of her.

'It's lovely to see you here,' said Natalia, only half lying. She stirred the remains of her coffee.

'I doubt it,' said Tomas, with another chuckle, 'but I'm handling the extraction, assuming all goes to plan?'

He left it as a question. Natalia raised her eyebrows. 'You had my report. I expect to be successful, but there are sometimes with these deals . . . unforeseen issues.' She dropped the spoon on the saucer.

'As a friend,' said Tomas, his smile thinning, 'I'm advising that there are no unforeseen issues.' He crouched his huge frame lower, leaning in conspiratorially. 'Your record is precarious, my dear Natalia. You are under elevated scrutiny, since . . . you know.'

Natalia knew. The big black mark against her name. 'They don't trust me? Why send me?'

Tomas shook his head, taking a swig from his water glass. 'They do trust you. You're one of their finest, one of their most valuable.'

Natalia shrugged.

'We watch our valuables more closely than we watch our other possessions, *da?*'

Natalia narrowed her eyes. Tomas didn't know about her personal surveillance of Alex Madison. He might know about Pavel, but had chosen to keep it to himself.

'What are they saying? Specifically?'

Tomas shook his head again. 'Nothing to me, but the wind has changed – we can all smell it back home. The circle is getting smaller. Our activities are being curtailed.' He swallowed. 'Something's going on, Natalia, and I'm warning you, from one ugly worthless handler to one beautiful prime asset. Be careful.'

He held her eye for a few moments and Natalia saw the warning pass between them. She nodded, putting her hand up, calling the waiter for the cheque.

'On the matter at hand,' she said. 'These traffickers. You have some contingency plans?'

'I do,' said Tomas. 'We know all of their properties in the city. If they move the girl, we'll know where.'

She nodded.

'But we're under instruction not to force this. Not yet,' he said.

She stood, leaving cash on the table. Before she left, she leaned in and pecked Tomas on the forehead, leaving a smudge of lipstick against his pale skin.

'Thank you, my friend,' she said. 'And you're not ugly, though I meant it about your hips.'

She patted him on the shoulder and his chuckle returned.

'*Da.* I'm going to find that ham restaurant. I'll call you later.'

Tomas's subtle warning had shaken Natalia more than she wanted to admit. For him to expose himself like that – issuing such a warning could earn him severe punishment – meant he was serious. And yet he'd said almost nothing of use.

She trusted his instincts. Pavel had come out of the East, and now the handlers were getting twitchy. They were normal men and women, but exposed to so much of the inner workings of Nova that their hunches were often correct. If Tomas thought change was afoot, she needed to tread very carefully. Pavel might be taking an interest in Alex Madison, but that might not be his sole reason for exposing himself.

In the safety of her room, Natalia considered the variables. Would Eva survive? Months of what would seem like torture, but Natalia hoped the young girl could come out the other end. She'd be changed irrevocably, but still alive. And what other options did she have? She'd been discovered, and now her secret was out, the other players in this game would be far worse in their dealings with her. Natalia wished Eva had never been found. Life in a Western institution might seem like prison, but it was a comfortable existence compared to so many others.

There was no choice, not any more. Natalia must see it through and do her best to ensure Eva's smooth transition. Close observation would be impossible, and discouraged, but Natalia was senior enough to engineer some means of keeping an eye on the girl.

She slipped out of her dress and headed to the bathroom, turning the shower on. While she waited for the water to heat, she checked her email. Nothing significant. A medical report from the Westpoort experiment with a more detailed description of the clinical objectives in creating Eva. Background reading, for her eyes only.

Or perhaps not.

A dangerous thought struck her. Insurance, of sorts. A breadcrumb trail. She considered and dismissed it, but it followed her into the shower and played on her mind as the water washed away the sweat and dust of the city.

CHAPTER THIRTY-SIX

Eva was left in the room for a long time after Alex's departure. Evidently, the bidders had been left satisfied. What they had made of her last comments, she could only imagine, but Naylor didn't appear. Perhaps she could avoid any further spells of punishment in the coffin.

She had a brief moment of panic when Alex left. It burst through and she almost cried out, begging him to return. Safety. But no, she was firm in her commitment. The shock of the Russian woman's revelation was still sinking in, but with every passing second Eva's resolve increased.

An origin. A family, perhaps. Eva's eyes glazed as she realised she didn't even know what her family looked like. Vague scraps of memory – a voice, a smell. She knew what a mother *felt* like, but it was abstract. Warmth, comfort, belonging. Not even real memories: inventions. She saw Natalia's face and wondered if she shared a similar anguish. She was kin, of a kind. Perhaps that was on offer – a family of sorts. With people who understood her, were *like* her. Perhaps she could offer Natalia kinship in return.

She forced the dreams away. She became thirsty but held back on her desire. She needed to think. She'd heard whispers of more bidders and needed to stop the auction. Engineering her own sale to the Russian woman was a disturbing but necessary next step. It was the only outcome she could accept.

She could use the doctor, Alex. Telling Naylor the English police were here would surely disrupt the sale, but would that mean Natalia was cut out too? And what would happen to Alex? Tendrils of guilt snaked in. He wanted to protect her, so how could she feed him to the wolves?

She wouldn't. She thought of the first bidder, the disgusting man with torture on his mind, seeking her as a tool for his brutal activities. Perhaps in reality that hadn't been what she'd seen. Perhaps he was from the police too – the Spanish police, ready to shut them down.

Maybe that's what she'd tell them. But she still had the same issue. Must undertake it with care. Try to make it work.

What other choice did she have?

Naylor entered the room with a man, both of them shielding their faces with their hands.

'Look away,' said Naylor, her voice firm, but with the same waver in it as earlier. She was nervous, stressed. Even as Eva turned away and her chance to read Naylor evaporated, she detected the anxious tones of a woman on the edge.

Perhaps Eva could help push her over it.

A blindfold was pulled tight over her eyes. She resisted the urge to lash out and controlled her ever-present anger, reflecting that in this short time she was getting better at it. Lashing out in the hospital had had few consequences; this place was a different matter.

'You asked to speak to us,' said Naylor.

Eva licked her dry lips. 'May I have some water?'

'After we've finished talking,' said Naylor. 'What do you want?'

'I want to get this over with,' said Eva, keeping her voice calm and humble. *Appear defeated and the message will deliver much more easily.*

'That's not for you to decide,' said the man, with a thick Spanish accent.

'The Russian woman will pay the most,' said Eva. She waited, but there was no response. Good. They were listening.

'She didn't want me to know – she tried to hide it. But she has money. She'll beat any other offer. Set your price and they'll pay it. I'll go with her.'

She heard Naylor and the man breathing heavily, considering her statement.

'So what?' said the man finally. Eva presumed he was speaking to Naylor. 'Then we continue as planned. We have more interested parties. Keep the price going up.'

'Agreed.' Naylor's voice. This wasn't the reaction Eva had hoped for, but she was prepared.

'You don't have time,' she said, hoping this would work. 'The first bidder, the Arab. He's not who he says he is.'

She heard a shuffling on seats. The man, on alert. She'd grabbed his attention.

'They underestimated me, or didn't understand what I am,' said Eva, keeping her voice low and timid. 'I read him before he knew what was going on. I don't know if he's from the normal police, but what I saw was uniforms, weapons. He was thinking of gathering evidence, arrests and bringing down the Vipers, whatever that means.'

Eva continued, chewing her lip, aware of the sound of a phone being switched on, the almost imperceptible tapping of a finger on glass.

'They don't want me. I'll be put into care, somewhere in the system. He guessed I'd be in a brothel within a year. He didn't seem bothered. He was hateful towards me. He only cared about you.'

She breathed, hoping she hadn't waited too long. Her final gambit. A risk, but one she was dying to take. She looked in what she knew was Dr Naylor's direction.

'He thought about you, Dr Naylor,' she said, 'and about the money he owes you.'

She turned her face, stifling a sob, the first fake one of her trip, trying not to push it any further. She had no idea if she was managing to appear convincing, but the sound of a chair being shoved back on the floor and the door swinging open suggested she'd had some effect.

She heard the man shouting. Naylor had jumped up, but remained in the room. Her squeaky breathing grew desperate, louder and closer now.

'You stupid fool, Eva,' whispered Naylor, 'you have no idea what you've just done.'

Eva froze, and swallowed. More shouts in the corridor and a rush as several people entered the room. Naylor backed away.

'Take them.' A muffled voice before her arms were grabbed and Eva was frogmarched from the room.

As she was dragged away her heart fluttered.

Too much, or just right?

CHAPTER THIRTY-SEVEN

'We have a problem.' Josh was tapping at his laptop with increasing urgency, his face creased with worry.

'What's up?' said Laurie, joining Josh at the dining table. They conferred in hushed tones.

Alex remained on the sofa, where he'd slumped for most of the day so far. He couldn't shake the vision of Eva. Her face. Her words. Her ability.

You don't need to save me, like you did her.

Since returning to the apartment he'd been lost in a flurry of competing thoughts and emotions. Without the benefit of his extensive personal library, he was left inside his own head and with what he could research online.

Laurie could see his state of mind and was checking on him periodically. When she'd asked how the meeting had gone, he'd just shaken his head.

'She can do it,' he said, but refused to expand. He needed time.

Time, unfortunately, was fast running out.

Alex had seen Eva's face. This was no cold reading, not even close. She had to be an empath. He'd already dismissed that, and was still inclined to do so. Empathetic accuracy combined with super-senses . . . building intuitive insights and a full mental picture of the other person . . .

But it was so *fast*. Conversational almost, the way she had acknowledged and then dismissed his innermost thoughts. Eva was not Mia, her condition different in so many ways, and yet . . .

'Alex,' said Laurie. She clicked her fingers.

'Hmm?'

'Trouble.'

The room came back into focus. The heat seeped across his body. The noise of the city outside the window crowded into the flat.

Eva was a genuine mind reader. The first of her kind, and quite possibly the last.

And she was in mortal danger.

He heaved himself off the sofa and joined the others. Terry and Hannah were examining their phones. Alex read everyone's face at a glance.

'Did we lose?' he said.

Josh blew his cheeks out. 'Yes and no. The auction has closed. Gone. Shut down. We lost. Maybe everyone lost.'

Hannah switched from her phone to her laptop and nodded in agreement. 'That site on the Dark Web has gone. The contact number we had has been disconnected.'

They all looked at Laurie, who chewed her lip.

'When?' she said.

'Within the last few hours,' Josh answered.

Laurie looked accusingly at Alex for a moment before her expression changed and she shook her head. 'It wasn't you,' she said.

Alex frowned. Laurie's faith in him was undeserved. His performance with Eva had been poor and had been cut short. He'd had no idea as he'd left what she thought of him or what she wanted. She could have run straight to her captors and told them he was with the police. That was the simplest explanation. He'd screwed up.

'They wouldn't have let you walk,' said Laurie. She was watching him. 'I can see the battle in your head, Alex. Trust me. If they thought you were a cop, you wouldn't be standing here right now. Whatever happened, happened later. Another bidder, perhaps. Either that or the Spanish police have got wind of it.' She turned to Terry.

Terry shook his head. 'Nothing on the chatter. I haven't picked up anything on the radio about this.'

Moments of silence, with each spinning their own thoughts, plans and solutions.

Eva is alone, thought Alex. He'd failed her and failed the team.

'Check all your contacts,' she said to the table. 'I need to know if our cover has been blown. Speak to our friends in South Africa – tell them to be on high alert. Hannah – check flights. See how quickly you can get us out of here.'

Hannah nodded, turning to her keyboard.

'The apartment block,' said Alex. 'We have to go back.'

Laurie raised her eyebrows. 'No. No way. Even if they're still there, which I doubt, we are not going anywhere near that place.'

Alex opened his mouth to protest, but Laurie cut him off.

'We're unarmed and operating illegally. There's nobody we can call on here except the people around this table. Even if we could barge in there and grab Eva Jansen and Dr Naylor, we'd never get her out. The Vipers are a huge organised crime syndicate. The plan banked on us buying Eva first – so the Vipers wouldn't give chase. We'd never make it as far as the airport, let alone the border.'

Laurie paused, her frustration evident. 'What the fuck happened?' she cursed under her breath.

'We can't just leave her,' said Alex. He glanced at the faces of the other officers around the table. None would meet his eye.

'Laurie,' he said, 'tell me we're not done here.'

Laurie closed her eyes, her chest rising and falling in deep breaths. She placed her hands on the table.

'OK, we sit tight and we listen,' she said. 'For now. But pack your stuff up – we need to be ready to leave within one hour if I give the order.'

Alex couldn't believe his ears. Was this it? Failing this fast was not something he'd considered for even a second. Were they really prepared to let Eva slip away, just like that? Was he?

As he slumped back on to the sofa, his heart racing and his thoughts spinning, he realised there was absolutely nothing he could do about it.

CHAPTER THIRTY-EIGHT

The car sped through the suburbs in the early-morning sun. Eva watched the housing blocks thin out into industrial parks and wasteland. She tried to read the men in the car. Three of them, each avoiding eye contact with her. Maybe they'd been told about Eva's special talent, maybe not. They weren't bothering this time with restraints or the hood.

Their language was alien, but emotions and intent were universal. The words tumbled away, meaningless on their own, but the sparks in their minds and the ripples through their bodies gave away so much. The threads were still there. Her ability to read people of other languages and cultures was constrained, but not removed. It was a struggle, but that was her future.

The mood had changed rapidly. The tempo had increased as Eva was marched out of the building. She'd heard Naylor shouting behind her, the doctor's protest of innocence sounding hollow in the small room. It turned to pleading before Eva heard the slap of a hand against skin. Naylor's skin. Eva's smile remained hidden and her heart jumped. Eva had been locked away for the night, then dragged out early morning, into this waiting car with the three men.

She wondered if she had done the right thing. Had she gone too far? Disrupting the auction had been her only way, hadn't it? Trying to force the sale to the Russian woman was the right choice, she was sure, but she'd got greedy. She'd seen a way to make Naylor suffer and taken it without a thought as to the consequences.

That was yesterday.

Today she would face the consequences.

The men were all determined in their focus; they were under instruction and very little would stop them achieving it. She turned to the man next to her, examining the side of his face – tanned with rough stubble, clenched jaw, eyes hidden behind sunglasses. His hair was tight and curly, slicked back with gel. Or sweat.

He didn't turn towards her but maintained his stare between the front seats. In his head was a clock. Time was ticking, and he was responsible. If he missed the deadline, he'd face trouble. His stomach clenched at the thought, butterflies driving him to shuffle in his seat.

Eva couldn't get a clear picture of where they were headed. The motion of the car, the heat and her fatigue were taking their toll.

They lurched around another corner and she lost his train of thought. He was examining the buildings, counting in his head.

'*Prisa*,' he said to the driver, who waved his right hand in the air, muttering a reply. Eva couldn't understand, but the sense of urgency increased, all three men releasing sweat and pheromones in response.

Time. They were running out of time.

The car slowed. A few buildings scattered across what looked like derelict industrial ground, wire fences and faded warning signs. A stray dog stopped to stare at the car. It raised its nose to sniff, tucked its tail between its legs and skulked away.

'*Aquí*,' said the man next to her.

The car turned off the road on to a dirt track which snaked through shipping containers and mounds of rubbish. They continued to a corrugated-iron structure – an old warehouse or storage unit. The car stopped.

'*Fuera*,' said the man, opening the door, grabbing Eva's arm and dragging her behind him.

He kept hold of her, closing the car door, while the other two came round the car to join him. Eva could feel his heart rate across the air, his sense of alertness. She looked around at the dusty concrete, squinting as the sun beat down.

The driver, dressed in a dark shirt and chinos, pulled an expensive pair of sunglasses from his top pocket and put them on. Eva could no longer see his eyes but saw a subtle transformation as his confidence increased. A façade, she thought. Hiding one's eyes made it much harder for anyone to read you. You could play a thousand different roles by hiding your eyes.

The third man stood at the back of the car. She heard the trunk pop open and a series of thumps. She turned, but the lid of the trunk obscured her view. The man was dragging something heavy out and on to the floor.

He slammed the lid and Eva gasped.

Naylor's face was bruised and bloodied. The gag was so tight it held her mouth in a grotesque rictus, her lips swollen and red. Her hands and ankles were tied, but the man reached around and now cut her feet free, pulling her to her knees.

Naylor struggled to see, her bruised eyes blinking furiously in the harsh daylight. Dust whipped up into her face. Eva had dreamed of seeing Naylor like this.

Naylor's eyes fell on Eva. A moment passed between them.

Anguish. Pain. Fear. Betrayal. Naylor was terrified, and the sight of Eva only increased her panic. She tried to talk; a muffled moan released against her gag.

Death, thought Naylor, her certainty overwhelming. Eva probed and her own heart leapt.

Both of us.

Eva paused.

They're going to kill both of us.

Naylor's despair was evident and all-consuming. Eva turned her head, whipping it towards the man holding her arm.

'Please,' she said, unsure if he could understand. Unsure if she did.

He turned, frowning, but held her more tightly. Eva tested his grip, straining against his hand, but it was no use. His hand was huge and vice-like. Given time, she might persuade him to let go, but time was not on her side. Besides, she was in no position to tackle all three of them.

'Please don't kill me,' she said, almost as a whisper. This couldn't be the end. This wasn't the plan. Had she screwed up so badly they'd decided to kill both of them? Naylor deserved it, but not her. Not her. The panic rose and the nausea followed. A derelict waste ground with no one to hear her scream.

She closed her eyes.

'Stop there.' The driver's voice was raised, but it wasn't Eva or his friends he was talking to. Eva's eyes snapped open and she followed the gaze of the others.

Hope.

It appeared in the form of a woman and a man. Natalia stood several feet away, near the abandoned iron building. Her appearance was relaxed, her stance firm but non-threatening. Her clothing, another tight-fitting suit, was immaculate and expensive.

To the left and behind Natalia was a giant of a man. His eyes, too, were hidden behind sunglasses, and his arms hung at his sides, muscles taut, ready to spring.

Both parties stared at one another in a flexing of muscle, of power and influence.

This was no execution. This was a sale.

Eva was being sold to the Russian, and the absurd thought filled her with hope, the sudden surge of relief flooding her until she sagged against the car, supported only by her captor.

'The fee has been transferred.' Natalia's voice cut across the hot air. The driver was studying his phone, waiting. Thirty seconds passed, his face glued to the screen. Finally, he swiped and nodded.

'Received,' he said. 'And you still want them both?'

'Yes.'

'Very well.' The driver nodded to his companions. Eva was thrust forward and released. She stood there for a moment, between her old owners and her new, in no-man's-land, staring at the dust, feeling the deafening silence of tension as it prickled in the air.

A thump beside her as Naylor was flung to the ground. The doctor lay panting, unwilling to move. A brief respite from the immediate terror of execution, now her mind was awash with confusion. She had no idea why she was being handed over.

Neither did Eva.

'Thank you, gentlemen,' said Natalia. 'Our business is concluded.'

The driver nodded. 'Our apologies for the nature of the transaction,' he said. 'This is not how we do business. Rest assured it won't happen again.'

'It won't affect the future,' said Natalia. 'Now, if you will leave us?'

The three men climbed back into the car. The engine roared into life and the car crawled away, picking up speed as it achieved distance. Eva heard it disappear on to the main road. She risked a glance back, but all she saw was dust.

Eva glanced at Naylor then at Natalia, who remained in the same pose, her face calm but with a definite air of relief about it. Eva stared into the woman's eyes, but the same wall of silence presented itself, eerie in its intensity. Eva had never experienced anything like it.

'I have a call to make,' said the man, turning and disappearing into the building. Natalia smiled and extended her hand.

◆ ◆ ◆

Eva was taken inside. It was better in the shade, although not cool, the metal walls and roof giving minimal benefit. Natalia gave her a bottle of water. She drained half of it in a few gulps.

They sat on plastic chairs next to a white van. The huge man sat in the driver's seat, talking into a mobile phone. The glass obscured Eva's vision and the sounds of his voice were silenced by the moans coming from Naylor, who lay on the floor several feet in front of the van, out in the full sun. Natalia hadn't offered Naylor any water. Eva watched in fascination, and her natural audacity came out of hiding, creeping back in from the shadow of the last few days. Her constant glances at Natalia were met with warmth and a feeling of kinship.

Safety. That was it. For the first time since leaving her hospital room, Eva felt safe.

And with that feeling came anger, bottled up and suppressed, her heart thudded as the usual noise came crowding in.

'That was a mess,' said Natalia, drinking from her own bottle. She smoothed her lipstick with her index finger. 'But you're almost home, Eva.'

Eva considered the choice of words. 'Where is home?' she asked.

Natalia stared across at the prone body of Naylor. 'Somewhere cooler,' she said. 'But before we go, there is something we must do.' She examined the plastic water bottle in her hand before crushing it in her fist. The sound echoed off the metal walls. A bird took flight from the rafters, dipping under the roofline before escaping into the open.

Natalia pulled a small black pistol from her waistband at the back of her trousers. She turned it over in her hands, held it by the barrel, offering it handle-first to Eva.

'Dr Naylor can't come with us,' said Natalia, 'but I can't let her go back to her old life. Her operation in the UK must end. I'll credit her with leading me to you, but her usefulness is over.'

Natalia waved in the direction in which the traffickers' car had departed, 'The people who held you – some of them are a necessary evil. But not this woman. She's a tumour that needs cutting away.'

Eva studied the gun. She'd never held one before, but didn't worry for one moment that it would matter. She pictured herself taking the gun, walking over to Naylor and pulling the trigger. Naylor had made Eva suffer. She deserved a hundred gunshot wounds, but also a hundred days of pain and fear. Eva didn't know or care much about the girls who'd gone before her, but she knew she wasn't the only one. Natalia was right: Naylor was evil.

She deserved a fate worse than death.

Eva paused and withdrew her hand. 'Can I do it my way?' she asked.

Natalia raised her eyebrows, revealing a brief flash of interest, concern even, but also curiosity. She tucked the pistol back out of sight.

'Of course,' she said, narrowing her eyes. She appeared to consider Eva for a moment. 'But take care, Eva. What you can do may harm you also. We all have our limits.'

Eva considered how little Natalia knew about her.

Maybe this was a good time to show her.

She rose to her feet, walking over until she was right on top of Naylor. Placing a foot on either side of Naylor's body, Eva crouched until she was kneeling, straddling the doctor, pinning her upper arms beneath her knees. She loosened the gag, removing it and throwing it into the dirt.

Naylor seemed drowsy. She clenched her jaw together, grinding it, licking her swollen lips. Eva emptied the rest of her water over Naylor's face and waited while she spluttered. Specks of blood hit Eva's chest and neck. She placed the bottle on the floor.

'Eva,' Naylor whispered, 'I only did what I thought was best.' Her voice was hoarse and dry. Her throat looked bruised. 'For me, yes, but also for you. You had no future. You were abandoned.'

Naylor tried to continue, but Eva clamped her left hand over Naylor's mouth, leaning in, putting her weight into it, ignoring the slime of blood, snot and water.

Eva didn't reply. There was nothing to say. She stared, letting herself relax as Naylor's eyes widened, resisting, before crumpling under her gaze.

Eva searched. She saw a layered exterior – a wall of pent-up aggression strengthened over the years. Superiority. A God-complex, the doctor's curse, exacerbated by her ruthless intellect and position. Mental health had been a natural home for her, where she could exert her dominance and control, playing with the lives of others. She relished it, needed it, her primal urge satisfied.

But Eva forced her way through, prising open the cracks, looking for the threads that would lead her inside.

Naylor blinked, trying to turn away, her brow furrowed with confusion. Eva brought her other hand up and clamped down on Naylor's nostrils long enough for Naylor to convulse in panic.

Eva had her attention again. Naylor writhed, but in her bound and weakened state, she lay helpless on her back. Her face open, her mind and body ready to answer.

'Why?' Eva whispered. A single word, but Naylor knew what she wanted and couldn't help the memories flooding her mind.

The threads formed – tangible, multiple strands. Slow at first, but as one spun out, the others unravelled in response, meandering towards Eva. The haze formed into clearer details and she pulled – an image etched into Naylor's memory. She saw a large room, dark wood panels, a library, a study. Books covered one wall, a small ladder leaning against the shelves.

Deeper.

A sofa. A couch, on which Naylor was sitting with her legs up. She wore knee-length white socks and black patent shoes. School shoes. Naylor as a child.

A memory of particular significance.

A shadow to her left leaned in. Female, a large woman, sitting close. She talked, asking Naylor questions about herself. About her schoolwork. About what she liked. About what had happened next.

What had happened before this point?

Eva paused. The box was open and Naylor's twisted history was seeping out. This wasn't all of it, by any means, but it was enough. Enough to cause a fracture of sanity, enough to create something different, something monstrous. To be abandoned as a child. Naylor never knew the reason, only that she had pleaded and they had rejected her. Left with that wound for ever, never to be healed, despite the best efforts of her doctor and her therapist.

What possible route would Naylor take? Seek out her parents? Never that. Confronting the people who had abandoned her would have taken more energy and courage than she was ever able to muster.

Instead she turned on her patients. The ultimate power, to take a young life and send it away, abandon it into the void. She had that power now.

Or at least, she used to.

Eva wrestled with what she saw. The similarity with her own memories wasn't lost on her. Was this her own future? To become twisted, warped and evil? To inflict on other children what had been inflicted on her?

Abused by the doctors, only to abuse in return?

She shook her head. *Never.* This wasn't the only path. Naylor had made a choice: she'd reflected on her damage and decided to exact it on others.

This had been Naylor's story, but it wasn't hers. Eva had her own story to tell.

Eva took a deep breath and looked into Naylor's eyes. She wanted to feel pity, but could find none. There was no sympathy here. Naylor must be judged on her actions. She must be punished.

And so Eva let it come.

She wrenched the threads from the depths of Naylor's mind, tearing the memories from their hiding place, teasing them out, making them simmer. Once they had surfaced, she twisted and knotted them, making them a permanent fixture in Naylor's waking consciousness.

She didn't doubt for a second that Naylor deserved it.

'They never wanted you,' she whispered, plucking at the visions. 'The doctor hugged you out of pity. Nobody wanted you.'

Naylor groaned, her eyes pleading as the whirlwind of emotions took her.

'You'll always be that girl on the sofa,' said Eva, 'and you'll always exist in that room. You'll never leave there. Abandoned and alone.'

Eva pushed the words home, repeating them in a whisper, leaning into Naylor's face, concentrating her efforts on the strands of pain within.

The damage was done within seconds. Naylor writhed with incoherence, her stream of consciousness disrupted, her ordered thoughts becoming chaotic and nonsensical. Eva grabbed more memories of Naylor's trauma and amplified them, playing them over and over, twisting and knotting, a fairy tale of desertion, played on repeat, hammering into her psyche.

The room. Always the room.

That's where you'll stay.

Slowly and surely, Eva was changing Naylor. The pathways were shifting, her mind forever altered. She would never recover, not in Eva's experience. Because Eva had done this before.

Naylor had taken Eva's freedom and now Eva was taking her sanity.

It didn't take much longer. Naylor continued to writhe while Eva probed and contorted, whispering her thoughts as they emerged, reflecting a perfect storm of emotion and twisted logic until Naylor's eyes rolled into the top of her head and the blackness descended once again.

And with it, Eva's anger flicked off like a switch. With the voices gone, her inner rage withdrew at speed, creeping back into the dark recesses of her mind, poised, waiting, but for the moment satisfied.

Eva released her grip. She watched Naylor's childlike face, panting with her mouth hanging open, dribbling.

Naylor would exist after this, for as long as her body survived out here. Maybe she'd even be rescued, physically at least, but she'd never be Dr Naylor again. She was just a shell now, with fragments of her mind bouncing around the interior, never to find their place. Always turned inwards, forever locked in the memory of her trauma. Forever in the moment she feared the most. Living her worst nightmare over and over.

It was everything she deserved. Eva gathered as much saliva as she could muster and spat it into Naylor's face.

She caught her breath suddenly and turned towards the van. Natalia and the man stood side by side, equally frozen to the spot, both of them staring. Natalia was holding her phone upright, recording? Her face was blank, her eyes curious. She walked over, holding her phone in front of her, focusing now on Naylor. She paused, zooming in on Naylor's face.

'Go to the van, Eva.' Natalia's voice had lost its warmth. Eva stood, raising herself up as if pulled by strings. She turned her back on Natalia. The rear door of the van stood open.

'In there,' said the man. He had a Russian accent. Thick and unwavering. He didn't look at Eva but climbed into the driver's seat.

As Eva climbed in, a single gunshot startled her and her head snapped to the front. Through the windscreen, she could see that Natalia's phone had been replaced with the pistol. She stood over Naylor, her right arm extended, the pistol still smoking in her hand.

Naylor's body twitched one last time as the blood seeped from her head into the dust.

CHAPTER THIRTY-NINE

Alex woke from a fitful nap. He peeled himself from the bedsheets, his sweat musky and stale. He stripped off his shirt and trousers and grabbed a towel.

With nothing to do but wait, he'd retired to his room and, under instruction, packed his few belongings into the suitcase. Laurie was preoccupied, focused on her team. She'd given Alex a reassuring smile and suggested he take a break.

Alex padded along the corridor to the bathroom and turned the shower on cold. He climbed in, shivering for a few seconds before lathering his hair and body.

With a towel wrapped around his waist, he brushed his teeth and headed back to his room. Laurie was coming the other way. She folded her arms and made a point of staring.

'I'm not too good at wolf-whistles,' she said, 'so you'll just have to imagine it.'

Alex smirked, self-conscious. He gripped the towel a little more tightly.

Laurie frowned. 'Sorry,' she said. 'That was . . . ahem.'

'Ahem?'

'You know.'

'Of course.'

Laurie's face broke into a smile. It was strained, apologetic. 'I'm sorry this hasn't worked out,' she said. 'You know it's not your fault. You had no time to shine. Work your magic . . . you know.'

'I'm not sure I have any,' he said. 'I'm not sure I'm qualified any longer.'

Laurie approached him. She touched his forearm. Alex felt a spark, the same spark he'd felt the year before when he'd done his stupid best to ruin their professional relationship. He'd pushed for something more between them, then abandoned her when Grace needed him. Except that Grace didn't want him like that, and he was still deluding himself.

'There's nobody qualified to deal with what you described, Alex,' she said, 'with what you've been through. But you're the best of the rest – no one else has your experience. Remember that.'

Alex nodded. He wanted to believe her. He should believe her. But it was hard when he'd failed Eva so badly.

'I'd best get dressed,' he said, putting his hand on top of hers, the briefest touch. He didn't know why he'd done it.

She glanced at his towel. 'Yes, you should,' she said. 'My team see enough horrors in their jobs without this.'

Laurie spun on her feet and strode off. Alex entered his bedroom and closed the door, his spirits lifted by a fraction, although not nearly enough.

His phone was charging on the bedside table. It vibrated twice: a text message. He sat on the bed and picked it up.

Alex stared at the screen of his phone. He didn't recognise the number, and the message was a single URL – a web address to a video-sharing site. He glanced at the door. The team were still busy, either packing things away or speaking into their phones in hushed tones, the anxious preparation creating a haze of tension.

He clicked on the link and a browser window opened.

The video was clear, high resolution in bright sunlight. It wobbled before focusing in on its subject.

Alex watched the video through once, then again. He started a third, pausing on a frame.

He stared at the image of Eva Jansen, dressed as he'd seen her the previous day, crouched in the dust, leaning over a figure he didn't recognise. A shiver ran through him. Where had he seen an image like that before? A person perched over a suffering body, writhing in trauma.

Mia, when she leaned over her victims, drinking in the pain. So similar, yet for such different reasons. Eva appeared as a predator over her prey, committing the same visceral violence.

There was no background other than concrete and dust, no landmarks. Just a body.

And Eva.

The final few seconds of the video focused on the face of the woman under Eva. Alex squinted as it became clear. Dr Naylor. Quite a brutal contrast from the photos Alex had seen before, but unmistakably her. She looked dazed, almost like an infant, her eyes glazed, rolled upwards, and her expression numb. Catatonic, if Alex wasn't mistaken, in a complete stupor, her body rigid. He remembered the police officer's report – the hospital record of the girl Eva had attacked at school. She'd been the same – catatonic, unresponsive, her mind in a waking coma.

Eva didn't just read minds. She destroyed them too. And someone wanted Alex to know about it.

The video focused in more closely before stopping, and the image went black.

He jumped as another message came through.

She is a monster, Alex. She is not for you to fix or to save.
Do svidaniya drug.

Alex swallowed. He checked the number, but it came up as unrecognised. A quick search revealed the final phrase to mean *Goodbye, friend*. It was in Russian.

A fresh chill swept through his body.

Sent to Alex's personal phone number. They knew he was here and what he was after.

But they'd called him *friend*. Hardly the behaviour of the man who'd chased him, the man whose whispers had pinned Alex to the wall of the elevator, twisting his insides in pain. This couldn't be the Nova who'd warned him away.

So then who?

He jumped up from his bed, grabbing the door handle.

'Laurie!' he shouted, holding his towel with one hand and his phone with the other. 'Quick.'

A moment later Laurie came racing towards the bedroom. 'What?'

'I need you to see something,' he said. He perched on the edge of the bed and brought up his messages. The screen refreshed the list and he waited for it to appear.

Nothing.

'What?' said Laurie.

'Wait,' he said. 'I . . .' Alex refreshed his messages again, but both of the messages had disappeared from the list. He switched to his browser. The page refreshed and showed him an error page: *This video has been removed.*

'No,' he said. 'Shit!'

He tried his messages again, then the browser. Nothing. It had all gone, vanished into the digital ether as quickly as it appeared. He knew it was technically possible to remove messages from somebody's phone, but he'd never witnessed it. The video had been removed just as cleanly.

'Alex, you're worrying me,' said Laurie. 'Do you want one of us youngsters to show you how to use your phone? Please don't Instagram our stay here. I shouldn't have to tell you.'

Alex dropped his phone on the bed. He looked at Laurie's inquisitive face. Amused, but concerned.

He had nothing to show her. He could tell her. And she'd believe him, wouldn't she? But how could he describe what he'd seen? In clinical terms, or in terms of what he remembered?

She looked like Mia. Eva looked like Mia.

A sudden dread crept in. He couldn't start down that path without the risk of revealing everything else, and possibly spending the rest of their trip in handcuffs. So what else? That the video showed Eva not as a timid young girl but as a monster, a product, a *weapon*?

How would Laurie react? Would she still want Eva back? The girl's UK citizenship would count for something, but Alex's initial worry about Laurie's motives now increased. If Laurie saw that video, she'd treat Eva as a dangerous individual, not a victim. Even if they could retrieve her, she'd be locked up, gagged and hooded until the slow wheels of the system began turning.

He played the possible course of events in his head, but remained torn. Naylor was down, Eva was gone, and Alex would follow. At what point did he invite Laurie in?

Not now.

Not yet.

He slumped, taking a few deep breaths. It was time for his Xanax – the little voice in his head warned him not to leave it too long. The delusions and the panic attacks wouldn't resolve through cold turkey. He needed his fix.

'It's nothing,' he said. 'I thought I had . . . I don't know. It was an idea, but it's gone. I think we're done here, aren't we?'

Laurie watched him for a moment. He saw her eyes flicker. She sensed something was wrong.

'We are,' she said. She glanced out into the corridor before sliding across and perching next to him on the bed.

'We were done the moment they pulled the auction,' she said, 'if I was being honest – which I like to be, on occasion, even with you.'

Alex smiled. He wished he could match her honesty, but kept his mouth shut. He was alone again in his world of secrets and shadows. He had no idea where to start, but at least he knew one thing: Eva was alive. Maybe not safe, but at least no longer in the hands of the Vipers. Nova had shown him they were still out there, and in more than one guise. He needed time to regroup and rethink.

'So are we going home?' he asked.

Laurie nodded. 'As soon as we can get flights. But you still haven't got any pants on.'

Alex glanced down. 'I promise to wear pants on the flight. You have my word.'

CHAPTER FORTY

The evening drew on. Eva was allowed to sit on the rear seats of the van, behind Natalia and the man who'd introduced himself as Tomas. His mind was less obscured than Natalia's, but still far from normal. He seemed to sense her probing. While his body movements and smell could not be masked, his thoughts were shielded. The few words she managed to pluck were in Russian and mostly incoherent.

Natalia, on the other hand, was utterly silent and closed to her, her calm face rigid with control; even her body gave nothing away. She spent the first couple of hours staring out of the window, occasionally playing with her phone, which she plugged into the cigarette lighter to charge.

It was such a curious experience for Eva, being in the presence of two people whom she could not read. The rage with which she'd destroyed Naylor had reduced to a simmer, then departed, and in its place was left a cold, vacant feeling. She had only her own thoughts and the sounds of the road to entertain her. This was soothing, although confusing.

'Where are we headed?' she asked. They'd fed her chocolate and crisps, promising more substantial food soon. She'd drunk Coke and water and demanded several toilet stops. Natalia had accompanied her into the bushes. Eva didn't plan on running, but she evidently wasn't trusted.

'East,' said Tomas, his face always turned firmly to the view beyond the windscreen and away from her. Natalia picked up her phone yet again. The screen was obscured from Eva's view.

'Who were you messaging?' Tomas wanted to know, now turning to Natalia.

Natalia turned her phone off quickly. Too quickly, thought Eva. Hiding something.

'Nobody,' she said.

'Earlier,' said Tomas. 'You sent something.'

Natalia glanced back to Eva before facing Tomas. 'I don't know what you mean,' she said.

Tomas gave an audible sigh. They drove in silence for a few minutes. Eva watched the pair of them. Neither turned to her.

'There was a red flag,' said Tomas. 'One of the other bidders.' He let it hang. Natalia remained facing him. He kept his eyes on the road. Eva sensed the warning from Tomas.

'You know who I'm talking about,' continued Tomas. 'Madison.'

The name conjured in Eva's mind the image of the man who'd tried to rescue her. Take her home. What did these people know about him? Eva leaned forward a little.

Tomas huffed, his big chest rising and falling. Natalia appeared rigid. She reached out for her phone again, seemed to think better of it and put her hands in her lap, staring forward.

'They're watching him,' said Tomas, turning to glance at Natalia, who shuffled in her seat. 'I thought you should know. Be careful.'

Eva saw something pass between them. The tension rose and the air thickened.

Another minute of silence. The car droned on and the light started to fade.

'I don't know what you mean,' repeated Natalia at length, 'but thank you, Tomas.'

◆ ◆ ◆

Eva let the tension fade. Whatever had happened was over. Alex Madison was on their minds, but Eva couldn't figure out why. She waited another hour before her impatience got the better of her.

'Who are you?' she said. 'Not your names – you?'

Natalia shuffled around in her seat. She appeared to consider the question. Her face was calm again, relaxed even, although Eva thought she looked tired. She bit her lower lip before answering.

'You'll be told soon enough. You're one of us now.'

'Us?'

Natalia frowned. 'Our organisation goes by many different names, Eva. You will hear it called Nova, but that is not everything it is. And now is not the time.'

'Why do they want me?'

Natalia looked uncomfortable. Her eyes darted across to Tomas.

'I've already told you why,' she said.

Eva frowned. She thought back to her first meeting with Natalia. The information that had been revealed. The impression she'd been given. Natalia had revealed Eva's origin, yes, but hadn't admitted to being part of the organisation that had made her like this. With a growing unease, Eva tensed, fists forming. She looked closely at Natalia's eyes, saw them narrow. 'My childhood?' she said. 'That was you? My . . .'

Eva felt the insides of the van shrink, the walls caving in. Flashes of the immersion tank filled her vision. She grabbed the top of the seat.

'Not me,' said Natalia. She reached out and held Eva's arm. 'Not me,' she repeated.

'Border,' came Tomas's booming voice from the driver's seat.

'What do you . . . ?' said Eva. Natalia's grip tightened.

'It will all become clear, Eva. Quiet as we cross the border.'

'But—'

'Shhh.'

The van slowed as the road spread into several lanes. Blocking each lane was a gatehouse and a barrier. Overhead gantries displayed signs with green arrows or red crosses, their light reflecting off the metal roof, shining on to the tarmac. Police swarmed over the roadway, checking in and under cars. Tomas steered towards an empty lane, bringing the van to a halt several feet from a barrier. One of the police officers approached.

'There are more than usual,' said Tomas in a low voice. 'Spain to France is normally a wave-through.'

'Stay calm,' said Natalia, and she shuffled closer towards Tomas as he lowered the driver's window.

Eva forced herself to listen as the officer addressed them. Both Tomas and Natalia responded. Natalia spoke slowly, her smile never wavering. The officer pointed to Eva, and Natalia leaned over, holding Eva's arm and patting it gently.

'*Ella no habla español*,' said Natalia, laughing.

'English?' said the guard.

Natalia shook her head. 'Sorry, Russian. *Prosto russkaya.*'

Eva watched the guard watching her. Now would be the time if she wanted to leave. Hand herself over and ask to go home. They'd send her, wouldn't they? Away from Tomas and Natalia and whatever concoction of truth and lies they were offering.

She experienced suddenly the same crushing feeling as before, the walls crowding her peripheral vision, her chest tightening. She had no choices. She was trapped.

The guard frowned. 'Are you OK, miss?' he said in English.

Eva froze in indecision. She opened her mouth, but the words refused to form.

'She's fine,' said Natalia, leaning over, almost on top of Tomas. She reeled off several phrases in Spanish, fast, her voice taking on a husky quality, much quieter than before. She paused before repeating them, this time more slowly. 'Let us through,' she said, in English.

Eva thought she heard something else, the merest whisper, uttered under Natalia's breath. To Eva it felt eerie, strange in her ears. Despite the warmth inside the van, her skin prickled. Her own thoughts drifted and she struggled to keep her head clear.

The guard paused and his expression changed from a deep frown to a placid, almost dreamy expression. His demeanour followed, his shoulders slumping as he stepped away from the van. He raised a lazy arm to a couple of other officers lingering at the gate. They waved, nodded and raised the red and white steel barrier.

'Go,' said the guard, tapping on the windshield.

As Tomas inched the vehicle along, Eva watched the officer. He was shaking his head, leaning down with his hands on his thighs. He stared at the ground for a few moments, swaying.

'What did you . . . ?' The thundering realisation came to Eva as Tomas gunned the engine. Natalia only stared forward, patting Tomas on the arm. Both of them ignored Eva.

She strained her neck to look behind them, but the guard had disappeared out of sight, as the van slipped across the border and into France.

CHAPTER
FORTY-ONE

Natalia tried to doze while Tomas drove. She offered to take the wheel, but he refused, insisting it was his job and his place. She should not have to bother herself with such things. And so the countries blended into one long motorway, a foreboding expanse of dark tarmac stretching into the distance.

Eva slept, the mild tranquillisers in her water keeping her in a pleasant slumber across the rear seat. Her questions, for the time being, were silenced, although Natalia worried about the girl's anger. It simmered so visibly, a background noise she couldn't control, waiting for a reason to unleash. Did she know how much her rage consumed her? Her treatment of Dr Naylor had been fascinating, but concerning. The girl did not understand or fully control what she possessed. Freak had been the same: a damaging force, rarely trusted and forever restricted. His activities these days were constrained to Russia – he was never allowed to roam. His promised freedom would never materialise.

It would make the future all the harder for Eva.

They drove all night and well into the next day, across southern France and into northern Italy, where the temperature dropped and the landscape changed from blinding yellows to greens as they climbed. Rain hit them during the night, great drops rattling off the roof of the van, keeping Natalia awake. Stopping her from dreaming.

The sun-kissed Spanish landscape was long forgotten as they climbed into the Alps, their raw features reminding her of her relative size against Mother Earth. Natalia was hit with a tinge of melancholy, these mountains recalling the frozen peaks of Siberia. They shouldn't be luring her in like this – she had absolutely no desire to return. Her cough tickled, as if in protest. She stifled the worst of it, feeling the dull ache deep down in her lungs.

They were approaching the Austrian border when her phone rang. She checked the screen, rubbed the sleep out of her eyes and sat up straighter.

'Yes?' she answered.

'This is Kostas,' came the reply.

Natalia resisted looking at Tomas. Kostas was another handler, and Tomas's superior. 'I don't understand.'

'I'm sending you an address. Eastern Czechia. I think you know it. Be there within twenty-four hours, please. Orders from above.'

Natalia's phone vibrated, and she checked the incoming message and brought up the maps. The blood drained from her face when she saw the location.

'Got it?' said Kostas.

Natalia zoomed back in and showed the address to Tomas, whose eyes widened, his mouth opening and shutting like a guppy. He composed himself and plugged the address into the satnav. He grunted, holding up nine fingers. Nine hours.

'Got it,' she said, her voice barely above a whisper.

Kostas hung up, and Natalia sniffed, a fresh shiver running down her back as she recalled her own memories of their revised destination.

Pavel's plan, whatever it was, now included them.

They'd been summoned to Starkov.

Near the Czech border with Poland, Starkov was one of Nova's largest laboratories, fashioned out of a Soviet-era nuclear bunker deep in the countryside. A vast warren of dark concrete passages and chambers, it had once held hundreds of scientists and patients, kept underground for months and years at a time. Natalia had been stationed there for over two years in her twenties while completing her training. She remembered how the rounded concrete walls reflected the screams, which would echo down the corridors for what seemed like miles, distorting with time and distance. She would lie in her bunk and hear the cries of the children seeping under her door. The shrieks would continue long into the night – time having little relevance underground. The lab operated in shifts, never stopping, never relaxing.

Daylight was a luxury afforded only to those who survived. Or the bodies of those who died.

Eva's experiments in childhood would pale in comparison to what awaited her at Starkov.

Natalia stared down at her phone, keeping the maps open, zooming in on Czechia, scrolling around, before she found herself panning back out. Poland, Slovakia, Germany and Austria shrunk as the rest of Europe came into view.

Of all the places on Earth, there were many that could hide a girl such as Eva. Within this one continent alone, she could be safe, untouched, *undamaged*. Natalia could do it.

It had been done before.

The hours passed, the mountains still teasing her. Another time, Natalia might have admired their imposing and relentless stature, let them wrap their spell around her, remind her what it was to be human.

Right now, however, they crowded in, suffocating her as the van wound through the narrow passes. Her head was full of conflict and increasing unease. For the first time in many years, she felt under threat, her grasp on her own fate growing increasingly unstable. And now they were headed to that hateful place. To Starkov.

As the hours passed and the mountains fell behind, Natalia managed a fitful doze, although she woke at each border – each one a new step, beckoning Natalia to her fate.

Czechia finally welcomed them, and they skirted the cities, losing themselves in the country roads, weaving through pine forests, climbing in altitude as they approached the eastern border.

Natalia turned to her ward on the back seat. Still fast asleep. Still safe.

But not for long.

'Twenty minutes,' said Tomas, tapping the satnav.

Natalia's heart started thumping long before the quiet road narrowed even further, weaving through the hills in the evening sun. Tomas slowed the van as they navigated a dirt track, before pulling over in front of a grey brick guardhouse. It was large, with two storeys and barred windows facing the road, a high fence all around. Next to the house was a high razor-wire gate, beyond which lay a single-width road. Natalia knew that, at the end of the road, hell waited.

Natalia took a deep breath before stepping out of the van. The wind was fresh, from the north. It brought a chill and she pulled her jacket tighter.

'Natalia.' A thin form appeared at the front door of the guardhouse. He walked up to her, arms spread. They kissed both cheeks and Kostas stood back. His appearance was in such contrast to

Tomas – small and wiry, but with a piercing glint in his eyes. She should trust him. She should trust all of them, but still she shivered.

'Congratulations,' he said, before turning to Tomas. 'I'll help you get her inside. Natalia, you have a visitor.'

Natalia left them to carry Eva. She entered the hallway, casting her eyes around at the decor, which was grey, like the outside, with rough plaster walls and no paint.

A door creaked open off the hallway and a dark silhouette beckoned her into the dimly lit room.

Tomas headed upstairs with Kostas to secure Eva in one of the rooms. His heavy feet thundered through the house, barely softened by the thin carpets, as the staircase groaned in protest.

Natalia followed the figure into a drab reception room, as bland as the hallway, but painted in a dirty beige and furnished with cheap fabric sofas around a small glass coffee table, a fake leather chesterfield chair to one side. Blinds were pulled against the windows. Her eyes adjusted to the gloom just as the person turned to face her.

'Natalia.' Pavel, this murky shade from her past, seated himself on the chesterfield, his eyes never leaving her face. He beckoned for her to sit.

'Pavel, sir,' she said, struggling to find her voice as her mind raced. 'Why are we here?'

Pavel examined her, his ancient face creasing with concentration. His eyes were old but sparkled with an intensity Natalia had always found unnerving. His immaculate tailored suit and shoes, his carefully groomed grey hair, did nothing to put her at ease. Carefully, she closed her mind, tensing her jaw, firming up her face, relaxing the rest of her body until she was in full control.

Pavel's features creased again, but this time in laughter.

'Good!' he cackled. 'Good, Natalia – always on the defence. We taught you well.'

Natalia kept her expression neutral. They *had* taught her well, through years of pain and suffering, not to mention a childhood of brutality and abuse. Teaching. Yes, that was what they'd called it.

'Would you like me to tell you about the girl?' asked Natalia. *Or Alex*, she thought. *Please don't ask me about Alex Madison.*

Pavel's laughter died. His face held the smile and he took a deep breath, letting it out through thin, chapped lips that quivered as they moved.

The air electrified in front of her as Pavel's words seeped into her psyche. His technique was exquisite, his words inaudible. His grip eased its way around Natalia's defences. She swallowed, forcing him out, feeling her head start to throb with the effort. A stampede at the back of her head, blood rushing to cope with the exertion. Her chest began to tighten, pressure creeping from her diaphragm, up and over her lungs. She held his gaze while her eyes burned and her jaw clenched even more tightly. A tooth cracked.

Pavel released her and nodded. 'Very good,' he whispered. He sniffed, pulling out a starched handkerchief, then dabbed the end of his nose before continuing.

'What would you like to tell me about the girl?' he said. 'Or anything that's happened in the last few days?'

Natalia drew a breath, held it until the tremor passed, then let it out. She turned the small fragment of tooth from the rear molar on her tongue and spat it on to the floor. She had done nothing wrong, fundamentally. Her own surveillance of Alex Madison could have been traced, but what would they find? She'd watched him. She'd warned him off. That was her job. Her connection to him was in her head. There was nothing Pavel could pin on her. Nothing substantial.

'It could have gone more smoothly, I suppose,' she said, 'but we were in and out with no force, no suspicions raised. We took care of the seller, Dr Naylor. There is no other risk.'

Pavel's expression didn't change. 'No other risk?'

Natalia considered her next words very carefully.

'Nobody significant,' she said, 'in my humble opinion. Nobody that'll be a problem. This is my job, Pavel. You know I take care of our interests first. Always.'

Pavel's smile returned to his mouth, but not to his eyes. He shook his head.

'I'd like you to take a few days off,' he said. 'Weeks, perhaps. You'll stay here, in this guardhouse. At Starkov, as my guest.'

Natalia tried not to let her reaction show.

'Pavel,' she said, 'I really must—'

'You *must*? Be careful, Natalia,' he said, taking his handkerchief once again and dabbing the corners of his mouth. 'This is a temporary shortening of your leash. Don't make it permanent.'

'But the girl,' she said. 'I'd like to—'

'The girl is going into Starkov,' said Pavel.

This time Natalia couldn't hide her reaction. 'But why?' She hadn't meant to plead, but couldn't stop the sound emerging.

Pavel frowned. 'You've earned the right to ask, but don't push me, Natalia. I have reviewed her records, examined her background. She's volatile – her talent unstable. She was never finished. Her treatment must continue under more . . . controlled conditions.'

'But you can't!' Natalia burst out. 'She won't make it through Starkov. That wasn't the plan for her. She was supposed to . . .' She saw his frustration increasing. He didn't have to explain himself to her, and it would do her no good to push it, nor Eva.

She took several deep breaths. She was no match for Pavel and her anger was of no use. Better to agree, and do it gracefully. She could try again. Eva might not be sent down immediately. There was always tomorrow, provided she obeyed him today.

She lowered her eyes, nodding her submission. She waited.

He kept her there for a few moments until she finally met his eye. 'You may go,' he said. 'There's a room for you upstairs with everything you need. You'll keep your privileges, your phone, your access. I'm not taking anything away from you, Natalia. Not unless you make me.'

Natalia stood, heading for the door.

'You have a future, Natalia,' he said, his voice turning to a croak. He coughed, clearing phlegm from his throat. 'But it's about choices. Your choices. Forget about the girl. And forget about Alex Madison.'

He left it hanging, his eyes piercing through her. Natalia nodded again, before turning and leaving the room.

CHAPTER
FORTY-TWO

The grey skies of a London morning greeted Alex. He checked his phone as the taxi swung into more traffic, switching it out of airplane mode, realising he'd forgotten after they'd landed. A couple of missed calls from Grace, but no messages. Having a police protection unit parked outside their house would have come as a shock, but at least they were safe. Angry, perhaps, but safe.

The sounds of London did little to lift Alex's mood. He stared out of the window, Laurie beside him, both quiet and lost in their thoughts. The journey home had been sombre and frustrating.

It wasn't your fault.

The standard line. Except he believed it now. Laurie's insistence was spot on, but Alex didn't tell her why. He wrestled with it throughout the flight, but his gut reaction was still the correct one.

'The auction was a failure, but she might still be out there somewhere, Alex,' said Laurie. 'They had no reason to kill Eva. We may still find her. Naylor, on the other hand,' she said with a shrug, 'we'll pick up when she returns to the UK – assuming she returns.'

Alex kept his composure and nodded, his gaze directed away from her.

'We'll debrief properly at the station,' said Laurie. 'I'll call you. Until then, go home, have a drink, play golf, relax, etcetera.'

Her voice was weary, a pale imitation of her usual banter. Alex figured the trip had affected her too, albeit in her own way. No matter how much exposure she'd had to this type of crime, she was still human. Losing a mark and a victim in one foul trip was bound to hit hard.

'You'll be relaxing? Drinking? Playing golf?' he said.

'Sure,' she said. 'The second one at least – maybe not so much the first. I don't play golf, because I'm not sixty or a loser.'

'Harsh,' said Alex, who had failed to convince Laurie that not all doctors played golf. He certainly didn't, and didn't even own a set of clubs, yet it was a standard insult from Laurie, lobbed at him whenever she could.

They stared through the traffic. The car in front honked, joined by several others. The lights changed and their car jerked forwards.

'We never did have that second drink,' she said.

Alex glanced at her. She continued to frown through the window. 'Last year – after you stood me up. Remember?'

Alex remembered alright, although 'stood up' wasn't quite how he would have phrased being kidnapped and held captive in an industrial park while searching for Mia. Laurie wasn't someone to offer easy forgiveness, that much was clear.

'I was a little tied up that day,' he said, 'although it was my fault, of course. Did I ever apologise?'

'I don't think so,' she said. 'You came up with some crap excuse at the time.'

She turned and smiled. He smiled back, despite the last few days. This was what Laurie excelled at – detachment. It was how she survived and how she enabled the people working with her to survive. She knew her skills and applied them brilliantly when needed. Alex envied her.

He also wanted to take her out for that second drink, but it felt wrong on so many grounds, not least of which was the growing list of secrets he held from her. First Mia, now Eva. Not exactly the basis for a professional friendship, let alone anything else.

'Maybe when this all blows over,' he said, not sure if he meant it, not altogether sure where Laurie was headed with her comments.

'Whoa, boy,' she said, helping to clarify. 'Remember, last time, I said you were a mess, and I was a mess, and that was a poor basis for drinking partners?'

Alex nodded.

'Has anything changed?'

Alex paused. His ego hated for him to be called a mess, but at this stage he wasn't in a position to argue, and especially not with Laurie. He'd lose outright. But was she really a mess too? Promoted beyond her peers, leading a team at the NCA, running covert police ops overseas? That didn't sound like a mess, although he knew her professional excellence was only one side of her. If you dared penetrate the armour plating of her exterior, there was a tender person inside with a whole heap of baggage. She hid it well, but Alex could see through the bluff – he'd been trained to see it.

But he never pried. That was not the nature of their relationship, or at least not yet. If he started to psychoanalyse Laurie, he'd find himself kicked off the police psych roster and literally booted out of the taxi.

Some people couldn't be helped until they asked for it. It was not his place to push her.

'I guess it hasn't,' he said, 'in which case we'll both be drinking alone tonight.'

Laurie nodded. 'I guess so,' she said, sounding none too happy about it.

'Feel free to text me if you run out of cider and want some grown-up wine.'

Laurie laughed and punched him in the leg.

'Thanks,' she said, her eyes sparkling. 'But cider will have to do.'

CHAPTER FORTY-THREE

Eva's grogginess faded in the cool air. A biting wind tore across the valley, whipping dust up from the road in front of her. Her eyes strained as she stared into the distance. Tree-topped hills stretched out as far as she could see, hazy where they blended with the dark skies.

She'd been led from the house before dawn. Natalia was nowhere to be seen, nor Tomas. *Don't worry*, they'd said. *You're one of us. You're safe now.*

One of us.

'This way.' A thin man led her along the road. He wouldn't meet her eyes and barely spoke. The road snaked upwards towards the higher ground before stopping abruptly in front of another small building, much smaller than the house they'd left, concrete this time, standing odd against the empty landscape, perched in front of an artificial-looking grass mound with a number of metal pipes protruding from the top. All around the mound was more concrete, empty and cold.

Eva followed, her feet scuffing as she dragged them, her head spinning with fatigue and confusion.

Daylight was breaking, although the time was hard to determine, the sky thick with cloud. The man was a good deal ahead of her. She turned, but there was nothing behind except a dense treeline, the single road escaping back into the forest.

A thump. A screech in the wind. Eva turned back to see the single metal door in the building swing wide. A light flickered on inside. As she approached, she saw a caged lift, the doors sliding open, welcoming them in.

The man nodded. He stepped into the lift and beckoned to Eva to follow.

One of us, she thought again.

Her choices had reduced with every hour, her resilience shattered – she supposed that was the intention. But she held on to the glimmer of hope that Natalia had given her.

Your life will be different from this point on.
There are others like you, and this is where you belong.
The answers are here, Eva. In this place.
These are your comrades.

The lift doors closed with no squeaks, no rust. It was clearly well used, but started with a jerk, the exposed chains and cables turning and flexing as the ground disappeared above them. The walls of the shaft were too dark to focus on, but Eva tracked their progress by the lights sunk into the concrete, flashing at one-second intervals.

Fifteen seconds and the lift slowed, jolting to a stop.

The doors slid open and a wall of figures appeared, framed by a dark tunnel that stretched into the distance behind them. Dim lights kept most of the faces hidden, until one of them stepped forward. He wore a long white coat with silver buttons and a stethoscope draped around his neck. His yellow tie was fastened loosely, the top button of his collar undone. A name badge was clipped to his chest. His face was pale and wrinkled, his eyes obscured by frameless glasses. What hair he had left was white and greasy.

Eva tried but failed to grasp his thoughts. Much as with Natalia and Tomas, she experienced a wall of white noise interfering with her ability. She sensed his anticipation, his excitement, but the words failed to form, his facial expressions and body language dulled and confusing.

His lips puckered, not in a smile, but with a flicker of recognition. The sight of him caused Eva to tense, her mind and body reacting to something primal – a warning triggered by memory.

Altogether different, and yet frighteningly familiar.

Eva gasped as the memories jostled for position.

'Eva,' he said. 'This way, please.'

Eva allowed herself to be led along the tunnel, shadowed by four orderlies in white scrubs, who stayed close, barring her exit, only enabling her to keep moving. The doctor paced along in front of her, whisking them through an increasing maze as the tunnels branched off in every direction. The left-hand wall along their route was stacked high with boxes, some open, containing shrink-wrapped packets, about the size of a pack of sugar. Several men were filling boxes, sealing the contents with rolls of plastic wrap and tape. She peered at them but was hurried onwards.

The group paused periodically at huge steel doors that were unlocked by armed guards to let them through and then locked behind them. The doors looked old, dug into the rock and concrete, creaking and screeching as they opened. Five barriers between her and the surface now, the number of men with guns increasing at each checkpoint, gaunt but alert as they sucked on their cigarettes. Her eyes remained on the doctor's back, trying to control the flashes of memory. Trying not to admit to herself that she'd heard his voice before, many years ago. That accent – thick, with a hard *g*. Not Russian, but harder than Spanish or Italian in sound. It teased her memory but didn't catch. Eva knew it, but couldn't place a name to it.

They walked for ten minutes or so, weaving left and right at crossroads in the tunnels before finally stopping. This particular tunnel opened out into a cavernous space where bright lights dazzled her eyes after the darkness of the tunnels. The walls had been painted white, but a long time ago, the paint peeling now from the floor up to waist height, the damp visible as a slimy sheen on the bare concrete beneath. A drip of water echoed in the background as Eva scanned the room. It was living quarters designed for many people, a long time ago. Now there was a long Formica table with wooden benches on either side, a kitchen area with a steel sink and oven, and an array of ripped and mismatched chairs lined up in front of a blank wall.

There was nothing else. No books or magazines. No toys or TV. Worse than the communal areas in the hospital by a long shot. Eva shivered.

'This is Section E,' said the doctor. 'Sleeping quarters are through there.' He pointed to the far side. Another tunnel. 'Fifth on the right, although most of the others are empty. I . . .' The doctor tailed off. He seemed distracted, reluctant.

'Where's Natalia?' said Eva. She noticed a couple of the orderlies stepping away, heading back the way they'd come. Two others remained behind her. The doctor frowned. Eva found her fists curling in fear and frustration. 'She said . . . she said she'd give me answers. Tell me what I am. What happened to me.'

The doctor cleared his throat.

'She said I might find out where my family are.'

The doctor looked shocked. He hid it well, but his eyes darted and he licked his lips. He glanced at one of the lights. Eva saw an almost imperceptible shrug of his shoulders. He stepped back and Eva heard one of the orderlies shuffling closer.

'I don't know who you're talking about,' he said. 'There's nobody here by that name, although . . . our organisation is large. I don't know everyone.' His expression switched as he gave a forced smile.

'But . . . answers, yes. We will give you those in time. When you've finished.'

Eva found the doctor's demeanour increasingly uncomfortable. He was scared and distracted, as if Eva was unwelcome. Where was the friendly greeting? Where were the comrades Natalia had promised? *Like-minded people*, she had said. *Come in from the cold to where you belong.*

This wasn't right.

'What do you mean, *finished*?' she asked.

His fake smile twisted and disappeared. He tilted his head. 'Your treatment, Eva,' he said. 'We never finished your treatment. That's why you're here. We've been told to start again.'

Eva didn't remember her reply. One minute the doctor was standing in front of her, the next everything went black and she woke on a hard mattress, staring up at a dirty concrete ceiling. A single lightbulb was covered by a wire cage holding several dead insects. A large cockroach carcass was curled into one corner.

Eva shivered and rolled herself awkwardly into an upright position.

A bedroom. A concrete box, although larger than the one in which she'd been punished by Dr Naylor. More like a prison cell.

Smaller than her room at the hospital, it held a metal bed, a metal chair and a metal cupboard, all fixed to the wall. The walls were blank except for two posters hung near the door. One looked to be instructional and was covered in red and white type, in Russian, Eva assumed. The other was in English – a film poster for *The Sound of Music*, faded and curling at the edges. The actress, Julie Andrews, held forever as she pranced in the centre. Eva knew the film. It was standard fare in psychiatric wards, played in the rec rooms on repeat until anyone still sane was driven mad, along with the others. The girls would all sing along, picturing themselves on the hills with Julie. Most couldn't sing to save their worthless lives.

The door to her room was open and she stood a while, listening. A rustling sound, the clink of a spoon against crockery. A low voice. Eva took a breath and followed the sounds back out into the large recreation area. The doctor and orderlies were nowhere to be seen, but a young girl in pigtails sat on her own at the table, spooning something into her mouth. She looked up as Eva entered and smiled a toothless smile.

Eva paused at the end of the table, with its cracked plastic finish, leaning forward, staring at this young girl, who couldn't have been more than nine or ten years old. She wore a floral dress, vintage blue with a white frilly collar. Her face was white, with small dimples, and marked all over with scars and scratches.

The more Eva stared, the wider the girl smiled. Her grin was unnerving, fixed and silent. Eva studied the child's face, the minute fast twitches and the slower pulsing of her chest as she sucked in small, shallow breaths. Eva realised within a few seconds this was no ordinary girl. She gave off flashes of emotion – curiosity and excitement – but these were muddled and flipped to fear and back again in the same breath. Words tried to form in Eva's mind, but they danced and disappeared. She huffed.

'You're one of the mirrors,' said the girl. Her voice was small and high-pitched, but friendly. She spoke slowly and firmly, placing her spoon on the table. Her cornflakes grew soggy in the milk.

'Mirrors?' said Eva. 'What do you mean?'

The girl tittered. She looked puzzled. 'There were three of us,' she said, 'but the other two . . .' She seemed suddenly disturbed, her head and eyes darting around, checking the corners of the room. She glanced at the lights. Eva read a deep fear pulsing out of her, violent and immediate.

She shook her head. 'No,' she said to herself, still shaking her head. 'I won't talk about that.'

Eva's skin tingled as she watched the young girl mutter to herself, catching the rapid flips in mood, but then she seemed to settle again and her head remained still. Her smile returned, wider than before.

'Like a monkey,' she said. 'A monkey yawning.' She tittered again.

'I don't understand,' said Eva, failing to return the smile, increasingly freaked out by the girl. 'Where are your parents?'

The girl's smile froze. Her eyes held Eva's and the noise crowded her once again, a flood of nonsense.

'My name is Autumn,' she said. 'Mirrors in our heads. Like the monkey. Monkey see, monkey do.'

Autumn picked up the spoon and started shovelling the cornflakes into her mouth. Milk dribbled out, splashing on to the table and her frock. She narrowed her eyes at Eva.

'From the right angle you can see inside,' she said. 'I can too. Have you not been to lessons yet? Silly me. You just got here. On a boat. In a car. From a house. From a van. From a hospital. From a . . . Mmm . . .' She tilted her head. 'Are you hungry?'

Eva staggered back, her head spinning. 'What did you . . . ?' It couldn't be. Eva couldn't allow it.

'I can do it too,' said Autumn. She studied her bowl. 'Yuk. All soggy.' She dropped her spoon in the bowl and rested her chin on her hands.

'Mirror, mirror, on the wall,' she said, and started laughing.

Eva swallowed, her stomach twisting. Is this what Natalia meant? Was this girl like her? Had she been through the same horrors? Could she do the same as Eva?

Autumn snorted. 'Oh no, I'm way better than you,' she said, turning to Eva. The glint in her eyes was terrifying in its intensity. 'I'm top of the class, they told me. You're . . . bottom, I guess. There are only the two of us now.'

She paused for a moment, looking pleased with herself, before her eyes suddenly widened in horror. She stared at Eva with renewed fervour.

'Oh, you're an angry one. Fabien was an angry one.' Her face dropped. 'But he's gone now.'

She gasped, slapping one hand to her mouth as if what she'd said was forbidden. She sank back into her seat, her small chest rising and falling with deep, rapid breaths.

Eva watched as Autumn descended into hyperventilation. She ran over, putting her hands on the girl's shoulders.

'Calm down,' urged Eva, trying to straighten the girl's body, but Autumn was bent almost double now, gasping for air. She brought her hands to her own face and plucked at her cheeks, digging her short nails into the fragile skin. Her existing scratches opened up and Eva could immediately see what had caused the scarring.

'Stop!' shouted Eva, seeing her fingers draw blood. 'Stop it!'

'I can't,' wailed Autumn, curling into a ball on the chair, head on her knees, her hands gripping her face so hard her knuckles turned white. Blood dripped from her fingertips and on to the pale skin of her legs.

Eva let go and stepped back. The shock of seeing Autumn hurt herself was only marginally more terrifying than what this girl must be.

Footsteps thundered in the tunnel. Eva had no idea what to do next and stood helpless as two orderlies headed straight for Autumn, lifting her off the chair in one swift movement and forcing her to the ground. One of them pulled a small syringe from his belt and plunged it into Autumn's leg, while the other held her hands away from her bloodied cheeks.

Whatever the drug, it acted fast. Autumn's eyes rolled backwards and she slumped, unconscious.

'Is she OK?' said Eva, shaking all over. 'Her face . . .'

Without a word, the orderlies picked Autumn up off the floor. One of them slung her over his shoulder and then they both headed back to the tunnel, the way they'd come in.

'Hey!' said Eva. 'I said, is she OK?'

They continued to ignore her, walking at pace. Eva followed at their heels, asking the same question over and over. She was met only with silence and the thud of their footsteps until they came to one of the steel doors. It screeched open and they went through. One of them turned to Eva and wagged his index finger at her. He lifted a syringe with his other hand.

Eva got the message loud and clear. She stopped abruptly and stepped back to let the door close, touching the cold steel before slipping to the floor. She tucked her knees into her chest and forced her breathing to slow.

One of us, she thought, Natalia's words bounding around in her head.

An angry one . . . but one of us.

CHAPTER FORTY-FOUR

Eva didn't see anyone for hours. She headed back to the communal area, trying hard to put the vision of Autumn's bloody face out of her mind. She distracted herself from the rising panic by hunting through the cupboards for food and found them well stocked with familiar cereals and bread, tins of baked beans and soups. She took a couple of slices of bread and forced them down with a glass of water. It tasted metallic, but was cold and refreshing.

A mirror, she thought. *One of several.*

Eva picked a chair, one with a floral pattern, the orange faded on the seat to a pale yellow, mixed with a dirty white. There were no books, no TV, nothing to occupy her mind. She wondered if that was the point.

They came for her just as she began to doze off.

'Walk with me, Eva.'

A voice behind her, startling her back into the present. She turned, her defences up. It was the same doctor as before, the same accent. He wore a blue tie this time, not yellow. She noticed his white overcoat was grey and stained. He looked tired. This was no NHS hospital. This was even worse.

'Where are we going?' she asked.

'To have a chat.' He smiled again, but made little effort with it. Maybe once upon a time his smile had been genuine with a patient. Not any more.

'We can have a chat right here,' said Eva. 'Where is Natalia?'

The doctor's smile never wavered but his eyes sank deeper into their sockets. 'I've told you already I don't know who that is.'

'Alright then . . . Where's Autumn?'

No response. The doctor beckoned for her to follow.

Eva paused. What would be the point of resisting? She'd come here out of choice. It was a limited choice, given the circumstances, but nonetheless she had agreed to follow Natalia.

She was one of them.

She glanced past the doctor and saw the white suit of an orderly, doing a bad job of staying out of sight in the tunnel.

'What's your name?' she said.

The smile dropped altogether. He glanced at the ceiling. 'I'm Dr Brown.'

Eva saw the lie but little else, his thoughts masked behind the wall of white noise. So they knew her name, but she wasn't allowed to know theirs.

Had Natalia been lying? Had Tomas?

Eva slid out of the chair and followed Dr Brown back along the dark tunnel to the first steel door. This time they turned right. The floor sloped downwards here, deeper into the earth. The temperature increased with each step, becoming warm and muggy.

They walked in silence for a few moments, only their footsteps echoing against the walls, out of time with the orderlies, who followed at a distance. As the floor levelled out Eva thought she heard another sound, a high-pitched scream, followed by a low sobbing. She stopped, craning her neck.

'Keep moving, please,' said Dr Brown. The sobs faded. Perhaps she had never heard them.

Eva nodded. Almost certain now, although it couldn't be. It had been such a long time ago; her memory must be playing tricks on her. That voice – she recognised the accent so clearly. Her heart skipped a few beats.

'What's down here?'

'A place we can talk.'

'Just talk?'

The doctor sniffed. He shook his head. 'Mostly. I need a baseline. Do you understand?'

'No.' Eva shook her head, although the word was familiar.

'We need to understand how far you've deteriorated. What you have left. Where to start. Do you see?'

'Deteriorated?'

Dr Brown kept walking.

'Why did she call me a mirror?' Eva repeated the question. 'That little girl. Autumn. It's what she called me.'

Dr Brown stopped in his tracks. He sniffed again, as if testing the air, before turning to Eva. 'She's bright,' he said. His eyes narrowed. 'She listens. So should you.'

'But what did she mean?'

The doctor tilted his head. He folded his arms, examining her face. 'You should know this. You were told, although that was long ago.'

Eva didn't remember, and the doctor seemed distracted. He swatted the air in front of him. 'Damn flies,' he said. Then more quietly, to himself. 'Even down here, the flies . . .'

Eva waited. Another faint scream echoed through the tunnels. Dr Brown's head turned in the direction of the sound.

'It's a blessing,' he said. 'Such a blessing. A miracle. Hyper-developed mirror neurons – so sensitive.'

Eva stared at his eyes. Their gaze flicked here and there, almost manic. Eva knew what people on the edge looked like, and he wasn't far off. The words meant nothing. She thought she knew what neurons were, but she'd never admit her ignorance. She knew what she could do.

He leaned in, his eyes darting all over her face, reflecting the harsh lights from the ceiling. 'Your cortex.' He tapped her forehead. 'It's incredible, yes?'

His eyes stopped somewhere around her nose.

'Why can't I read you?' she asked.

This seemed to amuse him. 'Ah,' he said, wagging his finger. He turned and strode off along the tunnel. 'We're not stupid, you know.'

The silence of the tunnel was gradually broken by a background cacophony of sounds. Eva heard the hum of machinery, the squeak and shuffle of feet and the unmistakable sound of young voices. Children's voices.

Footsteps approached. Light, but fast. The doctor paused, listening intently.

A boy hurtled out of the relative darkness, nearly bowling straight into Eva. He skidded to a halt and stopped to catch his breath. He was as tall as Eva, lanky, dressed in small shorts and a white vest.

'Don't run!' he hissed at Eva. His eyes were wide and bloodshot, his pupils dilated. He peered at her for a second and sparks went off in her head. She shuddered, her muscles twitching as he stared. Her ears started ringing.

'Whatever you do, don't run,' he repeated. 'They'll find you.'

He dodged to the side and sprinted onwards, screaming as the two orderlies stepped out to block his path. They threw their arms around him and wrestled him to the floor.

Eva gulped, watching as the boy was subdued, his arms brought behind his back, his face planted on the concrete. One of the orderlies produced a syringe, but Dr Brown stopped them.

'Let him be,' said the doctor. 'He'll calm down in a few minutes.'

The orderlies glanced at each other but released their grip on the boy, who jumped up and ran off.

'They always bring you back!' Eva heard him shriek as he disappeared along the corridor and out of sight.

Dr Brown continued, apparently unperturbed and not bothered about explaining any of this to Eva.

Eva registered her heart rate. Her palms were sweating and she wiped them on her trousers. The temperature increased. The darkness of the tunnel began to recede as it opened up, wider here, with several arched passageways leading into a series of large cavernous rooms carved out of the bare rock. Harsh lights hung from the ceiling and the whirr of machinery increased – huge fans set into thick metal pipes, blowing the hot air through the tunnels. The sounds of people talking and moving about now flooded her ears.

Dr Brown paused at the entrance to each cavern, allowing Eva to look, before leading her on to the next. The first was empty, just a brightly lit hole in the earth, about the size of a school hall.

Eva stifled a gasp at the second.

Similar in size, it held banks of wooden tables and benches, most of them empty. One long table was lined on both sides with small children, no more than five or six years old perhaps, seated shoulder to shoulder, all dressed in white shorts and vests. Each of them stared down at a clipboard holding a stack of papers with pictures on them. Eva stared at the tiny faces, the eyes focused in extreme concentration as they flicked through the sheets.

A couple of orderlies stood off to one side, talking in hushed tones. One held a tablet and periodically swiped the screen, pausing now and then to sweep her gaze over the assembled group.

The little ones looked scrawny and underfed, their hair long and unkempt. They were talking, but not to each other, whispering at the pictures in front of them. The collective sound of so many children murmuring sent a shiver through Eva with the rise and fall of their small lungs, the hiss of their tongues as the words escaped. The echoes bounced from the rocky walls, creating a stifling flood of sound that crept under her skin.

More than anything, however, Eva was swamped with fragments of emotion. The children radiated a complex and primal noise right across the spectrum. She sensed fear and terror, but also excitement and achievement – a bizarre blend of thoughts in their little heads – and Eva struggled with some fascination to filter the detail from the general clamour.

'Keep moving,' said Dr Brown. He was eyeing her curiously. 'We don't like to distract them mid-lesson. It takes forever to settle them afterwards.'

Eva tore her eyes and ears away, and finally her feet.

'What are they . . . ?' she whispered.

'They're orphans, bless them,' said Dr Brown, without looking back. 'We do what we can for them. This country doesn't have the services I expect you're used to. It's very sad.'

He indicated a third cavern off to their left, the steel door left open, flat against the wall. This time Eva peered in, scared of what she might see. The cavern was smaller than the first two, no bigger than a classroom.

A child was sitting there, all alone at a desk with her back to the door. She was taller, older than the others, with long hair down to her waist. Her head hung low and Eva could see the heaving of her chest.

'She's crying,' said Eva. There was no one else in the room.

The girl's head spun around. Her face was streaked with tears, her eyes wide and bloodshot. Her mouth hung open, with lips swollen and yellow teeth bared.

'Get out!' she hissed.

Eva took a step backwards, seeing and feeling the hostility. This girl was angry, with a deep fury that simmered, ready to boil over. Eva recognised it in an instant and her guard came up, her arms tensing. Eva knew that rage and what it was capable of.

'Come along,' said Dr Brown. 'Leave Mabel. She gets like this.'

Eva backed away slowly. Dr Brown spun on his heels and kept walking. Eva followed, checking behind her at intervals until she was sure the girl called Mabel wasn't following her.

'We can help,' said Dr Brown.

'With what?' said Eva.

'The anger,' he said. 'The rage. I know it's in you – I can see it. Trust me. So many of the children have it: a product of such a sad upbringing. Losing your parents at such a tender age takes its toll. We do what we can for the children placed in our care, so they can become strong and able citizens with a bright future.'

Trust him? The words almost made her laugh out loud. Almost. Eva hadn't trusted anyone since she was old enough to know what it meant. She rarely met anybody worth trusting. Only two people might have earned that privilege in the last year – the Russian woman was one of them, although, given the last few hours, Eva realised with a crushing disappointment that the trust had been misplaced. The second was Dr Madison, the man who had come to rescue her. He had innocent intentions. He would have been worthy of her trust.

She should have trusted him above all else – she could have done, but she'd chosen a different path.

Eva remained silent as the tunnel darkened again, narrowing until it terminated in a single door. Set into the wall on the right was an array of pipes and vents, all leading into and through the rock. They were labelled, but not in English.

The doctor released a heavy bolt and pushed, using his weight to swing open the door. Eva followed him through. The room was dim, but she saw people moving, orderlies and other doctors. They were fussing over something near the back wall, in the shadows. She waited while the doctor swung the door closed and turned on the light.

Eva's knees sagged. She staggered, reaching out for something to hold on to, but felt only the cold rock of the wall. She turned, but the door had already slammed shut, blocking her escape. Dr Brown guarded the catch, poised, his eyes wary.

In the periphery of her vision Eva saw three orderlies approach her. They held their hands out as if to corner a rabid animal, ready with a cage.

But they had something far worse than a cage.

Eva backed against the wall and a groan escaped her lips, as her breathing grew ragged. Her fists refused to clench, her energy sapped at the sight of the contraption they'd lured her down here for.

Her memories lurched forward, her vision clouding. Back full circle, back to her childhood nightmares. The doctor's voice was suddenly so clear. She hadn't wanted to believe it, but the scene in front of her was so vivid she had trouble knowing if it was real or memory. A vision of a room she'd been in so many times before.

She tried to lash out, or thought she did, but they were too fast and overpowered her quickly, her arms and legs pinned as they carried her away, stripping off her clothes and opening the hatch.

Eva was lowered into the immersion tank.

Her screams echoed for several seconds along the tunnels, reaching as far as the classrooms before fading into the darkness.

CHAPTER FORTY-FIVE

Choices. Pavel was right, and his threat wasn't lost on Natalia. She considered her position and listened to the incessant unease that had grown daily within her for months now – since well before her arrival in Spain and the discovery of Eva Jansen.

But was Eva even the tipping point? Was Alex? What Pavel wanted with Eva was obvious, but with Alex . . . that still eluded her. Nova was not known for its subtlety, and Pavel had clearly not achieved what he needed.

She'd spent the night in her room. It was large but cold, with a small bathroom of her own for privacy. The bed and pillows were new, as was the dressing table, the old guard bunks cleared out. The facilities weren't lost on her – it meant she could stay confined to the one room for several days, something she was used to, but nevertheless hadn't anticipated. Not yet.

The morning came and with it a deep sense of dread.

Natalia splashed her face with water and dressed, finding an array of new clothing in the wardrobe. They'd planned her stay here, prepared. She had to give them that. Raiding the dressing table, she stood at the window, pulling her hair back, securing it into a tight bun.

She looked out over the forest and the clearing of grass immediately behind the house, illuminated at night by floodlights, keeping the perimeter of the house secure.

She'd saved the girl only to bring her to this place, which crushed her. The feeling was deep and unsettling, increasing, whether she understood it or not, with every mention of Alex Madison.

She sucked in the anger, the betrayal. Had she known Eva was bound for Starkov all along, she might have taken a different path altogether. This was not what she had struggled for, and to wreck the young girl in this place was worse than killing her outright.

Her gut instinct had been correct, and it was time to start following it, time to lay a breadcrumb and see if he followed. She'd warned him off, but now found herself wanting him close.

There was one window of opportunity. Whatever Pavel was up to, securing Eva had diverted his attention, at least for now. His focus on Starkov might be used to her advantage.

Pavel hadn't killed Alex yet. Whatever his intentions, would he suspect she would draw him towards her? Bring him further into the fold? Use his tenacity to achieve both their goals? It might just catch Pavel off guard.

This wasn't about betrayal, but rather insurance. Securing yourself was the number-one lesson you learned as an asset, and it was time for Natalia to reach out.

She grabbed her phone, browsing through the recent documents and images – all of the material she possessed relating to Eva Jansen. Next, she drafted an email, attaching everything she had.

Alex had saved one. She might need him to save another.

She paused, waiting for her conscience to decide. Waiting for good sense to return.

It didn't.

She hit send.

CHAPTER FORTY-SIX

One of us.

The shakes didn't subside until her second can of cola. Autumn opened it for her and sat cross-legged on the floor while Eva uncurled herself in the chair.

'The sugar helps,' said Autumn, 'and I don't think they care about your teeth in here.' Another titter, but it sounded strange coming from a girl with wound dressings all over her face. Red weals on her chin marked some of the more minor scratches.

'Thank you,' said Eva. She sipped the warm fizzy drink, feeling her teeth go fuzzy, trying not to stare at the cuts.

'They don't hurt,' said Autumn. 'Oh, sorry,' she added.

'For what?'

Autumn shook her head. 'We're not supposed to read each other. None of us are supposed to do anything unless it's being studied. *Recorded.*' She glanced at the ceiling lights, then hunched down conspiratorially. 'I think they do anyway,' she whispered.

Eva followed her gaze, but couldn't see anything other than the dazzling bulbs, which seemed to pulse, her head starting to throb in return. The damp bare walls revealed nothing else. The smell of bleach was new, or at least she hadn't noticed it before. Antiseptic, medical. She shivered.

'I can't read you anyway,' said Eva.

This seemed to fill Autumn with delight. 'That's because I've been practising,' she said, smiling. 'I told you I was top of the class.'

Eva watched the bizarre mood shifts of this young girl, but couldn't shake off what had happened over the last few hours. The darkness of the tank still filled her mind, the abject terror still holding her in its grasp. She curled up again, putting the Coke to one side.

Autumn's face fell at the same time.

'They're testing you,' she said. 'Once you've been here a while, you might only get the tank once a week. The injections are every day, and the practice sessions are Tuesdays and Fridays.'

Eva swallowed but the lump got bigger. *One of us.*

'I can't . . .' she said, wondering what would happen if you didn't. 'I won't.'

Autumn uncrossed her legs and stood up, heading to the sink. Eva watched her stand on tiptoes to fill a glass of water. The young girl grasped the full glass with both hands and drank it down in one, leaving the glass on the side.

'You will,' she said, matter-of-factly. 'Everyone does.'

Eva shook her head. There was no way she was going back in the tank. They'd got her the first time, but she'd fight the second. She held that thought for a moment. Would it make any difference? Her anger and fighting had got her nowhere but here. Her world had been expanded to the point where she was no longer in control. Her comfort and superiority on the hospital wards was a distant memory of naïve arrogance.

This was her new reality. She looked at Autumn. She was one of them.

'What if I don't?' asked Eva.

Autumn rummaged through one of the cupboards. 'I wonder what's for dinner tonight?' she mused.

Eva sensed she wouldn't like the answer. She didn't push it, but wanted to keep Autumn talking, needing the distraction. To be alone with her thoughts might be too much for her. She glanced around at the empty room.

'Is it just us?' she said.

'Us?' said Autumn.

'You and me. This room. The bedrooms. Where are the others? Who else gets put in the tank? And who are those other children? I was told I was one of you.' The questions tumbled out.

Autumn grabbed the glass again, scraping it across the work-top. Her eyes darted and her shoulders tensed. Eva could feel her unease flooding the room. She'd said the wrong thing. Autumn was cowering under her troubling questions.

'They're in lessons,' Autumn whispered, barely audible. She glanced at the ceiling lights a few times. 'They're learning.'

Eva swallowed. The children in the classroom – learning what?

'Are you an orphan?' she asked, watching the young girl sink into herself. She quickly changed the subject, not wanting to be responsible for another attack of self-harm. 'Where were you before this?'

But that only made things worse. Autumn sank to the floor, shaking, but this time it was sadness radiating from her small body. Her hands stayed by her sides and she began crying in low sobs.

Eva slid off the chair to join her, feeling an unwelcome sense of responsibility for this strange young girl, who suddenly looked so normal, her eerie exterior and behaviour dissolving as she bawled her small heart out. Eva was no stranger to such things, having spent most of her life on wards with damaged young girls. Autumn was different to most of those, clearly, but Eva could recognise herself in her. How many times had she also given in to the tears?

How often had she sat and cried until all she wanted was the world to end, taking her with it?

Eva waited. Interrupting was pointless. There was no comfort she could offer – she was on the brink herself. She shuffled around, leaning against the kitchen cupboards, moving closer until, finally, their arms were touching.

Autumn's crying peaked and then petered out. She sniffed a few times before wiping her nose on the back of her hand.

'They won't tell me,' she said in the tiniest of voices. Her chest heaved with emotion, her small body wracked with grief, which oozed out uncontrollably, hitting Eva with the depths of her despair. Eva tried to read what was causing it – fragments of faces and words. The feeling of a hug, the closeness of a familiar body. The feeling of love lost.

'My mum,' Autumn whispered. 'My dad. They don't ever tell you what happened to them. They promise, but they lie. They never tell you . . .' The words faded as the sobs took hold again. Autumn buried her damaged face in her hands.

Eva watched, her stomach churning. Not that she expected the truth, not any more. Being forced into the tank again had seen off any hope of that, but to see this little girl suffering just like herself . . . To have her suspicions confirmed. Natalia had promised answers. Lies. All lies.

'Autumn.' The voice startled them both. Dr Brown, his clothing even more dishevelled than before, appeared in front of them.

Eva found herself tensing, automatically crouching in defence, while Autumn shrank back against the cupboard.

'We don't tell tales, do we, Autumn?'

Autumn trembled against Eva's arm. Slowly, she raised her face from her hands and shook her head.

'Do we?'

Autumn sucked in a deep breath. She quivered. 'No, Dr Brown,' she said. 'We don't tell tales.'

Dr Brown put his hands on his hips, towering over them like a bully. Eva knew how to deal with bullies, but she could sense Autumn's fear.

'Back to your room, Autumn,' said Dr Brown. 'Eva needs to come with me.'

Autumn nodded, shuffling away without a backward glance or a word.

Eva stared defiance at the doctor. She heard a door close somewhere down the corridor.

'Fuck you,' she said. 'You're a liar.'

Dr Brown's expression didn't change. 'I don't think so,' he said.

'I'm not going anywhere with you,' Eva said. Her leg muscles trembled, ready to spring.

'You'll come with me, Eva, every day until I say stop. Your behaviour last time was obstructive. We'll repeat until you get it right.'

Eva shook her head again. Her behaviour in the tank was nothing she could control. The claustrophobia was so extreme she'd become a different person. The red mist had descended and she'd screamed and thumped on the sides until the red had changed to black and the water had filled her lungs. She'd passed out in a fit, thrashing until her body gave up, but she couldn't control it.

Her anger was not her fault.

None of this was her fault.

Dr Brown moved closer. A crooked smile appeared at the corners of his mouth. Genuine, this time.

'Time for another dip, Eva,' he said.

CHAPTER FORTY-SEVEN

The care home was stifling hot, as always. Alex signed in at the front desk and trod the long corridor towards his mother's room. She preferred the solitude, so she said, during her more lucid moments, although the nurses wheeled her through into the common room in the afternoons, and for tea.

The corridor smelled of disinfectant and gravy, and Alex took small breaths. The care they provided was good – excellent, in fact – and his mum was in the best place possible. It didn't stop the guilt, though, of everything she'd been through. The dementia took away a lot, but some memories would never die.

Her bedroom door creaked open and the sound of the TV wafted out. Alex's mum was in her armchair, gazing in the direction of the TV, but not at it.

'Hi, Mum.' Alex didn't expect a reply, not immediately. He walked around and pulled another chair across to sit facing her, then turned the volume down a little on the TV.

'Sorry I haven't come to see you lately,' he said. He watched her eyes. They were heavy. Not a flicker. Not yet.

'And Katie's sorry too,' he added. 'She'll come to see you as soon as she can. We both . . .' He sniffed. Why bother making excuses? 'I'm sorry.'

He reached out and held her hand. It was warm and soft. He caught a whiff of something – perfume or shampoo. It was familiar, conjuring up a flash of memory – vague, just a feeling of childhood. It made him smile.

They sat for a few minutes in silence, then a few more. Alex shuffled on the seat, feeling the tiredness creeping in.

'I'm working with the police again,' he said. 'An important case.' Then, without knowing why he said it, 'There are more of them out there, Mum. I think there might be a lot more. I'm trying to track them down.'

He paused, swallowing, his mouth dry, starting to sweat in the heat.

A long moment passed before she responded.

'Be careful, Alex.' His mum's eyes focused on him. She blinked. She recognised him.

'Mum?'

'The past,' she said, screwing up her face, as if the words pained her. 'It was a different time. We did our best.'

Alex put his other hand out, cupping hers. 'You did a fantastic job,' he said, trying to think of how to keep the conversation going, to keep her in the moment. It would be fleeting, he knew it, but every second was worth it.

'It was a different time,' he said. 'You're right. You were very busy, looking after me, after Dad.' He paused, hating to mention his father, but the mention of him often helped. He'd only been gone a couple of years, but her deterioration since then had been rapid. The trauma of his death had been a major factor, her doctors were convinced of it.

'You held the family together, Mum,' he finished, running out of steam. He was so distant from her, so removed since he'd left home all those years ago. Their relationship had never been normal. His mum's mental health had seen to that, leaving him with his lifelong addiction to benzos, but he didn't blame her for any of it. Mostly, he blamed his father.

She smiled at him. 'Alex, dear,' she said, shaking her head, 'I loved you so much when you arrived.'

He smiled back. 'I expect I was a difficult baby,' he said, pouncing on the memory.

She was smiling still, although a flicker of uncertainty now crossed her face. 'I expect you were,' she said. 'I expect you were.'

Alex squeezed her hand. These moments were the hardest – when she saw through the fog and knew what she'd forgotten. Sometimes it irritated her, the confusion turning to anger, but today she seemed serene.

They sat for several minutes in silence. Sometimes he sat for an hour or more like this, just being there, thinking of things to say, starting conversations that quickly went nowhere. The clock ticked on the wall and the chat show mumbled on in the background. A bell sounded out in the hall. It was an alert for the carers – dinner would be served shortly, and they'd start to bring everyone through.

His mum jumped at the sound of it.

'Is your father with you?' she said, straining her neck, trying to see behind the chair.

'No,' said Alex, never sure how to answer. Sometimes she knew he was dead, sometimes she didn't.

'Oh,' she said, 'that's a shame. Dinner's nearly ready.'

She turned back, peering at Alex. He saw the recognition had disappeared in an instant. Her smile dropped and she pulled away her hand.

'Are you new?' she said. She shook her head, fragile and scared.

Alex swallowed the lump in his throat but managed to keep his smile. She might come back again today, she might not. He stood and leaned over, giving her a kiss on the forehead.

There was a soft knock at the door and a nurse poked her head in. She mouthed the word *dinner* to Alex.

'Love you, Mum,' he said, grabbing his coat. He'd wouldn't leave it so long until next time. 'See you soon.'

◆ ◆ ◆

Alex drove home in a flood of mixed emotions – the same way he always felt when leaving his mum. She was another of Nova's casualties – several times removed, but still a victim. His father had been consumed by his passion and his evil acts. His mother was a product – not in the usual sense for Nova, but still a product of their activity. Her mind had been destroyed through neglect, by a husband who treated her as a servant and ignored her needs. How was she expected to achieve anything else in such an environment? Alex had broken free, but that had been luck more than anything his father had done for them.

He slammed the front door, trying to contain his growing anger. His phone buzzed with a new email notification, a welcome distraction. He pulled it out and blinked twice, reading the sender. Spam, he thought, although why it hadn't been filtered out was a mystery – the sender's address was a string of random letters and numbers at a Gmail account.

But then he read the subject.

Eva.

Suddenly alert, he hurried through to the kitchen, grabbing a notepad. A mystery sender direct to his personal inbox. He had no doubt this came from the same sender as last time. Would this disappear, like the last message? There was nothing much he could do, except try to screenshot as much as he could.

He held his breath and tapped to open the email. The message was short:

Things are not as they appear. What are your intentions?

It was unsigned, but the email had an attachment. Keeping both eyes on the phone, Alex backed out and headed to his study. Not daring to put his phone down, he logged on to his laptop with one hand and opened his email. It was still there. He placed his phone on the desk and turned his attention to the laptop.

With a single click he downloaded the attachment – a formatted text file. He stared at the message again.

Rhetorical? A follow-up to the text message and the video? Or was it real and expecting a reply? What would happen if he didn't? What would happen if he did?

He swallowed and his left hand shook, rattling the space bar. He gripped his wrist, aware that his heart was racing.

Opening the attachment, he forced his elbows on to the desk and cupped his chin in his hands.

Westpoort Operations. Project Progress Report. August 5th, 2005.

Alex scrolled down, trying to make sense of what he was reading. It was translated into English, the words often jumbled and out of order, but the more he read, the more it made sense. More than sense, it was familiar. He'd read similar reports before, and his skin prickled at the memory.

This was a periodical medical report of a human trial, which took place in Westpoort, Amsterdam, some fifteen years ago. It was incomplete. There were no details of the subjects other than an alphanumeric reference, and the pharmaceutical details section was missing altogether. This report was observational. A behavioural update following a series of 'twenty-four-hour immersions'.

Immersion in what? Alex scrolled and found his answer: sensory deprivation tanks. For twenty-four hours? That was insane. He scrolled further. His phone buzzed in the background with an incoming call. He ignored it.

Subject A-13 confirmed elevated activity in the Broca's area on post-immersion EEG.

Alex frowned. The Broca's area was the language centre of the brain. Located in the posterior section of the left frontal lobe, it was normally examined for reduced function as a result of trauma, rather than elevated function. Brain tumours often caused damage to the Broca's area, resulting in severe language and speech issues.

It was frequently studied, but a lot remained unknown. As far as Alex could recall, this part of the brain was instrumental in coordinating the processing of speech prior to articulation – helping to put thoughts into words. It was the speech in your mind rather than motor functions that actually made your mouth and larynx move.

Alex held the questions forming in his head. From experience, this would be uncharted territory, and they would not necessarily record the details if it might mean later reprisals. This was fringe medicine, and highly illegal.

But the effect had been wider than in the Broca's area. Alex read on. The sensory deprivation combined with the drug regimen was giving the subjects an elevated empathetic affinity for bodily signals – physical micromovements, smells, sounds and an extreme sensitivity to electrical impulses. Alex skimmed through for further details. Just how sensitive, exactly? To the point of reading someone else's brain activity? But that was . . .

Alex had learned over the last two years not to utter the word 'impossible'. If this report was as genuine as the others, this experiment appeared to be rapidly conditioning the subjects' frontal lobes into becoming hugely overactive. That meant hyper language skills, motor skills, empathy, memory formation . . . The frontal lobe was responsible for most of the functions that made one uniquely human. To mess with that on such a brutal scale was frightening.

Here the report stopped. This was one month out of God knows how many, but the message was not lost on Alex.

Alex's phone buzzed again. He ignored it, scrolling on to the next section, which did nothing to ease the tension in his gut.

> *Noted side effects if different from previous batch and schedule.*

This section was longer than the previous one. It listed side effects in much the same way a drug packet from the high-street pharmacy would do, except what might seem worrying to most people seemed routine here, with ninety per cent of subjects suffering from a range of upsets to the nervous system. Alex scanned the list: *ataxia, disturbance in attention, dizziness, dysarthria / speech disorders, dysgeusia / disruptions to the sense of taste, drowsiness, headache, paresthesia / unexplained tingling or prickling of the skin, somnolence, tremors.*

Christ, he thought, and those were just the new ones. More disturbingly, two other effects were listed in bold with cautionary notes alongside them, indicating these were likely permanent and would not subside with cessation of treatment.

In other words: lasting brain damage.

The first was a permanent claustrophobia caused by extended forced sensory deprivation. All subjects were observed to have extreme anxiety, hallucinations, temporary senselessness and signs of depression within three days of commencing the new treatment. There was no suggestion these subjects would be excluded from the experiments, simply that they were suffering.

The second permanent effect made Alex sit a little more stiffly in his chair. He swallowed, his hand shaking, the tremor responding to the words on the screen.

Sudden-onset violent behaviour. Seventy per cent of subjects had random violent outbursts resulting in physical and psychological harm to themselves and others. Sedation was encouraged. The root cause was suspected as unspecified dysfunction of the frontal lobe, which on investigation appeared due to the unpredictable shift in cognitive-neuropsychological functions within the lobe. It was irreversible and would likely worsen with age.

The notes ended there, and a single black line across the page denoted the end of the report. Underneath were a series of boxes for dates, roles and signatures, all of them empty.

Alex let out a long breath, realising he'd been holding it. Eva after Mia after Victor – a series of products of brutal human experimentation. This one had got away, but someone was keeping her close.

Eva Jansen. A mind reader and a ticking time bomb of violence. *What are your intentions?*

CHAPTER FORTY-EIGHT

Natalia sat under the shade of a pine tree at the back of the guard-house. The evening was warm, the air pleasantly fresh and full of scent, yet still she shivered. Could she hear the screams of Starkov from here, or was it her imagination? She could almost feel the narrow tunnels squeezing her breath away.

As in Madrid, the deceptively calm surroundings were shadowed by the events unfolding within them. Moments of appreciation were few and far between, broken by the harsh reality of her predicament.

She took a deep breath, glancing at the screen of her laptop, wondering what to do with the file in front of her. In the last forty-eight hours one of her searches – a delve into the archives – had revealed something odd. Her access was still unrestricted: Pavel's trust in her remained intact. A shortening of the leash hadn't changed that.

She was still one of them.

For how long was up to her.

The file on the screen was a top sheet, referring to a paper archive buried deep in the vaults. She'd been staring at it for an hour and finally summoned the courage to reply.

She tapped out her message, asking for the full paper record to be retrieved and sent to one of her private mailboxes in central Munich, far away from here. It was probably nothing, but Natalia's world was based on information and the control of it. Whatever it revealed might be useful, depending on which way she eventually fell.

The winds of change were blowing, all the way from the freezing slopes of Siberia towards the west and beyond. Natalia sensed it in Pavel and the way in which he had crafted his meeting with her. Sending Eva into Starkov was an extreme message that would be heard far and wide. His personal interest in Alex Madison was a puzzle. The handlers were already twitchy and the assets were closing ranks. Natalia needed to draw her defences closer, check her actions and be very, very careful about her next steps.

Deep in thought, she headed back towards the house. Her phone rang and she checked the screen before answering.

'Tomas,' she said, ducking into the pantry near the back door. She pulled it closed and lowered her voice. 'It's good to hear from you.'

Tomas had been sent home, but said he was safe, as much as any Nova agent could be. Handlers were valuable too, and Natalia was confident he'd be reassigned soon enough. Another asset would be tracked down. Another product of Nova's historical activities would be judged worthy of joining the ranks. Another comrade to be *brought in from the cold*.

'I need to tell you something,' he said.

'What?'

'The girl. Eva.'

His tone put Natalia on alert. She checked the corridor and then the kitchen, before sealing herself back in the cool of the small pantry. The scent of vegetables and herbs filled the air.

'She's out of my control, Tomas,' she said. 'She's in Starkov and I've been stood down, as you have. Move on.'

Tomas cleared his throat. 'She isn't . . . that is . . . they're having a few problems with her.'

'I'm not surprised,' said Natalia. No one should be in that place, she thought, its tunnels of torment decades old, its testing rooms more abhorrent than the very worst torture chambers human history could offer. Natalia had survived, but she doubted its methods had improved. The decision to send Eva there had been vile and unnecessary.

'She's . . .'

'Uncooperative? Violent? I can't help. I wish I could.' Natalia didn't know why she hid her true feelings towards Eva from Tomas. Perhaps because they were so confused; perhaps they'd make her appear weak. All Natalia saw was a younger version of herself, and her new-found inability to affect her welcome into Nova was hitting her harder than she'd anticipated.

'Natalia, *listen*! They performed a baseline. It's not good.'

Natalia caught his tone. He had many, most of them jovial, but on occasion Tomas was deadly serious, his voice low, barely above a whisper. She leaned against the worktop of the pantry, suddenly wary.

'Why?' she asked, her stomach suddenly plummeting. 'What did they find?'

'Irrecoverable.'

He said it softly and let it hang. Natalia gripped the phone so hard it flexed in her hand. She turned, full of nausea, and slammed the other hand down on the worktop, the thud sounding hollow and pointless in the restricted space.

It couldn't be. Starkov was as bad as it could get, she was sure, the news hitting her like a blow to the gut, but she hadn't seen this coming. Not this.

'Irrecoverable?' Natalia's voice was raised, trembling. 'After all the shit we went through to get her?' Her shock turned to anger.

'Why? The fucking idiots. Monsters – they don't know what they're doing. Eva needs nurturing, welcoming. I told her she's one of us, for Christ's sake.'

'Whoa!' said Tomas. 'I'm only the messenger. All I know is what was on the wire. Damage to the pre-frontal cortex too extreme. Something to do with her early treatment – she was discarded too young, her medication incomplete. She has a talent, sure, but it's wrapped up in a whole violent mess of unfixable behavioural issues. Her second dunk in the tank revealed as much. They had to bring her in for obvious reasons, but they think it might be easier to start again from scratch.'

'Start from scratch?' Natalia whispered the words, clenching her jaw, because they still managed to shock her, even after all her years with Nova.

Tomas sighed. 'I knew you'd be upset. That's why I told you, rather than you hearing it later. I think Pavel was going to tell you after it was all over.'

Natalia tried to manage her myriad of emotions, but her heart was screaming at her. This was not finished. Natalia had once been in Eva's position. She'd survived Starkov, but could Eva?

'What are the chances of them changing their minds?'

A pause. 'I've never heard it happen before,' said Tomas.

'But the outcome isn't certain?' She pushed. 'What if Eva could be made to cooperate? If I could talk to her?' Natalia was grasping at straws, but felt a fresh surge of protection for the young girl she'd been responsible for bringing in. This wasn't about all their hard work going straight down the drain. It was about Eva.

'Nothing is certain,' said Tomas, his tone changed again. He knew what she was thinking.

They both fell silent for a few moments. Tomas knew her too well.

'Don't, Natalia,' he said. 'Don't go in there.' Tomas had no need to say that the risk was as much his as hers – he could be shot for having told her about Eva.

'I have to,' she said, trying to avoid revealing her own horror at the prospect, but she could see no other choice. The girl didn't deserve a life in Starkov, and she certainly didn't deserve to die there. Natalia had no firm idea of what she might do once she entered the bunker, but staying on the surface with her feet up was simply not an option.

'Goodbye, Tomas,' she said, hanging up before he could reply.

Natalia exited through the hallway and took one last glance into the garden through the rear door. She was about to turn away when a figure appeared near the trees. He was clear in the light, facing the other way, stooped and bald. Not Pavel, nor one of the handlers. Something about the man caused her to lean in, cupping her hands around her eyes against the glass to block out the reflections.

The man turned side on to her. He paused, sniffing the air. He wore wire-framed glasses. Thin, but not skinny. A slight paunch.

Natalia's heart skipped a beat. It couldn't be.

The man turned towards the house, staring straight at Natalia, his face in full view.

Natalia recoiled but met his gaze. They watched each other intently for several moments before his mouth broke into a twisted grin. He broke away finally and wandered across the back of the house and out of sight.

Natalia took a few deep breaths, shifting her gaze beyond the treeline, her curiosity mixed with apprehension.

What was Thirteen doing here? A person she'd hunted down herself, incarcerated and made damn sure would never escape again. The person Alex Madison had hunted with her. The person who had brought them together for the first time.

Ostensibly, they were comrades, but she made no move to follow him. That might be a mistake. His presence here puzzled Natalia, but her curiosity had already been stamped on once by Pavel. To question his deployment of assets might tip him over the edge.

One of the most dangerous products Nova had ever created – a mass murderer with a talent and disposition feared even by Natalia.

So what was Victor Lazar doing at Starkov?

CHAPTER FORTY-NINE

Darkness met Natalia as she stepped out of the lift and into the concrete bunker. The tunnels of Starkov would never feel familiar, but she remembered them. Her footsteps echoed against the floor, walls and ceiling, rattling into the distance, the sounds conjuring up all manner of buried horrors.

Brought in from the cold.

That's what they called it – a hangover from their Eastern origins in the frigid temperatures of Mother Russia. The tunnels weren't cold, and yet Natalia shivered with the memories. All the children shivered here. The temperature had little to do with it.

She'd told no one of her intentions, except for Tomas. With her training, covertly exiting the house and disappearing into the forest had been easy. She didn't break cover until the road terminated at the bunker entrance. Kostas would discover her absence in due course, and Pavel would decide what to do about it. Her presence in the tunnel complex at Starkov couldn't be kept a secret, but it was a test as to how far Pavel would go to keep her away. She was still a *păpușar*, and it carried authority wherever she went. Pavel could take it away in a heartbeat, but so far had not. His indecision was her opportunity.

The seed of a plan had formed as she walked, although the options narrowed in line with the tunnels. Natalia couldn't stay above ground and let this play out, let this poor girl die because of a lack of trying. Would Eva cooperate, or would Natalia need to consider a different course of action? For the first time in years, a realistic alternative to this life knocked at her door.

Could this be it? Could this be what her instincts had been telling her for months?

Natalia approached the next checkpoint, aware they'd be watching her on camera, the security in the tunnels rudimentary but robust. Heavily manned although barely automated, they relied on brute force and fear to keep people in. The odd child might escape, but the hunting parties were swift and brutal. A few of the escapees were brought back again; others were silenced in the woods.

The bunker complex was huge and layered. Four levels, each accessed from one of the surface lifts. During the Cold War all manner of official Soviet business had been conducted from the safety of these tunnels. Now, an altogether more nefarious empire had taken hold, using the bombproof security to train some of their most sensitive specimens.

The uppermost tier was reserved for other business interests operated by Nova. Lucrative fronts were run from here, some of them legal, most of them not, alongside the shipments of narcotics flowing all over the globe from this one hub. The drugs masked the real business of Starkov, and funded the research taking place on the lower three levels.

Children on one level would never meet those on another, and the deeper you went the more secure it became. Level Four was reserved for those who would never meet another soul until released or terminated – locked in a solitary cell while their treatment was administered. The screams from Level Four were rarely heard, but the children on the upper levels used to swear they could hear the vibrations through the rocks. Very few survived Level Four. Rumour had it, Pavel had been one of them.

Natalia remained on Level Two and hoped to venture no lower.

'ID, please,' demanded the guard. He sat perched on a rocky boulder protruding from the wall, sidearm in his holster. She'd only got this far because of the camera checks at the entrance. She was one of them. He didn't need to be too cautious.

Natalia waved her ID at him but knew she'd be studied on the camera. After a few seconds the guard listened on his earpiece and his eyes widened. He slid off the rock and stood to attention.

'Welcome, comrade,' he said. 'We weren't expecting you.'

'I'm here to see a patient,' she said. 'Eva Jansen.'

The guard relayed the name into his radio.

'Section E,' he said, giving her directions. 'Do you need a radio? Mobile phone boosters work, but there are many dead spots down here.'

'No,' she said, watching the door creak open. The rust was apparent, the paint long since peeling. It had struck her on the way down that the compound had fallen into disrepair. Her memories were of a place meticulously maintained, full of sharp-suited guards and throngs of people working, one of Nova's furiously productive laboratories.

Her impressions so far seemed to tell a different story. This place was a shadow of its former self. A large part of her felt optimistic at the fact.

It would make things easier.

The door swung back.

She followed the directions she'd been given. It was a ten-minute walk, during which she saw only a few orderlies pushing trolleys full of narcotics towards the lifts.

The sign for Section E was still up, bright yellow against the dark wall. The recreation area triggered a fresh wave of memories and Natalia shuddered as the long-buried anxiety tore through her body. It would never leave, but it had always been controlled. She forced a lid on it as she approached the long table at the centre. This type of room was replicated throughout the complex, a disgusting nod to normality.

Three children looked up, one girl and two boys, twins. Their eyes sparkled at the distraction, but they knew better than to speak to an adult, their learned caution keeping them crouched in their chairs, sizing her up, testing her with their immature skills.

The girl continued to slurp at a bowl of cereal, dribbling it down the front of her dress. The two boys had empty plates. One of them dropped his plastic cup, startling himself. The girl started to titter. Her face was covered in dressings.

All three were pasty and thin. Several months underground took its toll on small bodies, particularly ones punished by starvation, injected with fire and humiliated by ritual. Natalia supposed she'd once looked like this, but there were never any mirrors, back then. Appearance was not a priority until you had to venture out into the real world.

God, she hated this place, but could she follow through on the threat forming in her mind?

'Where's Eva?' she asked the three of them.

The two boys stared at the table. Natalia turned to the girl, raising her eyebrows in query.

'In her room,' she said, in a tiny, high-pitched voice. 'Will you play with me?'

Natalia smiled. 'Thank you. Maybe later.'

The girl's face fell. She dropped her spoon into the bowl and buried her face in her arms. Natalia left her sobbing as she made her way towards the sleeping quarters.

◆ ◆ ◆

The bedroom hummed with the sound of air being pumped through the ducts in the ceiling. The single harsh light blasted every crevice, reflecting off the metal surfaces. Natalia felt a headache coming on. She cleared her throat, unsure if the small figure on the bed was asleep.

'Eva?' she called. The figure stirred.

Eva turned over and opened her eyes, squinting. Her face was red and puffy, her eyes bloodshot.

Natalia waited for the recognition. It was swift, and she saw Eva's anger in a heartbeat. The girl shuffled backwards on the bed, hard against the wall, clutching her knees to her chest. Her eyes stared in hatred. Natalia knew she deserved it.

'Bitch!' whispered Eva, before clamping her mouth shut, grinding her teeth.

Natalia nodded. Anger was a useful emotion, and more productive than simple fear, which was all she had possessed when she'd first come here.

'I didn't know,' she said. It was worth a try, although she doubted Eva would believe it. Did she believe it herself? Bringing an asset in meant they would suffer somewhere, somehow. The tunnels of Starkov were among the worst, but there were others. Eva should have been spared this place.

The world should be spared this place.

But Natalia's battle had begun long before she'd been sent out to secure Eva. Bringing in another asset was just a job, but Eva had fast crystallised the doubt into certainty. Breathing in the damp, humid air of this room, Natalia knew she'd finally hit the tipping point.

'I knew you'd be taken somewhere,' continued Natalia, 'but I hoped to be with you. I was . . . waylaid by another urgent matter. For that I apologise.'

Eva's expression didn't budge and her shoulders shook with rage. Natalia would need to be on her guard. This girl was stronger than she looked, and with her type of primal psychological disturbance, once enraged she would be hard to calm down.

'I need to tell you a story,' said Natalia. It was important she knew. This is what Nova expected, what they would demand. Let the record show. At least she could say she had tried, and she needed to say it to convince herself of the next step. She sat on the far end of the bed, feeling the thin mattress hit the frame beneath. She cleared her throat.

'What you're going through is torture, I agree, but it is something all of the *păpușars* go through.'

She saw Eva frown at the word. Interested, curious. *Not dead yet.* There was an intelligence there that needed to be nurtured, far away from this place.

'*Puppet master*, Eva,' said Natalia. 'It was coined in the '80s by one of our faction and stuck. We control others – it's what I am, and it's what you'll become if you stay with us. That name is rarely used outside of closed doors, but it refers to the few of us who survived. Survived this . . .' she looked around, indicating the room, 'and much worse besides.'

She saw Eva's eyes narrow.

'Worse than this, yes,' said Natalia. 'But the results, if you *cooperate* . . .'

Natalia felt the words forming, the propaganda drummed into her at almost the same age and under very similar conditions. To survive and learn meant you would transcend all others, bringing in a new dawn of human development, ushered in by the few, transforming the multitude.

These are the words, Natalia.

She heard them in Pavel's voice. She felt his control washing over her.

The world is ours, Natalia. This is the natural path for us. Medical advancement has been stifled for too long by people too scared to push the boundaries and test the limits. Strangled by ethics committees and politicians bowing to public pressure, to the lowest common denominator. The proletariat doesn't know what it needs – it never has – and the people who do are corrupt to the core. Our organisation is following what mankind was always intended to pursue – our natural inclination to explore. Not the physical world, in our case, but the mental. The potential of the most complex machines in the universe – our brains – goes largely untapped, while the world struggles. We can end another millennium of global suffering by enduring a fraction of it ourselves. What we go through here is a means to an end, but it is the most glorious endeavour an individual can be asked to undertake.

You're one of us, Natalia. Your path has only just begun, but your cooperation is required.

Accept your suffering to save the world, Natalia.

Her eyes flickered with the memory, but the words stuck in her throat. Watching the terrified and angry young girl in front of her now, this *damaged* human, the propaganda evaporated to leave only nausea. Pavel had no influence in this moment. It was hers.

And this girl would never cooperate. She was past that point. *Irrecoverable.*

Mia Anastos would have been the same, had they brought her to this place. Natalia had had the foresight to let that one go, which had started her down this path. The foresight had been lacking where Eva was concerned, but better late than dead.

Eva's face was contorted, her anger simmering. Such rage was a frequent side effect of her treatment, and learning to control it would have involved trial and error, in an inexact science of medication and conditioning. But it was too late. Even if she were capable of cooperating and they changed their minds, Eva would be brutalised, taken to the edge and left hanging. Her anger might save her, or condemn her.

Natalia caught her breath. Pavel's words still echoed. It was her choice.

'I need to tell you . . .' What she said now could determine both their fates. Was it really as simple as this? To head down this path might finish both of them, right here in this dungeon. But Nova's promise was empty, any progress achieved directed towards something altogether different. Nova never planned to save humanity – instead it planned to dominate it. Eva's life was on the brink. Even if she survived physically, her life would never be her own. Natalia's own life so far had taught her that much – she remained a prisoner, with the whole world as her prison cell.

And it was time to break free.

Natalia couldn't allow Eva to die, but nor could she allow her to follow in her footsteps. She realised her decision had been made before they'd even arrived at the guardhouse. Before they'd even left Madrid. She knew why she had to make this call.

To save one life is to save the world.

'Here's what we're going to do,' she said.

CHAPTER FIFTY

Eva watched Natalia's behaviour unfurl, the woman's confidence descend into self-doubt and fear. The wall was still up, but less opaque than before, her emotions evident in her posture and fractured speech.

Eva fought to control her anger, listening to the confusing message as it played out. As Natalia continued, Eva found herself daring to hope that this fresh new hell wasn't the only option remaining to her. This woman had lied, but not to the extent Eva had thought.

Natalia talked for five minutes before falling silent, then leaned back against the wall, staring into nothing.

'Why?' asked Eva. The tears welled suddenly, and she sniffed, wiping her face on the back of her sleeve, a sudden rush of sadness washing the anger away. 'Why couldn't you have told me this before? I followed *you*. I trusted *you*.'

'I didn't know,' said Natalia. Eva saw her open up a fraction more. It was the truth. 'I would never have brought you in if I'd known.'

'You don't want me to die,' said Eva, 'and neither do you want me to cooperate with the people who created me. Having promised me this, you now want me to leave it. What about my childhood? You said . . .' Eva's voice cracked. Promises shattered, and yet this woman wasn't lying. There was no more deceit here.

Natalia shook her head.

'And you'd throw everything away for me?' said Eva.

'I didn't say that.' Natalia paused. 'But it's your best shot.'

'But why would he come for me?' Eva had refused him once. She didn't share Natalia's optimism.

'For the same reason he came for you the first time. But this must be your decision. If I make the call, hell will descend on this place, and when the time comes, you need to go with him. If you hesitate, they'll kill both of us.'

Eva watched the curves of Natalia's face. She was younger than she looked, but an interior battle raged. She leaked uncertainty, her rigid exterior finally cracking.

'You'll come with me?' said Eva.

Natalia shook her head. 'I can't,' she said. Her eyes dropped. 'Not yet. They're not ready for me. But you . . . this is the best chance for you, Eva.'

'You'll stay here,' said Eva, 'in this place?'

Natalia struggled and fell silent. Eva thought of all the children she'd seen. She wondered how many others there were in this labyrinth. How many like her. How many mirrors would be shattered if Natalia did what she said she was going to?

'I'll be betraying my organisation,' said Natalia. 'The people who created me, and you, and scores of others like us. They may not realise at first, but they will, and when they do, it's best if you're far away from me. Their revenge will be swift and brutal.'

Eva watched Natalia as she spoke. She radiated a brief flash of fear, but forced it away and composed herself, her mind closing once again. Eva felt it all, admired it, and wanted more of it.

But she understood, and her anger towards Natalia faded. This woman was not acting out of self-interest. She was acting out of empathy and fear and heartache and a dozen other emotions that Eva saw but couldn't grasp.

Most of all, she acted because she had the power to shift the balance ever so slightly in her favour. She realised that power and had decided to come back for her.

No one had ever come back for Eva.

'OK,' she said, easing her legs out, sliding to the edge of the bed. She rested her bare feet on the cold floor. It sent a shudder up her legs and into her spine.

There was no other path to take. To stay here would mean a fast death or a slow death, with nothing but torture beforehand. She had to leave, and Natalia had a plan.

'Let's do this,' she said. 'Call Alex Madison.'

CHAPTER FIFTY-ONE

Alex dropped the phone on the desk. Both hands were shaking this time, his heart thumping and his face flushed. He stared at the notepad, the scrawls he'd made during the thirty-second incoming call.

A location. Czechia, a set of coordinates, a single message.

Come and get her. Come and get them all.

The voice. Female, East European, smooth and silky, but urgent in her intention. Was it the voice – *her* voice? He thought so, and yet there was a fleeting feel to the memory of it. The more he tried to conjure up the sounds, the more they evaporated. He could barely recall the words, let alone recognise the person.

All he had was what he'd written down, and an overwhelming sense of urgency.

Come and get her. Come and get them all.

He forced himself to sit, screaming inside to keep the panic from taking over.

The Russian woman.

He'd attempted this so many times before, painstakingly picking apart those last few minutes when he'd lifted the bleeding body of Mia and staggered across the waste ground towards safety. This was the story he had never told – could never tell. The day he saved a murderer in the heart of London was not a tale anyone wanted to hear.

But, as with every attempt before this, his memory refused to deliver. All he could summon up were blurred fragments and incoherence. He knew what had happened, but had no clear memory of it. She'd spoken to him, offered her name even, but it was lost in the recesses of his mind, refusing to give itself up.

Deep down, he knew somehow that she wasn't acting on behalf of Nova.

She'd studied him, studied Mia, dismissed her colleague and made her decision. She'd *decided* to let Alex and Mia go free. Alex was out of options at the time, with a gun trained on his head, dead if she pulled the trigger.

Her choice back then had never made sense, but Alex had been happy to take his own life and save the girl. History was repeating itself, and this time he had nothing much to go on. The woman had offered Mia to him so he could save her. And now she was doing the same with Eva? She knew he'd come. She knew he wouldn't pass up a chance to find out more.

His heart thudded loudly as he popped out his pills and crunched one between his teeth. A muzzy head wouldn't help, but a failing body would be worse.

She'd said nothing about the police, which meant she'd expect him to use them. Alex was no Jack Reacher; he couldn't fight his way into a foreign country and save anyone. There was only one possible course of action this time.

He fumbled with his phone, finding Laurie's number. She answered on the third ring.

CHAPTER FIFTY-TWO

Conference room B in the NCA building in Vauxhall was already full when Alex walked in. Laurie stood at the head of the long table, on her phone as per usual. The screen behind her was switched off, the blinds drawn. She gave Alex the briefest of smiles and pointed to a spare chair.

Around her, Alex recognised Laurie's team from Madrid, plus a couple of new faces, who stared at him as he took his place. He'd surrendered his mobile phone on arrival and saw Hannah playing with it – connected to her laptop via a USB cable – trying to trace the call he'd received. Her expression suggested she wasn't having much luck.

The chatter died as Laurie ended her call. She turned and placed her hands on the table, staring at Alex with a wild expression, her eyes wide and her nostrils flared. She held his gaze for several seconds before turning away to address the room.

'Sorry for bringing you all in here so many times. That was my third call with Inspector Gabriel of Interpol's National Central Bureau in Prague. My first call was ignored, my second considered and rejected, and now, finally, we're talking business.'

Alex sat up straighter. In the three hours since he'd spoken to Laurie, the cogs had been turning.

'I have already shared with you Dr Madison's increasingly fascinating position of being in receipt of serious crime information before we are.' She once again stared daggers at Alex across the room. 'However, the sequence of events, the information he revealed, and the location sparked a series of high-level conversations between the UK and the Czech police. The Foreign Office was involved. Dr Madison may not realise this, but that location has sparked off an absolute shit-storm. It hit the fan and took a while to clean off. But we got there – we've agreed a way forward and it goes down tomorrow.'

The team kept their eyes on Laurie. Her tone was rousing and Alex sensed excitement levels rising all around him.

'I shared my views on the case of Eva Jansen and the antics of the trafficking organisation which we believe took her, along with the high probability that she's already been passed on to another crime syndicate. Nova.'

She looked at Hannah, who tapped Alex's phone and gave her a small nod. Alex swallowed. He needed water.

'It turns out – not surprisingly after talking to my colleagues upstairs – that the location given to Dr Madison by his mystery contact is well known to the Czechs. It's a huge narcotics hub with links to UK organised crime. Over ten thousand kilos of heroin stockpiled in numerous locations throughout the East comes into Western Europe annually through that route. This particular site' – Laurie rummaged through her notes on the table – 'Starkov, is a disused Soviet-era bunker, used as a primary storage hub, but until now, it has been largely *ignored* by our friends in Prague.'

'Ignored?' Alex couldn't help blurting it out.

'Ignored,' said Laurie. 'And I mean actively. My first two phone calls revealed as much. It was only when we got the Foreign Office involved that the Czechs reluctantly agreed it even existed.'

'You mean they know? And they do nothing?'

Laurie pulled her best *Ahh, bless him* face.

'Honestly, Alex. You'd think a few years of working with the police would have opened your eyes a little. Yep, they knew alright. It's big business and I expect it lines a lot of pockets at the local town hall, not to mention some rather bigger pockets higher up. The Czech government know all about it. They have done for years.'

'So what's changed?' said Alex, feeling his blood beginning to boil. The same sordid underbelly of humanity rippled through from Victor to Mia to Eva. First, his father's university, then a pharmaceutical company. Today, these people were operating in plain sight with police protection. Maybe Laurie was right and he was hopelessly naïve, but it still angered him.

'What changed,' said Laurie, 'is that following your tip-off – which we had no reason to trust, by the way – we told them that a British citizen, a young girl, may have been trafficked to Starkov, along with several others. It might have all come to nothing, except that the Foreign Secretary seems to have a particular bee in his bonnet about this one. He made it clear we're happy to make a public statement to the world media on how these people and drugs are seeming to find their way completely unchallenged across the Czech Republic. It'll be good for approval ratings and excellent for the party to hammer this sort of thing across Europe. The elections aren't far off.'

'So we've blackmailed them into admitting it?'

'No, we've *shamed* them into admitting it. The Czech Republic is a wealthy modern country with a booming industry. On the global stage they pretend these sordid elements are behind them – part of the old world. This could be a nasty PR issue for them and could damage their funding allocations from the European Union. Nobody wants to be called out for concealing human trafficking and drug running, period.'

Alex frowned. 'They're not suggesting they keep it covered up?'

'Subtlety does it, Alex, and no. Now this particular cat is out of the bag, the Czech government want to be the ones to reveal it. What they've suggested is a good old-fashioned raid based on an anonymous tip-off, which is not so far from the truth, with the Czech police at the helm. We'll go along as guests. If Eva Jansen is there when they bring it down, we'll bring her quietly home. If Dr Naylor is there, ditto, although from Alex's description, we don't know where she might be.

'Either way, we've forced their hand. If the operation is a success, the Czechs come out looking proactive and aggressive against organised crime. We get this young girl back and we do significant damage to the supply chain in and out of the UK.'

'So everyone wins,' said Alex.

'Exactly.'

'Except the people who've been protecting them all this time. They go free.'

Laurie shrugged. 'You take what you can get, Alex.'

Alex nodded, but he saw the same conflict as before. The police always reduced it to the simplest haul – grab the victim and arrest the most obvious bad guys you can find. Alex needed more. The woman who called him was not going to be one of the obvious bad guys. She was part of the bigger deal, part of the shared history his father had been intricately involved in, and yet still managed to keep hidden from beyond the grave. He found himself cursing his father's memory. Nova continued to play God and no one seemed willing to hold them to account.

'How far will we go?' he said.

Laurie stared through him again, seeing his soul. She shook her head. 'As far as the Czech police will let us,' she said, 'which means not as far as you'd like, Alex.'

He held her stare for a few moments before turning away, conscious of the puzzled looks from the rest of the table.

She was offering him a good result, but not the result he wanted.

The awkward silence in the room broke as Laurie's phone rang.

'Dismissed,' she said, before taking the call. Her team grabbed their kit and papers and filed out. Alex lingered.

Laurie rubbed her left temple, nodding, with the phone glued to her ear.

'Understood,' she said, hanging up.

'Trouble?'

'Hartley,' said Laurie. 'One of the doctors at St Anne's – Holly Morgan?'

Alex raised his eyebrows, his stomach sinking.

'She was found dead at her flat.' Laurie nodded to herself.

'I—'

'Nothing you can do, Alex. Not right now. I need you focused. If Eva Jansen is there, you're going to have to figure out what to do with her . . .' She paused. 'Within reason,' she added. 'Go home and grab what you need. We leave in six hours.'

CHAPTER FIFTY-THREE

'You're going where?' Grace had taken his call, her tone weary but still interested. She cared. He always called before going away. It was routine, plus he felt like he owed her.

'I can't say exactly,' he said, without knowing if it was true, 'but Eastern Europe. It's a human-trafficking case. They need me.'

'Is it related?'

'To?'

'To why your daughter and ex-wife are holed up in a pokey flat in London under police protection. Alex, we're worried . . .' Her voice cracked.

'It'll be OK,' he said.

'It's not OK, Alex! Katie is scared. I'm scared. You don't have any answers except to cover our house in cameras and watch us from the street. Human trafficking? It's creepy, Alex. It's gone too far. You're not yourself, you're . . . obsessed. Whatever you've got yourself into isn't good for you, and it's certainly not good for your family, whom you claim to love.'

Alex recoiled under the words. 'I do love—'

'I know, I know . . .' said Grace. 'I didn't mean that. I'm sorry.' She took a breath. 'It's just . . . we're on edge, and we're worried about you. This obsessive spiral of yours is destructive. I can't do this again. Katie can't do it again.'

Grace took a deep breath. Alex could hear her holding in her anger and he had nothing to say that could temper it. Had he really gone that far, so absorbed in his own work that he struggled to see it?

'Grace, I'll always love you and Katie. Nothing I do will change that.'

'But your *behaviour*, Alex. Christ, how many times? This is your profession, isn't it? How are you so short-sighted when it comes to your own actions?'

Alex couldn't answer. She was right, but she didn't have the whole story, all the facts. He'd shielded her from the worst of it – the revelations about his father, the true nature of Nova and all the events since then. If it meant she blamed him, it was a burden he'd just have to carry. He deserved it, but he couldn't fix it. Protecting her was more important.

'I wish I could tell you everything,' he said. 'There's more to it, Grace. There's a reason I'm working on these cases.' He stopped before the floodgates opened. Telling Grace everything wouldn't help either of them, but it would place a secret with Grace she'd be bound to keep.

'Because you want to, Alex. That's normally the reason you do most things.'

'No, Grace,' he said. 'Not because I want to. Because I *have* to.'

Grace fell silent for a few moments. Alex could hear noise in the background. Voices, a door slamming.

'Alex, I've got to go.'

'Everything OK?'

'Change of shift. Go on your trip, Alex. Please take care.'

'Can I speak to Katie?'

'Text her. She's in her room. She doesn't want to talk to you right now.'

Alex paused. 'I will,' he said. 'I'm doing this for her. I know that sounds crazy, but it's true. One day she'll understand.'

He heard Grace take a few deep breaths. 'Maybe she will, but be careful, Alex. She's less forgiving than I am. Don't push her beyond reach. She's weary – we both are. Do something about this. Fix this!'

'I'll try, Grace,' said Alex, wondering if finding Eva and the Russian would bring him any closer to a resolution. 'I'll try.'

CHAPTER
FIFTY-FOUR

The journey out of London was quick and by the book. Laurie was busy with constant reports and phone calls, removing any chance of a conversation with her.

She'd acknowledged his central involvement in this case, but he sensed her increasing distance. She saw a prize, and one worthy of her efforts, but Alex knew she wouldn't allow the same thing to happen as before. If Eva was there, Laurie would be the one to bring her back, not Alex. He'd provide the necessary psych support, and given the nature of her condition, that was essential. But beyond that, he read between the lines – if Eva also disappeared, there would be consequences.

The welcome at Prague Airport was cold and forced – an inspector from the NCB greeted Laurie at the gate and ignored the rest of the team. They were ushered away from the other disembarking passengers and into a Customs side room. The inspector offered them transport, a driver and one of his detectives. They'd be briefed on the two-hour journey east, then again in the staging position two miles south of the Starkov bunker complex.

Laurie was visibly frustrated at the lack of courtesy and involvement in the final raid, but the message was clear: you forced this on us, but we're in control. They were guests of the Czech police because their foreign office had insisted on it, and for no other reason.

They were given thirty minutes to track down their luggage and any refreshments. There would be no food at the forward base.

'They're jumpy as hell,' said Laurie as they headed towards the pick-up zone outside. Alex walked beside her with Terry, Hannah and Josh following close behind. The five of them had been given permission to come; the rest of her unit would be watching from the UK, keeping the top brass informed as the situation played out.

'It's too rushed,' said Alex.

Laurie shook her head. 'I think Inspector Gabriel is honest, but he knows this operation will have been leaked the moment we called them. If the people running Starkov haven't been tipped off about the raid yet, they will be soon – it's only a matter of time.'

Alex frowned. 'We can't lose her again, Laurie.'

'Which is why they're going in quickly. Within twenty-four hours is the aim – before everything can be cleared. They want the drugs and the people.'

'In that order?'

'Don't make this about you, Alex. They want both. None of the honest cops here want to see these shitheads get away with it . . .'

'But a pile of drugs looks good on camera,' said Alex.

'That it does,' said Laurie.

They climbed into a police minibus and the driver pulled away from the airport, heading in the direction of the Polish border. Beyond the airport and the industrial parks the landscape was blanketed by thick countryside as the east of the Czech Republic welcomed them. Evening drew in, and the fading sun and low cloud lent everything a surreal appearance in the hushed darkness. The roads were quiet and the drone of the engine sent Alex into a daze.

Laurie sat up front with the Czech detective. They talked in hushed tones for thirty minutes or so before turning to the rest of the group.

'They're going in at 1 a.m.,' said Laurie. 'Two armed units under the command of Interpol's NCB. Gabriel's calling the shots from central control in Prague.'

Hannah pulled a face, glancing over at Josh and Terry. 'Who's commanding on the ground?' she asked.

Laurie waved away the question, although Alex wondered why it was even an issue.

'Staging has been moved to a click south-east of the bunker entrance, on a dairy farm. We'll remain there until the bunker is secured. Once we're received clearance, we'll be driven to the site by Land Rover.'

Alex watched Laurie as she recited the instructions passed on by the detective, who sat looking frosty – not best pleased, perhaps, with his role of babysitting the British whistle-blowers. Was he one of the honest cops, or one of the corrupt? Alex stared until the detective glared back, forcing him to turn his glance away to Laurie.

'How long will this all take?' he asked.

Laurie opened her mouth to speak, but the detective took the opportunity to answer.

'These things take time,' he said with a thick accent, his English crisp but slow. 'Maybe hours. It's a large bunker.' He shrugged.

'How large? How do you know?' asked Alex, for no other reason than he'd taken a dislike to the man, who seemed to regard them as an irritation rather than the people who'd led them to a major Nova stronghold.

The detective shrugged and turned away, staring out of the window.

'Very large,' he repeated. 'Lots to find. You sit tight. We'll take you there when we're ready.'

Alex couldn't think of a polite response, and neither, it appeared, could anyone else. They hunkered down in their seats and waited as the minibus lurched forwards into the growing night.

◆ ◆ ◆

The open fields gave way to woods of spruce and pine. They arrived at the farm in darkness. In all directions lay black forest, broken only by the hive of activity in the courtyard in front of a large farmhouse, its perimeter visible as a low flint wall that glinted in the lights of the minibus.

Alex spotted four armoured personnel carriers and three Land Rovers parked up on the approach road. Spotlights on tripods had been erected around a pop-up tent and a series of trestle tables. Dozens of armed officers milled around, dressed in black combat uniforms with white identification patches on their arms and POLICIE written on their backs in reflective yellow.

'Looks serious,' said Alex, as he climbed out on to a mixture of gravel and mud, caking his boots. At least he'd had the foresight to dress appropriately, which Laurie had found annoying because she couldn't rib him for it.

'What did you expect?' asked Laurie. 'A couple of bobbies on bicycles?'

Alex realised the absurdity of his comment, but Laurie smiled. 'This is big-boy shit, Alex – that's partly why they don't want us going in with them. Partly . . .'

Alex caught her tone. 'Why else?'

Laurie shook her head. 'Like I said back in Blighty, there'll be people who don't want this to go down. They won't have any choice, but they could make it difficult.'

'How?' Alex watched a couple of heavily armed police give them a double take. It made him suddenly uneasy. Were they all on the same side here? The rest of the officers milled around in small groups, the red embers of cigarettes dancing in the dark.

Alex looked over at the L-shaped two-storey farmhouse. The curtains were all closed and the lights off. He had no idea if it was occupied, but it didn't seem as if they'd be allowed inside. Laurie pointed to a table to one side of the main tent which had been set up with urns of tea and coffee.

'Let's get a drink,' she said. 'There's nothing much we can do apart from sit tight and hope it goes off without too much trouble. If your mystery contact hasn't sent us on a wild goose chase, we may still get the chance to rescue that poor girl.'

Alex nodded. Mystery contact. Mystery woman? Alex wondered how far away she was at this moment, and whether Laurie's statement back in the UK briefing room could be true – there was no reason to assume the message he'd received was honest. If the message was indeed from the Russian, his trust in her was based on nothing but gut instinct – a desire to trust her, despite who she worked for.

And yet trust her he did.

He heard an order being shouted and watched the various groups of officers gather under the spotlights for a briefing, their cigarettes flicking on to the mud in a coordinated shower of sparks. Weapons were slung over shoulders, sidearms in holsters. They looked tough, ready, but Laurie was right – they were nervous, Alex recognising all the subtle signs in their body language.

But they were about to head into a firefight, and Alex could only imagine how that felt. It was probably just adrenaline, he thought, and far too late to do anything about it.

◆ ◆ ◆

At midnight, a whistle sounded at the command tent. A few barked orders saw the police jump into their vehicles and start the engines.

All four of the APCs and one Land Rover roared into life and took off along the farm road in convoy, heading to the final staging area in preparation for the assault. Alex followed their lights as they filed out on to the main road north, their tail lights disappearing as the winding forest road devoured them.

The minutes ticked by. The night was warm enough to be comfortable, and Alex alternated between sitting in the minibus and stretching his legs, drinking two more cups of coffee before deciding neither his bladder nor his nerves could take any more. He checked his pulse but resisted another Xanax. He'd loaded up before they left the airport. He'd save another for just before they left. His left arm quivered in protest.

With the armed units gone, Laurie spent most of the time on her phone near the makeshift command tent. Alex wanted to talk to her, but realised he had nothing new to say. She was in the zone – focused on not screwing up whatever part the UK police had to play in this. Alex would remain a sideshow unless they found Eva. Even then, he worried his part might be redundant as the police took over.

His heart thumping a little faster at the thought, he stood and paced outside the minibus for a few minutes, trying and failing to burn away the excess adrenaline. He jumped as his phone vibrated in his pocket, twice in quick succession. He leaned against the minibus and froze, the screen glaring in the dark.

> *Don't trust them. Meet me at this location, 30 minutes. Come alone.*

It was followed by a link. He opened his maps application, which showed a red pin in the middle of the forest, around half a mile from the farm. He tapped for directions and a ragged blue line appeared, snaking back along the main road, several miles out of his way. This location wasn't on any road or path. He dismissed the directions and stared at the map.

He glanced up, holding the phone to his chest. There was nobody in the minibus – all of the UK team were at the command tent, some fifty yards away. He counted the four of them, including Laurie, standing with their babysitting detective, studying something on the table. Two other Czech officers stood off to one side, smoking and chatting. He could have sworn there'd been another, but they could be in one of the Land Rovers, or inside the farmhouse. He couldn't see them anywhere in the vicinity.

Alex checked his watch. 12:53. The assault was in seven minutes. He had two options, but didn't for a second need to think about which one he'd take. After checking his boots and zipping his jacket, he slipped behind the minibus and out into the darkness.

CHAPTER
FIFTY-FIVE

Eva raced along behind Natalia, pausing as they approached each checkpoint, slowing to a forced saunter up to the cameras and guards. The tunnels seemed busier than before and Eva sensed an urgency from the orderlies they passed. The guards were scattered and their normal uniforms bolstered by thick black vests and gun holsters.

Natalia had destroyed her phone in the last tunnel, scattering the pieces into one of the vents on the wall. At the next checkpoint she spoke to the guard on duty, leaning in, a few sly words in a language Eva couldn't understand, but which transformed the guard's behaviour from suspicious to trustworthy. He pulled his mobile phone out of his pocket and handed it to Natalia. She whispered to him, touched him lightly on the arm, then proceeded through the open door, Eva in tow.

Natalia approached the sloping tunnel and Eva felt the nerves bite. Down here were the classrooms. And the other room. The room she'd been forced into three times before they threw her back into her quarters. Why must they go this way?

Natalia stopped. Up ahead a group of orderlies and armed guards surrounded Dr Brown, who was holding a walkie-talkie to his mouth. Now Eva understood. Against the far wall of the tunnel, children were lined up, heads down, ropes strung between their hands, all trussed up. After a hiss of static from the radio, Dr Brown issued orders to the guards, who grabbed the children and marched them further into the tunnels.

Eva could see Natalia counting the guards, judging them. She turned and leaned her palms against the wall.

'Shit,' she whispered.

'Where will they take them?' Eva said.

Natalia shook her head. She was torn, that much was obvious, a deep frustration simmering from her. She wanted to save more than just Eva.

A shout from the tunnel broke Natalia's indecision. Dr Brown was staring at them, walkie-talkie to his mouth. Two armed guards broke away from the main group and strode in their direction.

'Move!' said Natalia, pushing Eva back the way they'd come. They headed away from the familiar – the tunnels that led to the torture chamber – the tank, and the classrooms. Instead they took a series of left turns and sank deeper into the bunker, spiralling downwards. Eva could feel the air grow thicker and more humid with each step. The temperature rose and she pulled off her hoodie, knotting it around her waist as the sweat oozed from her skin.

'Wait.' Natalia stopped at a T-junction. There were two signs, one for each direction, but they meant nothing – just a series of Russian letters and numerals. Natalia closed her eyes. Eva sensed her sinking back into memory, her wall to the outside world fluctuating as she concentrated.

'This way,' said Natalia, and took off to the left, Eva skipping along to keep pace.

They kept going for a few minutes and Eva noticed the tunnel narrowing. The lights were dimmer here and a few didn't work at all. The fans seemed weaker, the air dirtier, stale and dusty.

'Here,' Natalia said, stopping as the tunnel terminated in rough-hewn rock, a narrow passage snaking off into undeveloped hollows. She pointed to a vertical shaft sunk into the right wall. An iron ladder was set into the concrete, its rungs spaced wide.

'It goes all the way to the surface,' she said. 'It's a tough climb. You go first. I'll be right behind you.'

Eva gulped. She ducked into the shaft and looked up. It was black: complete darkness.

'But what if I—'

'Don't,' said Natalia. 'Just focus on putting one foot after another.'

Eva gingerly placed one foot on the lowest rung, then grasped another with both hands and pulled herself off the ground. The metal was rough under her palms – rusty and damp. She gripped as hard as she could, reaching for a higher rung, lifting her feet to follow.

After a few yards the darkness engulfed her, all light quashed from the tunnel below. The air became heavy and she could hear nothing but her own breath echoing off the sides.

The tunnel grew narrower with each rung, the darkness over-powering. Her heart started to race and sparks flashed in her eyes.

'I can't,' she whispered, her hands growing damp and slippery. She gripped, but the strength had left her. Her feet trembled and she shuffled, sliding on the metal. Her calves froze and her knees locked.

'Please,' she said, 'let me down.'

Natalia climbed on to the rung below. She placed a hand on Eva's shoulder and gave it a squeeze. 'It never leaves you,' she said, 'but it does get easier.'

Eva nodded, but her body remained frozen. She wrapped her arms around the rungs and felt the shakes coming on. She gasped, blinking furiously in the dark until Natalia pulled out the phone and switched it on. The screen gave a low glow. Eva watched the shadows dance between them, straining her neck to look at Natalia's face.

'I can force you up there,' said Natalia. 'I can make it go away, but that's not the best way. It leaves a mark, always. You are marked enough, my young friend.'

Eva sucked in the hot air. She wanted to let go and throw her arms around Natalia. To make it all go away. To escape.

'Move, Eva,' said Natalia. 'Do it by yourself. Use your anger if you have to. If we're caught, this tunnel will be like heaven compared to what they'll put you through.'

The hand gave her another squeeze and let go.

Eva felt Natalia's mind filling the tunnel beneath her. It would be easy to reach out and beg. To throw it all away for a quick escape.

But Natalia was right, and they'd come this far. Eva dragged in a breath, feeling the dust and the moisture in her throat. She couldn't let them win. There was too much she must do. Too many questions left unanswered.

With a Herculean effort, she untangled her arms and forced her hands on to the rung above, then the one above that. She focused only on this – the rungs and her breathing. One breath, one rung, never counting, never opening her eyes, never looking at the walls.

It felt like an eternity, but eventually she reached out and hit nothing but air. Lowering her hands, she found the top of the ladder curving around and back into the concrete. She opened her eyes and saw the faint outline of a door. She was on the inside of a concrete shack, much like the one with the lift, albeit much smaller. Pulling herself out of the shaft, she waited for Natalia.

'The door will be locked,' said Natalia. 'Here, hold this.' She pulled out the phone and turned on the torch. Eva held it steady while Natalia worked away on the rusted bolt. It inched its way open, screeching in protest, but slowly relenting.

'Wait.' Natalia leaned on the door, swinging it open, peering out. Eva was disorientated for a second, expecting daylight to flood into the room, but only the faint glimmer of moonlight peeked through. There was a rush of cold fresh air and the sound of rushing water.

'Come,' said Natalia.

Eva followed her out into the night, where they paused for a few minutes to catch their breath. A stream flowed past the building, which otherwise lay hidden in a small glade surrounded by high trees, sloping sharply downwards to their left.

Natalia cocked her head, listening to the sounds of the forest. Eva listened too, and although she heard a myriad cracks and whistles drifting through the trees, Natalia didn't seem concerned.

They waited another five minutes before Natalia checked the phone and stood up.

'It's time,' she said.

CHAPTER FIFTY-SIX

Alex tried to keep one eye on his phone and the other on the dark ground in front of him. It didn't work, his night vision ruined by the bright screen. Instead he took a bearing, then tucked the phone in his pocket.

The moon poked out from behind the low cloud, penetrating the thick canopy in places, leaving others in complete darkness. It created an eerie patchwork through the trees.

The ground rose sharply and Alex was soon out of breath, but the minutes sped up as he slowed down. Half a mile in thirty minutes should have been easy, but Alex struggled with the terrain and started to worry he wouldn't make it.

He paused to check the location, taking a few breaths, aware of his hammering heart. The trees grew more densely here, the forest floor spongy with wet leaves and moss. He heard the rush of water and strayed over to his left to find a source. A small but fast-running stream cascaded through the forest. He stepped across, trying to keep his feet dry. His breathing was heavy, his footsteps even louder. He thought he heard something up ahead and held his breath for a few seconds, trying to listen over the sound of water and through the thudding of his ears.

Nothing – probably a rabbit or whatever creatures lurked in these woods. He kept walking, second-guessing his every step. Why hadn't he just told Laurie and the team? They could have warned the Czech police and headed to this location with back-up.

But he kept walking, unable to shake the feeling this was his task alone. She had contacted *him* three times – not the police, not Laurie, not Interpol, but *him*. The connection Alex felt to these people, however objectionable, was his alone. His questions couldn't be asked in front of a police force who would sooner lock them up for points than get at the real answers.

His father's legacy was only the surface. Nova went far deeper, and they teased him with their messages and their threats. He needed once and for all to confront them and end this dance. This could be his opportunity.

That noise again. A crack, branches being snapped. Too heavy to have been made by rabbits. Alex slowed, tucking in behind a tree, its bark wet and cold on his hand. Again the sound drifted in the air, eerie in the otherwise silent night. He pulled out his phone, shielding the screen against the tree. 01:15. The raid had started fifteen minutes ago. The location he'd been given was just over a hundred yards away now.

His foot caught in something under the mud. He pulled it free, tracing a line of barbed wire. It was old and trampled, a fence post rotten underfoot. This area had once been fenced in, or fenced out. Restricted. He must be close to the bunker.

Tucking the phone back in his pocket, he stalked onward, straining to see further than a few feet ahead, watching the dappled moonlight against the thick tree trunks, trying to make as little noise as possible, treading down first on the balls of his feet.

The sound of a silenced gunshot should have been alien to Alex, yet he knew it the moment he heard it. A muted bark, followed by rapid footsteps crunching through the wet undergrowth.

He sank to his knees, cowering behind a tree, holding his breath. But the footsteps were getting fainter now – whoever it was was headed away from Alex.

They were headed towards his meeting place.

He let his heart catch up, giving it a few minutes before daring to stand again. Should he go back? Laurie had said this was serious shit. He'd listened, but without any feeling of danger to himself, but now that danger was real. Who the hell used silenced weapons in a police raid? His flesh began to crawl.

Going back would mean his own safety, but what about Eva? If she was up ahead waiting for him, it could place her in mortal danger. Alex swallowed his natural inclination to run and made his decision. He crept forward at a fraction of his previous pace, trying to find the spot where he'd heard the shot.

It didn't take long. He saw the reflective armband of a police officer glinting in the faint moonlight. The body was prone, unmoving. Alex paused for several moments, scanning the darkness, before approaching the body.

He felt sick to his stomach as he knelt by the fallen officer. The man was dead – no pulse, eyes open, pupils fixed and dilated. The bullet had entered his neck just above his tactical vest. A careful shot. Friend or foe, whatever he was doing out here had ended his life. This could be Nova's doing, or one of his colleagues. Laurie had suggested that no one could be trusted here, but maybe even she hadn't realised the extent of the corruption.

The officer's gun was still holstered – he hadn't even drawn it, which meant he'd been taken unawares. Alex froze, listening to the muted sounds of the forest, trying to discern between the natural and anything that might indicate the killer. He must have waited for five minutes, hunched over the body, before straightening up. Before he did so, he unclasped the officer's revolver and turned it over in his hands. He'd never fired a gun, but found the safety catch – still on – and figured he could if he had to. Whoever did this was happy to kill cops, so wouldn't blink twice at killing Alex. Having a gun wouldn't stand him much of a chance, but at least it was something.

He took another bearing from his phone and stalked forwards, the gun in his right hand, pointing at the ground. He flicked the safety off as something darted in front of him, a small silhouette thrashing through the low branches. Alex pulled the gun away just in time and kept his trembling finger from pulling the trigger. The figure stopped, a young girl in a small dress. Her face was wild and cut, possibly from the undergrowth. She was barefoot, muddy and out of breath. She panted, moving closer to him until he could see her more clearly.

A small child running through the forest. Starkov. Alex shivered again.

He put his left hand out, palm up. 'It's OK,' he whispered. 'I won't hurt you.'

The girl tilted her head, examining him. The moonlight reflected in her eyes. Alex suddenly felt heat rising in his neck. It extended to his head, his temples sparking with tension.

'She left before me,' said the girl. 'They forced us out into the forest. Some made it to the trucks. I escaped.'

Before Alex could answer she dashed off, running as fast as her spindly legs could carry her. Alex spun round, biting his tongue, wanting to call after her, but fearful of what announcing his location might bring. The girl was out of sight already and the sound of her footsteps faded.

Her words weren't lost on Alex, and the sensation of her stare – his physical reaction – was beyond his comprehension. But she knew who he was looking for.

Once more he resisted the urge to call out. He was close to hyperventilating, events spiralling faster than he could manage. He looked at his hold on the gun – it was shaking so much he was in danger of shooting himself in the legs.

Deep breaths. Four in, four out. You're running out of time, Alex. You've made your choice. Stick with it.

A check of location. His phone glared at him, the battery meter on red. He was nearly on top of them now, the pin appearing to pulsate on the bright screen. He switched off the phone and raised the gun.

More sounds ahead, not isolated footsteps this time. He heard voices, low but rising in urgency – an argument, orders being shouted.

A few more steps saw him come to a natural clearing in the forest, no more than twenty yards across. He hid behind the last of the trees and watched. The break in the canopy allowed the moonlight to spill through, illuminating two figures.

A tall thin man with grey hair, his dark suit wholly out of place in this environment. In his right hand he held a gun, fitted with an extra extension to the barrel – a silencer. The gun was pointed across the clearing at a young girl.

Alex's eyes shifted. He watched the girl, cowering against the thick trunk of a pine tree.

Eva.

'I found you.' He whispered it under his breath, without thinking, the sound barely audible, but she turned her head in his direction.

Alex stepped forward into the moonlight, equidistant between the two of them. He kept his own gun trained on the ground, forcing his hand to stay steady, his throat tight with tension.

'Put your gun down, Alex.' The old man spoke without looking at him, but then twisted, revealing the side of his face.

Alex froze at the sight.

The grey man from the lift in the NCA building. The man who'd gone after Katie?

The agent from Nova.

Alex gripped the gun a little more tightly.

'I can't do that,' he said, raising the gun, pointing it at the grey man. He tried to mask the tremor in his voice. 'I'm with the British police. I need you to put down your gun and lie on the ground.'

The man laughed before reeling off a string of words in what sounded like Russian, hissing across the still air. He spoke like this for several seconds, his voice raising in pitch and speed. The sounds crowded Alex's mind until his ears began to ring. His vision wavered and he saw Eva stagger. She stayed on her feet, head in her hands, writhing from left to right. At the same time his own ears burned and a shooting pain stabbed through his forehead.

He recognised in a heartbeat what was happening.

Memories of the way Victor Lazar had grabbed him in his prison cell all those years ago. Like a puppet on strings, his body began to detach. His neural systems screamed in protest, but they were not his to control. His shoulders tensed and his arms dropped to his sides.

Time slowed.

'No,' he pleaded, but it was too late.

'No?' The man turned to face him. 'No, Alex?'

Alex gulped, white noise filling the air. The forest faded until there were only the two of them. He could hear the grey man's breathing and his voice, hissing in his ears.

'I gave you a choice, Alex.'

Alex tried to move, his body stiff, in slow motion. His eyes flickered, looking for Eva, but she'd melted into the shadows. He was going under, unwilling, unable to stop it. The trance was taking hold. He battled, his thoughts twisting, trying to escape.

'You could have stayed away – we *warned* you to leave it.'

Alex shook his head, trying again to free himself, but his mind and body remained rooted, bent to the grey man's will. Alex felt rather than heard the anger, his head shooting with pain, a growing numbness in his chest, his throat constricting.

'We would have let you stay on the fringe, prodding from your cosy little existence.'

The words hammered home and he was unable to ignore them. The fringe was where he had stayed for too long. His father had kept him out, but Alex hadn't wanted to remain there.

'And you still don't listen, do you, Alex? To anybody – your friends, your family. Let me ask you, have you ever truly listened to your daughter? Do you know what she wants? Does she know what you *are*?'

Twisting and probing, the grey man's words confused Alex. His body was tense, fixed, but his mind was spinning freely, exploring the message behind the words, feeling the sentiments crashing through his reality, what he knew to be true.

'But this is the end, Alex,' the grey man said, 'and you no longer get to make that choice. Not any more.' He turned, but then stopped. 'It's time to bring you in from the—' he said, his voice stuttering, the calm whisper cut out mid-sentence.

The voice wavered; there was interference. Alex's head throbbed and his ears popped. A tightness grew across his chest. A conflict raged inside him.

A whisper from behind. Another voice.

The words drove through. Confusion. The grey man's face filled his vision, his wrinkled skin tensing, stretching, his jaw clenching. He was angry, resolute, but a frown now appeared at the edges: curiosity.

'What are you . . . ?' he said.

Alex's body moved. But it wasn't him in control.

More whispers – soft and urgent, they seeped in, wrapping around his words before he could respond. But this wasn't the grey man; this was the second voice. One he'd heard before. It crept out from the forest behind him, waiting for its chance, and now it pounced.

Two voices in his head. They danced, dodging, chasing.

A battle of minds.

'Stop!' shouted the grey man, but his voice sounded hollow and his words had less power than before. He reeled off another string of Russian, hissing at him, the words incomprehensible to Alex but the urgency rising in his tone.

'Come to me, Alex.' The second voice, female, was delicate but unyielding, seductive in its power. He sought her out, listening, willing her closer, louder.

'Where are you?' The grey man's voice trembled as he realised. His hesitancy cost him his focus, and with that, his grip. Alex's body shook, trembling from head to toe as control was transferred.

The forest came back into view, the fog fading.

'You'll die for this,' said the grey man. 'Both of you.'

But the woman's voice was stronger now. She rattled off a string of commands, the sound barely rising above the wind, but screaming in Alex's ears. They popped again and a fresh wave of dread washed over him.

He watched his own arm rise and move to the left. A ghost, a phantom limb, it pointed at the grey man, his finger squeezing the trigger only as a remote sensation of force, barely registering. The sound of the gun was louder than he could have imagined, yet his reaction was almost non-existent. He held the gun raised and fired again, his finger squeezing the trigger all the way home.

He wanted to scream as the bullet passed through the grey man's neck, but his jaw was fixed, his breath held in, his body rigid as his shoulder absorbed the force of the second recoil. His collar-bone cracked in protest, but there was no pain.

Only his eyes remained willing, watching as the body of the grey man spun under the force of the two bullets, dropping his own gun as he fell, first on to his side, then his back, gasping for air as his body caved under the trauma.

Time sped up.

As fast as Alex had been forced under, the control disappeared and Alex's body surged with relief. His arm dropped to his side and the gun hung limp in his hand. He gasped for breath as he watched the body in front of him. It twitched one last time before falling still.

After the ear-shattering gunshot, silence descended on the clearing. All Alex could feel was the blood rushing through his body and the sense of lethargy, like the feeling immediately after a panic attack, when the body realises it's still alive and starts to recover. A new lease of life, but a fragile and timid one.

A crack of twigs underfoot. A shadow.

It was her.

Alex stared at the woman, and the longer he stared, the more the recognition danced at the edges of his mind. The dark features and chiselled cheekbones, her unrelenting stance. Her eyes were fixed on the grey man, but they were wide and swallowed him whole.

It had to be her.

'Alex,' she said, her accent familiar – a strange blend, Eastern European, not pure Russian. She stepped towards Eva, protective, helping the girl up from the floor, where she still crouched in fear. The woman tucked her own gun out of sight in her pocket.

'I'm sorry I had to do that, Alex,' she said. 'I had to wait until his focus was entirely on you. It was the only way.'

Alex met her gaze, mesmerised by the sight of her.

'What did you . . . ?'

'Set a trap. For both of you.'

'Who is he?'

'His name was Pavel,' said the woman, staring down at the body. The immaculate suit was crumpled now, dark stains of blood and dirt where he'd fallen. His shoes were covered in mud, the leather damp, forever ruined.

'He was . . . Starkov is his facility. Your raid caused chaos. We got out just in time, but he followed us, as I expected he would. He wanted us, but more than that, he wanted you, Alex. And that was his only weakness. It was the only thing I could use.'

She tilted her head, her eyes narrow with questions.

He wanted you.

Alex shook his head, trying to ease the chaos within. A million questions formed and dissolved. 'In England. The warnings. The threats . . .'

She stared, her eyes shining, penetrating. 'He was cleaning up. Eva's trail must go cold. But for you, Alex . . .' She shook her head, frustrated and confused. 'He had other plans.'

Eva now stepped forward. Still dressed in her black hoodie and jeans, the young girl looked tentative but willing. She too narrowed her eyes, gazing at Alex. He had no way of stopping her. She peered at him, then at the woman, her eyes searching.

'Am I going with him?' asked Eva. She glanced around at the forest. 'We don't have long.'

The woman nodded and began to back away.

'Wait!' said Alex. His hand tensed around the gun. She stopped, her own hand dipping towards her pocket.

'You can't . . . that is, I don't even know your name.'

The woman smiled, and it was genuine, her eyes sparkling with warmth. She closed them for a few seconds before stepping forward again.

'Natalia,' she said. 'I—' She stopped as muffled shouts floated through the darkness. They heard the cracking of branches underfoot. The shot sounded a second after Natalia's shoulder was wrenched backwards by the impact. She stumbled and Alex threw himself into a crouch, pulling Eva down with him.

'Shit!' Natalia bent to her knees and raised her gun, staring past Alex into the undergrowth. She let off a couple of shots, then winced, glancing at the torn clothing of her jacket. She reached up gingerly and touched the wound underneath.

'Follow me,' she hissed. 'Run. Now!'

She lurched to the right and took off into the trees. Eva jumped after her and Alex followed, with the briefest of glimpses in the direction of the gunshot. He could see nothing in the darkness, but could hear sounds from every direction.

'It might be one of ours,' he shouted after Natalia.

'It's not,' she hissed back, just as a branch snapped into his face. 'These are my people. We were followed. Pavel has unleashed his hounds.'

She picked up the pace, heading up the incline, away from the direction Alex had approached – away from the farmhouse and safety.

Alex pounded after her, a gun in his hand, his heart in his mouth.

CHAPTER FIFTY-SEVEN

A second gunshot rang out, echoing through the forest. Alex heard the thump of the bullet as a tree splintered to his right. Natalia stopped in her tracks and raised one fist.

'There are more up ahead,' she said, then paused, her face glistening in the low light. Her eyes remained resolute, but her jaw was clenched and Alex could see the glint of blood on her arm.

'This way,' she said, moving to the left, more slowly now and towards the sound of the stream.

Shouts from behind spurred them on, and the three of them crunched faster through the dense foliage. Alex had no idea where she was taking them.

A third gunshot sounded as they reached the treeline, where the forest opened into a clearing; in front of them stood the shadow of a small building. The sound of running water was louder now. Alex found himself crouching, fearful of the next bullet. He struggled to get a grip on himself, panting into the damp ground as Natalia pointed to the building.

'We have to go back in,' said Natalia, turning to Eva. The young girl shook her head, but Natalia grabbed her arm and dragged her. 'There's no choice. We stay out here, we die.'

Alex picked himself up and followed them into the shack-like structure. The door swung open with a creak and they piled inside. Natalia swung the door closed behind, blanketing them in complete darkness.

'Torch,' she hissed. Alex rummaged for his phone, realising he was still holding the officer's pistol. He tucked it into his belt and pulled out his mobile, shining the screen at the door. Together they worked the single metal bolt across. It was thick, with mounts welded into the door, but Natalia didn't seem satisfied.

'I can't go back down there.'

Alex turned to shine the light on Eva. She was staring at a hole in the ground with a ladder snaking up and over. An entrance to the bunker below.

'Is this it?' said Alex, trying to get some sense of direction and distance. It felt like they were a long way from where the raid was taking place.

'We stood no chance in the forest,' said Natalia. 'I'm sorry, Eva.'

Alex watched the young girl's face. She was breathing heavily, staring at the black hole, terrified at the sight. *Claustrophobia* – Alex recalled the medical report from Amsterdam. No wonder she didn't relish the thought of climbing into a narrow tunnel. Could he help her? Almost certainly, in the comfort of his office, with plenty of time and gradual exposure therapy.

Right now, he wasn't so sure.

'Down the ladder, Eva.' Natalia's voice was low and firm. Eva glanced at her. Alex caught a spark between them, tension, resistance. Eva sagged, letting out a small sigh. She stepped forward and started downwards into the blackness.

'You next,' said Natalia.

Alex didn't need coercing. He placed his feet with care, stepping down until his hands were on the rough metal of the rungs.

Rusty, but solid. He clutched his phone between his teeth, the beam of light dancing as he moved.

The temperature rose steadily as they clambered downwards. Twice Eva stopped. Alex saw her hugging the rungs, her eyes closed, resting her forehead against the cold iron before finding the courage to keep going. Alex didn't rush her, despite the growing threat from above. He'd been in danger before, had a gun pointed at him, but that was nothing compared to this – here they were heading down into the scorpion's nest.

After some time he heard Eva scramble on to the ground below. He joined her, casting his eyes around at the end of the tunnel they had arrived in, where the concrete terminated in solid rock. In the other direction, the space was dimly lit by bulbs sunk at intervals into the wall. Three yards high and a similar distance wide, the tunnel echoed with thumps, voices and unidentifiable sounds. Alex thought he heard shouting, but it was impossible to determine the direction or distance.

How big was the bunker? He'd read the briefing, but it gave no clear indication. The Soviets had had many years to dig down and extend this place. There could be miles of tunnels down here.

Natalia jumped to the ground to join them.

'They didn't follow,' she said. 'They'll secure that exit and the others.'

'So what do we do?' said Alex, feeling the bite of being trapped. Not claustrophobia, but cleithrophobia – the fear of being locked in, unable to leave this underground tomb.

'We hope,' she said.

'Hope for what?' said Alex, but Natalia had already headed off, Eva hot on her heels.

They weaved through the tunnels and their rapid turns at each junction, Natalia appearing to direct them from memory. The path appeared to incline slightly, and it widened and grew cooler as they climbed.

'There's an exit not far from here,' Natalia whispered, slowing at the next turn. Alex and Eva waited while Natalia peered around the corner. Shouts erupted and Eva leapt backwards, sinking against Alex.

He held her for a moment, trying to project calm, control. He realised he could barely keep his own breathing in check, and Eva must have sensed it, her eyes showing her understanding. 'Thank you,' she said, giving his arm a squeeze.

'No, that's blocked,' said Natalia, stepping back. She was beginning to look desperate. 'Back the way we came.'

They swung round to see two men take position behind them, fifty yards away or so, blocking their route, raising their guns. As they edged closer, Alex could make out their clothes – one was dressed all in black with a turtleneck sweater and smooth trousers – not the clothing of a guard.

'Stop!' The man spoke into a radio while the other kept his attention on them. Natalia whipped out her own gun, edging forward to stand in front of Eva and Alex.

'Leave us!' she shouted. 'You don't know what you're doing.'

Whatever Alex was expecting, it wasn't the reaction they got. One of the men even laughed. 'Your time's up,' he said. 'Pavel has called you in – you and the girl. You're both finished.'

Natalia wavered, her gun dropping for an instant. Alex saw fear and frustration etched on her face.

'Who are they?' he said.

'Trouble,' said Natalia. She appeared to think for a second, shaking her head, then tensed, adjusting her grip and firing three rapid shots in succession. She charged forward and fired twice more. One of the shots hit the man in black and he went down. The other man dived to the side of the tunnel and returned fire. The shots were deafening in the confines of the tunnel, but Natalia continued to run towards the two men, firing as she ran.

Alex saw the second man go down with a scream.

Natalia turned. 'Come on!' she shouted.

Alex raced after her, the gunshots still ringing in his ears, keeping Eva close by. They gave the fallen men a wide berth and Alex tried not to look as one of them writhed in agony against the wall. His radio hissed static with a burst of Russian voices as they passed.

They retraced their steps, making several turns before the tunnel sloped downwards and Alex once again was completely lost. The air grew thicker and Alex's sense of unease increased. The lights along the tunnel all flicked off for a second before coming back on and Alex wondered what would happen if the power failed. How long could they survive down here, running through the darkness? A faint breeze was tinged with the smell of diesel.

He checked his watch. 01:47. Where the hell were the police? He wondered how long it would take them to secure this place, assuming they even could. Assuming they wanted to. Alex felt another stab of regret at leaving Laurie.

The tunnel became wider and brighter, opening out into a crossroads with a huge elevator at the centre, its sides made of wire mesh. It sat at the top of its shaft, the cables snaking up and into the ceiling, which meant there were further tunnels below. Stacks of boxes were being moved by a forklift, out of the elevator and to the side. Other than the driver, the crossroads was deserted.

'Wait here.' Natalia strode ahead, approaching to the rear of the forklift.

Alex watched as she addressed the man in the cab, taking him by surprise. A combination of the gun and Natalia's powers of persuasion made him switch off the engine and step down from the vehicle. Alex couldn't make out what she was saying, but the man handed over a pass and then backed away. By the time Alex and Eva reached her, the man had disappeared, sprinting away up one of the tunnels.

'Get in the elevator,' she said.

Alex surveyed the metal contraption, swallowing his unease. Running on adrenaline this far, the thought of heading even deeper into the ground now caused a fresh surge. Eva stepped forward and pulled back the metal door.

'Where are we going?' Alex said, his voice sounding weak.

Natalia took her place alongside Eva, the pair of them gazing defiantly back at Alex.

'Level Four,' said Natalia.

The lift shuddered to a halt. There was a marked difference in atmosphere down here from the tunnels above. The air was still, dusty, tinged with bleach and other chemicals. The walls and floor were rough, dirty, the lights yellow in their mounts.

The sounds of the upper levels had faded, but a low hiss radiated through the static air.

Holding her head, Eva shuddered and fell against the wall, her breathing quick and erratic.

'You'll feel it down here,' said Natalia, and then frowned. 'It's too quiet.' She put her hand out to lead Eva away. 'We need to find somewhere to hide,' she added.

She walked slowly, as if frightened what she might meet. This was no longer the same frantic race as on the upper levels. Down here Alex could feel tremors in the air and the skin on the back of his neck tingled.

When they reached the first lab, he knew why.

The rock was roughly hewn here – large caverns connected by a single tunnel.

In the first cavern, a glass room had been erected. It looked clinical in style but was dirty, the glass smudged up to chest height with small, greasy handprints.

A row of beds stood there, metal-framed with slats where the mattresses should be. Alex counted nine in total, a couple with soiled cloth diapers draped over them. Black hoods lay discarded alongside old-style over-the-ear headphones, the cables snaking away to a single trolley in the middle, which held a desktop computer and printer. The computer monitor was still switched on.

Behind each bed stood a stand, each one still with its own full IV bag, the liquid seeping out from bloody needles on to the floor. Two of the stands had fallen over. There were no doctors or nurses. And no patients. Alex stepped up to the glass.

'Empty,' he said, a little unnecessarily, perhaps.

Natalia paused, before joining him. 'The clean-up has started,' she said. 'They had a head start.'

'So this is Nova,' Alex whispered. He closed his eyes and saw rows of test subjects, children, assets. A million questions formed, but none seemed appropriate to judge the magnitude of this place.

Natalia shook her head. 'You don't understand,' she said. 'Come on, we can't stay here.'

Still staring through the glass, Alex managed to tear himself away. Eva was across on the other side of the tunnel, refusing to look. Alex watched her reaction. Her ability, her bizarre affliction, had been manufactured in a place like this.

'How many more?' asked Alex.

Natalia shook her head. 'I don't know,' she said, 'but I think we're too late, even if we could help them.'

They left the glass lab behind and kept walking. The next cavern held a rudimentary toilet block, lined with stalls with bowls in them, some overflowing, the sewage spilling all over the floor. Child-size footprints were visible, so many their outlines were blurred. Alex shivered as the stench hit him.

'This is . . .' he said. 'We need to expose all of this. You have to . . .' He looked at Natalia, who silenced him with a glance and turned away.

'They're coming,' she said. Alex was about to question her, but then heard it for himself – muffled shouts and the metallic thud of the lift. They were being followed. Hunted.

'This way,' said Natalia.

They walked for another five minutes, stopping every now and then to listen. After the last confrontation, their pursuers were being more careful, no doubt wary of Natalia's trigger finger. Alex stayed close, while Eva walked along in a daze, cocking her head periodically.

They passed three more labs and two more darkened rooms, all empty, all seemingly evacuated in a hurry – the medical equipment scattered and several beds left overturned. Drinks cans lay on the floor, and the remains of a sandwich. An ashtray lay with cigarette butts still smoking.

Natalia entered one of the rooms and stared coolly round, then grabbed a bottle of bleach from a shelf behind one of the beds. She squirted it behind them as they walked, and the smell of the sewer was replaced with the smell of chlorine.

'In case they use dogs,' she explained.

'Where have they all gone – the children?' Alex didn't stop for an answer and Natalia picked up the pace as an alarm sounded. A low drone, it thundered through the tunnels. Alex felt the air shift and his ears popped.

'Shit!' said Natalia, breaking into a run.

As they rounded the next corner, a sheer metal door slid into place. It looked new, polished, in contrast to the doors on the upper surface – like the door to a safe, with no hinges, closed and locked, barring their way. Airtight and thoroughly impenetrable.

'No no no,' hissed Natalia, backing away. The shouts grew louder behind them. Their pursuers must be at the first glass lab by now, taking their time. Now Alex knew why.

'We're trapped,' said Natalia. 'They've sealed Level Four. The only way out is back the way we came.'

'Then we go that way,' said Alex, pulling the gun from his belt. It shook, the tremor in his wrist so violent he had to swap hands. 'We fight.'

Natalia shook her head. She gazed at Eva, whose face was a picture of fear and anger.

'I didn't do all of this for you both to die now,' she said, then sniffed at the air. Alex tasted something bitter.

'Gas,' she said. 'Quick! This way and to the right.' She glanced over at Eva.

Eva looked puzzled but followed. Alex watched her chest pumping with small breaths. She was clearly as close to panic as he was.

To the right lay one of the rooms in darkness they'd passed not so long before. Natalia entered and stood just inside, waiting for Eva. Once she was in, Natalia stood at the entrance, blocking their way out. She squirted more bleach on the floor, then fumbled for a switch on the wall and flicked it. Light flooded the room.

Three identical metal contraptions stood along the far wall, each the size of a small car, shaped like a hot tub with a dome over the top. Pipes ran from the bottom and top, along the side of the wall and into the tunnel. A series of pressure gauges sat on top of each metal dome.

'No,' whispered Eva.

Alex stepped forward. 'What are they?' he asked, then saw Eva's terror and realised.

Natalia checked her gun, pointing to the left-most tank. 'Get in,' she said. 'They have their own air supply.'

'No.' Eva backed up against the wall. 'I'd rather die.' Alex saw the tears forming in her eyes.

Natalia shook her head. 'But you won't die. It's CS gas and they'll take you and they'll . . .' She didn't finish her sentence. 'You'll suffer first.'

'I'll suffer in there,' Eva retorted. 'I have suffered in there. That's all I've done!' She coughed, hacking as the gas started to take effect.

Alex fumbled with his gun. To run out there and face them, or hide in the tank – his two choices. His nostrils started to burn.

'The others,' he said. 'What about the other children?'

Natalia shook her head and her eyes dropped. 'We were too late,' she said. 'Give me the gun. I need both.'

'Hide with us,' said Alex, but Natalia gave a weak smile.

'Then they'll find all three of us and kill us all,' she said. 'This is my mistake, my failure to see more than one step ahead. I thought perhaps the police would penetrate further than this. I thought they'd be faster, better.'

'They'll be here soon,' he insisted. 'We'll stand and fight.' He rubbed his eyes, which were starting to burn. 'You'll die too.'

She shook her head, grabbing Eva's arm and pushing them both towards the tank.

'CS doesn't affect me,' she said. 'Five per cent of the population. I'm a lucky one.' Another weak smile. 'I know you want more than this,' she said. 'But all I can offer you now is your life. Get in the tank. I'll lead them away. It's our only option.'

'I'm not getting in there without you,' said Alex. He still held the gun, but what could he do with it? Threaten her? She had the power to stop him in his tracks, and more besides. He was within a few feet of the only person who could answer all of his questions.

Natalia focused on his face. She reached out and touched his arm. It felt electric, even through his jacket, her presence overpowering.

'I need to know,' he said, begging her. All the questions he'd jotted in his notepad at home, all the searches he'd sent across the Internet, into the medical archives and the university libraries. All the dreams he'd endured, seeing this woman's face . . . he couldn't let it end here. The surveillance, the messages, the threats. All of it leapt from his mind.

But the clock was ticking, the sounds of their pursuers increasing in tempo and volume. The gas hit his throat.

Nova. This woman, Natalia, was about to slip away again.

Sacrificing herself to save Eva and Alex.

He grasped at thoughts as he backed towards the tank. Eva followed, protesting, but her body wouldn't obey her mind.

'My father,' he said.

Was that it? Was that the core of his search? He'd forced his father's deeds into the background for such a long time, but now it felt like the root of his angst. Even from beyond the grave, his father managed to torment him in his search for the truth. 'I need—'

'One step at a time, Alex,' said Natalia, taking the gun carefully from his hand. Her eyes were reassuring but melancholy. She whispered to him and the questions disappeared into the void, his anxiety faded, his heart rate plummeted.

He stepped towards the tank and lifted the lid. The heat of the water radiated outwards.

All around him the air froze and a bubble of silence engulfed him. On one level he knew what she was doing and tried hard to resist, but it was no use. Her hand caressed his body and her voice caressed his mind.

For a few moments he existed in another time, another world, his body in suspended animation as he drifted to her words. It was comforting, a blanket of calm holding him tight as his stress faded away, and his father's memory with it.

His vision was the last thing to go. Natalia's face, so prominent against the wall of darkness, began to fade until she became no more than a ghost. He tried to blink but was no longer sure if his eyes were open. It made no difference, and the blackness filled his world.

The last thing he heard was a message that jolted and lodged firmly in his memory – a nugget, carefully placed for later.

Be careful, Alex. Pavel is dead, but if we make it out of here, the others will be coming for you. They'll be coming for both of us.

The tank closed with a metallic thud.

And then silence.

CHAPTER FIFTY-EIGHT

Alex rubbed his temples, nursing the growing headache. His temples were on fire and his vision still felt off. A side effect of the isolation tank, or the gas. The English doctors couldn't decide which. Alex had other ideas.

'If I could charge you with obstruction, I would.' Those were Laurie's last words before slamming the door of the conference room. He'd endured the journey home to the UK in silence, only hearing the full extent of the bunker operation during the team debrief in their last session, back at the NCA headquarters in Vauxhall.

He hadn't replied, just stared down at his empty paper cup, spinning it in his hand.

The true extent of the chaos had only become clear once they'd been hastily ushered out of the country. Corrupt to the core, was how Laurie had framed it, screaming her frustration at her Czech counterparts over the phone in the debrief, who declined to answer any questions and effectively barred the NCA from any further discussion on the matter. Starkov was their problem and they'd taken care of it in their own way. Any further queries would have to be taken up through the ranks.

Except that the ranks quickly closed.

Interpol declined to comment further, citing the case closed, and the Foreign Office was busy running damage control, trying to distance the minister and any UK involvement in what had happened.

Once the details came through, Alex couldn't blame them.

The Starkov compound had been given plenty of warning. Rogue units within the armed response teams had done a thorough job of disrupting the approach, and one member of the force remained missing, presumed absconded with the drug traffickers.

The bunker complex itself had been rapidly emptied of both people and drugs, and as a final act, the air filtration system had been sabotaged.

The firefight provided by the drug traffickers had been drawn out and vicious with several casualties on either side, although the ballistics reports had been contradictory, and were then redacted – another thing for Laurie to yell about later.

The drug traffickers had used CS gas throughout the bunker and the police were underprepared, deciding to pull back until it had cleared, giving the occupants extra time in which to escape, given that the police lacked the manpower to secure all of the exits, three of which they claimed not to know about until afterwards.

By the time the bunker was secured and Laurie arrived with her team in the second wave, all that was left was a few kilos of heroin scattered on the concrete outside.

No other drugs. No trafficked victims. Not a single child was found inside except Eva, along with Alex, hidden in the deepest cavern, both in a trance-like state of consciousness. They'd been pulled out by the Czech police and brought to the surface, to be met by a furious Detective Laurie. Furious because she hadn't been allowed to enter the bunker herself, furious that Alex had given her the slip, and absolutely beside herself that back in the UK, comprehensive gagging orders were now in place.

Alex's story was not required. What he'd seen was not admissible, what he'd witnessed was not considered reliable, and no evidence of his claims could or would ever be verified. When Laurie called bullshit, the Foreign Office paid her a visit and decided it was best if her unit had never been there. That was the official story, at any rate.

The Czech police were ordered to retreat, sealing the inner chambers by orders of the Ministry of the Interior. They cited risk of contaminant leakage into the local water courses – during the Cold War the bunker had been used to store all sorts of chemicals and munitions. The orders were obeyed. Beyond the initial search, no details were documented about the lower levels. Nothing was catalogued, nothing was removed. Everything was effectively buried in concrete, the doors sealed by order of the government.

The blame was scattered and diluted until it was pointless even to ask. Laurie screamed until she was blue in the face, managing to insult each and every one of her team members, but reserving the best for Alex.

He deserved it, but regretted nothing.

And he kept quiet. He had no choice. The police trail needed to end there. Pavel's name was never mentioned – the man who'd pursued Alex, threatened him and his family, killed Larry, Susan, Dr Morgan and God knows who else. One of the leading members of Nova was dead, by Alex's hand, guided by Natalia, the ghost who'd once again drifted back into the darkness.

Alex's burden had grown, but with it, a sense of satisfaction. For if he could bring about the downfall of a place like Starkov and a man like Pavel, then the rest of Nova surely lay within his grasp. He'd won a significant battle. The war was within reach.

And then there was Eva.

She remained in secure custody downstairs. Alex was confident she was safe, but wanted her out of this place as soon as possible, and under his care. There were plenty of private facilities nearby, none of which would have experience of this particular condition, but nonetheless could offer a secure and comfortable period of rehabilitation for a girl who'd been stolen, sold and brutalised.

'She won't talk to me,' Laurie had said, her face still like thunder, but without quite so much energy. She squeezed her eyes shut for a few seconds.

'She's angry,' said Alex.

Laurie raised her eyebrows. 'No shit.'

'Not because of what happened,' he said. 'It's underlying, part of her – a result of all the experiments. She's highly unstable, borderline delusional.' Alex totted off a list of issues in his head that would need addressing. He thought back to the medical file he'd been sent. The anger would increase with age. A high dose of antidepressants might be necessary from the outset. He wondered what else he'd need to put in place.

But they had a pact, and he'd see it through. Once she'd healed, she'd be valuable, and Alex would be right there waiting for her.

'Why?' said Laurie. 'I don't mean Eva – I mean why to the rest? I know I asked you already, but why, Alex? We could have had her. We could have had them both.'

Alex shook his head and gave the same answer he'd given on the journey – the same as he'd repeated in the conference with everybody else present.

'I had to,' he said. 'That was the deal. Me alone.'

Laurie shook her head. She didn't bother repeating her own response – that going in alone was never the right way. Going in alone meant having no back-up at a moment's call. You had to trust your colleagues to do the right thing, the legal thing, the *sensible* thing, when dealing with an unknown force in an alien situation.

She sagged against the desk, letting out a huge breath, her anger appearing to dissipate at last.

'I know you only got half the prize, Alex.'

Alex stared at her. She stared back. She knew what he was after, what he'd always been after. But he had nothing new to tell her, and nothing old to reveal. Natalia had disappeared; no female bodies had been recovered. That didn't mean much, given the relationship with the Czech police, but it gave him a glimmer. Just a glimmer.

'You couldn't have brought her in,' he said. 'Even if she'd come willingly, you had no jurisdiction. She'd have been taken by the Czech police and then . . .'

'You don't even know her name,' said Laurie, 'Do you?'

Alex shook his head. 'She's not the threat.'

Laurie frowned. 'Excuse me?'

'To my family. To me. It's not her.'

Laurie screwed her face up. 'I'd say that's exactly who. She managed to find out all your personal details, tap into your phone, even *remove* stuff from your phone. She knows far too much about you, Alex.'

They'll be coming for both of us.

The final words that had formed in his head. Her message to him.

'I need to move Grace and Katie,' he said. 'Somewhere more permanent. Nova is coming for me, Laurie.'

Laurie sniffed. 'It's already in motion. You'll have our finest on it.'

'And you?'

Laurie snorted. 'Not me, Alex. I have a month of paperwork to complete. I've got a bizarre young woman downstairs who's experienced the most brutal few days imaginable. Her story is incredible but also, for the most part, unprovable. The fact we found her in Starkov is almost irrelevant at this stage, given we weren't even there.'

'You've agreed to go with the story?'

'What story? We didn't go there. We didn't participate. The UK police doesn't involve itself with corrupt forces or governments, even so-called allies within Europe.'

Alex saw the frustration building again in her face. It mirrored his own, albeit for different reasons. Laurie saw a failed and screwed-up police operation, and she blamed herself.

'I've got nothing concrete, Alex,' she said. 'Nothing. Hartley doesn't know what to do with Eva Jansen. My super doesn't know what to do with her. They've agreed to release her into your private therapy only because you're a rich git and will pay for it all. You won't tell me what's really going on – who these people are or what they want. And more importantly, what *you* want. I can't force your secrets out of you, Alex, but I can't help you either, if you keep them.'

Laurie was frustrated, but it was Alex who was left with the threat, and beyond securing Eva, his family was the only thing that mattered.

The others will be coming for you.

'My family needs protection, Laurie,' he said. 'That's all I need from you.'

It came out wrong, his choice of words insulting. Laurie had been his biggest ally and had risked a lot based only on his word, his demands. His rationing of the truth hadn't been the reason it had ended the way it did, but he felt guilty regardless. Laurie was only trying to do her job, but she was right and the secrets would remain his.

Alex met her gaze. He saw frustration, along with sadness. He saw someone who'd gone out on a limb for him, been pushed to her limits. Her eyes burned and he knew what she felt, because he had caused it.

'If that's all you need, Alex,' she said, standing to leave the room. 'If that's all you need.'

◆ ◆ ◆

Alex stepped out of the Vauxhall building. The air was thick and electric, the grey clouds darkening overhead. A storm was coming, and Alex shivered in anticipation.

His left arm cramped, the tremor peaking before subsiding. It was accompanied by the worsening of his headache, with a sharp stab in his temples.

He stared at the screen of his phone for a few moments before dialling. He'd already called Grace to tell her about the police protection. He couldn't explain any more than he already had, but could only continue to offer apologies, which he did. Grace had calmed down somewhat – the new unit would let them go home, with a mixture of private security and police squad cars. Their life could resume, albeit under surveillance, with reassurance from the police that it would not be permanent.

But Katie was different.

'Hi, Dad,' she said, her small voice cutting through the fog. His shakes subsided in response.

'Hi, sweetie,' he said. 'I'm home.'

'I wish we were.' A brief stab – sombre, but not malicious.

'You will be,' he said, 'soon enough.' Alex could offer no advance on that promise, but it didn't feel empty, at least.

'Mum's told me the deal,' she said. 'Are you OK?'

'Am *I* OK?'

'Your work is important, Dad. The bad people, the criminals. Mum told me about the traffickers – that's young girls, isn't it? Like me. I Googled it. Are you sure these people can't hurt you?'

Alex opened his mouth to answer, then thought better of it. Enough with the lies.

'I'm not sure,' he said, 'but I'm doing my best. The police will be watching you and they'll be watching me. The bad guys will have one hell of a job to hurt either of us.'

'OK,' she said, then in a firmer voice, 'OK. I guess I didn't really understand before, but I do now – about the therapy and stuff. You've got a lot going on. Most of my friend's dads have boring jobs. I guess yours is pretty important.'

Alex smiled, marvelling at her maturity, how she was rising above the inadequacies of her father. 'But I promise not to lie about that again. I will go to therapy when the time is right, but that time is not now. You understand?'

'I suppose,' she said. 'Everyone has their own way of dealing with things. You're just weirder than most. You'll take longer to fix.'

He laughed. They both paused in a comfortable silence as his past actions were filed away. Not forgotten, perhaps, but one day forgiven.

'And you'll still come around?' she said.

'If you want me?'

'Of course. Mum hates sci-fi. There's a new series on Netflix. Maybe we could start it on Saturday?'

He accepted with tears in his eyes, knowing in that moment that his family was in equal parts as close and as distant as ever. Life would go on in spite of his actions. His relationship with Katie was strong enough to withstand anything.

'Katie?' he said.

'Yes, Dad?'

'I promise to do better.'

He heard her sigh. 'Just do me a favour, yeah?'

'Anything.'

'Next time you start to lie to me, just stop and think about it. I'll always love you, Dad, but I can't take that.'

357

Alex paused. It bit, but he deserved it. Therapy from his own daughter. He'd taught her well.

'Deal,' he said. 'I love you, Katie.'

Another pause. 'Love you too, Dad. See you Saturday.'

Alex hung up and the beginnings of a smile played across his face. He paused on the street, taking in the cool air before heading back inside, enjoying at least a moment of calm in the chaos of the last few days. With his family in police protection, as safe as they could ever be, he had the confidence to continue – to pursue his newest ally, wherever she might be, to the ends of the earth if necessary.

To win Eva's life and at the same time lose Nova. That was his burden, his challenge. A significant victory was his, yet the final goal seemed as distant as ever.

He checked his watch. Time to see Eva. He'd promised to speak to her before he left for the day. She was fragile, but recovering. They had a lot to talk about, a lot to plan.

But at least she was safe.

CHAPTER
FIFTY-NINE

The sun shone through the upper window, casting a pleasant warmth over Eva's bed. The door to this room was locked, but for the first time in as long as she could remember, she felt protected. She glanced down at her new clothes, picked out by a friendly officer, and across to the dinner tray. She'd eaten the sandwich but left the yoghurt. She hated apricot.

Eva took a deep breath and closed her eyes.

He'd come back for her, like he said he would. Natalia had disappeared into the long night – a disturbing mixture of memory and reality, but she'd done the right thing, the only thing, and had given Eva her life.

She'd given both of them their lives.

Those first few minutes in the tank had almost consumed her. She'd stumbled in a waking dream, not understanding how futile her resistance was until Alex had explained it.

And then she'd broken.

Resisting the screams had been the hardest part, fearing their pursuers would kill Natalia and then come looking for them. But the seconds had dragged into minutes, the air had continued to pump through the isolation tank, the water had continued to be filtered and heated, and they sat on in the darkness.

She was never meant to be in a chamber like that with another person, and in those minutes she saw deep into Alex's soul, crystallised in the silence, all of her senses removed until he spoke to her, bringing her down from the edge.

With Alex came an understanding that went deeper than he realised. She might not have much control over the next few weeks and months, but the prospects under Dr Madison were an altogether different proposition than her past, where she had been pushed from pillar to post, the odd child, the freak. The curiosity that could be sold to the highest bidder.

He had learned her history, and she already knew his. She had read him until she could bear no more, the threads of his own demons deep and festering – and for now, best left alone. They would unravel in time, she'd seen as clearly as her own, when the red mist descended and the voices consumed her. When she'd clawed at the mind in front of her, savaging it until it stopped.

Alex had a darkness in him she'd seen before, and she saw again. But she would leave it, and wait. It would be there when she needed it.

They had no plan, but with each passing minute, as he talked her down, she began to believe in a different future – in a life beyond the institutions. He had encouraged her anger, controlled, examined and managed it. As it reappeared, she had welcomed it like an old friend and kept it at bay, realising how practised she was becoming at doing so. She had a friend now, an ally, but the roots still burned inside. She'd been brutalised and terrified, but her history had been laid bare, and it was time to fill in the blanks. The list was long. Just as the other girls in the hospital wards had learned not to fuck with Eva Jansen, now the rest of the world would learn.

A pact. They'd made a pact.

Locked in their shared mission, Alex and Eva, together in the darkness when she thought she'd burst. It was the pact that had saved her.

Eva was no longer an asset. She was a person, an equal, and would be treated as such. She would be free. Free to seek out answers, free to seek out revenge. Eva's days of hospital wards were over. Her days as a child were gone. It was time to make her mark on the world. Time to do what she was good at.

She took a deep, contented breath, turning to the door as the lock clicked open. A loud thump followed as the bolt withdrew and the door creaked on its hinges.

'Oh,' she said, her smile fading. 'I was expecting someone else.'

The man nodded, closing the door behind him. He was bald, with wire-framed glasses and scruffy clothing. He peered at her for a moment.

'Eva Jansen,' he said. His accent was thick, similar to Natalia's but harsher, and his throat hoarse. He emitted a small but confusing wave of darkness, his thoughts knotted and tied too tightly to undo. A small shiver ran down Eva's back.

'Are you a doctor?' she said. 'A police officer?'

As the man approached, Eva realised he was neither. Her sense of safety came tumbling down and she drew breath, tensed, ready to fight. The man was murmuring as he approached, spitting out several words in quick succession that meant nothing to Eva, yet they slammed into her eardrums, piercing in their intensity.

Eva gasped, her jaw locking open as she tried to speak, to scream. Nothing would come out, her throat sealed, clenched, as if in a vice.

Her hands were free and she tried to raise them up, but they were heavy, too heavy, and slumped by her sides. All the while the man talked, his voice lowering into a whisper, his foreign tongue hissing across the air to her, embracing her, suffocating her with his words.

The sensation was vaguely familiar – when Natalia had spoken to the border patrol, Eva had experienced a similar if much gentler phenomenon, aimed at the guard. A feeling of lifting outside of her body, floating, observing herself from afar.

But this wasn't gentle. With each passing second the sensation became tighter, more restrictive, unbearable. Whatever he was doing had captured Eva's psyche, and was slowly but surely bending it towards his will.

Eva moved her eyes, the only physical part left of her that would obey. She watched as the man slid his hand into his pocket, producing a small, sharp kitchen knife. The blade glinted under the lights as he turned it, pushing it handle first towards her on the bed.

'Take it, Eva Jansen,' said the man, his English breaking through the myriad of other sounds. His voice was calm, never wavering. His eyes peered through his glasses in evil indifference.

Eva stared down, incredulous as she watched her right hand extend and grasp the handle of the knife. Her fingers were numb, yet she could feel the weight of the steel and the smoothness of the handle. She raised it up, placing it against the skin of her neck.

The man exhaled, his foul breath reaching Eva's nostrils. He ceased his whispers, pausing, adjusting his posture. Then he smiled. It was a deep, knowing smile, bringing with it a flood of knowledge into Eva's mind.

He opened up, and it only took a moment for her to read what would happen next. Her eyes filled with tears, but all they did was blur the inevitable.

'Irrecoverable,' said the man. 'Goodbye, Eva.'

CHAPTER SIXTY

The man perched at a bus stop, easing the ache out of his right leg. He dabbed the blood splatters on his shirt, pulling his jacket tighter to hide them. He'd left the knife in her hand.

His head throbbed – it did all the time these days, but it was familiar and proper. It was his balance, a careful one, an early warning of damage.

And damage was an absolute certainty.

His task had been straightforward, if not simple, but it wasn't finished. It was rare he came this far west, but the winds had changed and his leash had lengthened immeasurably. A product himself once, he'd been kept at bay for long enough. He'd always been the best, if only he could keep the demons away.

He'd convinced them that was the case.

Send a message, they'd told him. A clear message in the wake of recent events that would strike at the heart of all who were watching – the police, the intelligence services and any government who dared imagine they might affect the aims of his organisation.

To take out one of their directors was to wage war. Pavel's death would not go unpunished.

It wasn't by chance he'd been given this assignment, far from it. He'd been here before, his own personal assignment delivered by the gods, but thwarted by his own kind. His last visit to London had delivered revenge and anguish in equal measure, his targets all guilty, forgiven and laid to rest.

All except one.

Dr Alex Madison had been spared on his last visit, considered an unnecessary casualty in the havoc he'd wreaked on this city. The man's own organisation had come for him and spared the good doctor. A mistake, as it turned out, but not one that couldn't be remedied.

The decision had been slow to come – puzzling and frustrating, for his organisation was normally swift to action. People had been removed for far lesser transgressions than the crimes of which Alex Madison was guilty. They had delayed for reasons they wouldn't share, but he knew better than to push, and when the decision finally came, he welcomed it.

Pavel had had his own agenda, but that had died with him. Alex Madison was now deemed *irrecoverable*.

Victor Lazar pushed himself away from the railing and blended in with the foot traffic.

The girl had been taken care of. Her death would serve as a reminder to those who second-guessed Nova's decisions. The second target would take longer to execute. There was no rush, only certainty.

He had a plan to make, a message to craft, a stage to create. When the time came, the deaths of Alex Madison and his family would once again cement Victor's position as a master. The first and most powerful *păpușar* of Comănești.

And then Alex's world would burn.

EPILOGUE

The grey skies of London were matched over the streets of Munich and a small café tucked away in the Gärtnerplatz district, which was bustling at all hours, but especially now, as the office blocks emptied at the end of the day.

Natalia pushed the bowl of ice cream to one side, an unnecessary indulgence but one she couldn't resist. She took a small sip of her coffee, stifled the beginnings of a dry cough, and eased her left shoulder, feeling the swelling under the wound and the click of the joint. The bullet had passed straight through. She'd heal, given time.

She stared at the newspaper in front of her.

The article was tucked away in the international news section, a brief snippet describing a successful police operation in the Czech Republic, a minor drugs bust and a series of arrests. The article ran to fewer than five hundred words and would be forgotten instantly by anyone who read it. A non-event. This was the only paper to carry the story – Natalia had searched the Internet and, despite a few smaller websites running the headline, none of them had any details.

Natalia was one of the few who could fill those in herself. She had made it out with her life, taking several others in the process, and drawing her remaining pursuers straight into the path of the few police officers who were honest enough to put up a fight. She'd submitted to them, been arrested and placed under the guard of a single young officer, who, after a brief conversation, had escorted her dreamily out of the bunker towards his Land Rover and gave her the keys. As she drove off, the officer stared after her with a mild puzzled look on his face, and the beginnings of a headache in his temples. He'd be fired the next day, but would swear he didn't know what they were talking about. He had never arrested Natalia. He had never let her go. His mind would spin in circles forever on the matter.

As for the raid, no significant quantity of drugs had been recovered (the bunker had been mostly empty), but three children had been caught roaming the forest on the following day, been rounded up by local police and quietly ushered into the care system.

One of the children was called Autumn. Her parents had died in a car accident three years earlier – tragic, and unbelievable if you knew where to look.

But three souls weren't enough for claims of a trafficking bust, and besides, it had already been decided by the Czech government that the Soviet bunker at Starkov had never been used for such a thing. Not in their country.

Nova was letting the children be, for now. They would come for them in time, just as they came for everyone in the end. Those three children might enjoy a few years on the outside, in the cold, in some state institution, looked after by doctors and nurses who didn't understand what they were dealing with, before being hunted by those not lucky enough to escape that night.

Once you were *one of us*, there was no escape.

Nothing about the interior of Starkov had been mentioned in the article. No experiments, no questionable activities that might embarrass the government. The cleaners, in the few days after the raid, had been very thorough and the bribes had taken care of the rest, penetrating through to the very highest levels. As far as the Czech government was concerned, without even a trace of humour, stories of that bunker would be buried.

Starkov was quietly finished. Pavel was finished. Natalia had seen to that. It was a huge victory, yet must go uncelebrated. Now she had picked a side, she had no doubt the next battle would be much larger. You didn't take out a major Nova operation, you didn't kill someone like Pavel, without facing a war, and they already knew the enemy.

But she'd done it – saved another, and even one life was worth it.

Mia had been the first, given to the good doctor because Natalia couldn't bring herself to torture the young woman any further. And now Eva, rescued from a bleak future that would most likely have ended in those tunnels, with only her screams to remind the mountains of what had happened.

And now Natalia was alone. Subconsciously, she'd been preparing for this moment for many years, during the small hours when she woke in a sweat and cried into her pillow at the thought of another long day. But her trajectory had now altered permanently, along with her allegiances. She'd be on their watch list and they'd be coming for her. A bullet in the head in the middle of the night, or something rather more dramatic, to send a message to the other assets, to toe the line and hold it. Examples must be set, and Natalia's fight could only end in death.

She sipped her coffee, now cold, and tucked the paper to one side, retrieving instead the faded manila envelope from her bag, the one she'd retrieved from her private mailbox in central Munich a few hours before.

She had the booth to herself, but still gave the café a brief scan before carefully folding back the cover of the medical file. It was old, dated just over forty years ago, the cover sheet handwritten in Russian with English scribbles, translating it for the next reader.

The layout was familiar, the clinical notes followed by the weeks and months of treatments and observations, of drugs and reactions. It was all here, documented, filed, stamped classified – the red ink faded to a dark rust – and hidden in the vaults.

That Natalia had access to this *particular* file had been an oversight, a careless lapse in security hinting at more than a mistake. Nova was becoming careless, its inner circle fractured. Her access to the file would eventually be discovered, if it hadn't been already. Alarms would sound, action would be taken. Handlers would begin to clean up, and assets would decide how to punish the guilty, but once the cat was out of the bag . . . Natalia couldn't resist a smile as it all began to fall into place.

The subject's photo clipped to the cover was faded almost beyond recognition, the colours blended and the lines blurred, but the small baby boy had stared at the camera, eyes wide, his fingers grasping at the air, unaware of the unique future he would experience.

The boy's name had changed many times before being redacted, but he wasn't called that now, of course. This boy had been given to a proper family, an English family, tucked away in wealthy suburbia, the experimentation on him using an altogether different approach, reflecting his unique position as the child of one of Nova's foremost scientists.

But that scientist was now dead, killed by one of their own. And this boy was a grown man.

He didn't know – he couldn't. This boy, this man, was ignorant of his past, and therefore of his future, but Natalia's connection to him had been written in the stars, and their paths were always meant to collide. Her affinity with him was not by chance. It was a meeting of minds.

That's what Pavel had wanted. He had never wanted to kill Alex Madison. He had wanted to bring him in from the cold.

Because Alex is one of us.

ACKNOWLEDGMENTS

Once again, I am indebted to a huge number of wonderful people who helped to get this story out of my head and on to the page.

My agent, Julie Fergusson, continues to be a brilliant friend and advisor on every aspect of my writing, shaping this series and squeezing the absolute best out of me at each and every stage, from idea to publication and beyond. She suffered through the early drafts and told me exactly what I needed to hear.

A huge thank-you to my editor Jack Butler and the Amazon Publishing team, who are a fantastic and energising bunch of professionals. Jack has the rare talent of making me hit the deadlines while keeping the whole process super fun and stress-free. Special mentions to Laura Deacon, Eoin Purcell, Martin Toseland (whose structural edits transformed this book in the later stages), Monica Byles, Harriet Stiles, Nicole Wagner, Alexandra Levenberg and Jodi Marchowsky – all of whom have been dedicated to this series and added their magic at every stage.

Thank you to the Amazon authors I've had the pleasure of meeting over the last couple of years. They are a friendly, supportive group (and extremely talented) and I'm honoured to join the ranks.

Continued thanks to my parents, Brian and Mary, and my sister, Lucy (and Tim, Charlotte, Millie and Alice), for their encouragement and kind words.

Thank you to my wonderful wife, Kerry, and my daughters, Isla and Daisy, who continue to provide the perfect home in which to write, offering love, patience, time and the motivation to keep going.

And the biggest thank-you of all to you, the wonderful readers.

ABOUT THE AUTHOR

Adam Southward is a philosophy graduate with a professional background in IT, working in both publishing and the public sector. He lives on the south coast of England with his young family.

Printed in Great Britain
by Amazon